STAR TREK®
THE EUGENICS WARS

STAR TREK®
THE EUGENICS WARS

The Rise and Fall of Khan Noonien Singh

VOLUME ONE

GREG COX

Based upon STAR TREK® and
STAR TREK: THE NEXT GENERATION®
created by Gene Roddenberry,
STAR TREK: DEEP SPACE NINE®
created by Rick Berman & Michael Piller,
and STAR TREK: VOYAGER®
created by Rick Berman &
Michael Piller & Jeri Taylor

POCKET BOOKS
New York   London   Toronto   Sydney

This book is a work of fiction. Names, characters, places and incidents are products of the author's imagination or are used fictitiously. Any resemblance to actual events or locales or persons, living or dead, is entirely coincidental.

 POCKET BOOKS, a division of Simon & Schuster, Inc.
1230 Avenue of the Americas, New York, NY 10020

 STAR TREK is a Registered Trademark of
Paramount Pictures.

This book is published by Pocket Books, a division of Simon & Schuster, Inc., under exclusive license from Paramount Pictures.

ISBN 13: 978-0-7434-0642-0
ISBN 10: 0-7434-0642-7

First Pocket Books paperback printing April 2002

10   9   8   7   6   5   4   3

POCKET and colophon are registered trademarks of Simon & Schuster, Inc.

For information regarding special discounts for bulk purchases, please contact Simon & Schuster Special Sales at 1-800-456-6798 or business@simonandschuster.com

Printed in the U.S.A.

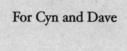

For Cyn and Dave

Acknowledgments

As history teaches us, nobody fights the Eugenics Wars alone. Thanks to my editor, John Ordover, for enlisting early on; to my agents, Russ Galen and Anna Ghosh, for securing vital defense funding, and to the entire Malibu Lunch Group for providing countless hours of R&R during the war years.

I also want to thank Sumi Lee for German lessons, Kim Kindya for fashion tips and Cuban profanities, Josepha Sherman and Amy Goldschlager for eyewitness reports on Lenin's Tomb, Marina Frants for tips on Russian grammar and vocabulary, the Star Trek Timeliners for advice regarding stardates, and, of course, Robert Lansing, Teri Garr, and Ricardo Montalban for inspiration.

Finally, thanks to Karen Palinko, for careful proofreading and keen editorial insights, and to Alex, for having a much better attitude than Isis.

"We want no Caesars."

—Jawaharlal Nehru,
     first prime minister of India

PROLOGUE

Captain's log, stardate 7004.1.

Under top-secret orders from Starfleet Command, the Enterprise *is en route to the Paragon Colony on the planet Sycorax, to evaluate that colony's recent request to join the United Federation of Planets. At issue is one of the Federation's fundamental principles, a centuries-old taboo perhaps second only to the Prime Directive in its scope and sanctity. . . .*

"GENETIC ENGINEERING? ON HUMANS?" DR. LEONARD McCoy was utterly, and audibly, aghast. He stared across the conference table at his friend and captain, James T. Kirk, as if he couldn't believe what he was hearing. The doctor's sagging, careworn features looked even more vexed than usual. "Have the brass at Starfleet lost their paper-pushing little minds? Human genetic engineering has been banned throughout the Federation since its very founding—and for good reason!"

Kirk smiled at his friend's predictably cantankerous response. Along with Mr. Spock, the three men were alone in the ship's primary conference room, Starfleet regarding the full particulars of this mission to be on a strictly need-to-know basis. Kirk sat at the head of the long, rectangular table, with Spock and McCoy facing each other across the polished brown surface of the table. *I should have known McCoy would react this way,* Kirk thought.

"Calm down, Bones," he instructed McCoy. "Nobody's talking about lifting the ban right away, just re-thinking it a bit. After all, it's been three hundred years since the Eugenics Wars; a case could be made that people are a lot more civilized these days, that we wouldn't necessarily make the same mistakes our ancestors did."

"Even when those mistakes nearly destroyed all life on Earth?" McCoy shook his head vehemently. "Civilization may be more advanced, but I'm not sure people themselves are any smarter, especially when it comes to messing around with our own genetic blueprint." The doctor gave Kirk a probing look. "Good Lord, Jim, you met Khan. Don't you remember what sort of a monster he was?"

Kirk nodded, his expression growing more sober at the mention of that name. Only four years had passed since the captain had made the mistake of reviving the genetically enhanced crew of the *S.S. Botany Bay,* all of whom had been trapped in suspended animation since fleeing the Earth in the 1990s, following their disastrous defeat in the infamous Eugenics Wars. Their charismatic leader, Khan Noonien Singh, had briefly captured the *Enterprise*—and nearly killed Kirk—before the captain had managed to turn the tables on Khan and his fellow supermen, stranding them on a primitive planet somewhere near the Mutara Sector.

That was a close call, Kirk remembered; he couldn't blame McCoy for citing the very existence of Khan as a compelling argument against the sort of genetic tampering under discussion.

"Your point is well taken, Doctor," Kirk assured him. "In fact, it's our firsthand experience with Khan and his followers that persuaded Commodore Mendez to assign this fact-finding mission to the *Enterprise.* Our recommendations will carry a lot of weight with the Federation Council when they meet to decide the future of the colony on Sycorax."

"You mean, *your* recommendation is the one the Council will listen to," McCoy insisted without any rancor. The doctor seemed somewhat mollified now that his misgivings had received an attentive hearing by Kirk. "So what's the story with this so-called Paragon Colony anyway? How in blue blazes did we end up with a community of genetically engineered humans here in the twenty-third century?"

Kirk let Spock fill McCoy in on the background of the colony. "The galaxy is a large place," the Vulcan explained, "and spacious enough that those who object to their society's policies can establish their own communities far beyond the boundaries of any controlling authority. To be more specific, the Paragon Colony was founded over a century ago, outside the Federation's sphere of influence, by individuals who sought to create a genetically engineered society. The colony has had little or no contact with the outsiders until very recently, when they discreetly appealed for membership in the Federation. In exchange for said membership, they offer the Federation generations of expertise in human genetic engineering."

"Which just happens to violate one of our oldest and wisest laws!" McCoy pointed out acerbically. "And the higher-ups back home are seriously considering this notion?" He rolled his eyes heavenward. "God help us!"

"To be honest, Bones," Kirk confided in him, "it's Starfleet that's most interested in the colony's proposal, for reasons of galactic security. Even before this Paragon business came up, there had been some highly hush-hush discussions about repealing, or at least loosening, the restrictions on human eugenics programs. A few of our top strategists have called Starfleet's attention to the fact that humanity is threatened by species such as the Romulans and Klingons, who are physically superior to ordinary humans in many ways. They argue that we need to close the 'genetic gap' by breeding enhanced humans who can stand toe-to-toe with whatever alien species we encounter. There are even rumors that the Klingons have already launched covert genetic-engineering projects of their own, and that we may be falling behind in a genetic arms race."

McCoy looked positively appalled. "The Klingons are rushing over an evolutionary cliff, so we have to hurry up and join them? That's the kind of reasoning that nearly blew humanity to kingdom come centuries ago." A passionate urgency crept into McCoy's voice as he leaned toward Kirk. "I can't speak for the Romulans, Jim, but I'm darn sure that we poor humans aren't ready to play God with our own chromosomes just yet. Good Lord, we're talking about the very stuff that makes us human in the first place."

His slender fingers steepled before him in a contemplative pose, Spock took a more objective perspective. "Despite humanity's own unfortunate experiences, a number of other sentient species have indulged in eugenics without suffering the adverse consequences recorded in your history. Take the Hortas of Janus VI, for instance: Once every fifty thousand years, they choose the best of their generation to be the sole mother of the next generation of Hortas, thus employing selective breeding to steadily improve their species." Spock directed an ironic glance at McCoy. "As you yourself can testify, Doctor, this process has produced a remarkably civilized and intelligent life-form."

Kirk repressed a smile, amused as ever by his friends' familiar antagonism. He could always count on Spock and McCoy to land on opposite sides of every issue; that was just one of the reasons he made it a rule to always listen carefully to both of them.

"I should have known you'd be in favor of this lunatic proposition," McCoy drawled, eyeing Spock dubiously. "What else could one expect from someone whose people have done their damnedest to breed honest emotion out of their own blood and bones?"

Spock was characteristically unfazed by the doctor's outburst. "The Vulcan repudiation of emotion," he corrected McCoy, "is the result of over two millennia of intellectual and philosophical discipline, and not a matter of mere biology. Furthermore, I did not say that I supported the Paragon Colony's petition to join the Federation; at present, there is insufficient data on which to make that decision. I merely observed that, on the basis of galactic history, genetic engineering and the selective breeding of sentient beings cannot be considered socially irresponsible by definition."

McCoy sighed wearily. "Why do I even try to talk sense to you, you pointy-eared, walking tricorder?" He

sank back into his chair and regarded Kirk quizzically.
"What about you, Jim? What do you think about all
this?"

Good question, the captain thought. His initial response to the commodore's classified communication
had echoed McCoy's: Why risk creating another Khan?
On further reflection, though, he felt obliged to give the
matter deeper thought. The original ban on tinkering
with human DNA had been drafted by a generation for
whom the atrocities of the Eugenics Wars were still recent history; it could be argued that such sweeping and
unconditional legislation had been an overreaction to
the crimes of Khan and his contemporaries. Perhaps it
was time to take another, less emotional look at the potential pros and cons of human genetic engineering . . . ?

"I believe it was Samuel Hopkins of the First Conti-
nental Congress who said he had never encountered an
issue so dangerous that it couldn't be talked about,"
Kirk stated firmly. "With that in mind, gentlemen, I intend to keep an open mind until we arrive at Sycorax
and hear what the colonists have to say. I also want to
see for myself just what a genetically engineered society
looks like." He rose from his seat at the head of the
table. "That concludes this briefing. Thank you for
coming, Bones, Mr. Spock. You may return to your duties now. Please keep the specifics of our mission to
Sycorax confidential for the time being; there's no
point in stirring up controversy before Starfleet has decided on a suitable course of action."

"Whatever you say, Jim," McCoy agreed, standing up
and stepping away from the table. "I don't envy you the
decision you have to make; talk about being on the hot
seat." Automatic doors whished open as McCoy

headed for the exit; he paused in the doorway to look back at Kirk. "You know my door is always open if you want to talk about it."

"Thank you, Bones. I'll keep that in mind."

Spock lingered behind while the door slid shut behind McCoy, cutting off the sounds of the busy corridor outside. "What can I do for you, Mr. Spock?" Kirk asked.

The *Enterprise*'s first officer stood behind his seat, his impeccable posture and dignified bearing betraying his Vulcan roots as surely as the tapered points of his ears and the slightly greenish cast of his complexion. "A word of advice, Captain. While I do not share the good doctor's excessively visceral reaction to the matter at hand, his suggestion that you look to the history of your own world is not without merit. As we have learned through our own experiences in the past, the latter part of the twentieth century was an extremely volatile period in Earth's history, in which, besides Khan and his fellow genetic tyrants, a number of crucial variables were at work, including, for example, the covert activities of Gary Seven and his associates."

That's right, Kirk thought. Seven, an undercover operative for an unknown alien civilization, would have been a contemporary of Khan, more or less. Indeed, Kirk recalled, Spock's subsequent research had revealed that both Seven and his partner, a young woman named Roberta Lincoln, had ultimately played key roles in the cataclysmic drama of the Eugenics Wars. "I wonder what Seven's take on the Paragon Colony would be."

"That we can only speculate upon," Spock observed. "His actions in the past, however, are a matter of historical record." He stepped away from the conference table and headed for the door. "The future of the human race remains to be charted, Captain, but a fuller knowledge of the past can only inform your decisions in the days to come."

Kirk nodded solemnly. "An excellent suggestion, Mr. Spock." He glanced at the triangular computer node rising from the center of the conference table. "How long until we reach Sycorax?" he asked his science officer.

"At our current rate of speed," Spock reported, swiftly performing the necessary calculations in his head, "approximately seventy-two hours, thirty-four minutes."

Time enough to do a fair amount of historical research, Kirk concluded. It dawned on him that it had been years since he had last reviewed the grim, tumultuous saga of the Eugenics Wars, and that there was much he still did not know about that fateful era. "Please take the bridge, Mr. Spock. I believe I'll remain here for a while more, doing just as you advised."

"Very good, Captain. I will leave you to your studies."

Spock left, and Kirk found himself alone within the sloping blue walls of the conference room. With only his thoughts to keep him company, he listened for a few moments to the steady, reassuring hum of his starship, then took a seat midway down the length of the table. "Computer, access Earth historical records for the late twentieth century. Begin with the first citation relevant to the topic designated 'Eugenics Wars.' "

The miniature viewscreen facing Kirk flashed in acknowledgment. "Processing request for data," stated a familiar feminine voice, the voice of the *Enterprise* computer. "Beginning historical display now. . . ."

CHAPTER ONE

ROBERTA LINCOLN PACED NERVOUSLY OUTSIDE THE Russian Embassy, hugging herself against the chill of the cold night air. The monumental stone edifice, built in a stolid, neoclassical style, loomed behind the young blond woman, silent and dark. Roberta peered at her wristwatch; it was ten past two in the morning, only ninety seconds later than the last time she'd checked her watch. *What's keeping Seven and that darn cat?* she wondered anxiously. *They should be back by now.*

Restless and apprehensive, she strolled down the sidewalk, wincing at the sound of her own heels clicking against the pavement. The echo of her footsteps rang out far too loudly for Roberta's peace of mind. The last thing she wanted to do was attract the attention of the local cops or, worse yet, one of the innumerable informants working for the Stasi, the dreaded East German secret police.

Fortunately, Unter den Linden, the wide city boulevard running north past the embassy, seemed deserted at this ridiculously late hour. The only traffic she heard was an elevated train rattling by a few streets over. Roberta clung to the shadow cast by the huge building, keeping a safe distance from the streetlamps at either end of the block, while also maintaining a careful lookout for any sign of trouble. "C'mon, c'mon," she muttered impatiently, wishing Seven could hear her. *You'd think I'd be used to this sort of thing by now,* she thought; after all, she'd been working with Gary Seven, alias Supervisor 194, for nearly six years now, ever since that unforgettable afternoon in 1968 when she'd shown up for what she'd thought was an ordinary secretarial job, only to find herself caught up in a bizarre happening involving nuclear missiles, talking computers, and a starship from the future.

Heck, she mused, *what's a little East German espionage compared to some of the spacey shenanigans Seven has dragged me into over the last few years?* Nevertheless, she shivered beneath a heavy gray overcoat, and not just from the cold. The thick wool garment she wore was neither flattering nor fashionable, but it helped to preserve her anonymity while simultaneously warding off at least some of the winter's chill. A black beret and matching kerchief, the latter tied below her chin, concealed most of her tinted honey-blond hair, while her gloved hands were thrust deeply into the pockets of her coat for warmth. Her fidgety fingers toyed with a thin silver device, snugly stowed away in the right pocket, that looked and felt like a common fountain pen. A mere pen, however, wouldn't have reassured Roberta nearly as much as this particular mechanism, even as she prayed devoutly that she wouldn't have need to use the servo before this night was over.

A pair of headlights approached from the north and Roberta turned her back on the empty street. *Probably just a delivery truck making a late-night run,* she guessed, stepping deeper into the gloomy shadow of the embassy, but her heart raced a little faster anyway. Roberta held her breath, while casting a wistful glance southward toward the lights of the Brandenburg Gate, only a block and a half away. The imposing marble arches, along with their attendant armed border guards and vigilant watchdogs, marked the frontier between East and West Berlin, making the safety of the Allied Sectors seem tantalizingly close by.

Granted, those brown-uniformed guards were under orders to shoot any would-be escapees on sight, but Roberta couldn't help experiencing an irrational urge to make a run for it. *Don't be silly,* she scolded herself. *It's not going to come to that. Seven will be back any second now . . . I hope.*

A covered truck rumbled past her, and she breathed a sigh of relief as the unassuming vehicle rounded the corner two blocks farther up the boulevard, disappearing down the adjacent cross-street. *That would be Friedrichstrasse,* she remembered, mentally calling up the maps she'd memorized for this mission. Her briefing had been exhaustively thorough, but no amount of preparation was going to help her, she realized, if she got caught on the wrong side of the Iron Curtain.

A rueful smile lifted the corners of her lips. She could just imagine trying to explain her situation to a stone-faced Stasi interrogator: *No, no, I'm not affiliated with the CIA or the U.S. government at all. I'm actually working for an independent operator trained by a bunch of secretive extraterrestrials who want to keep humanity from nuking itself into extinction.* . . . Boy, wouldn't that go over great with the Commies! She'd probably end up in a Soviet asylum, if she wasn't simply shot at dawn.

"Guten Abend, Fräulein," a voice whispered in her ear.

Gasping out loud, Roberta spun around to find a stranger standing beside her. Where the heck had he come from? In her effort to evade detection from the passing truck, she had completely overlooked the newcomer's arrival. *Sloppy, sloppy,* she castigated herself for her carelessness. *Some spy girl I am. Emma Peel would never let someone sneak up on her like this.*

Thankfully, the speaker did not look like much of a threat, at least not on the surface. To Roberta's vast relief, the man wore neither a police nor an army uniform; instead he looked like a middle-aged accountant or shopkeeper, out for a post-midnight stroll. The man was short and jowly, his balding head exposed to the frigid night air and a pair of plain, black spectacles perched upon his bulbous, somewhat florid nose. Like Roberta's, his hands had sought the warmth of his coat pockets, but, despite the cold, his face was flushed and red. *Germany's the beer-drinking capital of the world,* Roberta recalled. Maybe the stranger was just heading home after an especially long night at his favorite bar?

"Er, hello," Roberta replied uncertainly. She spoke in English, but her automatic translator, ingeniously disguised as a silver pendant shaped like a peace symbol, converted her awkward greeting into perfect German, just as her matching earrings conveniently translated the stranger's every utterance into English. *Beats a Berlitz course any day,* she thought, grateful for Seven's advanced alien technology.

"You shouldn't be out so late, pretty girl," the man warned her ominously. The avid gleam in his eyes, as well as a sinister smile, belied the cautionary nature of his words. Peering past the stranger's spectacles, Roberta flinched at the sight of the German's glazed, bloodshot eyes. *I haven't seen eyes that crazy since the last time Charlie Manson was on TV,* she thought, stepping backward and away from her unwelcome visitor. "Don't you know it's not safe?" he taunted her. His left hand emerged from his pocket, clutching the ivory handle of something that looked alarmingly like a closed switch-blade.

Just my luck! Roberta lamented silently. *You try to do a little innocent night's spying and what do you get? Attacked by some sort of psycho/mugger/ rapist!* "Stay back!" she whispered hoarsely, afraid even now to raise her voice so near the soldiers guarding the gate. "I'll scream, I swear it!"

She was bluffing, of course. She didn't dare raise an alarm. That could compromise the entire mission, putting Seven in danger as well, not to mention the cat.

"Go ahead," the German said, licking his fleshy lips in anticipation. With a click, a silver blade sprang from the ivory handle, catching the light of the streetlamps. "Old Jack likes screams, especially from pretty young things who know they're about to die."

Roberta fumbled in her pocket for her servo, briefly losing track of the pen-shaped weapon amid a clutter of loose change and wadded-up Kleenex. Before she could seize hold of it again, her assailant's knife slashed across the outside of her coat, slicing through the fabric and sending the contents of her pocket spilling onto the sidewalk. Roberta's eyes widened as the slender silver instrument bounced twice upon the cracked, uneven pavement, then rolled to a stop only a few inches away from the slasher's feet.

The man caught the hopeless yearning in her gaze and glanced downward. "Hah!" he laughed at the sight of Roberta's errant servo. Saliva sprayed from his mouth as he mocked her. "What were you planning to do, *Fräulein?* Write Old Jack a nasty letter?"

"Hey, the pen is mightier than the sword, or the switchblade, or whatever," Roberta answered defiantly, yanking her hand free from the perforated pocket and assuming a defensive stance. "Or haven't you heard?"

Her glib response elicited an angry scowl from the knife-wielding German. His ruddy features took on a bestial appearance as he advanced on Roberta with premeditated slowness, waving his blade back and forth before her watchful eyes. The yellow radiance of a distant lamp glinted off the shining, sharpened metal. "You ought to be more afraid, harlot. You should scream, scream for your life!"

Nothing doing, Roberta resolved, guessing that the psycho probably got off on his victims' fear. Struggling to maintain a confident expression, she raised her hands before her, karate-style. "Watch who you're calling names, you cornball creep. Who do you think you are, Jack the Rip-Off?" *That was a good one,* she thought, the wisecrack bolstering her courage. *Too bad the gag's probably lost in translation. . . .*

The German smirked, as though at a private joke of his own. "You have no idea who you're dealing with, you stupid trollop, but I'll slice the impertinence from your bones, bit by bloody bit!" He lunged at Roberta, stabbing at her wildly while growling like a rabid beast. A string of drool trailed down his chin while his blood-streaked eyes bugged from their sockets. "Die, harlot, die!"

If he expected Roberta to shriek or run away, he was to be severely disappointed. Six years of covert missions alongside Gary Seven, facing everything from radioactive mutants to cyborg zombies, had taught the twenty-four-year-old woman how to take care of herself.

As her assailant stabbed his knife at her belly, she pivoted to the left, dodging the thrust, while parrying the blow with her right arm. Then she used her left to block and trap Jack's own arm long enough for her to grab on to his knife hand and steer it away from her body. As the German snarled in frustration, Roberta pressed her left arm against his elbow, forcing him to the pavement with a flawless forearm takedown. Dropping her knee onto his hyperextended arm freed her left hand, allowing her to wrestle the knife from his grip. *Guess all those jujitsu classes finally paid off,* she thought triumphantly.

Jack suddenly found himself facedown upon the asphalt, unarmed and at her mercy. Her knee kept his arm pinned to the ground, while both hands held on to his captured arm. She could have broken the limb easily from this position, but settled for pulling back on it painfully. Twisting his head, the crazed German stared back over his shoulder at Roberta, blinking in confusion. Clearly, he had not anticipated that his attractive young prey would offer such stiff resistance, let alone refuse to be intimidated by his threats and vicious attacks. "How—?" he murmured, breathing heavily from his exertions. His spectacles dangled precipitously upon the tip of his nose. "Who—?"

"I am woman, hear me roar," she stated, après Helen Reddy. Had that song been a hit in East Germany, too? Roberta wasn't sure, but she hoped that her twisted adversary had gotten the message. *That'll teach this lunatic to underestimate us liberated American chicks!*

A rustle from above caught their attention. Still sprawled upon the sidewalk, Jack looked upward, past Roberta. His jaw dropped at the sight of a man in a business suit rappelling down the front of the embassy.

About time, Roberta thought.

The bottom end of a black nylon cable struck the sidewalk only seconds before the man himself touched down on the pavement. A tall, slender individual in a conservative gray suit, he looked to be in his late thirties, with touches of gray streaking his neatly trimmed brown hair. Shrewd gray eyes coolly assessed the situation: Roberta's torn coat, the knife-wielding stranger on the ground.

"Trouble, Ms. Lincoln?" Gary Seven asked calmly, arching a nearly invisible, faint-brown eyebrow. As if his dramatic entrance were not incongruous enough, a sleek black cat was draped over his shoulders. A white collar studded with sparkling transparent gems glittered against the feline's glossy fur.

"You might say that," Roberta conceded. The cat squawked at her indignantly, as if criticizing the human female for her carelessness in attracting the likes of Old Jack. *And hello again to you, too,* Roberta thought peevishly, glaring back at her four-legged nemesis, who sprang from Seven's shoulders onto the pavement, looking grateful to be back on solid ground. *Mrraow*, the feline squawked once more.

"Quiet, Isis," Seven addressed the cat. "I'm sure this wasn't Ms. Lincoln's fault at all."

All of this was much too weird for the dumbfounded slasher; with a burst of unexpected strength, he threw Roberta off him and scrambled to his feet. Abandoning his knife, he darted away, eager to make a hasty exit. *No way!* Roberta thought angrily. *You're not getting away from me that easily.* Snatching up her servo from where it had fallen, she set the weapon on Subdue and fired at the fleeing bad guy.

Despite his frantic haste, Jack was still in range. Watching his scurrying figure slow down, then collapse onto Unter den Linden, Roberta started to take off toward the tranquilized maniac, only to feel Seven lay a restraining hand upon her shoulder. "Not now, Ms. Lincoln," he advised. "We have no time for this."

"But—?" she blurted. The man was a menace to women everywhere. She couldn't just let him off with a warning.

"Leave him to the local authorities," Seven instructed firmly, no doubt anticipating her outraged arguments.

As if to prove his point, a shrill whistle suddenly blared from the vicinity of the gate. *"Achtung!"* a harsh voice cried out, followed by the sound of boots pounding on asphalt. "Put your hands up and stay where you are!"

Oh, no! Roberta realized that her altercation with Jack had finally drawn the attention of the border guards. Lights came on in the previously darkened windows of the embassy. Voices inside shouted in Russian, even as an enormous searchlight, mounted atop a sentry tower just before the Brandenburg Gate, swung in their direction, exposing all three of them—Roberta, Seven, and Isis—to a blinding glare that lit up the entire block. The spotlight stretched the trio's shadows out like taffy behind them.

"This way," Seven instructed. Leaving his rappelling gear behind, he scooped up Isis and began running up the boulevard, away from the onrushing soldiers. Deciding that maybe Old Jack had hit on the right idea after all, Roberta needed no further urging to sprint after Seven, servo in hand.

"Halt!" she heard someone yell less than a hundred yards behind her, accompanied by barking dogs and running feet. More whistles shrieked in her ears, summoning reinforcements? "Stop or we'll fire!"

Time to make like Secretariat, Roberta realized. Knowing that surrender was not an option, Roberta galloped north as fast as her well-exercised legs could carry her. Seconds later, a shot rang out and a bullet whizzed by her skull, nearly winging her beret. *A warning shot,* she wondered anxiously, *or just lousy aim?* A welcome surge of adrenaline gave her an extra burst of speed, so that she nearly caught up with Seven and Isis. *How come the kitty gets a free ride,* she thought resentfully, *and I have to run my butt off to keep from becoming an international incident?*

More bullets whirred past her, making her flinch with every near miss. No matter how many times it had happened to her over the last few years, she'd never gotten used to being fired upon. The *rat-at-tat* report of machine guns echoed across the spacious boulevard as she hurried desperately toward the sheltering darkness beyond the incandescent reach of the searchlight. *That's it,* she thought in well-deserved exasperation, staring balefully at the retreating back of her employer. *I definitely have to talk to Seven about hazard pay. . . . !*

"After them! Don't let them get away!"

Corporal Erich Kilheffer of the East German army ran alongside his fellow soldiers as they pursued the fleeing suspects. His heart pounded in excitement even as an acute sense of responsibility gnawed at his already taut nerves. The incriminating cables dangling outside the Russian Embassy had not escaped his notice; the fleeing man and woman must have been engaged in an act of espionage or worse, which made their capture absolutely imperative. He knew that his superiors, not to mention their Soviet bosses, would not look kindly on him if he permitted known spies to escape under his watch. These days border guards could be court-martialed simply on suspicion of having deliberately missed while firing upon anyone making a dash past the gate; Kilheffer didn't want to think about what might happen to him if even one of the two suspects got away.

That's not going to happen, he vowed, clutching his Makarov pistol as he charged down the middle of the street. A few yards ahead of him, a trio of barking German shepards strained at their leashes, literally dragging their handlers behind them in their eagerness to chase after the fugitives. "Release the dogs!" he ordered on the run. "Try not to shoot the hounds!" he added to the rest of his men. Given a choice, he'd rather take one or both of the suspects alive, but, one way or another, he was going to present their bodies to his commander.

Running up the boulevard, past the austere gray facades of the adjoining buildings, Corporal Kilheffer tried to anticipate the fugitives' escape route. To the left, only a few blocks away, were both the British and U.S. embassies. Might the exposed spies make for the foreign consulates, in a brazen attempt to claim political asylum? *Not while I'm on the case,* Kilheffer resolved; he'd gun the miscreants down on the embassy steps if he had to.

To his surprise, however, first the man, then the woman, turned right on Glinkastrasse instead. "Idiots," he muttered under his breath; didn't they know they were heading straight for the Berlin Wall? A knowing smirk signaled Kilheffer's mounting confidence in the outcome of this nocturnal chase. Even if the fugitives made it to the border crossing popularly known as Checkpoint Charlie, a couple of blocks southeast, there was absolutely no way they could make it past the East German forces stationed there. *We've got them trapped,* he thought smugly, regretting only that he might have to share the credit for the capture with his counterpart at the checkpoint.

As he jogged around the corner, however, slowing his pace somewhat now that he knew his prey was hemmed in, he was surprised to find the swiftest of his troopers milling about in confusion, as were the resourceful guard dogs, who only moments before had been intent on running down their prey. Quizzical yelps escaped the bewildered hounds as they pawed the asphalt and turned agitated brown eyes toward their handlers. "What is it?" Kilheffer demanded. "Where are they?"

Shrugs and silence greeted his urgent queries. The corporal scanned the narrow street ahead of him, searching for some sign of the missing fugitives. Unlike Unter den Linden, this particular avenue was no major thoroughfare. Darkened storefronts faced each other across an unremarkable strip of asphalt, interrupted here and there by vacant lots strewn with rubble left over from the Allied bombing nearly two decades ago. Several Trabis, the ubiquitous state-produced automobile, were parked against the curb on both sides of the street, still and driverless, but of the elusive suspects there was no trace at all, only an odd blue mist that seemed to glow with its own faint luminosity. Kilheffer watched the strange, phosphorescent smoke dissipate as he struggled fruitlessly to figure out where in the name of the people's government his quarry had disappeared to.

In the distance, at the far end of the street, barbed wire and concrete testified to the utter impassability of the Wall. A no-man's land of mines and crossed steel girders preceded the Wall by several meters, carving out a zone of death that two suspicious fugitives could not possibly traverse with impunity.

But where else could they have gone? Despite his desire to maintain a stoic expression before his men, Kilheffer gulped involuntarily. His superiors were not going to be happy, and neither would the Stasi. He eyed the looming Wall, suddenly calculating his own chances of slipping past the security at Checkpoint Charlie. However the mysterious spies had vanished, and wherever they had vanished to, Corporal Kilheffer found himself fervently wishing he could join them.

"Corporal!" Two of his men caught up with him, huffing from exertion. Between them, they supported the limp body of a homely little man in a rumpled brown coat. His hairless head lolled flaccidly above his shoulders, as though he were badly intoxicated, and his droopy eyes and insipid grin belied his current predicament. His flushed, red face still bore the cracked imprint of the pavement. "We found this drunk lying on the street near the embassy," Sergeant Gempp reported. "What do you want us to do with him?"

Kilheffer suddenly glimpsed a chance to salvage his career. "Drunk? What drunk?" He snapped a pair of handcuffs on the unlucky inebriate's wrists. "This man is clearly the leader of the spy ring, and a dangerous enemy of the state. Place him in custody at once, and let no one else interrogate him. I intend to personally extract his confession."

The poor sot continued to grin idiotically, completely oblivious of the hot water he had mistakenly landed into. *Probably completely harmless,* Kilheffer thought, with just a twinge of regret, but what did that matter? Someone had to take the blame for tonight's fiasco.

Chances were, this innocent dupe would not see the light of day for a long, long time.

CHAPTER TWO

811 EAST 68TH STREET, APT. 12-B
NEW YORK CITY
UNITED STATES OF AMERICA
MARCH 13, 1974

THE SWIRLING BLUE FOG COMPLETELY FILLED THE empty, vault-sized chamber. Empty for the moment, that is. Seconds later, a breathless young woman emerged from the mist, followed by a somewhat older man carrying a cat. *Home sweet home*, Roberta thought as she stepped out of the vault into the office beyond. Overhead lights came on automatically, revealing a tidy office decorated with contemporary furniture. Framed paintings, mostly on a feline theme, hung on the walls, except where cedar bookshelves occupied one entire wall. Roberta breathed a sigh of relief; it was good to be back.

She was still winded from their headlong flight from the East German troopers. Only seconds before, she and Seven had been running down that lonely side street in Berlin, with the determined Grepos hot on their heels; good thing Seven had managed to transport them all out of there just in time. *Those guards are probably still scratching their heads over our abrupt disappearance,* she reflected. *Serves them right for shooting first before even trying to find out who we were.*

Its timely rescue complete, the shimmering azure mist faded. A heavy iron door swung closed, sealing the vault away for the time being. Wooden panels slid out from hidden recesses on both sides of the vault, concealing the sturdy, impenetrable door behind three shelves of cocktail glasses. Within moments, all traces of the secret fog chamber had vanished from sight, so that Gary Seven's private office now looked entirely ordinary, and deceptively devoid of any eye-catching alien hardware.

Isis leaped from Seven's arms, landing nimbly on the plush orange carpet, where she promptly set to work licking the smell of East Berlin from her fur. His arms now free, Seven extracted a plain manila envelope from the interior of his jacket, laying the package upon a polished obsidian desktop. "A good night's work," he commented, loosening his tie as he turned toward Roberta. "By the way, who was the rather agitated-looking fellow with the knife?"

"Oh, just your run-of-the-mill mad slasher." She shrugged out of her heavy winter coat, then plopped down on the comfy orange couch against the far wall. Beneath the coat, she wore a red turtleneck sweater and a pair of faded bluejeans. "Too bad we had to leave that creep behind."

"I suspect the East German authorities will deal quite harshly with him," Seven assured her, "especially if they make him a scapegoat for our unauthorized visit to the Russian Embassy." He removed his jacket and hung it on the back of the black suede chair behind his desk. "In any event, we had more important things to do than respond to a random street crime. Catching a minor psychopath was not what our mission was about."

I guess so, Roberta thought, although she didn't like the idea of not knowing whatever happened to Jack. *Oh well, I'm sure he'll get his just deserts eventually.*

Seven sat down at his desk and removed a thin sheaf of papers from the manila envelope. His brow furrowed in concentration as he studied the documents he had just "borrowed" from the Russian Embassy. Judging from the scowl on his face, he didn't like what he was reading.

Roberta considered pointing out to Seven that it was nearly eight-thirty in the evening, Eastern Standard Time. Frankly, she was inclined to call it a day and head home to her apartment in the West Village. Instead she switched her watch back to New York time and waited for Seven to finish reviewing the purloined papers. For better or for worse, irregular hours were part of the job, even if zapping around the world via radioactive smoke confused the heck out of her body's circadian rhythms. *Do I want dinner or breakfast or what?* she speculated, leafing through a copy of *People* magazine she found on the endtable next to the couch. *Hmmm, I wonder if this* Jaws *movie is going to be any good . . . ?*

She was just finishing up yet another gloomy article on the Watergate scandal when Gary Seven looked up from the Russian documents. He stared blankly at the framed paintings on the wall, obviously deep in thought.

"Bad news?" she prompted him; despite their close association since the late sixties, her enigmatic employer could still be maddeningly tight-lipped at times.

"Perhaps, Ms. Lincoln," he replied. Concern weighed down his words and deepened the solemn lines of his face. "According to these classified reports, the Russians have misplaced several of their top geneticists and biochemists. Pavlinko, Lozinak, Malinowycz . . . close to a half-dozen of the top Soviet researchers in the field have gone missing in the last year or so."

"Maybe they defected?" Roberta suggested.

"Possibly, but to whom? I know for a fact that none of the missing scientists have been recruited by the Americans or any of the other major Western powers." Seven eyed Roberta gravely. "Unfortunately, these latest disappearances are only part of a much larger and more ominous picture. Many of the world's top scientists, particularly those specializing in applied genetic engineering, have seemingly dropped off the face of the Earth."

Seven paused to let Roberta assimilate what she had just heard. *Genetic engineering?* she wondered. She was familiar with the basic idea, from newspaper articles and the occasional sci-fi novel, but she'd thought that modern science was still years away from actually being able to tamper with anybody's DNA. Then again, most people didn't know about extraterrestrial social workers or instantaneous matter transmission either. "So what do you think this is all about?" she asked Seven apprehensively, not entirely sure she wanted to hear the answer.

"It's unclear whether the missing scientists have been abducted or if they have vanished of their own free will," Seven stated, "but I have to assume that some form of ambitious genetic-engineering project is in the works." The worry lines on his craggy face deepened noticeably. "This could have very disturbing consequences. Your people are nowhere near ready for that sort of control over your own genetic makeup."

How come whenever the human race screws up, they're suddenly "my" people? Roberta thought, not for the first time. Seven had an annoying tendency to forget that he was human, too, even if he and all his ancestors had been raised on some weird alien planet somewhere. She couldn't resist the temptation to tweak Seven a little. "Correct me if I'm wrong," she began, "but aren't *you* the product of generations of selective breeding and fancy genetic tinkering?"

Her pointed observation did not faze Seven; heck, it didn't even scratch the surface of his preternatural composure. "That's an entirely different situation," he replied with complete conviction. Self-doubt was not numbered among Gary Seven's personal failings. "My sponsors know what they are doing."

"As opposed to us primitive, twentieth-century Earthlings?" Roberta asked, trying to muster up a show of righteous indignation of behalf of the rest of the human race. She crossed her arms semi-belligerently and beamed a no-nonsense stare in her boss's direction.

"Exactly," he confirmed matter-of-factly.

There was a time, back when she first hooked up with Seven, when she might have accepted an answer like that, deferring to Seven's superior knowledge of such matters, but not anymore. "No way," she objected. "You have to do better than that. Why shouldn't we humans improve our chromosomes if we feel like it? What's the big crime?"

To her satisfaction, and mild surprise, Seven appeared to give her pestering questions serious consideration. "The problem, and the danger, Ms. Lincoln, is genocide, of one form or another, and the very real possibility of genetic warfare. Galactic history teaches us that once a species succeeds in creating a 'superior' version of themselves, it's then one very short step to viewing the rest of the species as unworthy, obsolete, and, ultimately, disposable. Just as their baseline contemporaries often regard the genetically or cybernetically augmented as monsters to be destroyed." He shook his head sadly. "It's an ugly, tragic situation that has devastated more civilizations and species than I like to recall. The Voixxians. The Ryol. The Minjo. The Borg. . . ."

"Okay, I get it, I guess," Roberta said, surrendering for the time being. "Thanks for the history lesson." In some ways, though, Seven's explanation was more frustrating than satisfying. "It's not exactly fair, you know. You're always winning arguments by citing incidents on planets I've never heard of, and can hardly check up on." She eyed him quizzically from across the room. "How do I know you don't make up half of this stuff?"

Seven looked backed at her with amused gray eyes. "On that, Ms. Lincoln, you'll just have to trust me." Perched on the back of the plush chair nearby, Isis mewed in agreement.

No surprise there, Roberta thought ruefully. Sometimes she suspected that the ever-present black feline knew more about what Seven was up to than she did; the rest of the time she was sure of it. *Yeah, but I've got opposable thumbs and she doesn't, at least not at the moment.*

Even after six years of working with Seven (and Isis), she knew frustratingly little about the mysterious aliens behind this little operation, just that they had snatched up his great-great-great-ancestors some six thousand years ago, trained their offspring for umpteen generations, then sent good old Supervisor 194 back to Earth to keep his fellow Homo sapiens from starting World War III. Whenever she asked Seven about his superiors Up There, he told her that she didn't need to know anything more, that greater knowledge of the Aegis (as he sometimes called them) would not assist her in the field, and might actually compromise the aliens' grand design should the information fall into the wrong hands. *Well, maybe,* Roberta mused; just the same, she would like to know whether she was working for a bunch of superintelligent bugs or birds or big giant brains. *Just so long as they don't have tails or whiskers,* she thought, with a suspicious glance at Isis.

One of these days, she vowed, she would pry the full scoop out of Seven. Now, however, did not seem like the right time to press the issue. The boss had more pressing matters on his mind, like these inexplicably AWOL chromosome counters.

Seven finally glanced at his own wristwatch. "All right," he said reluctantly. "There's nothing more we can do tonight. Starting tomorrow, though, finding out where all these scientists have gone to is our top priority." He leaned back into his chair, massaging his forehead with his fingers in a rare moment of human vulnerability and fatigue. "With any luck," he sighed, "we can nip this dangerous experiment in the bud before it goes too far."

Roberta figured she was probably still missing some of the deeper implications of this whole Mad Scientist business that had Seven worried, but she hoped he was right anyway. About it not being too late, that is.

CHRYSALIS BASE
LOCATION: CLASSIFIED

Selective breeding is effective as a means of evolution, but it takes too long, especially where human gestation periods are involved. Tedious as it sometimes was, deliberate genetic manipulation sped up the process immeasurably, or so Dr. Sarina Kaur kept reminding herself as she pruned yet another collection of human embryos. *With luck, there won't be too many rejects,* she thought, studying each embryo individually beneath a powerful electron microscope.

The sterile, air-conditioned laboratory resembled a gleaming, high-tech kitchen. Black acid-proof counters shined like polished obsidian against bright mango-colored walls. Equipment ranging from simple column chromatography setups to sophisticated liquid scintillation counters sat atop the counter, alongside agar-filled petri dishes and folded nitrocellulose filters. Spare test tubes, beakers, and pipettes were stacked neatly in open shelves above the counters, while a shining steel stool gave Kaur someplace to rest her legs while she inspected the embryos. A traditional Indian raga played softly in the background, soothing her nerves over the course of a long day's work.

Despite her fatigue, the thirtyish scientist felt an undeniable sense of accomplishment. The two dozen embryos arrayed upon the counter, each one no more than a few millimeters long and each suspended in a sterile dish containing an artificial growth medium of her own invention, were the end of a long and meticulous process of elimination and experimentation, expressly designed to create human embryos genetically superior to those created through the random genetic shuffling of ordinary reproduction.

The process had begun by inducing superovulation in all of the project's female volunteers, including herself. The large and diverse assortment of eggs yielded by this procedure had then been inseminated artificially and allowed to incubate at a temperature of precisely thirty-seven degrees centigrade, i.e., body temperature. Following fertilization, the eggs had been carefully examined for a wide variety of genetic defects or abnormalities, with all unsuitable eggs immediately terminated and disposed of. Kaur prided herself on developing, with the aid of her colleagues, selection criteria far more stringent than those employed by simple biology. To improve on Nature, after all, it was necessary to be harsher and more ruthless than Nature, so that only the most promising genetic combinations would survive.

The result of this early screening, however, merely guaranteed offspring free of certain inherited defects. A laudable outcome, to be sure, but one that fell far below the ultimate ambitions of the project. It was not enough to simply produce outstanding examples of conventional humanity; the Chrysalis Project aspired to create a new breed of man and woman, markedly superior to any who had existed before. To do so required adding new information and instructions to the genetic blueprint encoded in each egg's DNA.

The conventional wisdom of the time held that modern science was still decades away from performing such procedures with any hope of success, but, here at Chrysalis, the combined brilliance of Kaur and her associates, free from governmental interference and the timidity of the general public, had already taken the art and science of genetic engineering much further than the outside world could possibly imagine. *Someday,* she reflected, *the world will be astounded to discover all that we have been able to accomplish here.*

Take, for example, the unprecedented way they had learned to clone multiple copies of each surviving egg, thus increasing the odds of successful hybridization later on. Conventional science maintained that a fertilized egg could only be cloned twice before expiring, yet Kaur herself had developed a technique for producing dozens of identical copies of a single egg. *That was the key,* she recalled; invariably, applied genetics involved a certain degree of trial and error, heredity being fundamentally a matter of probabilities. But by generating so many ideal eggs to work with, the chances of achieving the desired genetic result increased dramatically—especially when the biological geniuses of the project knew exactly what modifications they wanted to make to the standard human genome.

Fragments of specialized DNA, built from scratch from the appropriate amino acids, then multiplied by polymerase chain reactions, were spliced into bacterial plasmids, which acted as vectors to transmit the recombinant genes to the nucleus of the egg itself. Not every plasmid-borne gene successfully infiltrated the egg's DNA, let alone at precisely the right spot in the sequence of codons, but that's what all those multiple copies were for. Enough hybridized eggs made it through the secondary screening process to provide a suitable number of samples for the *next* round of genetic augmentation.

In all, the process currently involved the introduction of seven distinct improvements to the basic human genotype. One such modification accelerated the formation of critical neural pathways, thus increasing intelligence. Another slight resequencing of the base pairs of a specific human gene had been found to substantially improve the efficiency of the lungs and respiratory systems, while the addition of a single new gene, adapted from one located in the DNA of the African gorilla, caused an increase in muscular density and resilience.

Now, after weeks of exacting effort, including the use of microscopic radioactive probes to confirm the presence of selected genes in various batches of modified eggs, only one last trial remained for this, the most recent crop of genetically engineered embryos. Careful screening of hundreds of test samples had winnowed the selection down to a mere two dozen eggs, which had then been allowed to develop into the embryos currently awaiting Kaur's final inspection. Of these candidates, only those she judged suitable would be implanted in the surrogate mothers who had agreed to carry the babies to term.

Only the best of the best of the best for our proud corps of moms-to-be, she mused, smiling. Many of the women involved were simply peasant women paid a generous sum for their cooperation and silence; since the surrogates made no genetic contribution to the children they carried, the project didn't need to be too picky when it came to recruiting extra wombs. As long as the women stayed healthy and drug-free, and agreed to be monitored on a daily basis, they were good enough to serve as human incubators for the vastly superior beings gestating within them.

One of these days we really have to develop some workable artificial wombs, Kaur reflected. That would place yet one more crucial stage of human development under deliberate scientific control, not to mention sparing the project the burden of having to constantly recruit new surrogate mothers. She patted her abdomen, already bulging slightly beneath her voluminous white lab coat; in the meantime, she, along with nearly every other female member of Chrysalis, was glad to volunteer her own body as a biological petri dish in which the future of humanity was growing day by day.

She removed a cell sample from Subject #CHS-453-X and inspected it through the electron microscope, paying particular attention to the chromosomes as they paired off during cell division. Something didn't look quite right about one pair, so, frowning, she increased the magnification. Through the lens of the microscope, the paired chromosomes looked like segmented black worms joined at their midsections so that each pair seemed to form a squiggly X shape. Except for one pair, that is. To Kaur's chagrin, she saw that a piece of one chromosome seemed to have broken off and reattached itself to the wrong arm of the X, producing a distinctly lopsided and unsymmetrical set of chromosomes.

"Good heavens," she said in Punjabi. How on earth did *that* get through the screening process? Lifting her face from the microscope, she used a grease pencil to mark the embryo in question for immediate incineration. Probably just a random mutation, she surmised, of the sort that spontaneously occurred every now and then. Oh well; if nothing else, catching an aberration like this one justified the long hours she put in giving the embryos a final checkup.

Thankfully, the next cell sample, from #CHS-454-X, showed no apparent defects, while the fetus itself appeared to be developing normally. Peering at the tiny speck of pink protoplasm, she couldn't help marveling at the exquisite machinery tucked away in the nucleus of every cell in the fetus: nearly two meters of stringy nucleic acids capable of producing an individual who might someday change the world.

Just like its older brothers and sisters.

Her imagination pictured the struggling, chaotic world outside this pristine laboratory, an endangered planet filled with flawed, imperfect men and women. *If they only knew,* she thought triumphantly, *what tomorrow brings . . . !*

CHAPTER THREE

HOTEL PALAESTRO
ROME, ITALY
MAY 14, 1974

"WELCOME TO ROME, DR. NEARY," THE MAN AT THE front desk said. "May I see some identification?"

"*Sì,*" Roberta answered, fishing around in her handbag for her phony ID. Traveling under an alias no longer troubled her; she knew from experience that Seven's advanced Beta 5 computer manufactured the best forgeries on the planet, even if the machine's snobbish artificial intelligence had something of an attitude problem. She blithely handed over "Veronica Neary's" passport and driver's license.

Isis squawked impatiently from within the plastic carrying case at Roberta's feet. The cat's indignant outburst reached the ears of the hotel clerk, who leaned over the edge of the counter to check out Roberta's belongings. Amber eyes stared back at him defiantly.

"*Scusi,* Doctor," said the clerk, who spoke excellent

English, "but I'm afraid the hotel does not permit pets."

Roberta sighed inwardly. *It wasn't my idea to bring the damn cat along,* she thought. But Seven had insisted that Isis accompany Roberta to Rome, leaving the young woman to wonder who was supposed to be looking out for whom. "Maybe you can make an exception, *per favore?*" She slid several thousand lira in paper bills across the counter toward the clerk. "I'd really appreciate it."

The brightly colored bills, featuring high-powered denominations with plenty of eye-catching zeroes, were quite genuine. The Beta 5 was perfectly capable of producing perfect counterfeits, of course, but she and Seven tried to use real currency wherever possible, to avoid inviting the scrutiny of the world's various treasury departments. Fortunately, covering their expenses was no problem, since Seven's earthly predecessors had shrewdly invested in any number of developing industries and discoveries, from Kodak to cellophane. As the sole employees of a company supposedly devoted to "encyclopedia research," she and her taciturn boss had money to burn, which certainly came in useful at times like this.

The clerk looked about quickly, to make sure no one was looking, then pocketed the cash. "*Prego,*" he said, returning his attention back to her documents. He handed them back to her along with a set of room keys. "The elevator is to the right," he informed her. "Room 11-G."

Roberta nodded gratefully, then hefted both her suitcase and Isis's carrier off the floor. She yawned, pretending to be jet-lagged from the long flight from America. In fact, she and Isis had taken the Blue Smoke Express to a deserted back alley two blocks away, but there was no need to advertise that particular detail to everyone in the hotel lobby. As far as any curious onlookers might be concerned, she was just another newly arrived delegate to the International Conference on Genetic Research and Experimentation.

Two months of pursuing assorted useless leads had not brought her and Gary Seven any closer to solving the Mystery of the Missing Scientists. This conference was one of their few remaining hopes for locating the vanished researchers, a not-quite-last-ditch ploy entrusted to Roberta while Seven followed another line of inquiry back in the States. *Let's hope this little expedition pays off,* she thought as she lugged her baggage across the lobby to the waiting elevator. *Or that Seven has better luck with his investigation.*

Her mission in Rome was twofold: keep a sharp eye out for any of the absent geneticists who might be tempted to attend the conference, while simultaneously presenting a likely target to whomever was responsible for the scientists' disappearances. *Just call me bait,* she thought, a role she was all too familiar with from prior undercover operations; the hard part was going to be passing herself off as an up-and-coming Ph.D. for as long as it took to attract the right (or wrong, depending on your perspective) kind of interest.

The weight of her suitcase tugged relentlessly on her arm and shoulders. Besides three days' worth of clothes and toiletries, the overstuffed bag also bulged with the latest scientific journals, along with a couple of weighty tomes on the theoretical applications of genetic engineering. She had started reading up on the subject after that eventful visit to Berlin, but she'd still brought along plenty of homework to keep her busy in her spare time, the better to impersonate a topflight biological whiz kid.

No moonlight excursions to the Fountain of Trevi this trip, she thought, sighing wistfully. *No time for sight-seeing while the fate of the world hangs in the balance.* Unlocking the door to Room 11-G, she stumbled inside. Her suitcase landed with a thud on the carpeted floor, giving her tired arm a break, but she couldn't help wishing that she were in Rome as a tourist, not a secret agent. *So what else is new?* she mused, liberating Isis from the confines of the plastic carrier. Without so much as a meow of thanks, or even a backward glance, the jet-black feline scurried away to check out the bathroom. A few seconds later, the door to the bathroom closed behind the cat.

At least she's housebroken, Roberta thought. Heck, Isis didn't even need a litter box; human facilities more than suited her needs, for reasons Roberta knew only too well. "Don't take all day in there," she called irritably to Gary Seven's so-called pet. "You're not the only one who wants to freshen up."

Roberta heard the toilet flush, followed by the sound of water pouring into the sink. Isis seemed to take her own sweet time washing up, but eventually the bathroom door swung open and the cat padded out onto the carpeted floor. Ignoring Roberta completely, Isis sprang onto the windowsill and settled down to watch the city streets below. *Fine,* Roberta thought. She didn't feel like sparring with the cat anyway. . . .

Shortly, after kicking off her shoes and making herself comfortable, Roberta retrieved a sheaf of folded papers from her carry-on bag, then stretched out on the queen-size bed to give them a closer look. No doubt the exact schedule for the conference had changed since this tentative itinerary had been mailed out, but there was time enough to look into that later this evening. Right now she just wanted to refamiliarize herself with the programming options available to her.

Even the titles of the various panels and symposia were fairly daunting: "Replication of Chromosomal Segments by Means of Enzymes derived from *Escherichia coli*," "Further Applications of Prokaryotic Bacteriophages as Transgenic Vectors," "The Use of Recombinant DNA in Multiclonal Antibodies" . . .

Let's see, Roberta thought, underlining some of indicated seminars with a colored pencil. Traffic noises drifted upward from the busy streets outside. *If I was a brilliant scientific genius on the cutting edge of the genetic frontier, where would I go?*

The ten A.M. presentation on "Tomorrow's Medicine: The Genetics of Health" was being held in a crowded lecture hall on the hotel's mezzanine. Roberta arrived early to get a good seat, right up front where she could be nice and visible. The better to attract attention, she had also worn a stylish polyester shirtdress in a cheerfully bright red-and-white print. A bit more conservative than her usual style—she felt like Florence Henderson on *The Brady Bunch*—but, then again, she wasn't attending the conference as herself. Isis, thankfully, had been left behind in their hotel room, to watch Italian TV, call for room service, or do whatever insufferable alien kitties did to amuse themselves.

Roberta couldn't care less; she had bigger things to worry about.

As discreetly as she could, Roberta scanned the audience as the hall rapidly filled up, looking for one or more of the missing geneticists, whose photos she had committed to memory. So far the only faces she recognized, though, were from the dust jackets of some of the scholarly tomes she'd perused the night before. *Would I spot the others if they were in disguise?* she wondered; the Beta 5 had tracked down the best photo reference available on all of the missing scientists, but in some instances, the results had been decidedly sketchy, especially for most of the Eastern Bloc subjects. In those cases, all Roberta had to go on were some blurry, black-and-white photos, sometimes years out of date. *I might not even spot some of those characters if they sat down right beside me.*

The conference was definitely drawing a real international crowd, she noted, munching on *biscotti* as she waited for the lecture to start. Among the hubbub of voices surrounding her, she identified American, French, German, Dutch, even Haitian and Pakistani accents. Her automatic translator was getting a workout, even though she had deliberately picked a talk that was being delivered in English, just to make her mission simpler. *It was as good a criterion as any,* she thought. *Besides, this one sounds more general than some of the others.*

At approximately five minutes to ten, not one of the absent geneticists had made the scene, and Roberta seriously considered skipping over to one of the other events to scope out the crowd there. That seemed a little *too* conspicuous, however, not to mention rude, so she settled back into her seat, posed with her pencil poised above an open notebook, and prayed that her eyes would not glaze over too obviously.

To her relief, the lecture, delivered by a Nobel Prize nominee whose name Roberta recognized from a couple of her marked-up scientific journals, was more accessible and interesting than she had feared. The good thing about gene splicing and cloning and all, it occurred to her, was that, since nobody could actually *do* all that stuff just yet, it was a lot easier to discuss their implications in the abstract than to get bogged down in all the messy little details.

"The promise of gene therapy holds the hope of preventing—and even eradicating—a wide variety of human diseases and frailties," the Famous Professor said after a ninety-minute survey of hereditary disorders and their genetic causes. "Cystic fibrosis, muscular dystrophy, mental retardation, sickle-cell anemia, juvenile diabetes, hemophilia, ADA deficiency, also known as 'bubble boy' disease—these and many other grievous human ailments will be stricken from the annals of mortal suffering once we can use recombinant DNA techniques to correct the chromosomal defects that cause such conditions. By splicing healthy genes into the germ cells of individual parents, whose families may have carried one of these harmful mutations for generations, we will be able to lift this curse from their children, their grandchildren, and all their descendants to come. Thank you."

Sounds good, Roberta admitted, joining in a round of polite applause. Her initial gut response to this whole gene-tampering business had been one of wary skepticism; messing around with people's DNA sounded a little too close to *Brave New World* for comfort, and

Gary Seven's dubious attitude toward the endeavor (even if faintly hypocritical) had only heightened her suspicion that maybe genetic engineering was one of those things that mankind was meant to leave alone, like nuclear missiles and streaking.

On the other hand, she had to concede that the F.P. had made a good case for the medical benefits of selective genetic repair work. Roberta had known a girl with muscular dystrophy back in junior high; poor Tina had already been forced into a wheelchair by seventh grade, and her condition had only deteriorated over the years they went to school together. In the end, she had died early in her twenties. Roberta remembered attending her funeral, and thinking what a waste it was that such a bright and talented person hadn't lived to fulfill her full potential, all because of a genetic accident that occurred before she was even born. *If gene therapy could have cured Tina's MD,* Roberta thought, *or maybe even fixed the problem in her parents' genes before she was ever conceived, then maybe conscientious chromosome-splicing isn't as bad as Seven makes it out to be?*

But now was no time for hesitation or indecision, she realized; if she wanted to reach the people behind the big project Seven feared was in the works, then she needed to place herself firmly and publicly on the side of bigger and better DNA.

She waited for the applause to subside. Then, as soon as the F.P. asked for questions from the audience, her hand shot up faster than a Saturn V rocket.

Her quick reflexes (and snappy fashion sense) must have done the trick. "Yes?" the F.P. prompted, calling on her. "What is your question, please?"

Roberta stood up in the first row of the auditorium,

feeling the collective gaze of the entire assembly turn upon her. *Good thing I'm not prone to stage fright*, she thought as she cleared her throat. *Well, here goes nothing.*

"So far all you've proposed is fixing preexisting defects in the genetic makeup of a few individuals whose DNA isn't quite up to code. What about making overall improvements in the ordinary human genome? Increasing life expectancy, for example, or intelligence?" She raised her voice, trying to sound inspired and enthusiastic. "Why settle for curing a handful of inherited disorders when you can use genetic engineering to create a better and more advanced form of human being?"

Her remarks didn't exactly elicit gasps—this was a pretty savvy crowd where such notions were concerned—but Roberta thought she detected more and louder murmuring going on all around her, thanks to her bold (and, to be honest, wildly reckless) proposals. *So much for making a splash on Day One*, she thought, sitting back down in her seat. *Here's hoping somebody takes the bait.*

She didn't have long to wait.

Roberta first noticed she was being followed later that morning, while strolling through the Eternal City in search of lunch. After her successful infiltration of the conference, she'd figured she was entitled to a break and a little of the local cuisine. *Why save the world if you can't stop and smell the pizza once in a while?*

The two men—one Asian, one Latino—started shadowing her shortly after she left the hotel and had been keeping her in sight ever since. They were being discreet about it, naturally, but years of spy games with

Gary Seven had given Roberta very good instincts when it came to being the subject of covert surveillance. *You're good,* she silently granted her secret admirers, *but I've been tailed by the best, including invisible aliens from Devidia II!*

She paused in front of a window display on the Via Sistina, ostensibly to check her reflection in the glass, but actually to take a closer look at the two strangers as they lingered on the sidewalk across the street, apparently engrossed in an Italian newspaper. The front-page headline said something about the Red Brigade and terrorism, but she doubted that the men were actually paying much attention to any news articles at the moment.

The Asian man looked vaguely familiar; Roberta thought she'd seen him around the conference. He was a slender, handsome man, about her age, wearing a somewhat battered tweed jacket over a Godzilla T-shirt. His long hair and sideburns made him resemble some long-lost Japanese cousin of the Partridge Family. Roberta caught him peeking at her from behind his companion's newspaper, but pretended not to notice. From his lapse, she guessed that he was new at this, and not a professional spook.

The other man was a whole different story: he was almost freakishly large, maybe seven feet tall, a yard across the shoulders, and a good deal more intimidating. *Just like that robot Bigfoot up north,* she thought, *only a lot less shaggy.* Indeed, the second man was a walking endorsement for Darwin's theory of evolution, complete with sloping brow and a noticeably prognathous jawline. Tinted sunglasses concealed the giant's eyes while the bottom half of his broad, square face maintained a stony expression. A black silk suit was draped over his imposing frame and a marine-style crew cut bristled atop his oh-so-simian skull. *And they say the Neanderthals have all died out. . . .*

Roberta could readily believe that the first man was another visiting scientist, in town for the conference; there was something mildly nerdish about his appearance and body language. The big gorilla, on the other hand, looked more like an enforcer than a geneticist. *Talk about your Odd Couples,* she thought. *These two make Felix and Oscar look like identical clones.*

Turning away from the reflective glass, she let them tail her for a few more blocks, until curiosity, not to mention an empty stomach, prompted her to see what would happen if she presented a stationary target for a while. Just how long would they be willing to hang out, she wondered, waiting for her to start moving again?

Lunch was a slice of pizza, a can of Fresca, and, for dessert, a small helping of fresh gelato. Roberta sat on the Spanish Steps overlooking the city, enjoying the warm spring weather as she gazed out at the rose-colored rooftops spread out before her, nestled snugly between Rome's famed seven hills. Throngs of tourists flowed up and down the steps, posing for photographs and admiring the view, while portrait artists, flower vendors, and portable snack carts competed for their attention. Roberta politely declined several roses, plus the opportunity to be immortalized in colored chalk or watercolors, and resisted the temptation to look back over her shoulder to see what her mismatched pursuers were up to. The pizza crust was thin and crispy, just the way she liked it. *Your move, guys,* she thought.

"Excuse me, miss," a friendly voice greeted her within minutes. Roberta looked up, but the glare from the midday sun whited out the face of the speaker. Squinting into the blinding sunshine, all she could make out was a single male figure standing on the step just above hers.

"Hang on," Roberta urged through a mouthful of pizza. She scrambled to her feet, nearly knocking over her soda in the process. "Just give me a second here." *Is this it?* she wondered, her heart speeding faster in anticipation. *Surely I can't have hit pay dirt so soon!*

Raising her hand to shield her eyes, she saw that the speaker was the Asian guy, minus his hefty partner. "I'm sorry to bother you," he said with a smile and a slight Japanese accent, "but I wanted to let you know that I was impressed by your remarks at the presentation this morning."

Bingo! Roberta felt a surge of triumph, then struggled to hold on to a more cautious attitude. *Let's not jump to conclusions,* she warned herself. *It's just possible that he might only be trying to pick me up.*

"Thank you," Roberta answered in English. The more she thought about it, the more she thought she recognized this guy from the talk on gene therapy. "I thought it was a fascinating topic." She started to offer to shake, then realized that her hands were full of pizza and gelato. *Oops!* She hastily placed the half-eaten gelato between her feet, switched the pizza slice to her left hand, wiped off the right on her skirt, then stretched out her open and not-too-greasy palm. "Veronica Neary, but you can call me Ronnie."

If the cheesy residue on her hand bothered the young man, he gave no sign of it. "Dr. Walter Takagi," he introduced himself, giving her hand a firm shake. "Pleased to meet you."

"Ditto." Roberta shifted right to put the sun fully behind her, hoping to locate her other shadow. Looking up the stairs, past Takagi, she spotted his enormous partner near the top of the steps, having his portrait sketched by one of the ubiquitous street artists. Rather ominously, he kept his shades on while posing seated upon a stool that looked two sizes too small, his opaque gaze studiously directed away from Roberta and his accomplice. *Now, this guy's probably a pro,* she surmised, wondering why they had decided to let the amateur make the first approach.

"So, you're here for the conference, too?" she asked, as casually as possible. Now that she had possibly hit the jackpot, she wasn't entirely sure what to do next. *Just play it by ear,* she told herself. The most important thing now was not to scare either of the two men away.

"Exactly," Takagi said warmly, as though they were old friends. "You're American, correct?"

"That's right," she said. "From the University of Washington, in Seattle." She lied confidently, knowing that Seven had already established a paper trail backing up her fictitious identity, just in case anyone felt inclined to check up on her. There was even a fully furnished apartment in Seattle's U. district, complete with a working phone number, newspaper and magazine subscriptions, photo albums, diplomas, and all the other accoutrements of Ronnie Neary's imaginary existence.

"That was a pretty brave position you took this morning," Takagi observed, "especially given most people's irrational aversion to radical genetic engineering for its own sake." She noted that he did not volunteer any information about where he was working these days. "Not everyone would be willing to go out on a limb like that, particularly at so public a forum." He eyed Roberta hopefully. "Were those your actual views on the subject, or were you just playing devil's advocate?"

Roberta told him exactly what she figured he wanted to hear. "Not at all. Recombinant DNA research is the most exciting thing to come around since the discovery of the wheel. I really think it can change humanity—for the better, of course."

"Me, too!" Takagi exclaimed. His dark brown eyes lighted up at the prospect. "We may be the first generation to actually take control of our own biological destiny. It's a chance to create a whole new world, full of better, healthier, and more intelligent people."

"A veritable genetic golden age," she suggested, finding Takagi's optimism and enthusiasm surprisingly infectious. He certainly didn't seem like the sort of person to be mixed up in the kind of sinister experiments Seven envisioned, let alone the abduction of his fellow scientists. *Maybe we're barking up the wrong tree here,* she mused.

"Hey, I like that!" he said encouragingly. "The Golden Age of Genetics, that's a good phrase." He pulled a small spiral notebook from his pocket and jotted the slogan down. "Sounds like we're on the same wavelength," he continued. "In fact, I may know about a project that might intrigue you." He paused momentarily, glancing upward at his burly . . . bodyguard? Baby-sitter? "I'm really not at liberty to discuss the details right now, but perhaps we could discuss it later, over drinks or something?"

"I'd like that," Roberta said, trying to sound interested, but not *too* interested. "Are you staying at the Hotel Palaestro?"

After another hesitant pause, Takagi revealed that he was indeed rooming at the same hotel as Roberta. They agreed to meet later that evening at the hotel bar. "Great," he concluded, giving her a parting nod. "I'll let you finish your lunch then. Nice meeting you, Dr. Neary."

Without a backward glance at either Roberta or his former companion, he marched down the wide marble steps to the piazza below, swiftly disappearing into the milling crowd of tourists, artists, and flower vendors. She waited to see if Mighty Joe Young would take off after him, but, no, the other man didn't budge from his perch at the top of the stairs. *Looks like I've still got a shadow,* she realized. *He's probably waiting to see what I do next.*

It was kind of a frustrating situation. Roberta would have liked to run after Takagi and tail him back to the conference, if that indeed was where he was heading, but that was hardly an option while she was under observation herself. A mental image of King Kong following her following Takagi produced a rueful smile. Nobody ever said international espionage was going to be easy.

Instead she had no choice but to play it cool and let the idealistic young scientist go, confident that they would meet again as planned. *If he wanted to make a break for it,* she assured herself, *he didn't need to make an appointment with me first—unless that was just to lull me into a false sense of security.*

She glanced at her wristwatch. It was nearly one P.M.

Over six hours to go before she hooked up again with Takagi. She sighed loudly; it was going to be a long, anxious afternoon, most likely with the world's largest secret admirer for company. Washing down one last bite of pizza with a swallow of Fresca, she started down the steps. Producing a compact from the depths of her macrame purse, she peeked in the mirror at Magilla Gorilla. Sure enough, he started moving again as soon as she did, thrusting a handful of lira at a surprised artist and leaving his unfinished portrait behind.

Just to play it safe, she turned left when she reached the Bernini fountain at the foot of the stairs, heading off in the opposite direction than Takagi had. The distinction between roadway and sidewalk turned out to be a blurry one, and she had to step briskly to avoid collisions with the ever-present Vespa motor scooters. Not too surprisingly, her large and silent pursuer managed to keep up with her. *Yep,* she thought. *Definitely a long day ahead.*

4

CHAPTER FOUR

THE SIGN ON THE OUTER DOOR NOW READ AEGIS
Scientific Supplies, Inc., a small but essential detail in
the sting operation Gary Seven had taken pains to set
into motion over the past two months. Now, if fortune
was on his side, his efforts were about to bring him one
step closer to the answers he sought.

"Mr. Offenhouse to see you, sir," his newly hired
temporary receptionist informed him over the intercom. Unlike Roberta, this young woman, whom he'd
hired for the morning primarily to maintain appearances, had no idea that Seven and his business were
anything more than they appeared.

"Thank you, Allison," he replied. "I'll be right out."
He depressed a concealed switch on his desk and the
nearby Beta 5 computer station, all gleaming steel and

brightly flashing display panels, swung inward, vanishing into a hidden recess in the wall. As the futuristic terminal disappeared, an ordinary-looking bookcase rotated into place, concealing the Beta 5 entirely from sight. Scientific manuals and catalogues now occupied the bookshelves that had, up until recently, held encyclopedias and reference tomes: yet another part of the misleading facade Seven had carefully constructed.

He took a moment to survey the office, confirming that its trappings were all 1974-standard, then straightened his tie and headed out to the foyer to greet his visitor.

"Good morning, Mr. Offenhouse," he said. A clock on the wall revealed that it was exactly 9:05 A.M. The newcomer was punctual, if nothing else. "Thank you for coming by."

"Let's hope it's worth my time," the other man answered brusquely. An American businessman in his late thirties, Ralph Offenhouse strode forward and took Seven's hand, squeezing it forcefully. *Standard alpha-male behavior,* Seven recalled, *not unlike a Klingon greeting ritual, although somewhat less bloody.* He squeezed back with equal force, as the customs of this era expected him to. "Why don't we step into my office and get down to business then," he suggested. "Allison, please hold my calls."

Aside from Roberta or Isis, he wasn't really expecting to hear from anybody, but Seven judged that it was important to present the appearance of a thriving business.

"Sounds good to me," Offenhouse agreed. He stepped through the interior door into Seven's personal office. Shrewd brown eyes inspected the room's furnishings, assessing their worth and state of repair. "Not a bad place you've got here," he conceded eventually. Without waiting for an invitation, he sat down on the couch and waited for Seven to take his place behind the obsidian-and-walnut desk. A translucent green cube sat like a paperweight atop various phony reports and invoices.

"Can I offer you a drink?" Seven asked.

Offenhouse shook his head. "No thanks," he said, glancing at an expensive Rolex wristwatch. "I'm a busy man, so let's not waste time with formalities." He stared across the room at Seven, establishing eye contact. "Like I said on the phone, I saw your ad in that magazine. Are those prices for real?"

Knowing that any project involving large-scale genetic engineering would require quantities of specialized equipment, Seven had placed a prominent ad in a number of popular science and medical trade magazines, offering sophisticated biotech apparatus at discount prices. Most of the inquiries generated by the ad had come from institutions and individuals that checked out as entirely aboveboard and innocuous; those deals he had quietly allowed to fall through, except for a few especially deserving clinics and research projects that he didn't mind subsidizing indirectly. Offenhouse was different; from their earlier discussions on the phone, Seven had sensed something covert, evasive, and promisingly illicit about the man's approach.

Subsequent biographical research had revealed that Offenhouse was a self-made entrepreneur with a history of faintly shady dealings. Marketing thalidomide in the Third World, for instance, long after the mutagenic tranquilizer had been discredited in the more advanced industrial nations, and investing in primitive cryogenics projects that sold a dubious promise of prolonged existence to the desperate, the fearful, and the terminally ill. Furthermore, he possessed no known connection to any reputable scientific organizations. *Assuming Offenhouse doesn't want the equipment for himself,* Seven wondered, *whom is he fronting for?*

"The prices are as advertised," he informed Offenhouse, removing his servo from his coat pocket and fiddling with it as though it were merely an ordinary silver pen. In this manner he instructed the crystalline cube on his desk to record the conversation for future reference and analysis. Later on, after Offenhouse departed, he could then examine his visitor's voice patterns to determine when and if the pugnacious businessman was telling the truth.

"Is that so?" Offenhouse said. Beneath bushy black eyebrows, dark eyes regarded Seven suspiciously. "What's your angle, Seven? How can you afford to unload this gear so cheap?"

"Excess inventory," Seven lied smoothly. "It costs too much to store this quantity of equipment on a long-term basis. In addition, I'd rather sell off the majority of my stock now, before the next generation of technology renders my inventory obsolete."

Offenhouse appeared only partly appeased by Seven's explanation. "What about quality?" he demanded. "I'm not going to pay good money for junk. I insist on inspecting the merchandise before payment."

"Of course," Seven agreed. "My instruments are all state-of-the-art and in excellent condition, as you can certainly see for yourself upon delivery."

Offenhouse glanced around the office, as if half-expecting to see a stockpile of electron microscopes or gel electrophoresis units tucked away in a corner of the room. Rising from the couch, he removed a folded sheet of paper from the inside pocket of his jacket and handed it to Seven. "Here's a rundown of what I'm looking for, and in what quantities. You think you can meet this order?"

Seven unfolded the document and scanned its contents. He nodded to himself, seeing more or less exactly what he had expected. *If I wanted to perform serious genetic resequencing using twentieth-century Earth technology,* he thought, *these are the rather crude instruments I would need to obtain.* The large volume of apparatus requested was also ominous, implying experimentation on a disturbingly ambitious scale. "A quite impressive list," he commented. "May I ask what you need all this equipment for?"

"Frankly, that's none of your business," Offenhouse stated bluntly. "Mine either, for that matter. All you need to know is that I've been commissioned by a private consortium to handle various business transactions for them, preferably without attracting a lot of attention."

Seven feigned a worried expression. "This isn't anything illegal, is it?"

"We're not talking South American drug lords, if that's bothering you." Offenhouse never took his intent gaze off the man he was trying to convince, almost daring Seven to contradict him. "This is all about science, and research, and not letting some other crew of eggheads get the jump on you before you're ready to go public with your big-deal discovery. Between you and me, Seven, I don't care if my clients are trying to cure the common cold or clone Elvis Presley, just so long as I get my commission. If you're smart, you won't worry about it either. Just take the money and run."

"I don't know," Seven hedged, hoping to draw more information from his visitor. "It all sounds a bit . . . unorthodox."

Offenhouse slapped his palms down on the desktop between him and Seven, thrusting his scowling face forward. "Look, Seven, let me put all my cards on the table. I'm willing to pay you *twice* what you're asking for everything on that list, provided there are no questions asked. So, do we have a deal or not?"

The more he heard, the more convinced Gary Seven was that this brash, overbearing businessman provided a link to whatever secret project was responsible for the disappearance of so many of the world's top scientists. All he needed to do now was to let Offenhouse lead him one step closer to the truth.

"Very well, Mr. Offenhouse," he said readily. "You've got a deal."

CHRYSALIS BASE
LOCATION: CLASSIFIED

"You asked to see me, Director?"

"Yes," Sarina Kaur answered from the midst of Chrysalis's communal garden. Cool water sprayed from the lotus-shaped fountain at the center of a tiled courtyard surrounded by ferns and fragrant orchids. Now six months pregnant, Kaur sat upon a white cane bench beneath the leafy bough of a mango tree, genetically engineered to bear refreshing fruit all year long. Solar lamps installed in the high domed ceiling simulated the light of a pleasant spring afternoon. Kaur found the tranquil atmosphere of the garden highly conducive to contemplation; she often came here when, as now, there was a difficult decision to be made.

"Thank you for coming, Dr. Singer," she continued, putting aside the plate of chicken *tikka* she had been having for a late dinner. Despite a distinct Indian lilt, her English was impeccable. "Especially at such short notice, and at this hour."

"Sure, no problem," Joel Singer said a little too quickly. His white lab coat was stained from the day's experiments and he shuffled nervously, not quite making eye contact with his superior at the project. "Er, what's this all about anyway?"

Kaur inspected the youthful American biochemist. A slender white male with curly black hair, Singer had come to them directly upon completing his postgraduate studies at Columbia and Johns Hopkins. At the time, he had seemed like quite a catch: talented, enthusiastic, and committed. Now, however, she had reason to doubt their initial assessment, especially where the latter trait was concerned. *Too bad we have yet to isolate a gene for loyalty.*

A manila envelope rested beside her on the bench. She picked up the envelope and handed it to the younger scientist, who had to step forward to receive it. "I was hoping you could explain this," she stated.

The temperature in the garden was cool and comfortable, yet beads of perspiration broke out upon Singer's unlined brow. He gulped as he opened the envelope and drew out the documents inside: several sheets of stationery marked with his own handwriting.

Beneath a carefully cultivated tan, the American's face went pale.

"How did you get this?" he blurted. "You've been reading my mail?" He tried to muster an air of righteous indignation, with only partial success. "You had no right . . . this was private, personal!"

Such predictable behavior saddened Kaur. "Now, Joel, you know we have to maintain the tightest security here. Secrecy is essential to the project. You were told that from the beginning." *Perhaps we chose him too hastily,* she thought with more than a twinge of regret. *If so, then this is partly our fault.*

"But it's just a harmless letter to a friend, an old classmate from Columbia," Singer insisted. He waved the sheets like a paper fan before the seated woman's eyes. "Read it yourself. It's all just small talk."

Kaur was not swayed by his protestations. "First off, all contact with the outside world was to be strictly supervised. Those were the rules. Second, you and I both know that this letter is not nearly as inconsequential as you meant it to appear." She gave Singer a rueful look. "Did you really think we'd forget that cryptography was a special hobby of yours? It's in your file, Joel."

Confronted thus, Singer looked unsteady on his feet. He tottered slightly, looking about plaintively for some sort of support amid the flowering bushes. Finally, he staggered backward and sat down awkwardly upon one of the lotus-shaped fountain's sculpted marble petals. "I can explain," he murmured weakly. "It's not as bad as it looks."

"It took us several weeks to crack the code," Kaur admitted, paying little attention to Singer's feeble denials, "but what we found is disturbing. Very disturbing." She did not need to reclaim the actual letter to recall the most damning passages. "In this letter, you confide to your friend that you were having 'second thoughts,' that you had accidentally discovered something that disturbed you." A look of extreme disappointment surfaced on her face, rising up from deep within her. "I thought you shared our devotion to the future, Joel."

"I do!" he exclaimed immediately, then caught himself holding contradictory evidence between his own fingers. "Mostly, I mean."

"But—?" she prompted him, wanting to conclude this matter as efficiently as possible. *If it were done when 'tis done, then t'were well it were done quickly,* she thought, referencing *Macbeth*, but first it was important to learn just what had led the young researcher astray, if only to prevent future mistakes—and sacrifices—of this nature.

Mercifully, Singer did not waste any more time proclaiming his innocence. "Look, I was nosing around on Level Four, hoping to scope out something more exciting than the routine stuff I've been working on lately, when I stumbled onto what looked like one of your pet projects." He raised his voice, hoping to claim the moral high ground. "What the hell are you doing breeding antibiotic-resistant streptococcus? Don't you know how dangerous that is? I saw lab rats in the final stages of some kind of complete cellular breakdown. The bacteria were literally eating away at their flesh!"

"Naturally," she replied serenely, unruffled by the young scientist's accusations. "That was the intent." She made a mental note to increase security on Level Four. "You needn't worry, though; all of our special children possess a genetic immunity to all forms of streptococcus."

"At the moment, I don't care about your precious whiz kids!" Nervous trepidation gave way to anger as Singer vented his previously hidden qualms. He rose from his seat on the edge of the fountain and began to pace upon the courtyard's red cement tiles. "Hell, I'm smarter than average, ninety-ninth percentile and all that, and even I'm freaked out by these pint-sized mega-geniuses we're manufacturing, especially that precocious little four-year-old of yours, the first creepy chip off your block." His gaze drifted automatically toward the director's swollen belly, as if envisioning an even more unnerving prodigy to come. "But what about the rest of us? What about the billions of ordinary people out there? Do you know what this super-bug could do to them?"

"Of course I do, Joel." She waited patiently for him to put the pieces together, mildly surprised that it was taking this long. Was he, perhaps, not really as bright as advertised, or was he just in denial? She suspected the latter.

But no amount of willful self-delusion could shield him from the ugly truth forever. She could literally watch the realization sink into his consciousness as the blood slowly drained from his face. It made an interesting case study in somatic responses to psychological stress.

"Oh my god, that's what this is all about, isn't it? Pruning the herd to make room for your Master Race? In with the new, out with the old." His entire body was shaking now, rocked by tremors of shock and remorse. "Nobody told me about this part! I thought we were working to *help* humanity . . . !"

"That depends on how you define 'humanity,' " she said, carefully probing his responses. In truth, she was more interested in analyzing the turncoat scientist than converting him. "The future of the species is here at Chrysalis."

"No, it's inhuman! I see that now. There's nothing human about this entire insane project." His tone swung between outrage and pleading. "We're talking about a flesh-eating bacterium here. Millions of innocent people wouldn't stand a chance."

Ah, I see, Kaur observed, understanding at last. *A misguided reverence for individual human lives, married to excessive identification with a soon-to-be-obsolete mode of humanity. We'll have to watch out for that in the future, especially with American candidates.* If nothing else, his volatile, highly emotional reactions made it clear that certain aspects of the project's long-term agenda should remain known only to the upper echelons of Chrysalis's leadership. Why burden the likes of Singer, or even Walter Takagi, with foreknowledge of the dreadful sacrifices to come?

Unfortunately, she judged, there was little that could be done to salvage Singer himself at this point; his counterproductive prejudices were doubtless deeply rooted. "Thank you for speaking so freely," she told him sincerely. "You've provided me with everything I need to know."

The finality in her tone reached him even through his mutinous outburst. "So, what now?" he confronted her. "Are you putting me on the first plane back to the States?"

Kaur shook her head. "I'm sorry, Joel. I wish I could." She removed a small brass bell from her pocket and rang it once. In response, two massive Sikh security guards appeared at either end of the garden, blocking both exits. Stern, unforgiving faces regarded him from beneath both turbans and bristling black beards. Their uniforms were blue, the color of the unstoppable monsoon. Automatic pistols in hand, they converged on Singer, who began to shake uncontrollably as his mind grasped the rapidly shrinking shape of his future.

"Wha—? No!" he exclaimed, his eyes darting back and forth in a futile search for an escape route. Kaur quietly retrieved a sharp kitchen knife from her discarded dinner, in the event that the condemned scientist attempted one final act of fruitless violence before the guards took him into custody. "You can't do this!" he shouted hoarsely, tears streaming from his eyes. "I'm an American citizen! I haven't done anything!"

Kaur refused to look away from the pathetic spectacle of the youth's final moments. She felt she had an obligation not to shield herself from the consequences of her own decisions, no matter how unpleasant they might be. *To surpass Nature,* she reminded herself once more, *I must be crueler than Nature.* That painful truth was rapidly becoming her mantra.

"Please," Singer begged as the guards flanked him on both sides and began to drag him away. The scene was not unlike, she thought, a defective piece of DNA being sliced from the main sequence by a pair of specialized enzymes. "I won't tell anyone anything, I promise! Just let me go and you'll never hear from me again."

I can't risk that, she thought, her face a mask of cool detachment. No final appeal was possible; she had already consulted with the other senior members of the project and they had all agreed to abide by her ultimate decision. Singer was talented, but not irreplaceable; they could not allow him to endanger the future of human evolution.

The youth's pleas for mercy echoed in the garden's stillness even after the guards took him away, or so it seemed. Sarina Kaur sat alone with her thoughts, inhaling the genetically enhanced aroma of the orchids surrounding her. *What a tragic waste of fine genes and an excellent education,* she realized sorrowfully. Her only consolation, besides the certainty that everything that must be done was utterly necessary, was the knowledge that Singer's superlative DNA, his natural mental and physical gifts, would continue to contribute to the project long after the man himself, with all his confusion and misplaced sympathies, had ceased to exist.

What a shame that we can't change minds as easily as we rearrange genes. She felt the developing fetus stir within her, reminding her in a very visceral fashion of all that was at stake. *I can only hope that our next recruit will prove worth the risk of bringing him or her into Chrysalis.*

CHAPTER FIVE

OKAY, WHERE ARE YOU, WALTER? ROBERTA THOUGHT impatiently, nursing an overpriced glass of 7-Up. Perched on a stool near the entrance to the hotel bar, she scanned the crowded lounge for any sign of Takagi, but couldn't locate head nor hair of the young man she had met on the Spanish Steps earlier that day. *Ready when you are,* she urged the tardy scientist, while "The Way We Were" played loudly over the bar's Muzak system.

Not that she was alone, exactly. Takagi's silent partner, the Son of Kong, was only a couple of yards away, just as he had been for most of the afternoon. At the moment he was taking up pretty much an entire booth at the rear of the lounge, nursing a single glass of dark red wine and smoking a cigarette. Roberta wondered if he was tipping generously for the privilege of camping out in the booth indefinitely.

Doing her best to ignore her apparently constant companion, she peeked at her watch. To be honest, she was a bit early. Since parting company with her target at the Spanish Steps, Roberta had felt the last six hours drag on interminably. At first she'd tried to attend a few more scientific panels, just to maintain her cover, but her intriguing encounter with Takagi had left her too keyed up and restless to even pretend to concentrate on the finer points of nucleic-acid hybridization.

Instead she had used the modern (and then some) miracle of matter transmission to zap back to the office to check out "Walter Takagi" via the Beta 5. It had been not quite eleven A.M., New York time, when she arrived, and Seven had apparently left the office on some errand, but she used her voice-activated typewriter to dictate him a quick report on her progress, which she left on his desk. Checking her office calendar, she'd seen that Seven already met with a Mr. Offenhouse earlier that morning. Hopefully, Offenhouse had proven just as promising a lead as Takagi looked to be.

She'd been annoyed to discover evidence of an interloper at her usual desk, but guessed that Seven had sent the temp home right after his meeting with Offenhouse, which was just as well; at least she didn't have to explain to some clueless newbie how she'd materialized without warning in Seven's office. The last time that happened, she'd had to tranquilize that poor girl prior to rearranging her memories, a delicate and distinctly unnerving process that Roberta was in no hurry to repeat.

The modified Smith-Corona dutifully transcribed her verbal account of the day's events. By the time she finished the update, the Beta 5 had dug up everything there was to know about the youngish Japanese geneticist.

Turned out Takagi was his real name, and he was an up-and-coming expert on microbiology, currently on sabbatical from the University of Osaka. He was also, Roberta learned, unmarried, the oldest of four siblings, an avid bridge player, right-handed, a dues-paying member of the Official Gamera Fan Club, and allergic to shellfish. (The Beta 5 was nothing if not thorough.)

Nothing terribly incriminating there, she had concluded, but then again, they had never known for sure that there was anything overtly illegal going on. It occurred to her that she still couldn't be certain that there was a link between Takagi and all those missing scientists. *But there's definitely something rotten in Rome,* she reminded herself. Why else would someone go to the trouble of having her followed?

She'd lingered a bit in the empty office, hoping to catch Gary Seven should he come back. She was reluctant to page him via her servo unless it was a genuine emergency; who knew what he was up to at the moment. Eventually, though, she had to transport directly back to her hotel room in Rome, just in time to order a plate of *il pesce* for Isis, change into a snazzy little black dress, discover her shadow still lingering in the hall outside her room, and hurry down to the bar to wait for Takagi.

And wait, and wait. As torturous minutes passed without any trace of her quarry, Roberta grew increasingly anxious. Had she given herself away somehow? She compulsively replayed their entire conversation upon the steps, searching for any minor gaffe that might have aroused Takagi's suspicions. What if this whole prearranged rendezvous was merely a ruse by the seemingly friendly scientist to keep her occupied while he skipped town? How on earth would she ever track him down again? She sure couldn't spend the rest of her life attending scientific conferences in the hope of running into Takagi one more time. *If I let him get away,* she thought, *Isis will never let Seven forget how I screwed up.*

Granted, she still knew exactly where Takagi's companion, the gigantic Latino, was, but she could hardly expect him to lead her to the truth as long as he kept sticking to her like glue. *How do you spy on the person spying on you?* she thought, wincing at the notion. Paradoxes made her head hurt. *Better to stick to Plan A, and make nice with Takagi, assuming he ever shows up!*

Her gaze was fixed so intently on the entrance to the bar that she failed to notice anyone approaching her from behind until someone tapped gently on her shoulder. Roberta spun around on her stool, hoping to see Takagi.

To her surprise and disappointment, however, the tapper turned out to be a blond woman, in her early twenties, with a strained and distinctly desperate smile on her reassuringly wholesome-looking face. "There you are!" the golden-haired stranger said loudly, then leaned in to whisper to Roberta, "Please, let me pretend we're together."

What the heck? Roberta wondered, caught off guard. Looking past the other woman, though, she spotted a small pack of young male scientists hovering only a few feet away, scoping out both women as though they held the cure for cancer hidden somewhere in their cleavage. Each man was clutching a bottle of beer, and they were strutting and posing and trying to look as cool and debonair as a bunch of inebriated science nerds can be. *Oh, I get it,* Roberta thought, grasping the situation in an instant.

"About time you got here!" she exclaimed, playing along. She patted the empty stool next to her, which she'd planned to keep free for Dr. Takagi. "Here, I was saving you a seat." She leaned sideways to address the lurking party animals. "Sorry, guys, but we've got a lot to catch up on here. Girl talk, you know?"

Disappointed, the amorous biologists drifted away in search of other prospects, leaving Roberta alone with the new arrival. "Thanks!" the younger woman said, her voice clearly identifying her as an American. *A college student,* Roberta guessed, *attending the conference on her own.* "Gillian Taylor," the grateful stranger identified herself.

"Ronnie Neary," Roberta supplied, shaking Gillian's hand. "And no problem. We American chicks need to stick together, especially abroad."

"I'll say!" Gillian agreed. Her rosy cheeks, pearly smile, and corn-fed good looks clearly marked her as a daughter of the American heartland. For a second, Roberta was briefly reminded of those robot housewives she and Seven had stumbled onto in Connecticut earlier that year—Gillian was *that* cheerleader pretty and well groomed—but it was also clear that there was a lively and genuine personality behind her cheerful auburn eyes. "Some of these wild and crazy geneticists are a little too eager to pass on their DNA, if you know what I mean."

"Tell me about it," Roberta said sympathetically. She'd had to fend off a few unwelcome advances herself. "I think the male-to-female ratio at this conference is about ten to one. Reminds me of a science fiction convention I went to once; in fact, I think I recognize some of the same faces."

"You're probably right," Gillian laughed. The bartender swung by and she ordered herself a glass of wine. "So, are you here for the conference, too?"

"Definitely," Roberta said sincerely, before bending the truth a little. "Genetic engineering is my favorite pastime; at least, I hope it will be someday."

"Really?" Gillian asked, sounding intrigued. "I'm into marine biology myself, but I'm fascinated by the notion of preserving endangered species through cloning. There's talk of starting a genetic repository, where we can save tissue samples from any of the hundreds of species threatened with extinction, from the bald eagle to the humpback whale. In theory, someday it might even be possible to bring back a species that has already died out, provided there's enough leftover genetic material to work with. The Russians are even talking about resurrecting the woolly mammoth, using DNA harvested from frozen carcasses in Siberia."

Roberta was impressed by Gillian's obvious passion and enthusiasm for wildlife preservation; she'd have to ask Gary Seven if this mammoth-cloning idea could really work. "Sounds like a worthwhile goal," she said.

"I think so," Gillian stated. "Human progress has wiped out so many other species' natural habitats; it would be nice if we could use our ingenuity and technology to actually preserve some of the other living creatures on the planet. Once a species goes extinct, it's gone forever, at least until somebody invents a working time machine." Her wine arrived, and she paused to take a sip. "How about you? What kind of projects are you working on?"

"Oh, you know," Roberta fudged, "your basic chromosome counting and amino-acid mixing." She felt bad about lying so blatantly to her new friend, and was trying to figure out a way to divert the conversation from her own alleged career in genetic research when Walter Takagi came running into the bar, out of breath and apologizing profusely.

"Sorry I'm late," he said, huffing. He wore the same tweedy jacket as before, but had changed into a fresh T-shirt, this one featuring a brightly colored illustration of Astro Boy. "There was sort of a crisis on the project I mentioned, which meant a lot of long-distance phone calls." Roberta offered him a drink from her 7-Up, which he accepted gratefully. "Everything's fine now, though. I hope you weren't waiting too long."

"No problem," Roberta assured him. *Long-distance calls from where?* she wondered. "I had company." She introduced Takagi and Gillian to each other, then started to make her apologies to Gillian. "I'm afraid Dr. Takagi and I have things to talk about."

"That's fine," Gillian insisted. She finished off her wine, then looked around the bar. "I think maybe I'll migrate to a less predator-infested environment. Room service and an early bedtime sounds like seventh heaven at this point." The youthful marine biologist surrendered her seat to Takagi. "Thanks again for playing chaperone."

"Anytime," Roberta said. "Good luck saving the whales and all."

Once off his feet, Takagi's labored breathing quickly returned to normal. He took advantage of his second wind to keep on burbling apologies for his late arrival. "It was completely unavoidable, I promise."

"I know how that goes," Roberta said sympathetically. She was just glad that Takagi had shown up at all,
although she tried to hide the extent of her relief from
the voluble scientist. After all, he shouldn't know that
she'd come all the way to Rome just to track down
some eager-beaver genetic engineers. *That might scare
him off for good,* she thought.

Interestingly, Takagi's appearance on the scene
seemed to liberate his former associate from his obligation to keep an eye on Roberta. While Takagi ordered
a beer, she watched out of the corner of her eye as the
ever-present colossus finished off his wine and exited
the lounge, leaving the stub of his cigarette smoldering
in an ashtray. *Time for the night shift to take over,* Roberta
deduced, judging that Takagi was clearly considered
competent enough to keep tabs on her on his own.

She wasn't too displeased to see the other man go;
the friendly young microbiologist was far and away better company. She couldn't help wondering, though,
where exactly the mammoth Latino was going to.

Carlos Quintana, CIA-trained survivor of the Bay of
Pigs, knew all too well where Veronica Neary's hotel
room was located, having spent a good part of the day
keeping it under observation. So far the attractive blond
woman seemed to be exactly what she claimed to be—an
American scientist sight-seeing in Rome—but Carlos
was not satisfied yet.

Pausing in front of the door to Neary's room, he surveyed the hall from left to right. There was no one else
in sight. *Good,* he thought. He knocked gently on the
door, but no one answered. Confident that the room
was empty, and that he was not being watched, he re-

moved a thin silver rod from his pocket and inserted it into the keyhole. The security at the hotel was hardly state-of-the-art, so he picked the lock easily and let himself in, ducking his head to fit through a door which, like everything else in the world, was much too small for him.

He made sure the door had closed completely behind him before flicking on the overhead light. To his surprise, he found a pair of golden eyes staring at him inquisitively. The luminous orbs belonged to the sleek black cat curled in the center of the room's single queen-size bed. Raising its head from the neatly made bedcovers, the cat squawked at him with obvious indignation. A jeweled collar sparkled around the animal's neck.

What the hell? Carlos thought. Nobody had said anything to him about a cat. He had observed Neary ordering room service less than an hour ago, but had simply assumed that she'd wanted a quick snack before meeting Takagi in the bar. The half-eaten plate of fish on the floor, however, suggested another explanation. This cat obviously lived well.

The unexpected feline stalked imperiously across the quilt to confront Carlos from the edge of the bed. Pearly fangs flashed as the cat hissed at the gigantic intruder, ebony fur rising up all along its spine. Worried that the stupid animal might start yowling loud enough to attract unwanted attention, Carlos rushed forward and seized the cat none too gently. Leather gloves, worn to prevent leaving fingerprints, also served to shield his hands from the cat's angry claws and teeth. Crossing the room with long, giant-sized strides, he hurled the squirming feline into the adjacent bathroom, then pulled the door shut firmly, trapping the troublesome beast in the other room, where it could scratch and hiss all it wanted.

That's better, he thought, irritated by the unforeseen complication of the cat. He'd been tempted to throttle the miserable creature, but that would have raised too many questions once the American woman discovered her pet's brutal demise; Carlos's goal was to check out Dr. Neary's belongings without her knowing that anyone had ever been here. He knew he could search her things without leaving any clue. Surreptitious breaking-and-entering was a specialty of his, even before the Experiment, and one of the primary tasks for which Chrysalis employed him.

Knowing that Takagi was awaiting his go-ahead regarding the woman, Carlos inspected the small room quickly. Aside from the oddness of transporting her pet all the way from America, he observed nothing overtly suspicious about Dr. Neary's personal possessions. Impressive-looking scientific journals, of the sort one would expect a potential Chrysalis recruit to read, were stacked upon the bedstand, while her suitcase contained merely a couple of days' worth of clothes. A tag attached to her luggage cited a home address in Seattle, Washington. Carlos scribbled the address down for future reference, in the event that Chrysalis wanted to send another operative to search Neary's permanent residence. *So far, so good,* he reflected, finding nothing to indicate that the American was anything other than what she purported to be.

Just to play it safe, though, he planted listening devices in the phone receiver and behind the headboard of the bed; the bugs would insure that Chrysalis heard everything discussed in the room. Rescrewing the plastic mouthpiece back onto the phone, Carlos took a moment to wonder about the other blond woman, the one Dr. Neary had met in the bar earlier. As far as he could tell, it had been merely a casual encounter, but it probably couldn't hurt to check out the second woman as well. He made a mental note to find out where she was staying in Rome.

According to his watch, it was past 7:30. Takagi would be contacting him soon, to find out if he should proceed with the cautious courtship of this new candidate. Glancing around the room, Carlos decided to take one last look at the woman's luggage, just in case he had missed something earlier.

Kneeling on the floor beside the open suitcase, his massive head still towering over the adjacent bed, he carefully reached beneath Dr. Neary's folded garments to pat the inner lining of the bag. A knowing smirk lifted the corners of his lips as he felt the outline of a hidden pocket within the buried padding. *Aha,* he thought. *Sneaky, but not sneaky enough.* Taking care to memorize the position of each item of apparel, he began lifting the doctor's clothes from the suitcase. It was quite possible, he realized, that the existence of the secret pocket meant nothing at all; chances were, the built-in hiding place merely housed the woman's passport and traveler's-check receipts, like any other paranoid tourist's. Nevertheless, he was not going anywhere until he found out what Dr. Veronica Neary had to hide.

He placed the last of the American's clothing onto the floor, then groped with his fingers for the zipper of the secret compartment. *There it is,* he thought smugly, at the very moment that twelve pounds of angry feline landed on his shoulder, hissing and biting.

"*Carajo!*" he swore, as the cat's claws raked across his cheek, drawing blood. He leaped to his feet, but the accursed beast clung to his back like a giant furry tick. *How in the world—?!* he thought. The cat had been locked tight within the bathroom; there was no way it could have gotten out on its own! Claws like fishhooks dug into the flesh of his left shoulder and small, sharp teeth locked on to his earlobe, making him shout out loud in pain.

Eyes wide with shock and surprise sought out the door to the bathroom, finding it unaccountably ajar. Gloved hands struggled to take hold of the wriggling cat even as Carlos charged into the unlit bathroom, half-expecting to find that the cat had a human accomplice hiding within. "Where are you, you filthy *cabrón?*" he snarled.

The cat escaped his grip by springing to the floor somewhere behind Carlos. More concerned with locating whoever had let the cat free, the Cuban operative tore the shower curtain aside, only to find an empty stall. He spun around in confusion, clutching his wounded face. There was no one else there! The cat had freed itself, as if by magic.

His cheek and ear stung like the devil, and his fingertips came away from his face stained a bright shade of red. He staggered out of the bathroom, bumping his head on the doorframe, and discovered that, somehow, the lights in the main room had been turned off. Blinking in surprise, he peered into the darkened hotel room, trying futilely to spot the midnight-black feline amid the murky, umbrageous shadows. Lights from the street outside filtered in through the drawn curtains, providing only a hint of illumination.

Feeling his way along the wall, he groped for the light switch, but the cat found his leg first, its claws sinking into his calf even through the expensive fabric of his trousers. Hissing like a demonic teakettle, the savage animal added its fangs to the attack, tearing both limb and slacks to shreds.

To hell with this! Carlos thought, growling like a mountain gorilla. He kicked his leg violently, but could not shake the enraged cat free. Malevolent yellow orbs glared up at him from somewhere below his knee. *This is just too plain loco,* he decided. *I'm getting out of here!*

He swung at the cat with a clenched fist, forcing it to leap away to avoid the blow. That was good enough for Carlos, who took advantage of the momentary respite to grab on to the doorknob and make a hasty escape from the lightless torture chamber Dr. Neary's hotel room had become. He could still hear the cat's ferocious hissing, and the scratching of determined claws against the other side of the door, even as he hurried away down the hall. Thankfully, the corridor remained unoccupied, so that nobody witnessed his humiliating retreat.

With any luck, he thought desperately, *the lady scientist will blame her own psychotic kitty for messing up her clothes.* At least that's what he wanted to assume; the alternative meant going back into that hellhole again.

His meaty hand hovered over the doorknob as he briefly debated reentering the American's room. The electronic *bing* of an elevator stopping farther down the hall, followed by the sound of approaching footsteps, made his decision for him.

"Stupid cat!" he grumbled beneath his breath, striding away from Room 11-G and its loathsome feline guardian. Chrysalis definitely owed him for this job, big time. His leg and his face competed to see which could hurt more. "Hell—ouch—damn!"

"Excuse me," Takagi said, looking at his watch. "I have to make a quick phone call. It'll only take a minute, I promise."

Roberta watched the Japanese biochemist exit the lounge. Curiously, he ignored an available pay phone right by the door, apparently preferring to make his call elsewhere. Roberta sighed; sadly, that was the most suspicious thing Takagi had done all evening.

She toyed impatiently with a plastic straw, tying it into a bow. So far her rendezvous with the good-looking young scientist had been a total bust, at least as far as her undercover mission was concerned. Despite her gentle prompting, Takagi had confined their conversation to small talk—and a one-way exchange of information. Under the guise of casual chitchat, he'd grilled her about the particulars of her personal life: friends, family, marital status, etc. Roberta had done her best to sound promisingly unattached, but couldn't help wondering if this was just a pickup after all.

No, she assured herself. Her instincts and intuition, what she called her "vibe detector," told her that she was on the right track. Takagi was mixed up in something big, she knew it. Why else would he have her tailed all day? And what about that extremely hush-hush project he'd alluded to on the Spanish Steps? *Let's not give up just yet*, she resolved. *Rome wasn't infiltrated in a day. . . .*

Paul McCartney's "Live and Let Die" was playing

loudly over the bar's sound system when Takagi returned a few minutes later. "Sorry about that," he shouted over the music. Rather than climbing back onto his stool, he glanced around the smoke-filled bar, which had begun to empty out as both conventioneers and natives drifted away in search of a typically late Roman dinner. "Are you hungry?" he asked her. "Why don't we go someplace else?"

Roberta thought she detected something new and more assertive in Takagi's manner, as though he'd reached an important decision during his brief absence. *Have I passed some sort of test?* she speculated. If so, she had no idea how she'd done so, but she wasn't about to look a gift biochemist in the mouth. "Sounds great," she said, playing it by ear. "I saw a nice little restaurant earlier, down by the Fountain of Trevi."

Takagi shook his head. "I know someplace better. Less touristy. More private."

This is sounding more and more promising, she thought. *Maybe we're finally getting somewhere.*

Then again, it could always be a trap.

Wherever Takagi was leading her, it was definitely off the beaten track. Leaving the larger and more frequented avenues behind, they wandered through a bewildering maze of back alleys and side streets until Roberta was thoroughly lost. Occasionally, she caught a glimpse of the Colosseum in the distance, its imposing, floodlighted facade providing at least one unmistakable landmark to navigate by, but Roberta doubted that she could retrace her path back to the hotel even if her life depended on it—which could be exactly what Takagi intended.

"Er, are you sure we're in the right neighborhood?" she asked doubtfully, seeing no reason to conceal her apprehension. No doubt "Veronica Neary," if she actually existed, would find their current surroundings just as nervous-making. Italian graffiti, ranging from the political to the obscene, festooned the narrow walls and shuttered back windows of the latest dismal little alley. Litter spilled over from dented trash barrels onto the rough, uneven pavement. Greasy puddles reflected the glow of a solitary streetlamp that seemed far too distant, not to mention wildly inadequate to the task of lighting the alley as much as Roberta would have liked. Horns blared several blocks away, but the alley itself was eerily silent and deserted. As inconspicuously as possible, she fished her servo out of her handbag, clutching the silver pen tightly between her fingers.

"Don't worry," Takagi said confidently. Roberta found it unfair, and more than a little annoying, that he wasn't also afraid for his life. "We're almost there."

"There" turned out to be a hole-in-the-wall trattoria located in the basement beneath a shut-down auto repair shop. A sign hanging in the doorway said CHIUSO, Italian for "closed," but Roberta spotted a glimmer of light coming through a glass pane in the basement door. Ignoring the handprinted sign, Takagi hiked down a short flight of cement steps and knocked on the door. "It's me," he called out, his voice seeming to echo in the lonely side street. "Takagi."

The door opened a crack, and a flashlight (or was it a candle?) shined on Takagi's face. A moment later, Roberta heard a chain rattling and the door swung inward, revealing little more than the shadowy entrance to the restaurant. "Here we are," Takagi said cheerfully, looking back at Roberta, who hurried down the steps to join him.

Once inside, after ducking her head to get through the low doorway, she thought the nameless restaurant looked surprisingly cozy—in a run-down, uninhabited, closed-by-the-health-department sort of way. Checkered tablecloths covered about a half-dozen empty tables, maybe a third of which had lighted candles sitting atop them, glowing like small islands of illumination cast adrift in a pitch-black sea. As far as she could tell, there was only one other customer present, a lone figure sitting in the far corner of the basement, his face hiding outside the feeble radiance of his candle, perhaps deliberately.

Who? Roberta wondered. *And why doesn't he want to be seen?*

"Okay, this is just too weird," she exclaimed, figuring some sort of freaked-out reaction was called for. She gazed about the vacant trattoria with open perplexity, her wide eyes failing to penetrate the nocturnal murk concealing much of the restaurant. "Don't tell me we've got this whole place to ourselves?"

"Sort of," Takagi admitted, shrugging his shoulders. "Come over here, there's someone I want you to meet."

"Who? Deep Throat?" she asked. So far, no one had asked them for their password yet, but that was about the only thing missing from this whole cloak-and-dagger scenario. "The Watergate snitch, I mean. Not the porn movie."

A raspy chuckle emerged from the gloom-shrouded figure in the corner. "I am afraid, young lady, that neither description applies to me," said an elderly-sounding voice with a distinct Eastern European accent. Takagi guided

Roberta to the rear table and they sat down opposite the other man. Her eyes strained to penetrate the event horizon of the enveloping shadows, but his features were still difficult to discern.

"This is Dr. Fyodor Leonov, my colleague and mentor," Takagi explained, gesturing toward the stranger. Roberta didn't recognize the name from her recent research, but that wasn't too surprising; she could hardly be expected to have memorized the name of every scientist working in the field of genetic engineering. "Dr. Leonov, this is Veronica Neary, of the University of Washington."

"A pleasure to meet you, Doctor," Leonov greeted Roberta, bowing his head slightly in her direction. The candlelight provided a glimpse of thinning, snow-white hair. "Walter speaks highly of you."

A waiter, unsmiling and cadaverous in appearance, approached them from beside the front entrance and silently handed out a trio of shabby, laminated menus before retreating into the kitchen area. "Please feel free to order whatever appeals to you," Leonov stated. "The dinner is atop me."

"On me," Takagi corrected him.

"Yes, of course. *On me.* My apologies." The older scientist had a courtly, avuncular manner that Roberta found charming. He spoke slowly and deliberately, but without excess formality. "My English, I fear it is not so good." He glanced over at the swinging metal door that led to the kitchen. "We may speak freely, though. The staff here speaks English not at all."

"Why so hush-hush?" Roberta asked.

"Our work is not without controversy," Leonov said solemnly, "as I am sure you must know." As her eyes gradually adjusted to the dim lighting, Roberta saw that

Leonov was wearing a dark suit and tie, as well as a pair of spectacles. She got the vague impression that he was in his sixties or seventies. "Walter tells me, however, that you are quite an advocate for exploring the full potential of new breakthroughs in genetic manipulation."

"Oh yes!" she gushed, much as she had earlier with Takagi. "The possibilities are just astounding. Cracking the genetic code opens up all kinds of new opportunities in medicine and human development. I firmly believe that we're on the verge of a social and scientific transformation that will make the Industrial Revolution seem like a minor hiccup."

"Me neither," Leonov agreed, not quite getting the expression right. "It is good to meet a young person with such enthusiasm for the future." A rueful tone entered his voice. "Those of us who have lived through the . . . upsets . . . of this century can only hope that the generations that follow us will know a safer, saner world."

Oddly enough, Roberta thought that Leonov sounded a bit like Gary Seven, who frequently opined that modern-day humans had not yet lived up to their full potential. "Oh, I'm sure they will," she insisted. "You can't stop progress."

She didn't even need to fake her optimism. Having actually met a couple of very likable individuals from at least one possible future, she had a lot more confidence these days that the human race might actually—what was that phrase again?—oh yeah, live long and prosper.

Assuming Seven and I don't screw things up, of course.

Their zombified waiter reappeared to take their orders, although his drawn, emaciated countenance hardly filled her with confidence regarding the restaurant's cuisine. She struggled with the menu (her automatic translator no help when it came to printed material), but eventually ordered the spaghetti with clam sauce. She declined any wine, however, wanting to keep her wits about her. Were Takagi and his so-called mentor buying any of this?

Apparently so, since Leonov leaned forward to smile at Roberta, bringing his face within the scope of the candlelight for the first time. "American courage and optimism at its finest," he said approvingly. "A most admirable trait, especially for a scientist."

Roberta's eyes nearly bugged out once she got a glimpse of the man's face. *Oh my goodness!* she thought, her poker face slamming into place. *Keep your cool*, her brain screamed. *Don't give yourself away.*

She had good reason to be excited, though. The man sitting across the table, whom Takagi claimed was somebody named Leonov, was actually Dr. Viktor Lozinak, a celebrated Ukrainian geneticist who had vanished from sight over a year ago. As far as Seven and the Beta 5 had been able to determine, Lozinak's whereabouts had been unknown to both the American and Soviet authorities since he disappeared from his modest dacha in Kiev last fall.

Roberta had no doubts. There was no mistaking the thoughtful brown eyes behind the man's bifocals. Wisps of snow-white hair lay flat atop the elderly man's cranium, just as they did in the grainy photograph tucked away in a folder in Roberta's hotel room. Now that she was looking for it, she even noticed a slender wooden cane, of the sort Lozinak reportedly used, leaning against the older scientist's chair. *You can't fool me, Doctor,* Roberta thought triumphantly. *I've got your number.*

It occurred to her that Lozinak certainly didn't look

as though he had been kidnapped against his will; perhaps all those missing scientists had their own reasons for dropping out of sight?

"Oh, I'm sure we Americans haven't got a monopoly on positive attitudes," she commented lightly, aiming to return the compliment. "I bet there are plenty of gung-ho researchers back in the Ukraine."

Lozinak blinked in surprise and Roberta realized she had made a mistake. He leaned back into his chair, putting a little more distance between him and Roberta. His eyes narrowed as he peered at the American woman through his glasses.

"How do you know I am Ukrainian?" he asked her, not in a hostile way but clearly more interested in her answer than maybe he should be. He exchanged a worried glance with Takagi, who looked somewhat baffled and caught off guard by the edgy turn the conversation had taken, as innocuous as it seemed to be.

Roberta kicked herself mentally. "Just a lucky guess," she improvised. "I dated a Ukrainian guy in college once, when I was a freshman." *Is he buying this?* she wondered, sweating beneath her increasingly clingy dress. "Your accent sounds a little like his."

"Ah," Lozinak replied. He mulled her explanation over for a heartbeat or so, then appeared to relax to a degree. He slid his chair closer to the table, coming back into the constricted circle of light. "I see."

An awkward silence followed, mercifully interrupted by the arrival of the appetizers. After they had sampled the antipasti, which weren't as bad as Roberta had feared, Takagi got to the point. "What if I told you—hypothetically, of course—that human genetic engineering was a lot closer to happening than most people realize, that many of the world's finest minds were already working on the project?"

"I'd think that was very exciting news," Roberta said carefully, aiming to act just as curious as Dr. Ronnie Neary would be at this point—and no more. "How much closer are we talking here?"

"Very," Takagi said emphatically, his eyes gleaming. Roberta guessed that he was just aching to tell someone about this mysterious project, and had probably been biting his tongue since the conference began. "Let's just say that old-fashioned evolution is in serious danger of becoming passé. Why, even now, at this very minute—"

Lozinak coughed, interrupting Takagi before he could spill too many beans. Clearly more cautious than his somewhat chattier colleague, the incognito geneticist rerouted the conversation. "Perhaps Dr. Neary will be so kind as to tell us more about her own work?"

Uh-oh, Roberta thought. *Looks like we've entered the job-interview portion of the evening.* Thank goodness she'd done her homework!

"Well, lately I've been experimenting with new ways to subdivide DNA into sections, using restriction enzymes," she said, praying that Lozinak wouldn't quiz her in too much detail; as far as she was concerned it was a minor miracle that she'd picked up enough genetic know-how to be able to string coherent sentences together. "I also want to find a better technique for pasting the isolated gene sequences into bacterial plasmids, so I can use the altered bacteria as a vector to deliver foreign genes to a host cell."

Lozinak nodded thoughtfully. To Roberta's relief, he didn't look like he found her imaginary experiments too implausible. "A promising field of study," he commented. "How are you able to tell whether the recombination has succeeded or not?"

Is this a trick question? Roberta worried. "I can't—yet." She recalled reading about some new technique that hadn't quite been perfected yet, and dredged her memory for the details. "Er, ideally, I'd tag the recombinant plasmid with a radioactive probe, but I still haven't found the right sequence to use as a carrier."

"We may be able to offer you some assistance in that area," Lozinak replied slowly. Judging from his benign expression, and the encouraging tone of his voice, she hadn't flunked the exam so far. "What is your opinion of the function performed by introns?"

Introns, Roberta remembered hastily, were segments of DNA—nucleotides, to be exact—that appeared to contain no useful genetic information. There were various competing theories as to what purpose they actually served, including the notion that they were nothing more than microbiological filler. *I can probably B.S. my way through this particular question,* she thought, *but I've got to find a way to turn this chat around, before the old guy catches me on something stupid.*

"Wait a second," she protested. "What's with the third degree? To be honest, I'd like to know a little more about this project of yours before I submit to some sort of entrance exam."

"Oh, it's nothing like that," an abashed Takagi insisted unconvincingly. "Please believe me, we thought we were just talking shop, not conducting some sort of interrogation. Good heavens, no."

Takagi probably would have kept on burbling denials, but Lozinak held up his hand, silencing the younger man. "No, Dr. Neary is correct. This was in-

deed a—how you say it?—an interrogation." He gave
Roberta a penetrating stare. "Forgive an old man his
suspicions, but there is much at stake, and it is important that we be certain that you are for real what you
appear to be."

"Look who's talking . . . Dr. Lozinak," Roberta said,
letting the elderly scientist's true name out into the
open. Takagi's jaw nearly dropped into his salad, but
Lozinak himself merely nodded and scratched his chin,
examining Roberta with a new mixture of respect and
wariness.

Blowing the old man's cover was a calculated risk,
but it was the best way she could think of to turn the
tables and place Lozinak on the defensive instead. "Did
you really think," she continued, "that I wouldn't recognize the celebrated Dr. Viktor Lozinak? Come on!"

He smiled ruefully and removed his glasses, placing
them upon the tabletop. "Guilty as charged, I'm afraid.
The others, they said it was too dangerous for me to
come to Rome in person, but I was certain I could keep
a sunken silhouette."

"Low profile," Roberta corrected him. "So where
have you been for the last several months?" she asked,
going for broke. "Aren't you supposed to be missing or
something?"

Lozinak sighed and shrugged his shoulders; evidently,
he felt that matters had gone too far to hold back now.
"You must understand, my American friend, that there
are many people in this world, some of them highly
placed in government, that are very afraid of where science has brought us. They hear 'genetic engineering'
and they think eugenics and Hitler and Frankenstein.
We who wish to lift mankind to a new level of advance-

ment, by rewriting the genetic code that makes us what we are, must do our work in great secret."

"You don't have to tell me that," Roberta pretended to commiserate. "Trust me, I've heard every single 'mad doctor' crack there is, sometimes from my own colleagues at the U.W."

Lozinak shook his head mournfully. "It is no joking matter. If the people and their political leaders knew how far we have come, they would take drastic measures to halt our work. That is why my colleagues and I have been forced to go—what is the expression, beneath blankets?"

"Undercover," Roberta supplied, being extremely familiar with the concept.

"Yes, undercover, thank you," the venerable Ukrainian researcher continued. "We must go into hiding, conduct our work out of the world's sight, and conceal our progress even from our fellow scientists, such as yourself."

"What progress?" she pressed him, wishing she'd thought to carry a concealed recording device on her person. Seven would want to hear all about this. "How far *have* you gone?"

There was another long pause as Lozinak once again considered how much to divulge. Roberta held her breath, as did Takagi, and she wanted to scream in frustration when their waiter chose that minute to return bearing their entrees, thus prolonging the suspense even further. Once the waiter left them to their meals, however, Lozinak finally broke his silence.

"Let us call it the project," he said, "and I truly believe it is our world's best hope for survival. Our technology has evolved faster than our ability to use it wisely. The only solution is to create a superior human being, more intelligent and better able to contend with the challenges and opportunities of the future. This is what I, and a number of my fellow scientists, have devoted the remainder of our lives to accomplishing: the next step in the evolution of humanity."

"Pretty fantastic, huh?" Takagi blurted. A plate of hot calamari sat in front of the younger scientist, as yet untouched. "I couldn't believe it myself the first time I heard about it."

Roberta's wide-eyed amazement was only partly faked. "And all this is actually happening somewhere?" she asked, leaning forward avidly. "Now?" She decided a bit of cautious skepticism was in order. "How do I know this isn't just hype? I like to think I keep up with the cutting edge of things, and what you're talking about, that's decades away. Real twenty-first-century stuff. No offense," she added hastily.

"None taken," Lozinak assured her. Giving her a conspiratorial smile, he reached beneath the table and brought forth a small package, about the size of a shoebox, covered with a dark velvet cloth. He placed the bundle gently on the tabletop between them. Roberta thought she heard something skittering inside and gulped involuntarily. Images of tarantulas, rats, and even ickier creatures raced through her mind. *Oh boy,* she thought, *what have I got myself into now?*

"We anticipated your skepticism," Lozinak explained. "Thus, a small demonstration." With a theatrical flourish, he whisked the cloth off the mysterious item, revealing a rectangular glass case housing a single white mouse. Wood shavings carpeted the bottom of the case while a wire mesh lid let air pass freely between the case and the outside world. Inside his cozy domicile, the tiny mouse scurried back and forth, excited by his new surroundings, or perhaps by the smell of their dinners.

Okay, a mouse I can live with, Roberta thought, grateful that Isis was not around to frighten the little guy. "Umm, he's cute enough," she commented, unsure about what exactly the pint-sized rodent's presence was supposed to prove, "but, er, I don't know about you guys, but I can't really see his DNA from here."

Maybe he's super-smart, she speculated, *like the mousie in that Cliff Robertson movie?* Roberta remembered crying when the mouse died in the motion picture.

"Patience," Lozinak counseled her. Lifting a corner of the metal grille, he fed the mouse a piece of cheese from his plate. "The demonstration has not yet concluded." He lowered his head until his lips were level with the flickering yellow flame of their candle. "Behold."

He blew out the candle, casting the table into utter blackness—or almost so. To her surprise, a soft white effulgence, coming from inside the glass case, caught her eye. She gasped out loud as she realized that the mouse itself was glowing in the dark, radiating a cool, constant phosphorescence even as the unconcerned animal contentedly nibbled on the piece of cheese that the older scientist had dropped onto the floor of the case. "Oh my goodness!" Roberta exclaimed.

Takagi leaped in eagerly to explain. "We isolated the gene for bioluminescence in an ordinary firefly, then spliced it into the DNA of this mouse's mother. At least half of the offspring glow like this." He could barely contain his exuberant glee at being able—finally—to share this discovery with someone. "Isn't it amazing?"

"I'll say," she admitted, her gaze glued to the sight of

the luminous rodent. Intellectually, she realized that it would be possible to fake this display, simply by dipping an unsuspecting lab animal in radioactive, glow-in-the-dark paint, but, in her heart, she knew this wasn't a hoax, not with all the high-powered scientific talent involved. "Talk about show-and-tell." She looked up from the case to Dr. Lozinak, whose head and shoulders were only faintly discernible in the descended gloom. "Okay, I'm convinced," she said, totally serious. "What now?"

Drawing a matchbook from the pocket of his jacket, the elder spokesman of two scientists relit their candle, then placed the velvet cloth over the mouse's case before returning it to its place beneath the table (where, frankly, Roberta doubted that it was the only mouse thriving upon the floor of this particular restaurant). Lozinak regarded Roberta thoughtfully, looking her directly in the eye.

"The project needs young people like yourself and Dr. Takagi," he began, "to see it safely into the decades to come. To be candid, we have already investigated your credentials and found them to be more than satisfactory."

"Thanks," she said nervously, relieved that the phony background Seven had manufactured for Veronica Neary had apparently survived some sort of rapid-fire background check. "You guys move fast."

"With modern civilization racing ever more recklessly toward the abyss," Lozinak lamented sadly, "we can hardly afford to do otherwise." The irony inherent in the old man's words, which could have just as easily emerged from Gary Seven's own lips, was not lost on Roberta as the elderly scientist cut to the heart of the matter. "I am offering you the opportunity to join the project, take part in our work, but I must deliver a warning as well. If you join us, you must be prepared to disappear as we have. You must be willing to cut yourself off from the outside world, sharing your secrets and successes with only your fellow members of the project, as well as those few individuals we employ to guard our operations and handle various logistical arrangements."

He leaned forward, letting the flickering light of the candle reveal the deadly seriousness in his expression. Beneath knitted gray brows, his eyes held Roberta's, and he emphasized every syllable of his dire admonition. "Please understand me, once you choose to accept our offer, there can be no turning back. This is your last chance to—what is the expression?—rear exit."

"Back out," Roberta translated. Despite the mangled English, she got the message. The only question, she thought privately, was whether she would really be allowed to leave if she said no. Neither Lozinak nor Takagi seemed terribly dangerous, and she figured she could take them both if she had to, but it was hard to imagine that they would truly let her go free after she had learned as much as she had. Roberta glanced anxiously at the dented metal door cutting them off from the kitchen, and wished once again that she knew what had become of King Kong. "I don't suppose I can take a few days to think about it?" she stalled.

Ultimately, she might never know what the two scientists' backup plan was, since she could hardly refuse a chance to infiltrate this mysterious project all the way. *Just wait until Seven hears the news,* she gloated silently. *This undercover gig is working out even better than we planned!*

"You have tonight," Lozinak informed her. He used a

ballpoint pen to scribble an address onto a paper napkin, then turned the piece of paper facedown. "If you wish to join the project, meet us tomorrow night at the time and place specified on this note. Come alone, and bring only that which you deem absolutely essential. We can arrange to pick up your belongings in Seattle at a later date. Do you understand?"

Roberta nodded slowly. *Don't want to seem too eager,* she remembered. *Ronnie Neary would be a little overwhelmed right now.* "At least I get to sleep on it," she murmured hesitantly. "It's a lot to think about, though."

"I certainly hope you'll decide to join us," Takagi urged her. His youthful face beamed at the prospect, and his voice conveyed a sincere warmth and cordiality. "It would be great working with you."

I'll bet, Roberta thought, wondering what the male-to-female ratio at the project was like. *Probably a lot like the conference, I'm guessing.*

"I wish as well that you give our offer serious thought," Lozinak added. He started to slide the upside-down napkin across the table, then paused, his bony, liver-spotted hand still holding down the vital piece of paper. Roberta bit down on her lip to conceal her impatience, even though the suspense was killing her. "My apologies," the old scientist said, "but before we proceed further, I must ask you one more thing: Do you have any skeletons in your closet?"

"No," she lied breezily. "Just a cat."

CHAPTER SIX

ISIS WOULD NOT CARE FOR THIS PLACE, GARY SEVEN thought, several hours later, standing at the corner of two dimly lit, rather unattractive streets. This particular corner of Brooklyn looked neither cozy nor clean enough to satisfy the feline's fastidious standards. By day a busy commercial district, the neighborhood had been all but abandoned after hours. Lowered steel gratings, bedecked with graffiti, covered the closed ground-floor storefronts, while unspooled razor wire ran along the edges of the rooftops, discouraging prowlers. A light breeze rustled the litter strewn upon the streets and sidewalks; Seven glanced down at his feet to see portions of a discarded newspaper blow against his ankles. An inky black headline informed him that authorities continued to search for kidnapped heiress-turned-terrorist Patty Hearst. "FBI TO 'TANIA':

TURN YOURSELF IN!" shouted the *New York Post*. Seven shook his head, admitting to a bit of culture shock himself. Even after six years living among primitive humans, he still sometimes found himself discomfited by the rampant squalor and irrationality of this era. Twentieth-century Earth was a far cry from the enlightened community, many light-years from here, where he'd been born and trained. Sometimes he found himself nostalgic for that urbane and smoothly run utopia, where a stimulating mixture of sentient species managed to challenge each other to achieve their highest potential, without all the pointless aggression and competitive nonsense that seemed to color every relationship on Earth, from the personal to the political. He missed the regular company of old friends and colleagues, not to mention the numerous small comforts and conveniences that came from living in an advanced technological society. Why, this planet was still centuries away from developing such necessities as personal replicators or portable nano-intelligences. . . .

On the other hand, he admitted, *I can't deny that precivilized Earth is strangely fascinating in its own right, no matter what Isis says.*

A northbound subway rattled beneath his feet, causing minor tremors in the pavement. The occasional automobile whizzed through the deserted block, barely stopping for the broken traffic light at the intersection. Seven glanced at his watch; it was about five minutes to midnight. *Late enough,* he judged.

Making sure that he was unobserved, he approached the entrance to a five-story brick office building. He examined the metallic numerals posted over the doorway, checking them against the address listed on Ralph

Offenhouse's business card. In theory, the man's professional offices should be located on the top floor of the building.

He tried the door, confirming that it was locked, then withdrew his servo from his jacket pocket. A pair of delicate targeting sensors sprang like antennae from opposite sides of the slender instrument. Seven selected the appropriate setting, then aimed the servo at the rigid doorknob. A momentary hum was followed by the satisfying click of a door unlocking itself. Seven waited for a passing car to drive by before letting himself in.

He took the stairs to the fifth floor, where the servo granted him access to a closed office bearing Offenhouse's name. From outside he had observed no lights in the upper windows, let alone the rest of the building, so he felt confident that the businessman's chambers would be unoccupied; nonetheless, he listened briefly at the door until he was certain that there was no activity within.

Once inside, he adjusted the servo so that it emitted a beam of light well within the visible spectrum. The miniature spotlight revealed all the accoutrements he expected: an expensive walnut desk, telephones, a separate desk for a secretary or receptionist, a couch for visitors, recent editions of the *Wall Street Journal,* and file cabinets. Seven sighed at the sight of the latter, anticipating much time-consuming grubbing through paper. *Hopefully,* he thought, *someone on this benighted planet will get around to inventing personal computers shortly;* it would make this sort of covert information-gathering much easier.

Earlier that day, after Offenhouse's departure from Seven's office on Sixty-eighth Street, the Beta 5 had conducted a thorough voice analysis of the business-man's statements to Seven, a process far more accurate than the ridiculously unreliable polygraph devices em-ployed at this point in human history. The computer had concluded that Offenhouse had told the truth, as much as he knew it, but Seven felt that there was still more to learn from the combative capitalist, hence this nocturnal expedition.

He began with the file cabinet located directly across from Offenhouse's own desk. The top drawer was locked, which struck Seven as extremely promis-ing. His servo opened it easily, and he discovered sev-eral dated folders labeled "Chrysalis Project." Seven nodded in satisfaction, quite certain that the files per-tained to the same mysterious project that Roberta had been asked to join several hours ago in Rome; thankfully, the time difference between here and there had given her plenty of opportunity to brief him on her meeting with Lozinak. *Our separate investigations appear to be converging rapidly,* he thought. *This can't be a coincidence.*

Starting with the most recent folder, he was gratified to find invoices and shipping bills for large quantities of scientific apparatus: everything from test tubes and petri dishes to computers and X-ray diffraction equip-ment. *As Roberta would say,* Seven reflected, *bingo.*

Much of the hardware and medical paraphernalia, he saw, had been purchased through a series of dummy companies, thus obscuring their ultimate destination, which appeared to be a location somewhere in north-west India. *Interesting,* Seven thought; the Indian sub-continent had already produced several outstanding biochemists, most notably Har Gobind Khorana, a co-winner of the Nobel Prize for his research on the chemistry of the genetic code and its function in protein synthesis. Only four years ago, Seven recalled, Khorana had successfully assembled an artificial yeast gene from its raw chemical components, an important first step in the development of genengineering technology. Khorana himself was not among the roster of missing scientists, but perhaps some of his countrymen were determined to take his work to a dangerous new level?

As if the threat of reckless genetic manipulation weren't worrisome enough, Seven was dismayed to discover shipping manifests for large quantities of peptone, a substance used to cultivate bacteria. The amount of peptone being shipped to India was far more than was needed for ordinary research purposes; a typical university course might use maybe one liter of peptone a year, yet, according to his records, Offenhouse had arranged for over two thousand liters of peptone to be shipped to India in nearly two hundred large metal drums. There was only one purpose, Seven realized, for which anyone would need to propagate that much bacteria: full-scale biological warfare.

Genetic engineering mixed with germ warfare? What kind of nightmarish scenario was Chrysalis working toward, he wondered anxiously, and what sort of viper's nest were Roberta and Isis trying to infiltrate?

"All right, Seven. Get away from those files."

The harsh command, accompanied by the sudden illumination of the overhead lights, caught Seven by surprise. He looked up from the documents to see Ralph Offenhouse standing in the doorway, pointing a semiautomatic pistol at the snooping alien operative.

Seven cursed himself for his carelessness. He had

been so engrossed in Offenhouse's highly informative files that he hadn't even heard the gun-wielding businessman arrive. But what in the cosmos was Offenhouse doing here after midnight? This entire block had given every indication of being closed for the night.

"I said, get away from my files," Offenhouse repeated angrily. He seemed just as surprised as Seven to find the other man here, and a good deal more indignant. "I thought we had a deal: No questions. So what the hell are you doing in my office?"

Given the hour and the neighborhood, Seven did not find it remarkable that Offenhouse had arrived armed with a weapon. Not wanting to provoke the man into shooting, he raised his hands and stepped away from the files. His servo remained gripped in his right hand, its narrow spotlight rendered unnecessary by the room's interior lighting. He rolled the silver wand between the pads of his fingertips, making a minute correction to its setting. His face maintained a neutral expression as he watched the irate Earthman carefully.

"You heard me, Seven. I want some answers and I want them now." The muzzle of Offenhouse's pistol followed Seven as he moved away from the metal filing cabinet. "I'd be within my rights to shoot you," Offenhouse warned. "This is breaking-and-entering, you know."

"Nothing is broken," Seven stated calmly. "As for the rest of it, I'm a government agent, investigating a suspected threat to national security." When in doubt, he had learned, appeal to this era's paranoid nationalism.

His false declaration seemed to undermine the man's belligerence and self-confidence. "National security?" Offenhouse echoed uncertainly, sounding like a man with plenty of reason to be concerned. Then his aggressive bravado reasserted itself, as though he'd resolved to brazen his way through this confrontation. "How do I know this is on the level?" he asked accusingly.

"I can show you my identification," Seven replied, lowering his hands gradually. He routinely carried phony CIA credentials for just such circumstances. Not to mention FBI, NSA, IRS, and assorted national and international press passes, each concealed in its own hidden pocket.

Offenhouse didn't buy it. "Keep your hands where I can see them!" he barked, gesturing upward with his gun. His teeth ground together noisily as he debated with himself as to what to do next. Seven was not surprised that summoning the police did not appear to be among the options Offenhouse was considering; the unscrupulous businessman had too many of his own secrets to hide.

"Fine," Seven agreed, raising his hands once more. "Let me give you a phone number for my superior officer. You can verify my credentials yourself." He fixed a stern gaze on the so-called entrepreneur. "Trust me, Mr. Offenhouse, it's in your best interests to cooperate. You don't want to get in deeper trouble than you already are."

Despite his obvious efforts to present a firm and unworried facade, Offenhouse's Adam's apple bobbed nervously. "All right," he said after a couple of moments, sliding a blank memo pad across the desk toward Seven. "Just write down the number. Don't try anything else."

"I wouldn't think of it," Seven promised. He lowered his writing hand until the tip of his "pen" was aimed directly at Offenhouse's skull. "You won't regret this," he lied.

The servo hummed for less than a second, but the

effect on Offenhouse was immediate. His eyes glazed over and his tense expression relaxed into blissful contentment. His shoulders sagged and he began to slump toward the hardwood floor. Returning the servo to his pocket, Seven stepped forward briskly and removed the loaded pistol from the other man's flaccid grip, then gently guided Offenhouse to a seated position against the doorframe. "Just stay right there," he instructed the anesthetized businessman, who wasn't going anywhere. "I'll be with you in a second."

Seven engaged the safety on the pistol before placing it atop Offenhouse's desk, safely out of reach. He turned off the lights, to avoid piquing the interest of any passing police cars, then crouched down beside the sitting man so that he could look directly into Offenhouse's dreamy, unfocused eyes. *Might as well make the best of the situation,* Seven decided; the servo's tranquilizer beam induced a highly suggestible state, much like sodium pentothal, but without any of the crude chemical side effects.

"Tell me more about Chrysalis," he prompted. "Who are they? What do they want?"

"Bunch of egghead do-gooders," Offenhouse murmured, slurring his words slightly. "Trying to make a better world through chemistry, or something. Don't know, don't care. Making a bundle, though. Tax-free. Plenty of venture capital, just like I need. Got big ideas for that dough, big ideas. Gonna be a millionaire before I turn forty. . . ."

Seven scowled. When was the human race going to learn that there were more important things than profit? He tried to steer the other man's reminiscences down less financial avenues. "Chrysalis," he reminded.

"What are their names? Where can I find them?"

"Whole thing's run by this Indian woman," his un-witting informant revealed. "Don't know her real name, only met her once. Really scary broad, supergenius freak. Has secret lab in India somewhere. Everything goes through Delhi, her people take it from there. New shipment going out this morning, from JFK. . . ."

This morning? Seven thought. That had possibilities. He was about to press Offenhouse for more details when the phone rang unexpectedly. Seven raised a quizzical eyebrow. A call after midnight? This office kept decidedly strange hours.

The answer occurred to him suddenly. *India,* he real-ized. There was a ten-and-a-half-hour time difference between Brooklyn and India; it would be approxi-mately ten-thirty in the morning there now. *That's why Offenhouse came in so late. He was expecting this call.*

The phone rang again, its piercing alarum reaching Offenhouse even through his hypnotic daze. He stirred fitfully, making a half-hearted attempt to rise to his feet. Seven placed a firm hand on Offenhouse's shoul-der, blocking his ascent. "Don't worry," he assured the tranquilized businessman as he pressed Offenhouse back down onto the floor. "I'll get it."

He wasn't lying this time. If this call was indeed from Chrysalis, as he had deduced, then Seven was very in-terested in finding out who was calling and why. He reached for the phone. "Hello?" he said, in a flawless impersonation of Offenhouse's own voice. Expert vocal mimicry was yet another skill the Aegis had taken pains to teach Gary Seven.

"Offenhouse?" said a masculine voice at the other end of the line. Seven heard a distinctly British accent. Upper-class, Oxford maybe, or Eton. "This is Williams. Just calling to confirm that today's shipment is on schedule."

According to Offenhouse, it is, Seven remembered. "Everything's set," he said, imitating the businessman's brusque tone. He rifled through the most recent folder, looking for the pertinent details. "From JFK, right on time."

Williams sounded nervous, as though constitutionally unsuited for espionage and intrigue. A scientist, not a spy. "You're sure this line is still secure, right? There's no chance anyone's listening in?"

"That's right," Seven improvised, guessing that Offenhouse had indeed taken precautions against wiretaps. The recent Watergate scandals had made the entire nation alert to the dangers of incriminating audiotapes. "You can speak freely," he encouraged Williams.

"I hope you're right," Williams said, sounding only slightly more at ease. "Did you get the replacement parts for those high-speed centrifuges? It's a bloody bother when the blasted things keep breaking down."

"No problem," Seven answered. "They're on the way." *Ah, here it is,* he thought, locating the relevant itinerary among Offenhouse's papers. A private jet, leaving John F. Kennedy Airport at two A.M. for Delhi, with a stop in Rome en route. *For Roberta and her new employers?* he assumed. *All roads do indeed seem to be leading to India, but where does the equipment go from Delhi?*

"I have to go now," he told Williams. The longer they spoke, the more chance he stood of making a careless mistake and raising Williams's suspicions. He glanced down at the Xeroxed document on the desk. "Expect the shipment at four-thirty tomorrow morning, your time."

You can expect me there as well, he thought. Performing

the necessary calculations in his head, he deduced that Williams, or his agents, would be meeting the flight roughly seventeen hours from now. Thankfully, Seven knew a faster way to get to Delhi, even if Roberta was in for a long flight. *I imagine she'll be very surprised to hear she's going to India.*

"Wait!" Williams interjected hurriedly, before Seven could hang up. "What about that uranium? I promised the director that I would remind you just how urgently we require that processed ore."

Uranium? A startled expression transformed Seven's ordinarily inscrutable features. He hadn't seen anything about radioactive materials among Offenhouse's files, unless that particular cargo had been disguised somehow. He quickly leafed through the manifests until he found one highly suspicious item: a large shipment of lead "construction materials." *That must be it,* he concluded, but what were Offenhouse—and Chrysalis—doing with potentially fissionable uranium? The discovery added an alarmingly nuclear dimension to what Seven already deemed to be an extremely hazardous situation.

Genetic engineering, germ warfare, nuclear proliferation. *Sometimes,* he brooded, *it seems positively miraculous that humanity hasn't destroyed itself already. . . .*

"Huh? Wha—?"
Ralph Offenhouse came out of a daze to find himself in his Brooklyn office, seated behind his desk. Groggy and confused, he blinked and shook his head, trying to clear the fog from his thoughts. A lingering sense of blissful well-being swiftly faded from his mind, giving way to uncertainty and bewilderment.

I must have fallen asleep at my desk, he guessed. The

funny thing was, though, he had no memory of actually sitting down here, or even of turning on the lights. The last thing he remembered was climbing the stairs to his office; after that, his mind was blank. *Weird,* he thought. *I haven't been working that hard lately, have I?*

For a second, he feared he'd had a stroke; heart disease ran in his family, so that wasn't a completely unlikely scenario, even though he hadn't even turned forty yet. He wiggled his fingers nervously, checking for paralysis or tremors. "Hello," he whispered, making sure he could still speak.

Everything seemed to check out. What's more, he didn't feel weak or impaired. If anything, he felt more relaxed and better-rested than he had in weeks. He didn't even have a hangover, which ruled out an uncharacteristic drinking binge. *So what the hell happened to me?* A thought occurred to him and he groped for his pistol, only to find it safely stowed away in his side pocket, right where it belonged. *That's a relief,* he thought. *Can't be too careful these days, especially in this part of town.*

Raising a hand to wipe his brow, he caught a glimpse of his Rolex. *Wait a second, what time is it?* He peeked urgently at the face of the watch.

One-fifteen . . . well after Williams at Chrysalis was supposed to call for an update on this morning's shipment. "Damn," he muttered. Had he missed the freaking call?

There was only one way to find out. Bending over, he pulled out the lower right-hand drawer on his desk. Inside, beneath a spare ashtray and a box of Kleenex, was what appeared to be an ordinary cigar box. He cleared the stuff on top, then lifted the lid of the box, revealing the tape recorder hidden inside. According to a numerical display on the machine, the machine had already taped one call tonight, even if Offenhouse had absolutely no memory of any such call. *This keeps getting stranger and stranger,* he thought. When he first started taping his calls, with an eye toward having something to hold over Chrysalis later on, he'd never thought he'd need the tapes to fill in a gaping hole in his own memory. *How the heck did I end up with my own personal eighteen-and-a-half-minute gap?*

He rewound the tape until the beginning of the last call, then hit Play. "Hello?" he heard his own voice say, then listened in amazement as he and that jittery Brit, Williams, carried on a conversation that Offenhouse didn't recall at all. He was particularly surprised to hear himself tell Williams that those stupid centrifuge parts were on the way when he hadn't yet managed to get any of those components at a decent price.

That's not me, Offenhouse realized, with a certainty that came from somewhere deep inside him. The voice on the tape sounded exactly like him, but he knew somehow, on an almost subconscious level, that he had never said those words. Somebody else had taken his place. *Doped me probably,* he guessed, *then pretended to be me on the phone.* Somebody who now knew all about the shipment flying out of Kennedy in less than an hour.

His heart pounding all of a sudden, he switched off the recorder and grabbed the phone, hastily dialing his contact at Chrysalis. "Williams?" he said a few moments later. "This is Offenhouse. I think we have a problem. . . ."

CHAPTER SEVEN

"OUCH!" ROBERTA EXCLAIMED AS TAKAGI PRICKED HER upper arm with his hypodermic needle. She flinched involuntarily, then flashed the young scientist a sheepish smile. "Sorry. I don't like needles, which is pretty funny for a biochemist, I guess."

"Not at all," he assured her, deftly withdrawing the hypo. He leaned over Roberta, bracing himself with one hand against the back of her first-class seat, just in case the plane they were travelling on encountered any unexpected turbulence. As midair inoculations went, his technique was smooth and almost painless. "I don't like getting shots myself, but these vaccinations are a good idea, considering where we're going."

"Wherever that may be," she said ingenuously, even though she knew full well that this jet was ultimately bound for Delhi. When they'd compared notes late last night, Seven had given her as much of the itinerary as he'd managed to glean from that guy Offenhouse's files, but, of course, she had to play dumb as far as Takagi and Lozinak were concerned. *There was a smallpox epidemic in India a few months ago,* she recalled, *which probably explains their insistence on these shots.*

Unless, that is, this had something to do with the secret germ warfare program Seven suspected. She still found it hard to believe that her two new friends, Walter and Viktor, could possibly be involved in something so sinister and barbaric. Breeding superbabies was one thing, that was arguably a positive goal, but growing bacteria by the ton? How did that fit into the utopian vision of what Seven had called the Chrysalis Project?

The shades had been drawn over all the windows in the passenger compartment of Chrysalis's private jet, presumably to prevent "Ronnie Neary" from tracking the plane's progress over Europe and Asia. The pressurized cabin smelled faintly of cigarettes, but at least she had plenty of legroom. With only four passengers aboard—herself, Takagi, Lozinak, and the huge Latino, whose name she had learned was Carlos—they each had a row of plush leather seats to themselves, with another row to spare for Isis and her molded plastic carrying case. First-class all the way; Chrysalis clearly had money to burn, not to mention a need-to-know mentality bordering on the paranoid. *I hope they're not planning on blindfolding me once we get to Delhi,* she thought.

"That's all," Takagi announced cheerfully. Placing a rubber tip over the point of his hypo, he returned the syringe to the black leather doctor's kit resting on the seat next to Roberta's. He then buckled himself into his own seat, across the aisle from hers. "You might as well get comfortable," he warned her. "We have a long flight ahead."

Tell me about it, Roberta thought glumly. It was at least a seven-hour trip from Rome to Delhi. Rolling down the sleeve of her blouse, she snuck a peek at her wristwatch. After arriving from New York, the plane had departed Rome at about four P.M., which meant she still had about six-and-a-half hours to go. She tried to calculate their arrival time in Delhi, but the tricky time differences just made her head spin. *Probably just as well,* she concluded. Ronnie Neary would have no idea how long this trip was supposed to last.

"You sure you can't tell me where we're going?" she pleaded, intent on staying in character. "It seems to me that I've taken a lot on faith at this point." She gave Takagi the most plaintive expression she could muster. "So when are you folks going to start to trust me?"

The amiable Japanese researcher squirmed uncomfortably in his seat. "It's not that we don't trust you," he insisted. "It's just that, well—" He chewed nervously on his lower lip as he struggled to find the right words. "I mean, you know, the way things are—"

"No," Carlos grunted from the seat behind her. "Don't tell her anything." The unsmiling Latino had been introduced to Roberta as Lozinak's bodyguard and "security consultant." In turn, she'd pretended not to have seen him before, since Ronnie Neary would never have noticed being followed all over Rome by the huge, silent phantom. *Pretty darn careless of me,* she admitted, *but, hey, I'm just a whiz-kid geneticist with no street smarts.*

"Nothing personal," Takagi added hastily. "Our friend Carlos is just very conscientious when it comes to security." He shrugged sheepishly, then made a painfully obvious attempt to change the subject. "Did you know that Carlos is literally one-of-a-kind? He was the subject of one of our very first attempts at adult transgenic therapy. DNA from the African mountain gorilla was spliced into his chromosomal sequence, causing increased muscular and skeletal development. Really! Believe it or not, he used to be my size, back when we first sprung him from some awful Cuban prison."

Ohmigosh, Roberta thought in amazement. *The big bruiser really is part gorilla!* She had to resist a sudden temptation to peek over the back of her seat to take a closer look. *I knew it! So what does that make him anyway? A Homo simian?*

"Unfortunately," Takagi confessed, a note of regret slipping into his voice, "on the whole, the experiment was not a tremendous success. Of the fifty initial subjects, all rescued from life sentences in prisons throughout the world, only Carlos survived the entire procedure, and he ended up sterile, pretty much killing any chance of passing on his newly acquired characteristics that way."

Carlos growled warningly from the backseat, suggesting that the tactless Japanese scientist was perhaps treading upon a touchy area. Roberta could see where the ape-man might be sensitive about certain issues. "Still, we've made enormous progress since then," Takagi added.

Such as? Roberta wanted to press Walter for more details, but she also remembered that Ronnie Neary still hadn't gotten an answer to her original query. "That's all very fascinating," she admitted, "but you can't distract me that easily. All I want to know is where this darn plane is flying to."

Takagi's lips parted encouragingly, but, before he could speak up, an older, Ukrainian-accented voice interrupted from one of the seats in front of Roberta. "My apologies," Dr. Lozinak said slowly but firmly. "We have indeed asked much of you, but you must grant us this much more. Please believe me, it is much safer for everyone if you do not learn the actual location of our primary facility until we have all arrived safely at our destination."

"Good," Carlos growled in agreement, his voice several octaves lower than Lurch on *The Addams Family*. Roberta had noticed the claw marks on the bodyguard's face when they met at the airport. Evidence, no doubt, of a recent run-in with a certain feisty black feline, and proof, as far as Roberta was concerned, that the surly Missing Link was indeed the culprit who had invaded her hotel room, bugged her phone, and rifled through her things. *Like I wouldn't notice traces of such obvious snooping!* she thought indignantly. *I bet I would have found that bug all on my own, even if Isis hadn't raised a fuss about the phone the minute I came through the door.* Fortunately, she and Seven hardly needed phones when they could use their servos as communicators—and without paying long-distance fees.

"Sorry," Takagi said with an apologetic shrug. "But Dr. Lozinak is right."

Frustrated, Roberta fought down an urge to swear out loud. "What exactly are you afraid of?" she asked, figuring she could probably press the issue a little further without blowing her cover. "That someone's going to interrogate me as soon as we get off the plane?"

"Perhaps," Lozinak admitted. She couldn't see his face from where she was sitting, but she could imagine the sober, slightly rueful expression on the older scientist's grandfatherly features. "Or we could—what is the English phrase?—lose trace of you somewhere between the airport and our base. Please understand, by informing you prematurely, we would be risking not only ourselves, but also our colleagues at the project, and all we have worked for these many years." He paused, probably to let his careful explanation sink deeper into Dr. Neary's consciousness. "You see, it is not a decision we can take lightly."

"Oh," Roberta said weakly. "I guess when you put it that way—" She let her voice trail off, making a strategic decision to let the matter slide. After all, she reminded herself, she already knew a lot more than any of her fellow passengers realized, including the fact that Seven would be waiting to greet the plane in Delhi.

She felt a stab of envy, directed at her aloof and enigmatic supervisor. Unlike her, Seven wouldn't need to cool his heels aboard a jet for seven hours just to get to far-off India. *Transporters have definitely spoiled me for air travel,* she realized. *What I wouldn't give for a cloud of glowing blue smoke right about now!*

Isis must have been thinking along the same lines, because she suddenly let out an ear-piercing wail from the confines of her cramped plastic carrier. No surprise; Carlos had earlier insisted that the cat remain locked up for the duration of the flight. Despite the feline's innumerable snubs and slights, Roberta couldn't help feeling a twinge of sympathy for the claustrophobic kitty-cat.

I know how she feels, the young woman thought. A paperback copy of *Jonathan Livingston Seagull* rested in her lap, its slender spine and meager page count suddenly striking her as grossly insufficient to get her through the tedious journey ahead. *I should've brought something longer,* she realized.

A lot longer.

CHAPTER EIGHT

BALAM INTERNATIONAL AIRPORT
DELHI, INDIA
MAY 17, 1974

THE METAL DETECTORS AT THE ENTRANCE TO THE
International Arrivals and Departures terminal were a
fairly recent innovation, being a necessary response to
the recent global epidemic of skyjackings. Gary Seven
handed a blue-clad airport security guard his servo,
along with a key ring and a handful of small change,
before stepping through the primitive scanning device. Circumstances, it seemed, were going out of their
way to remind him of the twentieth century's pen-
chant for senseless violence. *And these people think they
have the wisdom to rewrite their own DNA?* he marveled,
incredulous. *They can barely keep the skies free of terrorism
and extortion.*

More or less indistinguishable from a fountain pen,
the servo elicited no suspicions on the part of the security officer, who blithely handed Seven's personal arti-

cles back to him. Tucking them back into the pockets of his gray suit, Seven walked calmly but briskly toward the gate mentioned in Ralph Offenhouse's files, following signs printed in both Hindi and English. It was a little after four A.M. In theory, the plane would be arriving from Rome in less than half an hour, bearing, among other things, Roberta Lincoln and her newfound associates, not to mention a supply of processed uranium intended for purposes unknown.

Despite the early hour, the terminal was a typically Indian scene of hubbub and congestion. Milling families bid farewell to departing relatives with variable combinations of tears and jubilation, while those stuck waiting for flights slumped in worn plastic seats, dozing uncomfortably or struggling to stay awake. Irate flyers, perhaps discovering that their flights had been delayed and/or overbooked, argued loudly with airline personnel at the check-in counters in front of several of the gates. Worn-out babies cried incessantly, and a Hindi pop tune blared over the din, showing little consideration for those unlucky travelers hoping to catch a little shut-eye before boarding their planes, and the spicy scent of hot *chai* tea rose from more than one cup or thermos bottle clutched in the grip of a prospective passenger.

For himself, Seven was intensely grateful that he'd been able to bypass a grueling fourteen-hour flight from America, thanks to his matter-transmission vault. *I could transport from Vulcan to Alpha Centauri,* he marveled, *in a fraction of the time it takes a primitive 747 to fly halfway around this planet.*

Unfortunately for the mass of late-night flyers, none of the cafeterias, snack shops, or newsstands had opened for business yet. Weaving his way through the packed terminal, while doing his best to ignore the nerve-fraying crowding and commotion, Seven reached the designated gate within minutes. Since this was strictly a private flight, there were no airline employees in attendance. Rows of seated passengers, most likely waiting for the next scheduled departure from this gate, flanked the unmanned check-in station guarding the closed door that blocked access to the jetway. Peering through wide glass windows, Seven saw that the plane from New York had already landed. A BAX-146 jetliner, he guessed, taxiing toward the terminal. The jet was painted a bright shade of orange, contrasting sharply with the cobalt blue insignia adorning the plane's tail fin. The stylized logo resembled a butterfly spreading its wings. *Newly hatched from a chrysalis,* he surmised, recalling the name of the mysterious organization Offenhouse fronted for. A chrysalis, of course, was another name for the cocoon in which a caterpillar metamorphosed into a butterfly. An appropriate symbol for an outfit that appeared to be dabbling in genengineering, he decided, and not quite so obvious as, say, a double helix.

Seven watched as Roberta, Isis, and their three fellow passengers departed the plane via the jetway. Roberta looked exhausted from the long flight, but otherwise fine. Ditto for Isis, who silently bore the indignity of her claustrophobic pet carrier, currently held aloft by the straining muscles of Roberta's right arm. Seven was curious to hear what either operative might have learned during the trip from Rome, but now was obviously not the time to debrief them. Perhaps later, if one or both of them managed to slip away from their distinguished escorts long enough to contact him on their private frequency, they could bring each other up to speed on their respective missions. At the moment, his primary goal was to find out more about what Chrysalis *wasn't* showing Roberta, even if that meant making his own way to their ultimate destination.

Is the peptone being used at the same facility that Roberta and Isis are being transported to, he wondered, *or is Chrysalis's presumed biological warfare program being carried on elsewhere in India?* The only way to find out was to stick with Offenhouse's damning cargo until the end of its travels.

For now, he contented himself to nod discreetly at the two female agents as he briefly made eye contact with them across the crowded waiting area. If nothing else, he wanted them to know that, as planned, he was at large in India and pursuing his own lines of inquiry, which appeared to be dovetailing with Roberta's undercover operation at a remarkable and encouraging speed. At this rate, he, Roberta, and Isis might well be converging on Chrysalis's hidden base practically simultaneously. Then, unfortunately, the most daunting part of their joint mission would begin.

How far along is Chrysalis in their experiments? he worried once more. *And what will we find once we've finally penetrated their dense layers of intrigue and misdirection?* Dealing with Chrysalis's creations, he feared, would be infinitely more challenging than uncovering their secrets.

Turning his attention from Roberta and Isis to their companions, Seven recognized Viktor Lozinak right away, despite the lowered brim of the man's fedora. The missing scientist limped slowly beside his fellow travelers, pausing occasionally to catch his breath. Walter

Takagi, whose boyish face matched the photos Roberta
had retrieved from the Beta 5's copious database, helped
the older gentleman with his luggage, carrying a suitcase
in one hand and a black valise in the other. The third
man, who carried the remainder of their bags, was unfamiliar to Seven, although he accepted Roberta's initial
assessment of this large, muscular individual as some variety of professional spy or mercenary. He repressed a
knowing smile at the sight of the parallel claw marks
streaking the man's left cheek. *Good girl, Isis,* he thought,
assuming she had her reasons.

None of the party, including Roberta, appeared to be
carrying any of Ralph Offenhouse's scientific contraband, which was presumably still residing in the aircraft's cargo hold. *Very well,* he thought, as Roberta and
the others were quickly swallowed up by the crowd. *I'll
follow the merchandise while the women stick with our suspects.* He waited for the plane's flight crew to depart,
then surveyed the layout of the surrounding terminal.
How to get down to the plane? The jetway was tempting,
but probably not stealthy enough. A more roundabout
route was called for; fortunately, Seven knew just where
to go.

Past experience had taught him that the food service
and catering personnel tended to be the weak link in
airport security systems. Arriving and departing passengers might be checked out thoroughly, but cooks,
bartenders, waitresses, and busboys often had the run
of the place, simply because they served a necessary
function in keeping impatient flyers happy. Conse-
quently, Seven circled the nearest, conveniently closed
cafeteria until he found an inconspicuous rear entrance, then used the servo to let himself in.

Still hours away from opening, the restaurant was empty and cloaked in shadows. Seven weaved past silent booths and tables, taking care not to attract attention from anyone who might be walking by outside. He slipped behind the serving counter, then made his way into the rear storage area, where, as expected, he found an elevator next to a stack of empty tanks of soft drinks. He smiled knowingly. *Going down,* he thought.

In an ideal world, of course, he could have transported directly to the tarmac below; sadly, though, he couldn't risk having the powerful matter-transmission beam interfere with the fragile electronics in the nearby planes and air traffic control towers. Hence he had needed to materialize in a parking garage safely outside the airport itself. Yet another small concession to the primitive technology of the time—and the need to maintain a low profile while going about one's business on a precivilized planet.

The elevator took him down to a loading dock only a short flight of steps above the actual airfield. Stepping out of the air-conditioned environment of the airport, he was struck immediately by the sweltering heat and smog of the Indian night. Hours before sunrise, the temperature had to be at least eighty degrees Fahrenheit, while the humid air smelled of dust and diesel fumes. *Apparently the monsoon season hasn't arrived yet,* Seven concluded. Probably just as well. Torrential rainfall would only make this mission even more uncomfortable than it already was.

He ducked behind a large, rusty Dumpster while he surveyed the scene. Several yards away, airport baggage handlers were unloading numerous large wooden crates from the orange-and-blue jetliner and onto the back of an unmarked black Jeep pickup. Large, stern-faced men in dark suits stood by, supervising the procedure. Hired thugs, undoubtedly, or goondas as they were known in these parts. Seven wondered briefly how Chrysalis expected to get all that expensive equipment (and disguised uranium) past the Indian customs authorities.

Smog obscured the moon and stars, but elevated floodlights illuminated the airfield. Diverting his gaze from the black pickup and its cargo, Seven aimed his servo at the nearest lambent white orbs. One by one, in a matter of seconds, the lights went out, casting the area immediately around the parked plane into murky darkness. Startled voices cried out or cursed angrily, sounding more irritated than alarmed. From the weary tone of some of the grumbling baggage handlers, Seven guessed that power outages and blown bulbs were not entirely unheard-of at this airport. *All the better*, he thought with satisfaction.

Moving swiftly to take advantage of the blackout, he dropped silently from the loading dock onto the tarmac and scurried toward the rear of the plane. Some of the more alert baggage handlers had already retrieved personal flashlights, but Seven ducked low to avoid their searching beams. If he was lucky, the airport workers and their watchful supervisors might not even realize that there was an intruder among them.

His eyes, operating at the peak of human capability, adjusted to the darkness almost instantly, guiding him toward the waiting pickup and through the gang of disoriented workers. A solitary light shone from the interior of the jet, several feet above the airfield, but Seven was careful to stay clear of its limited radiance.

Reaching the rear of the truck, he nimbly climbed into the already cramped confines of its open bed. He squeezed himself into the space between two heavy crates, then crouched down and pulled a protective canvas tarp over his head and shoulders. Not exactly the most comfortable seat he had ever assumed on a primitive twentieth-century vehicle, but hardly the worst either; once, on one of his earliest missions on Earth, he and Isis had needed to hide themselves in the trunk of a white Plymouth sedan in order to reach a launch gantry at McKinley Rocket Base. Now, *that* had been claustrophobic. Isis had squawked about it for weeks thereafter.

A door opened noisily on the passenger side of the pickup and Seven heard a familiar British accent. "What the devil?" Williams exclaimed, clearly agitated. "What happened to the bloody lights?" He paced nervously upon the tarmac, only a few feet from where Seven listened intently. "This is all Offenhouse's fault, I know it! How could he possibly compromise our security like this?"

Flashlight beams bounced off the concealing tarp as the baggage handlers got back to the interrupted task of transferring Chrysalis's precious cargo from the plane to the truck. Seven waited expectantly, impatient to discover the uranium's ultimate destination. Then, without warning, the canvas was yanked away forcefully, exposing him to the harsh glare of multiple flashlights. The incandescent beams struck him in the face, forcing him to blink and raise a hand to shield his eyes. Seconds later, brawny hands dragged him out of the bed of the truck and onto the pavement. Scowling goondas drew their guns, placing Seven squarely in their sights. "Don't even twitch," one of them growled redundantly.

Williams himself, who turned out to be a balding, pear-shaped Englishman with ferret-like features and yellowing teeth, frisked Seven roughly. He dressed like a remnant of the British Raj, complete with pith helmet and khaki-colored safari garb. Although coming away with the other man's wallet, the nervous, middle-aged Brit seemed surprised not to discover any obvious weapons on Seven's person; he looked at the wary gunmen and shrugged his shoulders. Borrowing a flashlight from one of the baggage handlers, most of whom looked extremely confused at this point, he turned the beam on Seven's ID. Fearful eyes widened with amazement as he read the name on his prisoner's phony passport, visa, and driver's license.

"Seven?" he blurted. "*The* Gary Seven, the one from America?" He glanced quickly at his wristwatch, looking extremely puzzled. "Offenhouse and his men were looking out for you at Kennedy Airport . . . how in blazes did you get to Delhi before our plane?"

"How do you know that I wasn't on the plane all along?" Seven replied, aiming to nudge Williams's imagination in the wrong direction. He saw no reason to advertise his access to a matter-transmission chamber.

Upset by the violent confrontation unfolding before their eyes, the alarmed baggage handlers began speaking loudly among themselves, while peppering Williams and his hired guns with shouted questions in at least three different languages. The clamor got to Williams, who already looked overwhelmed by events. "Somebody take care of these jabbering coolies," he barked at one of the gunmen. His shiny cranium glistened with perspiration and he swabbed at his brow with a crumpled handkerchief. A vein pulsed angrily against his temple. "Pay them whatever you have to to shut them up. Get their names, too, just in case we need to offer further persuasion later on."

Giving Seven one last parting sneer, one of the goondas, who looked more Indian in appearance than his colleagues, turned away to deal with the distressed workers. Unhappily, that still left Seven at the wrong end of two loaded firearms. "What do you want us to do with him?" another of the gunmen asked, nodding brusquely at Seven. Although somewhat Germanic-looking, he spoke in Hindi, perhaps assuming (incorrectly) that their American captive would not understand what he was saying.

"I don't know. Let me think!" Williams looked even more nervous and apprehensive than he had sounded on the phone hours before. He chewed on his lower lip and dabbed compulsively at his sweaty face and neck. "Who are you?" he demanded of Seven. At least a foot shorter than his prisoner, he had to tilt his head backward to look Seven in the face. "Who sent you? Whom are you working for?"

You wouldn't believe me if I told you, Seven mused, keeping his thoughts to himself. *Not that I'm about to do anything like that.*

His silence enraged Williams, who slapped Seven with the back of his hand . . . hard. The sound of angry flesh smacking against Seven's face rang out in the night like a gunshot. "Talk to me!" Williams practically screeched. "Whom do you work for? How much do you know about us?"

"Quite a lot," Seven said ominously. His cheek stung

where Williams had slapped it, yet he maintained an even tone and stoic expression. "However, now seems neither the time nor the place to continue this discussion."

The latter observation appeared to have an effect on Williams, who glanced around the darkened airfield with anxious eyes, as though suddenly remembering that he and his men were in the middle of smuggling radioactive contraband into India's busiest airport. His face twitched and his foot tapped restlessly against the pavement as he struggled visibly to reach a decision. Seven kept quiet, not wanting to push the stressed-out scientist too far. Despite the guns aimed at his person, and the torrid heat, he was sweating significantly less than Williams.

"The director will have to handle this," Williams announced finally, after several seconds of indecision. He sounded like he was trying to convince himself as much as his subordinates. "Besides, there are drugs back at the base. Those might help get him talking." He stepped away from Seven and headed back toward the front of the truck. "Right, tie him up. He's coming with us."

Seven repressed an urge to smile. So far, everything was going more or less as planned, ever since he'd let himself be recorded back at Offenhouse's office in Brooklyn. *Next stop: Chrysalis.*

He was looking forward to meeting the project's mysterious director.

CHAPTER NINE

ROBERTA HAD HEARD HORROR STORIES ABOUT THE slow, bureaucratic ordeal that was Indian customs, but, to her surprise and relief, she and the rest of her party whizzed right past the long lines and mobbed airport checkpoints, drawing indignant glares from many of the other new arrivals crowding the terminal. No one even asked to see her admittedly bogus passport. She figured she ought to feel a little guilty about cutting in line this way, but, then again, she was here to save the world after all.

The overpowering Indian heat hit her the minute she stepped outside the air-conditioned terminal onto the pavement beside the pickup lanes. *If it's this hot at four-forty in the morning,* she thought, *what in the world are the afternoons like?* She prayed that, wherever they were going, Chrysalis had plenty of air-conditioning.

Born and raised in the damp coolness of the Pacific
Northwest, she tended to wilt in extreme heat. Her
sweaty fingers clenched the handle above Isis's dangling
carrier, and she couldn't help wondering how the caged
cat was coping with the oppressively torrid temperature. Who knew what kind of planet the alien feline
was from?

Like the packed terminal, the sidewalk was a scene
of clamor and confusion, with dozens of overeager
porters and taxi drivers competing for the attention of
many harried, jet-lagged travelers. "Please, sir, miss,
boss, over here! Very cheap!" the drivers, known lo-
cally as taxi-wallahs, hollered at every potential fare,
grabbing at their bags and tugging the arms of every
new arrival. Miles-weary men in long white shirts, accompanied by women in brightly colored saris, looked
almost as overwhelmed as the more Westernized
tourists by the daunting challenge of navigating their
bags and persons through the shouting, jostling mob.
"No, no, you don't want him, boss!" a taxi-wallah
shouted, trying to steal customers from the competi-
tion. "A very bad driver . . . unsafe! Over here! Come
with me!" The insulted taxi driver responded in kind,
provoking many angry words and a brief scuffle before
airport security guards intervened, but not before a
third taxi-wallah managed to make off with their understandably shell-shocked fares. *I'll never complain
about Penn Station again,* Roberta vowed, taken aback
by the sheer noise and tumult outside the airport.

Carlos used his considerable bulk to bulldoze a path
for the rest of their party, and his intimidating, gorilla-
like proportions also seemed to keep most of the horde
at bay, so that they were not swarmed nearly as badly as

the other newcomers, who looked practically under siege by the rapacious throng of would-be helpers. "Over here! Over here! Very cheap!"

Even still, one particularly fearless young porter ran forward and snatched at the handle of Isis's carrier, and Roberta had to tighten her grip to keep from being physically separated from her unwanted partner-in-espionage. "Back off!" she called out, jerking the carrier back from the overly aggressive baggage handler. "The furball's with me."

The air was hot and moist and smelled of gasoline. Although they had to travel less than a hundred yards by foot, Roberta was a gasping, perspiring mess by the time they reached the waiting limousine. The chauffeur, a serious-looking Indian man wearing a clean, short-sleeved shirt and brown trousers, held open the door as she slid into the backseat between the Drs. Lozinak and Takagi. She balanced Isis's carrier on her lap as Carlos joined the chauffeur up front. The bodyguard looked back over the seat at Roberta. "Here," he said brusquely, thrusting a rolled swath of black fabric at her. "Put this on."

She unrolled the cloth, which turned out to be about the size of a large handkerchief. A blindfold? "You've got to be joking," she said.

"No," Carlos grunted, scowling. The claw marks on his face made him look positively villainous. "Put it on. Now."

As before, she appealed directly to the elderly scientist now sitting beside her. "Look, this is ridiculous. It's pretty obvious that we're in India somewhere. The Delhi airport, if I read the signs correctly. You don't have to tell me where we're going next if you don't want to, but there's no reason to keep me sitting in the dark the whole way. Even if we're stopped at the first intersection by the DNA Police, what am I supposed to tell them? That the project is somewhere on the Indian subcontinent? That's all I know, and, last I heard, India was a pretty big place."

Lozinak sighed and rubbed his eyes beneath his spectacles. Even though he had napped most of the flight, the all-night journey still seemed to have taken a lot out of the old man. His breathing was labored and his face was pale and drawn. "I don't know," he wheezed uncertainly. "Perhaps there would be no harm . . ."

"The director wouldn't like it," Carlos warned. He glowered at Roberta. "She knows too much already."

Says Mr. Breaking-and-Entering, Roberta thought huffily. Not even bothering to respond to the sullen bodyguard directly, she looked to Takagi for assistance. "Heck, I probably won't even know where we are when we get there. I've never been to India before, and wouldn't know the Punjab from the Taj Mahal."

This much was true; the present assignment was her first trip to India, although Seven had 'ported some maps and background material over to her the night before, which she had carefully read and reviewed before incinerating the incriminating papers in the wastebasket in her hotel bathroom. *I wish I'd had more time to prepare,* she thought. Despite her crash course in Rome, most of what she knew about modern India still came from childhood memories of Kipling and the occasional Satyajit Ray movie. *In other words, not much at all.*

"She has a good point," Takagi said, much to Roberta's satisfaction. The Japanese biochemist had emerged from the flight in better condition than his aged mentor, but still looked fatigued from the trip. His tweedy jacket was more crumpled-looking than usual, and he yawned as he spoke. "She's not going to be out of our sight until we reach the base."

"That's right," Roberta argued, glad to have Takagi on her side. "Who am I supposed to squeal to anyway, the chauffeur?"

Carlos wouldn't let the matter drop. "We should not take any chances," he insisted. "There's already that problem in New York, someone snooping around where he shouldn't."

Er, that would be my boss, Roberta thought, choosing to keep that observation to herself. Neither did she mention spotting Seven in the terminal as they disembarked from the plane, resorting to sarcasm instead: "C'mon, next you'll be asking me to put blinders on the kitty-cat."

Isis protested loudly at the mere suggestion.

"Perhaps, there would be no harm," Lozinak announced wearily. "We have a long drive ahead, and it would indeed be inhospitable to keep Dr. Neary blindfolded the whole way."

How long a drive? Roberta wondered apprehensively, hoping that Chrysalis's secret headquarters was not tucked away on top of the Himalayas or something. *I'm not dressed for mountain-climbing.*

"Let me have that, if you please," Lozinak said, taking the blindfold from Roberta and handing it back to Carlos. Despite his exhaustion, he made it clear the discussion was over. "You are a valued colleague, not a captive."

"Thanks!" Roberta said gratefully. "I was starting to feel a bit like Patty Hearst, before she was brainwashed." She grinned triumphantly at Carlos, who grumpily turned his back on the two scientists and their supposed new recruit. *Score one for the American chick,* she thought smugly, as the limo pulled away from the curb. *At this rate, I'll be running Chrysalis by Thursday.*

In theory, that is.

Lozinak had not been kidding when he mentioned the long road ahead. After several hours on the road, Roberta figured they had to be halfway to Pakistan by now.

The limousine's tinted windows and first-rate air-conditioning insulated her from the exotic yet torrid environment outside, something Roberta considered a distinctly mixed blessing. On the one hand, she wanted to see and experience more of India itself; on the other hand, her body kept reminding her that it was now long past midnight, Roman time, and that she had been traveling for at least eleven hours at this point. Under the circumstances, she found it all too easy to doze off for long stretches of the trip, waking abruptly whenever their driver slammed on the brakes or leaned on the horn, which seemed to occur with alarming frequency.

In fact, Roberta quickly decided that the less she saw of the traffic on the overcrowded, underlit roads, the better she'd sleep. India had one of the highest traffic fatality rates in the world, at least according to the briefing the Beta 5 had provided, and Roberta could easily see why. Buses, taxis, cows, bullock-carts, bicycles, water buffalo, motorbikes, trucks, and motorized rickshaws contended for space on the overtaxed highway, with right-of-way going to the biggest vehicles and the loudest horns. Convoys of ten-ton moving vans roared past the limo, carrying their freight from Delhi to distant parts of the subcontinent, while public buses swayed with the weight of the teeming human cargo clinging to the sides and rooftops of the rickety vehicles. The twisted and mangled ruins of numerous traffic casualties rusted alongside the road, appearing every thirty miles or so to provide mute evidence of past automotive catastrophes, far more regularly than Roberta would've preferred.

She couldn't help recalling that her immediate pre-decessors, Seven's original Earth-based operatives, had both perished in an unforeseen traffic accident. *Here's hoping history won't repeat itself,* she mused, wondering how Seven would react to her own unfortunate demise, not to mention the cat's. *Probably complain some more about the senseless barbarity of twentieth-century life.*

Their driver stuck to the highway, bypassing both the larger cities and small, rural villages. The slums and shantytowns south of Delhi gave way to mile after bumpy mile of congested roadways as the limo made its way across the open countryside, through rocky hills and shadowy ravines. In the darkness of the early morning, Roberta occasionally glimpsed distant bon-fires, the murky silhouettes of small farms and tem-ples, and, far less frequently, the glow of electric lights. Speeding trains occasionally ran parallel to the dusty dirt roads on which they traveled, and she got the im-pression that the limo was heading vaguely south, but didn't see much in the way of signage. *What's south?* she tried to remember, wishing she could have brought along a map without arousing suspicion. *Agra? Cal-cutta? Probably someplace more off the beaten track,* she speculated.

Breakfast consisted of a thermos of milky *chai* tea,

plus some tasty banana fritters that the chauffeur had packed for them. The tea was hot, spicy, and presumably caffeinated, but even that was not enough to keep her eyes open. Soon she was somewhere else, far away from the cramped and bouncing limo.

In her dreams, she was back at the dimly lit Italian restaurant, but this time the spaghetti on her plate came alive, the wriggling strands of pasta twisting into an intricate double helix that Roberta recognized from all the biology texts and articles she had forced herself to consume lately. The double helix, the essential human genome, rose up before her, rotating slowly around an invisible axis like an upright work of art upon a revolving pedestal. She gaped in wonder at the sheer elegance and deceptive simplicity of the coiled, ribbonlike structure, which appeared to glow with its own transcendent light. *So* that's *what the basic recipe for people looks like,* she marveled, wondering why anyone would want to tamper with such a flawless design.

Then the helix began to change. *Mutate.* Before her eyes, the genome unraveled, each luminous strand writhing like sparking electrical wires. The wriggling noodles snatched at each other, knotting themselves into a tangle of unlikely connections and chromosomal linkages. A new double helix swiftly formed, but unlike the graceful rungs of the original structure, this mutated helix was bound together by something that looked like a demented cobweb made out of pasta. *That can't possibly be right,* Roberta realized, aghast. She reached forward desperately, hoping to somehow untangle the mess and put all the mismatched genes and chromosomes back where they belonged, but the sinuous genome slithered through her fingers, eluding her grasp.

Ugly and distorted, the mutant double helix reared back like an angry cobra, then lunged for her throat. Roberta threw up her hands to protect herself, but the serpentine monster passed through her hands like a phantom before striking her in the jugular, where it dissolved into her own bloodstream. *Oh my gosh,* she realized in horror. *It's inside me now!*

Like venom, the mutant DNA coursed through her system, rewriting her own genetic code. Convulsive cramps and spasms racked her body. She could literally feel her bones and organs shifting and changing as the recombinant invader transformed her very identity. Visions of glowing mice and limbless thalidomide children infected her imagination, but when she looked down at her hands, afraid that all she would see were flippers, she discovered instead that her fingers were stretching before her eyes, growing longer and preternaturally more supple. New knuckles formed, one to each finger, and she found she was able to bend them in places she never could before. *Is this supposed to be an improvement?* she wondered, unsure whether to be amazed or appalled. Then extra fingers sprouted from her palms and she started to scream. . . .

"Dr. Neary? Ronnie?"

She awoke with a start to discover that the limo had come to a stop. Takagi nudged her shoulder gently while, on her lap, Isis squawked impatiently. "Sorry to disturb you," the younger scientist said, "but we have to get out of the car."

Roberta blinked in confusion. The chauffeur opened the back door of the limo, letting in a blast of shockingly hot air. She shook her head, glad to have awakened, but having difficulty throwing off the lingering unease generated by her nightmare. *Yikes, what a dream!* she thought, trying to remember the last time she had experienced anything so surreal. *Woodstock maybe, but who needs acid when your own unconscious mind can conjure up a head trip like that one?* She made a determined effort to come back to reality. "Are we there yet?"

"Almost," Takagi promised, climbing out of the limo. Peering past the exiting biochemist's back and shoulders, Roberta caught a glimpse of some sort of village right outside the car. "We just need to transfer to another mode of transportation."

Holding on to Isis's pet carrier, she clambered out of the backseat after Takagi, then looked around to inspect her surroundings, squinting against the harsh glare of the morning. The scorching sun, which had risen sometime during their trip, beat down on an isolated desert village composed of thatched adobe and yellow sandstone huts. Hot and dusty air, smelling of spices and camel dung, enveloped Roberta like a heavy blanket, albeit one doused in ginger and curry. Scrawny white cows and bleating goats wandered freely through the unpaved streets of the village, while women in brilliantly colored saris, some balancing clay pottery upon their heads, paused to stare at Roberta and the others with open curiosity. Barefoot children chased each other along dry dirt paths and around the village well, their high-pitched voices competing with the muttering and whispers of their mothers. Old men, whose white beards contrasted sharply with their wizened brown faces, sat on mats outside their homes, watching the new arrivals warily. Like their elders, the women and children kept their distance, quite unlike the hyperaggressive porters and taxi-wallahs back at the airport. *Must not get many visitors around here,* Roberta guessed, feeling slightly self-conscious. *Especially not blondes.*

Beyond the village, stretching away to a seemingly endless horizon, rolling sand dunes sprawled beneath a bright turquoise sky. Desolate patches of desert scrub struggled to survive amid the arid sandscape. "That would be the Great Indian Desert, I'm guessing," Roberta observed, relying on a photographic memory of her discarded map.

Takagi nodded. "The locals call it *marust'hali.*" He was already sweating profusely from the heat, but seemed perfectly willing to act as tour guide. "The abode of death."

How cheery, Roberta thought. Shielding her eyes with her hand (which, thankfully, had merely the usual number of fingers and knuckles), she regarded the vast desert thoughtfully. As far as she could see, the road they were on came to a stop at the edge of a sandy wasteland. Could this be the end of the line? No, she recalled, Takagi had said something about switching to another means of transport.

Nervously, her gaze wandered back to the camels grazing on a block of dry-looking straw beside the nearest thatch building. A male villager, wearing a large orange turban and a mercenary expression, gripped the reins of a pair of camels as he watched Carlos and the chauffeur help Dr. Lozinak out of the limo, which clearly had gone as far as it could go. *Please don't tell me we're making the rest of the trip on camelback,* she prayed wholeheartedly.

According to her watch, it was now a few minutes after ten in the morning, which meant she had already been in transit for at least thirteen hours, seven by air and then another six in the limo. No wonder she felt so wasted; Roberta considered herself a more than usually adventurous person, always ready to try something new, but right now the prospect of spending several more hours stuck between the bouncing humps of a plodding Indian camel was enough to induce genuine despair. "Is that our ride?" she asked, nodding glumly in the direction of their prospective mounts. A brownish lather dripped from the slowly masticating mouth of one of the camels in question.

Ugh.

"Perhaps some other time," Lozinak chuckled, leaning heavily on his cane. "At my age, I find I prefer a jeep." He looked to the horizon, where Roberta saw a cloud of airborne sand approaching over the crown of a dune. "Ah, here it comes now. Right on schedule."

She felt an undeniable surge of relief as the four-wheeled vehicle emerged from the desert, churning up a flurry of agitated dust and sand. The jeep came to a halt in front of the limo, and its driver—a bearded Indian man who looked like he could have been a cousin to the disappointed camel-owner—set about transferring the travelers' carry-on luggage from the limousine to the jeep. He also offered Roberta sunglasses and a straw hat to protect her from the sun, which she accepted gratefully. *Okay, it's official,* she thought, contemplating the desert from which the jeep had come. *We're definitely heading for the middle of nowhere.*

She just hoped Seven was keeping up.

CHAPTER TEN

IRONICALLY, GARY SEVEN FOUND HIMSELF TRAVELING to Chrysalis's secret base much as he would have had he not been discovered by Williams and his thugs: hidden beneath a canvas in the back of the pickup truck. *All things considered,* he thought wryly, *I think I prefer transporters.*

Bound and gagged and covered by the all-concealing tarp, he had been on the road for several hours now, time enough for the blazing afternoon sun to turn the back of the truck into a veritable oven. Through sheer bad luck, Seven's mission had coincided with the peak of India's hot season, when daytime temperatures could easily exceed one hundred degrees Fahrenheit. Even with his own superlative physical conditioning and mental discipline, the trip had still become a torturous ordeal. His shirt and slacks were soaked with sweat and he felt more than a little dehydrated. His dry mouth and throat pined for something to drink, preferably with ice. He could only hope that he would not be too debilitated by the time the truck reached its ultimate destination.

Lying on his side, with his hands tied behind his back with thick strips of duct tape, he could see only the base of the wooden crate directly in front of him. Despite this inadequate vantage point, however, he had nonetheless managed to derive some significant conclusions based on what he'd heard from the floor of the pickup.

First, and perhaps most intriguingly, he couldn't help noticing that the truck had cruised from the airfield onto a highway without any official delays or inspections. From this Seven could only assume that, as an organization, Chrysalis possessed considerable wealth and/or influence; the ease with which Williams's contraband had circumvented customs implied extensive, systemic bribery, as well as possibly friends in high places.

This was extremely worrisome news. Such resources vastly increased Chrysalis's potential for dangerous scientific mischief. *They're playing with fire,* Seven thought gloomily, remembering the strife and devastation that unchecked genetic manipulation had wreaked on so many other civilizations throughout the galaxy. *The Minjo are still trying to rebuild their society after that last round of gene wars. . . .*

Never mind all that uranium and bacterial growth medium.

As best he could, while simultaneously analyzing what he had already learned about Chrysalis, Seven also attempted to orient himself regarding the truck's journey and surroundings. Over the last few hours, the vehicle had migrated from Delhi's noisy, traffic-clotted streets to the only slightly less crowded highways beyond the busy, clamorous environment of the city and its outlying slums. The air, although no less hot and humid, had become mercifully less polluted, smelling more of eucalyptus trees and burning dung than of industrial effluent, leading him to conclude that they had placed Delhi's urban sprawl far behind. Over the course of hours, the traffic thinned as well, judging by the gradual decrease in honking horns Seven could hear from his uncomfortable berth in the back of the pickup.

Possessed of an excellent sense of direction, he estimated that they were traveling southwest. *Through Harayana state and onto Rajasthan,* he calculated. They had been on the road for at least six hours; by now the truck must be nearing the vast, inhospitable desert lying between India and Pakistan. A fairly remote location, to be sure. Chrysalis clearly made privacy a top priority. *What are they hiding?* he wondered. *And how far have they progressed?*

His servo, tucked away in one of his jacket's inner pockets, jabbed him in the side. Seven wished he could access the device, if only to communicate with Roberta or Isis, and inform them of his present location and circumstances. He had barely been able to do more than make eye contact with them back at the Delhi airport, and he couldn't help wondering how that slightly incompatible duo were faring on their own excursion through India. *With any luck, they're still getting the red-carpet treatment from Chrysalis,* he thought, hoping that his agents could maintain their aliases for a while longer; as he was learning through personal experience, Chrysalis's agents were not above kidnapping and threats of violence when crossed. *Then again,* he reminded himself, *Isis is perfectly capable of taking care of herself in hazardous situations, and Roberta, despite appearances, has her own unique talents as well.*

The truck paused at an intersection, and Seven thought he heard the bleats of goats or camels. *Must be passing through some remote Rajasthani village,* he surmised. It was unlikely that the truck would stop here for long, since it was hard to imagine what such a place would need with processed uranium and high-speed centrifuges. He hoped, for the sake of his own physical comfort, that it would not be necessary to travel the rest of the trip slung across the swaying back of an ambling camel. *After all, there's primitive and then there's primitive. . . .*

Fortunately, the pickup soon resumed its journey. The bucolic sounds of the unnamed village faded away as the vehicle logged yet more miles in this seemingly endless trek. The road grew ever rougher, jarring Seven's body with every bump, until finally the road itself more or less disappeared. Seven heard the truck's four-wheel drive struggle to maintain traction in the sandy dunes of what he assumed must be the Great Thar Desert. He could no longer hear the horns or engines of other vehicles, only the steady rumble of the jeep's transmission as it carried him deeper and deeper into the hot and arid solitude of the desert.

He swallowed hard, but his parched throat yielded no saliva. His cramped arms and legs ached from inactivity. Darkness encroached on his limited field of vision, but he employed a series of mental exercises, borrowed and modified from ancient Vulcan teachings, to avoid losing consciousness. Concentration required considerable effort, yet he managed to remain focused on his mission. He was anxious to meet Chrysalis's so-called director, most likely the "scary" Indian woman Ralph Offenhouse had mentioned back in Brooklyn.

Perhaps it's not too late to reason with these people, he thought, *to convince them to abandon their reckless experimentation.* Since first returning to the homeworld of his ancestors, Seven had learned enough about ordinary human nature to realize that reason was often not their primary motivating factor. It was worth a try, though, before he was forced to resort to more drastic measures to curtail their operation. Sanity was always preferable to sabotage.

The sun beat down on him, even through the welcome shelter of the canvas tarp. Seven knew that, advanced training or no, he couldn't last much longer without water. *How much farther is there to go?* he pondered, a question that was growing more urgent with every hour.

Finally, just as he found himself pining nostalgically for the subzero temperatures of the Bajoran icecap, the pickup rolled to a halt somewhere deep within the desert. Car doors swung open loudly, and Seven heard boots stomping through sand just outside the truck. Minutes later, the tarp was pulled back, exposing him to the full glare of the midday sun. Seven squeezed his eyelids shut against the blinding light, even as beefy arms grabbed him by the shoulders and dragged him roughly up and out of the enclosed truckbed.

Vertical again, for the first time in probably seven

hours, Seven felt his feet hit the desert sand. He tried to stand erect, but the grueling trip had taken too much out of him. His legs felt like uncooked Klingon *gagh* and he had to be held up by captors on either side of him. Someone grudgingly stuck the mouth of a canteen between his lips and he swallowed greedily. The water was lukewarm, but he had seldom tasted anything quite so refreshing. The liquid restored him, somewhat, and he gradually opened his eyes, letting his pupils adjust to the glare before attempting to take stock of his surroundings.

The truck was parked in front of what appeared to be the ruins of an ancient Rajput fort. Reddish-brown sandstone walls, scarred by centuries of erosion and decay, guarded partially collapsed watchtowers that looked out over miles of surrounding dunes and sparse desert scrub. The domed spires of sacked temples and palaces peeked out over the crumbling battlements of the silent citadel, which looked as though it had been abandoned for hundreds of years.

Such forts were not uncommon in Rajasthan, Seven knew, being the legacy of a martial tradition dating back to the sixth century, but he assumed that these particular ruins were far less desolate than they appeared, or why else transport all of Offenhouse's expensive equipment to this seemingly barren site? His eyes searched the battered sandstone walls, hunting for some hint of the high-tech lab facility he knew had to be lurking here. All that met his gaze was the ancient fortress, however, and rolling dunes that stretched out in all directions beneath a cloudless, sapphire-blue sky.

A familiar voice called his attention away from the enigmatic ruins. "I trust you had a pleasant trip, Mr.

Seven," Williams taunted him, withdrawing the canteen. His beady eyes glared at Seven; apparently he had not yet forgiven the prying American for complicating his life. "Perhaps you feel more like talking now?"

"You're fortunate that I can speak at all," Seven croaked, his voice hoarse from exhaustion and dehydration. "Where I come from, human beings would never dream of subjecting another living creature to a journey like that."

Williams scowled, visibly annoyed by Seven's defiance and superior attitude. That angry vein throbbed at the man's temple. "You're in no position to scold anyone. I don't know who you think you are, or whom you're working for, but you're in way over your head now, I assure you."

We'll see about that, Seven thought. Despite the physical privations required, he was exactly where he wanted to be—almost. "You brought me here to meet your director," he reminded Williams. "Let's get on with it."

At least a foot shorter than Seven, Williams clenched his fists and stared up at the other man with a mixture of frustration and uncertainty. His flushed, angry face was redder than the sunbaked walls of the forgotten fort. Anxious to achieve the upper hand, but evidently unsure how to do so, he stalled momentarily while searching for an appropriately witty and devastating riposte. The blazing sun, however, made any prolonged stay in the open impractical, and Williams soon conceded to the inevitable. "Er, perhaps we should get out of the sun," he mumbled weakly, swabbing his sweaty dome with a handkerchief while avoiding eye contact with Seven. "Come on," he said to his hired goons. "Let's take him inside."

Although the outer walls of the fort had been breached here and there by long-departed cannonballs, Williams led the party toward the citadel's open front gate. As he approached the decrepit stone archway, Seven noted several feminine handprints carved into a stone plaque beside the gate. These were memorials, he knew, to bygone generations of women who had performed sati, the ancient and barbaric rite of self-immolation, upon the deaths of their husbands. The sculpted hands had been partially wiped away by wind and time, but Seven could just imagine Roberta's reaction to the very notion of sati; it was hard to envision that independent young woman setting herself on fire for tradition's sake, a realization that gave him considerable hope that the human race was, in fact, advancing toward a higher degree of civilization, albeit slowly.

Passing through the main entrance, he saw that the walls had once been over a dozen feet thick, and still were in places. The gate itself opened up onto a vast, stone-paved courtyard strewn with rubble and stubborn patches of weeds. Beyond the courtyard, deserted temples and towers lingered in varying degrees of decrepitude, while a one-story edifice that Seven guessed had once been a foundry had collapsed inward, becoming nothing more than a sloping pile of debris. No tourist guide, Williams did not comment on any of these intriguing historical ruins as he proceeded toward the regal palace opposite the front gate.

The palace looked in slightly better condition than most of the surrounding structures, although Seven still spotted gaping cavities in the palace's upper dome. Once the residence of some mighty prince or maharajah, the palace ascended in tiers like an ornate wedding cake sculpted of marble and sandstone. Intricate lattice screens, that once shielded the women of the palace from view, filled many of the second- and third-story windows. Seven and his captors climbed a steep stairway to a pair of heavy granite doors carved to resemble wood. A single silvered handprint, resembling those embedded in the wall beside the fortress's outer gate, adorned the juncture where the two doors met. Williams placed his own right hand atop the apparently ancient memorial, his fingers matching the outlines of the sculpted hand, and Seven heard the rumble of concealed machinery coming to life. *Interesting,* he mused. There was clearly more to these ruins than met the eye.

Williams withdrew his hand as the massive doors swung open, seemingly of their own volition. Escorted by the three looming goondas, Seven followed the portly Englishman into a spacious yet shadowy rotunda lit only by swatches of sunlight that fell from the fractured dome high above onto the bare stone floor. Long stripped of the rich carpeting, jeweled mirrors, and other furnishings that would have decorated the chamber at the height of the palace's glory, the empty rotunda still contained hints of its former elegance. Fluted columns supported the high ceiling, while an ornamental frieze ran along the upper boundaries of the room. Small altars, each housing the idol of a separate Hindu deity, were tucked away in closet-sized alcoves stationed at regular intervals along the perimeter of the chamber.

The scene still looked deceptively antiquated, Seven noted, despite the jarring incongruity of those automatically opening doors. Chrysalis had obviously gone to great efforts to conceal their presence, even this far off the beaten track. Any stray travelers who might wander by, such as curious tourists on a camel-back tour of the forbidding desert, would perceive only yet another colorful old fort, neither as well preserved nor as impressive as, say, the more famous citadels at Jodhpur and Bikaner. *All this secrecy implies that Chrysalis has a lot to hide,* he worried, recalling all the peptone and processed uranium that Offenhouse had shipped to this site. *Just what is the long-term agenda of this entire conspiracy?*

Ignoring all the other idols, Williams headed straight for a murky alcove devoted to Ganesh, the elephant-headed god of wisdom and prosperity. A layer of artfully applied dust covered the bronze idol, but Seven observed that Ganesh's single tusk, curving upward beside his trunk, looked much less dusty than the rest of the shrine, so that he was not too surprised when Williams took hold of the ivory tusk and twisted it so that it now pointed downward. A metallic click accompanied the gesture, and the entire altar, idol and all, rose toward the ceiling, revealing a pristine white cubicle large enough to hold three or four full-sized adults.

Very ingenious, Seven thought, although the lack of dust on the elephant-god's tusk had been a bit of a giveaway. The whole setup reminded him of his own office in Manhattan, whose futuristic hardware easily disappeared behind a facade of twentieth-century interior decoration. Who knew what else these crumbling fortifications concealed?

Williams retrieved his pistol from the pocket of his sweat-stained jacket. "Right," he said curtly, addressing the assembled goondas. "You lot finish up unloading the new equipment, taking special care with the crates marked 'fragile.' " He jabbed Seven in the ribs with the muzzle of his Browning pistol, then stepped inside the previously hidden elevator. "You're with me," he ordered Seven.

I should hope so, Seven thought, following Williams into the elevator. "Going down?" he predicted confidently, seeing there was nowhere else Chrysalis's deadly laboratories could be lurking. Seconds later, the entire cubicle began sinking into the floor, and he waited patiently as his view of the forsaken rotunda swiftly disappeared from sight, replaced by the smooth black wall of the elevator shaft.

"You think you're smart now," Williams sneered, "but just wait until the director gets through with you." He kept a few feet away from Seven, the point of his Browning never veering away from his prisoner's chest. "You don't get something like Chrysalis off the ground, and keep it secret, without learning how to handle sneaky little spies like you. She takes no prisoners, I can tell you that."

Sounds like a Romulan commander I knew once, Seven thought. He could have disarmed Williams easily, of course, but that was hardly the point of the exercise. There would be time enough later to regain his liberty—after he reached the nerve center of this ambitious conspiracy. *If I'm not already too late.*

CHAPTER ELEVEN

SOFTLY, WITH ONLY A WHISPER OF A THUD, THE ELEVA-
tor came to a halt, and Roberta found herself deep inside an environment very different from the crumbling
ruins she had just left. *We must be hundreds of feet beneath
the fortress,* she estimated, judging from the speed of the
elevator and the length of their descent. *Talk about private!* she thought, making no effort to conceal her astonishment from Lozinak, Takagi, or even Carlos. *I've
been in bomb shelters that were closer to the surface.*

Even more impressive than its subterranean depths,
however, was the size of the installation that greeted
Roberta's awestruck eyes when the spotless white elevator doors slid open, revealing a spacious courtyard at the
center of an enormous vertical shaft that extended for a
mile or so above her head. "Wow!" she exclaimed, step-

ping out of the elevator to take it all in. Her jaw dropped and even Isis squawked in amazement. "I mean, wow."

"Welcome to Chrysalis," Dr. Lozinak said proudly, finally revealing the codename that Seven had already told her about.

Like the petals of some colossal lotus flower, five tunnels led away from the tiled courtyard, burrowing deep into the solid bedrock beneath the desert. Between the tunnels' entrances, sturdy ladders and catwalks rose up along the sides of the central shaft, apparently leading to multiple levels above the ground floor of the elaborate facility. Dozens of men and women, of diverse hues and ethnicities, circulated throughout the vast complex, going briskly about their daily errands. Roberta spotted technicians in white lab coats as well as maintenance workers wearing matching orange uniforms. Looking around, she was startled to see, one level above her, a group of small children being led along a catwalk by a trio of attentive caretakers in paint-smeared smocks. The babbling preschoolers looked happy and completely at home within the sprawling installation. *Chrysalis has even got its own underground nursery school?* she marveled. *This is bigger than I ever expected.*

One of the children, a neatly groomed Indian boy, maybe three or four years old, noticed the adults standing by the open elevator. Perhaps intrigued by Roberta's unfamiliar face, he paused upon the catwalk to stare down at the blond-haired stranger. Smiling back at the boy, Roberta was struck by the seriousness in the child's expression and the obvious intelligence in his dark eyes; in a strange, undefinable sort of way, this little kid reminded her of Gary Seven. Before she could put her finger on the precise quality the boy and her boss had in common, however, one of the boy's watchful caretakers tugged gently on his hand, urging him to keep up with the other children. Roberta watched as the entire class, perhaps on a field trip of some kind, disappeared into one of the upper tunnels. *So long, kid,* she thought.

Mounted sunlamps, far more gentle than the blazing orb Roberta and her companions had left behind, simulated daylight, while a silent and efficient ventilation system provided a gentle breeze that felt blissfully cool after the sweltering heat of the sunbaked desert. The marble tiles beneath her feet repeated the butterfly motif that she had previously noted on the tail of the private jet that had picked her up in Rome. *Nice design,* she observed; somebody had taken the trouble to make the secluded lair attractive as well as functional.

She felt oddly humbled by her futuristic surroundings; Chrysalis HQ made her and Gary Seven's own secret headquarters look like a high-tech lemonade stand. "Umm, does the Indian government know you've got your own little city down here?" she asked her fellow travelers.

Behind her, the elevator headed back toward the surface, leaving her with no obvious means of escape. Roberta tried not to look as trapped as she felt, even though the looming Carlos continued to watch over her as implacably as any prison warden. *He's sticking to me like Super Glue,* she thought irritably. *And me without any solvent.*

"Various individuals in the government have been paid not to know," Lozinak explained. His cane tapped against the blue-and-white tiles covering the floor of the courtyard. "Sadly, even in this brave new world we are entering, old-fashioned bribery remains a potent force."

"Chrysalis has really deep pockets, huh?" she observed, almost embarrassed to state something so manifestly obvious. From the looks of this place, Chrysalis had a budget comparable to NASA's.

"You'd be surprised how many successful billionaires and tycoons are willing to pay in order to give their offspring a better start, genetically speaking, than they themselves had," Takagi told her. "It's all about leaving a legacy, and guaranteeing that one's heirs are among the best of the best." He grinned mischievously. "I can even think of a few royal families that aren't above improving their precious bloodlines, provided it's done on the sly."

"All the advantages—and premium DNA—that money can buy, huh?" Roberta said, nodding. "I can see where that would be tempting to social-climbing rich folks with money to burn." She gave Takagi a conspiratorial wink as they headed for the arched entrance to a tunnel directly in front of them. "So who are we talking about here? Howard Hughes? OPEC? The Kennedys?"

Takagi looked like he couldn't wait to spill the beans, but, as usual, his more cautious colleague intervened before Walter could compromise too many secrets. "That is, I think, more than you need to know," Lozinak said, shrugging his stooped shoulders apologetically. He shot a warning glance at Takagi, who blushed visibly. Carlos smirked cruelly at the young scientist's discomfort. "At least for the present," Lozinak added.

Party pooper, Roberta thought, repressing a disappointed scowl. *I'm definitely going to have to try to get Takagi away from Lozinak at some point, preferably without going the full Mata Hari route!*

"Come," the old scientist said to Roberta, as they approached the glass doors at the mouth of the tunnel. "There is someone you should meet." A red telephone and a blank video screen were mounted on the wall next to the entrance, at approximately eye level. Lozinak lifted the receiver and keyed a numerical code into a shiny push-button display. Moments later, a woman's face appeared on the monitor. *A videophone,* Roberta realized. *Cool.*

"Viktor, welcome back," the woman said, her voice emerging from the screen. An attractive Indian woman, probably in her early thirties, she had large brown eyes and short, Twiggy-style hair. Roberta thought she looked familiar, but couldn't place the face just yet. Was this the infamous director that Carlos had invoked earlier? Roberta took a few steps closer to Lozinak, hoping to eavesdrop on his conversation more easily, but the aged Ukrainian pressed another button, silencing the audio so that he could converse with the woman more privately via the receiver. He lowered his voice and turned away from Roberta as he replied to the unidentified woman's greetings.

Darn, Roberta thought, unable to hear what was being said. Lozinak's successful attempt to protect his privacy made her nervous, mostly because it implied that the old scientist didn't yet trust her entirely. Had she blown her cover somehow? She crossed her fingers instinctively, praying that she could still count on the welcome wagon instead of the third degree.

After a brief, frustratingly inaudible discussion, Lozinak hung up the phone. "Excellent," he announced jovially, his warm tone going a long way toward allaying Roberta's paranoid fears. "It seems we're just in time to have lunch with the director." He smiled in her direction.

"No doubt you could eat a house after our long journey."

"I think you mean 'horse,'" she corrected Lozinak mildly. To be honest, she was more exhausted than hungry, but she wasn't about to pass up a chance to meet Chrysalis's fabled director face-to-face. Besides, it was almost noon anyway, so lunch was not a bad idea; several hours, and a couple of hundred miles, had passed since she'd eaten breakfast in the back of the limo. "Lunch sounds great to me," she agreed cheerfully. Isis meowed loudly, to remind all concerned that she required sustenance as well.

"Very good then," Lozinak declared. Glass doors slid open automatically to admit the party into the central tunnel. A moving conveyor belt ran along the left side of the enclosed corridor, and Lozinak stepped carefully onto the mechanized walkway, which carried him down the length of the tunnel, while Roberta and the others promptly followed his lead. Peering past Lozinak, she could not see any end to the tunnel, although they soon passed several intersections and diverging corridors. *How big is this place anyway?* she wondered, experiencing an irrational urge to leave a trail of bread crumbs behind her. *Hooking up with Seven down here is going to be like searching the Smithsonian on a crowded Sunday afternoon.*

She gave her arm a rest by placing Isis's carrier down on the conveyor belt in front of her. With nothing better to do than play tourist for the time being, she scoped out her surroundings as the moving sidewalk carried her deeper into Chrysalis's underground extremities.

For the secret headquarters of a bunch of card-carrying Mad Scientists, the installation around her was a lot less sterile and utilitarian than she might have expected. The walls of the tunnel were a bright turquoise, while regional artwork and tapestries adorned the corridor at regular intervals, providing a treat for Roberta's tired eyes. She particularly admired a robustly colored mural in which stylized peacocks, elephants, and camels gamboled throughout an ornately painted jungle of vines and blooming flowers. *Chrysalis could teach your average evil underground organization a thing or two about interior decoration,* she thought approvingly. Maybe this whole operation wasn't as much of a Bad Thing as Seven kept assuming? The more she saw of Chrysalis and the people behind it, the less certain she was that they needed to be stopped. Aside from a slight mania for secrecy, as embodied by the ever-present Carlos, everyone involved seemed to be motivated by only the best and most humanistic impulses. *I definitely need to have a long talk with Seven,* she decided, *before I start actively trying to sabotage the proceedings.*

Fluorescent lights in the ceiling, running parallel to the track below, provided plenty of illumination, making it easy to forget that they were actually hundreds of feet beneath the desert. "Where do you get the power to keep this whole place running?" she asked Takagi. "I thought there was an energy crisis going on."

"We have our own nuclear power plant," he explained, "located one level down." He pointed out a map of the entire base that was mounted on the wall just before the next approaching intersection. Roberta noted a glossy red You Are Here arrow indicating her current location, plus another level marked by the universal symbol for atomic energy. *Well, this accounts for that uranium Seven told me about, if not for all the germ-warfare equipment.*

"Fission or fusion?" she asked with a touch of trepidation in her voice. Gary Seven had frequently expressed his low opinion of humanity's present generation of fission reactors, which he considered dangerously crude and unreliable. *He's going to want to know about this reactor,* she realized, *if he hasn't discovered it already.*

"Just fission, I'm afraid." Takagi grinned at her sheepishly. "After all, we can't be trailblazers in every field, especially since we've sunk all our time and resources into zooming past the boundaries of modern genetic research."

"What? You mean you aren't an all-purpose scientific renaissance?" She feigned an exaggerated look of horrified disappointment. "I'm crushed!"

"Well, don't give up on us just yet," Takagi teased her back. "Wait until you get the full guided tour, not to mention meet the director." He looked ahead to orient himself. "Ah, here we are."

The moving track terminated in front of a pair of large glass doors inscribed with the image of an ascending double helix. Roberta flinched involuntarily, the etched symbol raising unwanted memories of her nightmare en route to the hidden base. In her mind she could still see the coiled chromosomes striking out at her like a cobra, infecting her own DNA with its mutating venom. *You don't need to be Sigmund Freud to interpret that particular picture show,* she reflected as the party approached the end of the conveyor belt; obviously, her unconscious still had problems with Chrysalis's whole *Brave New World* agenda, despite her hosts' persuasive sales pitches.

"Umm, I didn't talk in my sleep, did I?" she asked abruptly, suddenly afraid that she might have given herself away while dozing. "On the trip here, I mean."

"Not that I remember," Takagi assured her, "although I was pretty wiped out myself." He nodded at Isis's pet carrier, presently resting on the belt between him and Roberta. "You'd better pick that up, and watch your step."

Oh yeah, right, she thought, not feeling terribly guilty about letting the miserable cat slip her mind for a few minutes. She scooped up the handle of the plastic case just in time to step off the automated walkway right after Takagi and Lozinak. She was glad to see that, cane or no cane, the older scientist managed the transition onto stationary flooring without too much difficulty. Carlos followed after Roberta, shadowing her so closely with his intimidating bulk that she was tempted to ticket him for tailgating. *Will I be glad to give this bruiser the slip,* she thought impatiently. *When the time comes, that is.*

The double doors slid open, bisecting the decorative double helix, and the spicy, mouthwatering smell of Indian food reached Roberta even before she stepped inside. *Mmmm,* she thought, surprised at how hungry she felt all of a sudden. Maybe she wasn't too tired to eat after all.

The chamber she entered was a treat for the eyes as well. Cool, vanilla-colored walls enclosed a cozy living area furnished Indian-style. Instead of sofas or chairs, large mattresslike cushions rested upon the floor, along with an assortment of smaller pillows, all colorfully embroidered or encrusted with sparkling sequins. Lunch was laid out upon a low, beaten brass table that shone with a rich metallic luster. The floor upon which the table rested was marble inlaid with polished chips of turquoise and jade. *Wow,* Roberta thought, impressed by the elegant and exotic decor. *Not too shabby. . . .*

The only ominous touch—namely the presence of two looming bodyguards—was partially concealed by a set of upright wicker screens stretched across the far end of the room, behind one of the neatly upholstered cushions that surrounded the brass table on three sides. Through the pierced cane lattices, Roberta could glimpse only two tall, turbaned figures standing at attention. She couldn't help wondering if these new guards were any friendlier than Carlos. *Probably not,* she guessed. In her experience, security forces were paid to be uptight and suspicious. *Just look what happened at Kent State.*

The guards were presumably there to guarantee the safety of the room's only other occupant: a handsome Indian woman seated comfortably on the rear cushion. She was surprisingly light-skinned, making her large black eyes all the more striking. Roberta recognized her at once as the woman from the videophone, but was startled to see that the presumed director of Chrysalis was also several months pregnant. A voluminous white lab coat failed to conceal the telltale bulge below her waist. *First the kindergarten troupe, now this,* Roberta observed, slightly taken aback by the rampant fertility on display. *Nobody told me that this place was ground zero for the population explosion.*

"Welcome," the expectant woman said in lightly accented English, while gesturing toward the cushions waiting at opposite ends of the brass table. "I am delighted that you could join me for lunch."

Takagi and Lozinak removed their shoes before seating themselves upon the floor cushions, so Roberta did likewise. "Thank you," she said sincerely, more than a little overwhelmed by Chrysalis's nonstop hospitality. A twinge of guilt pricked her conscience when she considered how thoroughly she appeared to have deceived these relentlessly accommodating and generous people. *It's not fair,* she thought grumpily, as she squatted down on the left-hand cushion. *Why do they have to be so darn likable?*

"Dr. Neary," Lozinak began, "it is my privilege to introduce you to Dr. Sarina Kaur, the director of Chrysalis."

A surge of recognition rushed through Roberta, which she did her best to conceal. *Of course,* she realized. *That's where I've seen her before.* Sarina Kaur, Ph.D., was one of the names on Gary Seven's list of conspicuously missing scientists. Roberta remembered seeing a couple of old photos of Kaur, as well as skimming a brief biographical summary of the woman's career. Kaur was some sort of prodigy, Roberta recalled, who had burst on the scientific scene with a couple of remarkable genetic discoveries before dropping out of sight entirely. *A real rising star,* she reminded herself, deciding rapidly that "Ronnie Neary" would have heard of Kaur as well.

"*The* Sarina Kaur?" she asked, her voice full of professional admiration. "I always wondered whatever happened to you."

"Dr. Kaur studied under Khorana himself," Lozinak elaborated, while Kaur looked vaguely embarrassed by her colleague's fulsome introduction, "before striking out on her own to lay the groundwork for Chrysalis. More than anything else, it was Dr. Kaur's vision and determination, as well as her unique scientific genius, that made this project possible. As I believe you Americans say, she got the show on the ropes."

Show on the road, Roberta translated, not bothering to correct him. "In other words," she quipped, "yours is the mind that launched a thousand test tubes." She glanced around the opulent chamber. "I have to admit, I'm really impressed by what I've seen of this place so far."

"Thank you," Kaur replied. Graceful hands indicated

the enticing and aromatic feast spread out before them. "Please help yourself."

Lunch was displayed on a large metal platter atop the low table, with each dish and condiment in its own porcelain bowl: lamb in a spicy yogurt sauce, hot tandoori chicken, rice, chickpeas, and several inviting pieces of hot, fluffy bread. Roberta dug into the meal with gusto, piling a little of everything onto her plate. She also prepared a small dish of fresh yogurt for Isis, whom, with Kaur's permission, she released from the pet carrier. Out of the corner of her eye, she saw Carlos tense visibly when the cat escaped its case, but, for once, Isis was on her best behavior and did not create a scene.

As Roberta and her hosts enjoyed their midday repast, Dr. Kaur expounded on the philosophy behind Chrysalis:

"Someone once asked Gandhi—Mohandas, not Indira—what he thought of Western civilization. He replied that he thought it would be a good idea." She smiled sadly at the remark, which amused Roberta as well. "Like so many others of our generation, I nurtured dreams of making the world a better place. I soon realized, however, that a better world was impossible without better people to live in it. Democracy, socialism, psychiatry, religion . . . all these avenues to utopia inevitably run into the inherent limitations of human nature, at least as we presently know it. Only by improving the human species itself, through controlled genetic manipulation, can we ever hope to overcome the ills that have perpetually plagued the peoples of the world: poverty, war, disease, and so on."

Roberta sipped from a cup of ice-cold water. "I'm not sure you're giving ordinary human beings enough credit," she commented. "We've made an awful lot of progress over the last couple of millennia." *And we might have a pretty rosy future ahead of us,* she thought privately, *if Captain Kirk and Mr. Spock are any indication.* "Plain old folks can accomplish amazing things, even without having their DNA tweaked."

Says the girl working for an alien-bred do-gooder from outer space! she thought, feeling a tad hypocritical. Was Gary Seven's covert campaign to save mankind from itself any less radical or snobbishly elitist than Kaur's?

The ambitious Indian scientist looked happy to have her assumptions challenged. "Indeed," she agreed, "but how much of that is because of the impact of a few truly exceptional beings? An Einstein, or a Martin Luther King? How often can we depend on environment and heredity to produce such individuals at random?" She raised her open hands to indicate and encompass the vast facility surrounding them, and Roberta saw that Kaur had the butterfly logo of Chrysalis tattooed upon her palms. "Here at this state-of-the-art installation, we're taking chance out of the equation, producing an entire generation of superior individuals, capable of completely transforming civilization as we know it."

A chill ran down Roberta's spine at the future envisioned by Kaur. As much as Gary Seven meddled behind the scenes of current events, he had never actually tried to run the world. But imagine a whole army of Gary Sevens, each determined to make their mark on history . . . *The rest of us might just as well give up any hope of controlling our own destinies,* she thought, which didn't strike her as a terribly hopeful prospect.

She knew better, though, than to express her doubts too openly; after all, she was supposed to be a gung-ho new recruit. "You've got a point," she told Kaur and the others. "I guess I wouldn't be here if I didn't know in my heart that Chrysalis, or something like it, is what the world needs right now."

"I'm glad you feel that way," Kaur said, nodding in approval. Taking a sip of water, she peered at Roberta over the rim of a clear crystal goblet. "It looks as though Viktor and Walter have made an excellent choice in inviting you into our community." She contemplated Roberta speculatively. "Perhaps you can tell me more about your own singular talents and specialties?"

"Not after a fourteen-hour trip and no sleep!" Roberta answered hastily, anxious to avoid exposure. She shook her head and yawned theatrically, stretching her arms overhead until the joints snapped, crackled, and popped like freshly doused Rice Krispies. "Can we put off the full job placement exam until later?" she pleaded. "I'm so jet-lagged right now that I couldn't tell a peptide from a Pepsi."

Time to change the subject . . . fast! Roberta decided. "I can't help noticing that you're expecting a child, Dr. Kaur. If you don't mind me asking, is that part of the project, too?"

The mother-to-be did not take offense at her guest's query. Instead she gave Roberta a sly, Mona Lisa smile and placed a protective hand upon her bulging belly. "Of course," she replied. "As the head of Chrysalis, I could hardly ask other women to assist in the creation of a new generation of enhanced human beings without volunteering to do so myself." She dipped an air-puffed piece of bread into a bowl of mango chutney. "This is my second such pregnancy, in fact. You shall have to meet my first great triumph later."

"I'd be delighted to," Roberta said, although inwardly dismayed at the implications of what Kaur was saying. Did this mean that Chrysalis had already begotten some genetically engineered superchildren? *Seven's not going to like that,* she realized, wondering what in the world she and Seven could do now that the recombinant genie (no pun intended) was out of the bottle?

She suddenly remembered the party of toddlers she had glimpsed earlier, and, in particular, the dark, soulful eyes of one small Indian boy. Now that she thought of it, that boy bore a distinct resemblance to Sarina Kaur.

Equally dark eyes, possessed of the same fierce intelligence, appraised Roberta, taking obvious note of the American woman's youth and apparent good health. "Perhaps you too will see fit to bear one of the products of our collective effort?" Kaur suggested.

Roberta nearly choked on her *poori.* "Whoa there," she sputtered once she caught her breath. "I mean, I think what you people are doing here is great, and I can't wait to be a part of it, but you've got to give me a little time to get used to that last part. Lab work is one thing, but this . . . !" She shook her head doubtfully, looking to both Takagi and Lozinak for support. "I'm not sure I'm ready just yet to turn into a human incubator."

Kaur appeared undeterred by Roberta's horrified reaction. "We'll see," she said with unnerving confidence.

Neither of the other scientists contradicted her.

Where the hell are you, Seven? Roberta thought anxiously. *Things are starting to get just a little too creepy. . . .*

CHAPTER TWELVE

WHITE MICE SQUEAKED AND MONKEYS JABBERED AS Gary Seven awaited his audience with Williams's unnamed superiors. A menagerie of what he guessed were prospective lab subjects shared his captivity within a cramped storage area somewhere on one of the underground complex's lower levels. He did not find it encouraging that the Chrysalis's experiments had already extended to primates. *That's too close to human DNA for comfort*, he thought, knowing that only a few minor chromosomal differences separated Homo sapiens from its nearest simian cousins.

At the moment, he felt a more than usual kinship with Earth's great apes, given that he was locked inside a cage that smelled distinctly of chimpanzee. Straw carpeted the cement floor beneath his feet, while both wrists were handcuffed to the bars at the front of the cage. Thankfully, he had this particular cage all to himself, although a large Bengal tiger paced back and forth in the adjacent cell, occasionally snarling at its new two-legged neighbor. Unfortunately, the big cat was nowhere near the conversationalist that Isis was.

An imposing male guard, whom Seven quickly identified as a Sikh by the man's uncut beard, steel wristband, and ritual dagger, stood by watchfully outside the cage, along with Williams, who fidgeted impatiently near the entrance to the storeroom, glancing frequently at his watch. "Where is she?" Williams said for possibly the tenth time. "I thought she was coming soon." Even though they had escaped the punishing heat of the surface, the portly scientist was still perspiring heavily. "Can't you shut those bloody animals up?" he snapped at the turbaned guard. "All this caterwauling is giving me a splitting headache."

The guard shrugged philosophically. Clearly, quieting restless lab animals did not fall within his job description. Seven shared the Sikh's fatalistic attitude toward their mildly cacophonous surroundings; compared with some of the environments he'd visited in the past, on Earth and elsewhere, this zoological prison was fairly easy to endure. He was more concerned about what was going on beyond the walls of the storeroom.

His own watch had been taken from him, but Seven estimated that it was approximately 1:30 in the afternoon, Indian time, when the door swung open to admit a tall Indian woman in a white lab coat, carrying a black leather doctor's bag. He recognized her face immediately. *Sarina Kaur,* he mused. His eyes narrowed as he compared the missing prodigy to her photos. *Of course, I should have guessed she was the woman Offenhouse described.*

Her obvious pregnancy disturbed Seven. He hoped that Kaur had not been so rash as to practice genetic engineering on her own unborn child, but feared the worst. *That makes my task ten times more difficult,* he realized, *and puts the very future of this planet at much greater risk.* With effort, he tore his troubled gaze away from the woman's protruding stomach.

Kaur inspected him right back, looking more curious than concerned about her uninvited guest. "My apologies for your admittedly dehumanizing accommodations," she said calmly. Self-assurance bordering on arrogance suffused her voice, which spoke perfect English, presumably for his benefit. "I'm afraid this base lacks proper detention facilities. An oversight, in retrospect, but not one I ever anticipated we would have cause to regret." She sighed and applauded softly. "To be quite honest, Mr. Seven, you've come much further than I ever expected any outsider to get."

"Your installation is impressively remote," Seven admitted, returning the compliment, "not to mention admirably well concealed." If Kaur wanted to maintain a veneer of polite conversation over the reality of his imprisonment, he was willing to accommodate her for the time being. *I'll probably learn more that way.*

Two stern-faced bodyguards, in matching blue uniforms, stood attentively behind Kaur, crowding the already cramped storeroom. Williams fluttered nervously outside the perimeter defined by Kaur's guardians, watching their charismatic charge with an obvious mixture of admiration and anxiety. "It's all Offenhouse's fault," he gulped, trying his best to look indignant. "He let this spy find out all about the flight."

Despite Williams's hasty indictment, Kaur appeared

uninterested in assigning blame, at least for now. "Has he been searched?" she asked without looking at Williams. Her peremptory tone left little doubt as to where the pudgy Brit ranked on Chrysalis's pecking order.

"Yes, of course," he assured her. Retrieving a clear Ziploc bag from the original guard, he handed Seven's personal effects to Kaur, who gave her own black valise to one of the guards. "Just some odds and ends," Williams said dismissively.

Kaur carefully scrutinized the contents of the bag: Seven's watch, wallet, keys, and pen. "No weapon?" she asked, raising an inquisitive eyebrow. "That strikes me as unlikely."

"We searched him thoroughly," Williams insisted, tugging at the collar of his shirt. If nothing else, the director of Chrysalis had surely put the fear of God into her subordinate. "He's unarmed."

Kaur seemed unconvinced. "I wonder," she murmured. Seven watched as she opened the bag and personally inspected his belongings. His face betrayed no hint of extra attention when she got to his servo. "Nice pen," she commented, rolling the slim silver utensil between her fingers. "For taking notes on our operation?" she asked, giving Seven a quizzical look through the bars of his cage.

"Something like that," he answered tersely.

For a moment or two, he thought Kaur was going to put the servo aside without detecting its true nature. Then she gave the supposed pen a second look, twisting and manipulating its shiny silver casing until, with a electronic beep, a pair of metallic antennae sprouted from the sides of the device. A victorious smirk lent a somewhat malevolent cast to Kaur's refined features. "Well," she intoned archly, "what have we here?"

Williams's ordinarily ruddy face went pale. "I didn't realize—I mean, how could I?" He was obviously not having a good day. Kaur's personal bodyguards glowered at him scornfully, for compromising the director's security, while the original guard just looked glad that the other man was taking the heat. "The important thing is, we *did* confiscate the bloody thing," Williams blustered unconvincingly.

Kaur paid no attention to the Brit's excuses. Instead she pointed the tip of the servo at Seven as she fiddled with the controls. "You might want to be careful with that," he warned her sincerely, his poker face masking a degree of genuine apprehension on his part. From where he was confined, it was impossible to tell how Kaur might have adjusted the servo's settings; for all he knew, it was now set to kill. The twin antennae vibrated and beeped, targeting Seven. He held his breath, waiting.

At the last minute, right before she fired, Kaur shifted her aim to the tiger instead. Invisible energy hummed momentarily, and the tranquilized feline drooped onto the straw-covered floor of his cage, settling in for a long nap. Seven watched the animal's striped torso rise and fall with every sleepy breath, relieved that no one—including the tiger—had been seriously harmed.

"You might have killed it," he chided Kaur. "I thought tigers were an endangered species."

She deactivated the servo, whose antennae receded back into the silver casing. "At the moment, the most endangered species here is you, Mr. Seven." She contemplated the disguised servo with amusement, then placed it in the pocket of her lab coat. "Or should that be Mr. Double-Oh-Seven?" she quipped.

Kaur's little demonstration had served two functions,

Seven realized: to test the capacities of the servo, yes, but also to demonstrate just how far Kaur was willing to go to protect her project. *Very efficient,* he thought, making a mental note not to underestimate this woman.

"I am not a government agent," he informed her deadpan, "and this is not a movie." He looked Kaur squarely in the eye, determined to reason with his captor if that was at all possible. "What you are doing here could have very real consequences for the entire world."

"I should hope so," she replied. "Have you seen the current state of the world? It could certainly stand a welcome dose of rationality and superior intelligence." She patted her swollen belly in a way that confirmed Seven's most dire expectations.

"Be careful, Dr. Kaur," he cautioned. "The heedless pursuit of genetic superiority almost always leads to strife and attempted tyranny, pitting the worshippers of perfection against those judged to be inferior." He watched Kaur's face intently, hoping to discern some crack in the woman's forbidding self-confidence. *Too bad I can't tell her about the Borg,* he thought, considering them to be an excellent cautionary example, for all that they preferred cybernetics to genengineering. "Don't you think the people of the world are divided enough already, without adding new and artificial grounds for discrimination and conflict?"

Kaur frowned, perhaps lacking an immediate rebuttal. "I would be considerably more interested in debating such matters with you," she stated coldly, "if I knew who you are and whom you represent." She stepped closer to his cage, so that only the bars of the enclosure separated them. He could have grabbed her, had he been so inclined, if his wrists weren't handcuffed to the bars. "Enough chitchat," she declared, examining him as though he were a genetically deficient retrovirus. "Tell me who sent you."

"I work for myself," he said, which was true enough, at least on a terrestrial scale. His nearest supervisor was several light-years away, and not remotely human.

"Which makes you what?" she demanded. "A mercenary? An opportunist?"

"A concerned citizen," he retorted, "and one who has every reason to object to the reckless experiments you are conducting here." In fact, he had yet to determine the exact nature of those experiments, but he wanted to give Kaur and her associates the impression that they had nothing further to hide from him. *The more Kaur tries to defend her work, the more I'll learn.*

"There is nothing at all illegal about our research," she pointed out, "although I admit we've bent some rules here and there when it comes to financing and obtaining the necessary equipment. Last I heard there were no laws against creating superior human beings, not here in India, nor in your native America." She peered at him speculatively. "That *is* where you're from, Mr. Seven, isn't it? The United States?"

"I like to think of myself as a man without a country," he answered. *In more ways than one.*

"How very cosmopolitan of you," she observed sarcastically. Seven detected an edge of irritation in her voice. "I'm losing patience with your evasions, Mr. Seven, if that is indeed your real name." *It is on this planet,* he thought. "You realize, of course, that I cannot allow you to leave here before you have answered my questions. The security of the project depends on it."

Somehow I doubt that I'd be going anywhere regardless,

Seven thought. He detected in Kaur a ruthless streak that reminded him of too many of the fanatics and megalomaniacs he and Roberta had encountered over the last few years. *Is it the ever-present threat of nuclear annihilation that breeds these extremists,* he wondered, *or is this sort of ethical tunnel vision simply an intrinsic part of human nature?* For the future's sake, he hoped Kaur and her kind were just a temporary symptom of humanity's painful transition to true civilization.

"What about the vast quantities of bacteria you're stockpiling? Is that for the good of mankind, or just your own chosen heirs?" A flicker of surprise disturbed Kaur's composed veneer, alerting Seven that he had scored a hit, even though he had genuinely hoped he was mistaken. *Just like on Lanac VI,* he thought regretfully, chagrined to see history repeating itself once more. "What sort of vile biological toxin have you concocted, Dr. Kaur? How many people have to die to clear the stage for your miniature messiahs?"

Kaur did not waste time with denials. "Evolution is a cruel process, Mr. Seven. Why burden future generations with the crushing failure of our own overpopulation?" Although briefly startled by Seven's knowledge of her plans, her calm self-confidence swiftly reasserted itself. "Barring decisive action on my part, the population of India alone is expected to exceed one billion by the year 2000. Can you imagine the sheer daunting impossibility of trying to feed, clothe, and govern that many human organisms, let alone the rest of the world? That is not the legacy I wish to bequeath to my children."

"Extermination is no solution," Seven warned her, "only an invitation to extinction." He wished he could somehow plant a seed of doubt in Kaur's mind, but feared that nothing could grow there but her own unshakable convictions. "When do you intend to release the virus?"

"Bacterium," she corrected. "Genetically modified streptococcus, to be precise, capable of devouring soft tissue at an accelerated rate." Judging from the silent acceptance of Williams and the guards, none of this came as a surprise to Kaur's inner circle. "As for deployment, that's still under debate. To be honest, the contagion remains something of a work-in-progress; I am not yet entirely satisfied with its rate of communicability. We're almost ready to start testing the bug on selected population centers, though, so I'm currently negotiating with moles in the Soviet germ warfare program, Biopreparat, for a quantity of ICBM missiles equipped with specialized biowarheads."

Seven nodded gravely. Although the Soviet Union had only recently signed the Biological Weapons Convention, banning the development and use of germ warfare, he was not surprised to hear that the Russians were secretly continuing their efforts in that area. *Something to look into,* he acknowledged, *if and when I survive this current mission.*

"Ultimately, of course," Kaur continued, "there's no need to fully unleash the final version of our lovely, flesh-eating bacteria until the children of Chrysalis are ready to inherit the Earth." She patted her gravid belly. "Still, I must say, Mr. Seven, that your own success at penetrating our security makes me think that sooner might be safer than later."

"Please don't rush on my account," he told her dryly. "If I were you, I'd worry less about your security, and more about the long-term implications of what you're doing." Although willing to make the effort, he was rapidly abandoning any hope of convincing Kaur through logic and argument. *I need to contact Roberta and Isis,* he concluded, planning ahead to the next phase of this mission, *and find out what they've learned.* Touching base with the two agents was not going to be any easier now that Kaur had taken his servo, but Seven was confident that he could locate one or more of his operatives once he succeeded in escaping this cage. After all, he had once managed to track down Roberta in the middle of that fifth-dimensional maze of mirrors, so finding her in a multistory underground laboratory should pose only minimal difficulties. All he needed now was for Kaur and the others to leave him alone for a few minutes.

He resisted the temptation to start searching for an escape route already. *Not while Kaur is watching me so closely,* he knew. Hopefully, she would tire of this fruitless interrogation soon and give him a bit more privacy. He had no doubt that he would be able to outwit a mere guard or two.

"You seem to have a genetic predisposition toward stubbornness," she remarked with what Seven considered an encouraging degree of impatience. "An annoying trait, at least when harnessed to a reactionary desire to hold back the future." She stepped back from the cage to regard Seven from a greater distance. "Fortunately, we possess effective means to erode that stubbornness." She turned her head to address a guard. "The bag, please, Sanjit."

Seven didn't like the sound of that. Was Kaur really obsessed enough to resort to physical torture? That hardly meshed with the utopian vision she espoused, but, then again, she would scarcely be the first reformer in Earth's history who proved willing to build a paradise atop the bones of countless victims. Un-evolved humanity, Seven had learned the hard way, was capable of embracing appalling contradictions.

Fortunately, he had little to fear from torture except the actual physical discomfort. Carefully constructed psychological blocks, implanted in his mind well before he ever set foot on this backward planet, would prevent him from revealing any of the Aegis's most dangerous secrets, no matter how brutally he was treated. His only real concern, besides an innate instinct for self-preservation, was that his ordeal might leave him too weak to complete his mission, let alone come to the as-sistance of Roberta or Isis. *They've both had plenty of ex-perience in the field,* he reminded himself. *If worse comes to worst, perhaps they can neutralize Chrysalis on their own?*

"Maybe you should examine your methods as well as your goals," he said, trying even now to plant that seed of doubt in Kaur's mind. "If one is suspect, perhaps there may be something profoundly wrong with the other as well."

Kaur's implacable demeanor remained unperturbed. "You needn't worry about torture, if that's what you're thinking," she told Seven. "Physical coercion is a bar-baric remnant of the past." She reached into her bag and drew out a capped plastic vial and a hypodermic syringe. "As always, I prefer a more biochemical approach."

A dark purple fluid, the color of spilled Klingon blood, sloshed within the clear plastic tube. "Sodium pentothal?" Seven guessed uncertainly. The color didn't match any variety of truth serum that he was familiar with, and certainly nothing available on contemporary Earth.

"Nothing so crude," Kaur declared with pride, carefully filling the syringe with the contents of the vial. "We have something much better: an artificially synthesized neuro-transmitter that stimulates the, shall we say, *confessional* areas of the brain." She held the hypo up to the light, checking for unwanted air bubbles, then sprayed a small quantity of the serum through the point of the needle. "A useful by-product of our research into brain chemistry."

Handing the bag back to her bodyguard, she approached Seven once again, holding the syringe upright. The other guard stepped forward as well, responding to a subtle nod from the director. He reached through the bars of the cell and took a firm hold on Seven's right arm. "Please refrain from struggling," Kaur advised the prisoner. She waited patiently while the guard rolled up Seven's sleeve, exposing his lower arm. "It will hurt less if I can make a clean stick."

Seven did not try to yank his arm from the guard's grip. As long as he was handcuffed to the cage, not to mention outnumbered and unarmed, there was little point in resisting. *I guess we'll see now,* he mused, *just how effective Kaur's serum is.*

With her free hand, Kaur stroked the large vein at Seven's elbow, palpating the dull-blue blood vessel until it stood out prominently against his skin. He winced as the needle pierced his flesh, the brief sting being followed by an unpleasant burning sensation as the serum entered his bloodstream.

Pleased with the smoothness of the procedure, Kaur stepped back and consulted her wristwatch. "We shouldn't have long to wait," she explained to Williams and the others. "Judging from our results in the past, the drug takes effect within minutes."

I wouldn't be so sure, Seven thought.

CHAPTER THIRTEEN

"THAT'S IT: THE REACTOR CORE," TAKAGI SAID BOAST-fully. He and Roberta stared through a thick Plexiglas screen at a huge concrete cylinder, roughly a hundred feet in diameter. Enormous pipes filled with either coolant or heated gas connected the heavily shielded nuclear reactor with the massive steam-powered turbine and generator that provided virtually all of Chrysalis's electrical power, or so the Japanese biochemist eagerly informed her. "At peak capacity, the generator produces current in excess of twenty-five thousand volts."

Roberta stifled a yawn. Despite having slept for a solid fifteen hours the night before, taking full advantage of a private room provided by Chrysalis, she was still feeling kind of jet-lagged this morning. She was also concerned that she hadn't heard from Gary Seven since spotting him at the Delhi airport yesterday. She had tried to contact him via her servo, both this morning and shortly before turning in last night, but he hadn't responded to any of her hails. *I hope he's okay,* she worried, remembering the arid and inhospitable desert she had crossed to reach this location.

That he hadn't responded to any of her hails was inconclusive. Seven had been known to switch off the communicator function of his servo when he was conducting a particularly covert maneuver, lest a badly timed beep risk exposure, but he had seldom kept the pen-phone off the hook this long. Surely he must have had an opportunity to talk to her sometime in the last umpteen hours? *This isn't good,* she thought, fingering the servo in the pocket of her jeans.

They had spent the last forty-five minutes touring Chrysalis's laboratory facilities, which, to her inexpert eye, certainly looked impressive and state-of-the-art. She had oohed and ahhed over a generous assortment of electron microscopes, incubators, radiation counters, test tubes, petri dishes, titration setups, gas chromatography equipment, MRI scanners, and other apparatus she couldn't even begin to identify. As far as she could tell, none of the labs had been devoted to breeding great quantities of killer bacteria, not that she was sure she could tell if they were. Her legs were tired from trudging all over the underground base, yet she wasn't any closer to reestablishing contact with Gary Seven. *He has to have gotten here by now,* she surmised, *but what is he up to?*

"Ronnie? Dr. Neary?" Takagi waved a hand in front of her face, and she realized that she had let her mind wander a little too obviously.

Oops!

"Sorry about that," she apologized hastily. Her face assumed a more attentive expression. "The reactor. Right."

This high-tech control room, overlooking the reactor, was the latest stop on the tour. She and Takagi stood at the rear of the room while industrious technicians monitored an impressive array of lighted panels and gauges. Mounted schematics illustrated the internal workings of the reactor, currently hidden behind several feet of reinforced concrete. Her unfamiliar face drew a few curious glances from the workers present, but apparently Takagi's presence was enough to vouch for her status as a security non-risk. *If only they knew why I'm really here,* she thought, feeling guilty once more for taking advantage of these people's trust. *Undercover missions really suck sometimes.*

"I'm sorry again," Takagi emphasized, "that neither Viktor nor Dr. Kaur could join us this morning, but both of them have plenty of responsibilities to keep them busy." As a safety precaution, a badge-sized radiation tag was affixed to the front of his T-shirt.

"I'll bet," Roberta replied, wondering how she could shake Takagi long enough to go searching for Gary Seven on her own. She glanced around the control room, pretending to be interested in the various flashing lights and switches. The sterile white chamber, with its long banks of consoles and computers, reminded her of Mission Control at Cape Kennedy. "I'm afraid I don't know much about nuclear power," she lied, having defused an A-bomb or two in her time. "So where's the self-destruct switch?" she joked. "In the movies, there's always a button that blows everything up."

A serious expression came over Takagi's face, momentarily dimming the friendly young scientist's natural ebullience. "Believe it or not, there really is a self-destruct procedure, just in case some newly developed recombinant bacteria or virus is in danger of escaping into the environment. If the director judges the threat is serious enough, she has the option of triggering an irreversible chain reaction in the reactor core. In theory, the resulting atomic explosion would completely sterilize the area, preventing the bug from spreading."

"Like in *The Andromeda Strain,*" Roberta said, nodding her head in understanding. She had seen that creepy super-germ movie the year before. In the film, an overzealous computer nearly triggered a thermonuclear blast in order to keep the titular Strain from escaping a significantly more fictional underground lab. Of course, if Seven's dire theories were correct, Kaur and her colleagues were already whipping up some sort of Chrysalis Strain. "You aren't actually breeding any bugs like that, are you?"

Way to go, Roberta, she thought. *Real subtle.*

"Well, not on purpose, certainly," Takagi insisted, sounding quite sincere, "although it doesn't hurt to play it safe." He tried to lighten the mood by flashing Roberta a reassuring smile. "That's a completely last-ditch emergency measure, of course. It's never going to happen. We're extremely careful when it comes to handling hazardous materials, especially genetically modified microbes and such."

Why don't I find this terribly comforting? Roberta wondered, readily imagining a mushroom cloud rising over the Great Thar Desert. Maybe because she knew how easily at least one potential saboteur had already penetrated Chrysalis's supposedly airtight security?

Namely, me.

* * *

Kaur lied when she promised Seven that Chrysalis eschewed torture. Resisting the neurotransmitter's effects was proving to be an agonizing ordeal comparable to enduring the tender mercies of a Klingon mind-sifter.

He hadn't eaten or slept for hours, maybe even a day, and his jaw ached from the strain of keeping his teeth tightly clenched together. Kaur's supersophisticated truth serum had worked its insidious alchemy upon his brain cells, provoking an almost irresistible compulsion to reveal his secrets to whomever was listening, in this case Williams and one remaining guard. He couldn't even open his mouth for fear that vital intelligence, like Roberta's true identity, would start pouring out of him uncontrollably.

Seven kept waiting for the effects of the serum to wear off, but instead the compulsion only kept building, like floodwaters bearing down upon an overstressed dam. It was only a matter of time before the dam cracked under the mounting pressure; the tailor-made synthetic neurotransmitter seemed to have stimulated a reflex that would not disappear until it had been discharged. *Like a sneeze that won't go away,* he thought, *only a hundred times more insistent.*

As he had since the beginning of his ordeal, Seven relied on age-old Vulcan meditation techniques to resist the lure of the serum. *My mind is outside my body,* he chanted silently, seeking the ancient wisdom of *Kolinahr. My mind is under my command.* He sought to observe himself from a perspective of absolute detachment, viewing both the exhaustion of his body and the artificially induced obsession gripping his brain as he would any other external phenomena. *I cast out fear,* he recited over and over. *I cast out desire.*

His weary frame trembled with fatigue and mental exertion, but he kept his thoughts to himself, despite the relentless prodding of the foreign chemicals tickling his neurons. Escape, in his present compromised condition, seemed increasingly unlikely, so he knew he had to hold himself together long enough for Roberta and Isis to take whatever action was necessary. The cold metal handcuffs chafed painfully against his wrists, and his legs were numb from squatting in the same uncomfortable position for many hours, but he willed himself to ignore his physical anguish, just as he forced his resolve to stand firm against the cerebral extortion of the truth serum. *My mind is outside my body. My mind is under my command. . . .*

Kaur and her personal bodyguards had left several hours ago, leaving only Williams and one solitary guard to conduct the interrogation, but now the door to the storeroom swung open once more to admit the self-assured director of Chrysalis, who, unlike Seven, looked just as fresh and energetic as the day before. "Still no progress?" she asked of Williams. Her accented voice held both frustration and fascination.

Williams was merely frustrated. "Not so much as a peep," he grumbled. Stubble infested his unshaven jowls, and the remains of a partially consumed sack lunch rested upon his lap as he perched upon a metal stool that a guard had produced for his convenience. "If I couldn't see him breathing, I'd wonder if he was still alive."

"Intriguing," Kaur admitted, sounding impressed despite herself. "This level of resistance, sustainable for such a lengthy duration, is literally unheard-of." She knelt beside the cage to inspect Seven more closely. "We've never seen anything like this in all our clinical trials."

"Are you sure you gave him the right stuff?" Williams asked irritably. The Englishman had to be getting pretty fed up, Seven surmised, if he was willing to question Kaur so openly. The prisoner watched his captors' interactions from behind drooping bangs of hair and half-closed eyelids. Playing possum seemed like his best bet to avoid an even more grueling interrogation, at least for the time being, so he chose not to acknowledge Kaur's return.

"Quite sure," she replied to Williams's query. She took little note of his impertinence, seeming far more interested in the mystery of Seven's continued silence. "Can you hear me, Mr. Seven?" she inquired, poking his chest through the bars of the cage. He remained immobile, but she eyed him suspiciously, brushing the hair from his eyes with incongruous gentleness and attempting to look him in the eyes, which Seven kept resolutely fixed upon the floor, avoiding her gaze. Even still, he felt an almost overwhelming urge to tell her everything he knew. *I cast out fear. I cast out desire.*

She grabbed on to his chin and tilted his head back roughly, so that he could no longer look away from her unbearably inquisitive face. "Yes, I believe you can hear me," she said perceptively, "appearances to the contrary." She held his head upright and peppered him with questions asked almost more urgently than he could endure. "Who are you? Where did you come from? How are you able to resist the serum?"

He stared back at her as blankly as he could manage, but an agonized groan escaped through his clenched teeth. Each unanswered interrogative was like a fresh torrent of floodwater pounding against the crumbling dam he had erected inside his besieged psyche. His tongue twitched spasmodically between his jaws, aching to satisfy his chemically inspired craving to confess everything to Kaur.

"Who are you?" she demanded. Her face was only inches away from his, dissecting his will with her eyes. "Tell me. Tell me now."

My name is Gary Seven, he thought involuntarily, the words bubbling up out of his consciousness. *My designation is Supervisor 194, and I was born in a cloaked solar system fifty thousand light-years from here. I was trained by the Aegis and sent to Earth to insure that humanity survives its technological and societal adolescence. My primary operatives include Roberta Lincoln, a contemporary human of this era, and Isis, my*

"No!" he barked hoarsely, breaking his long silence. He bit down on his lip until blood flowed, choking back the revelatory deluge that threatened to gush from his lips. His entire body jerked convulsively as he struggled to hold back a cascading stream of verbiage beyond his ability to control or censor. *My mind is outside my body,* he thought desperately, straining to regain dominion over his mental processes. *My mind has been trained by aliens from—no! My mind is under my control.*

Kaur's dark eyes gleamed with triumph and expectation. "His throat is dry," she called out to Williams. "Give me something to drink. Hurry."

Dismounting awkwardly off his stool, the British scientist stumbled over to donate his liquid refreshment to the cause. He hastily offered a mug of lukewarm tea to Kaur, who lifted the rim of the cup to Seven's cracking and bleeding lips. "Here," she said solicitously. "Drink this."

The tantalizing scent of the *chai* was more than tempting. His entire body felt dehydrated, and he wanted to gulp down the tea nearly as much as he needed to fill his listeners in on the full particulars of his assignment on Earth. His parched throat, however, was his last defense against the malignant influence of the truth serum, so he knew he couldn't risk even a single sip. He tried to pull his mouth away from the cup, but Kaur held on to the back of his head with her free hand, keeping it in place. She tipped the cup slightly and he felt the tea slosh against his teeth and lips, which he kept locked tightly together. The warm, brown liquid dribbled down his chin and onto the front of his sweat-soaked white shirt.

My name is—my name is— To his extreme dismay, Seven felt the words forming in his mouth. His tongue twitched of its own accord and he realized that, despite all stringent discipline and conditioning, he was about to tell Kaur everything. Perhaps sensing her victory, Kaur leaned in closer. "Yes, that's right," she prompted. "Go ahead. I'm listening."

Only at the last instant, as his moistened lips parted irrevocably, did Seven realize there was still one way to hang on to his secrets. . . .

"[My name is Gary Seven,]" he confessed in Klingon. "[My designation is Supervisor 194, and I was born in a cloaked solar system fifty thousand light-years from here. . . .]"

Anger and acute frustration disfigured Kaur's elegant features. Despite her vast erudition, the guttural sounds emanating from Seven's throat made no sense whatsoever; to her earthbound ear, they sounded more like the growling of wild dogs than comprehensible human speech.

"Bloody hell!" Williams exclaimed. "He's gone barking mad!"

"No, I don't think so," Kaur said slowly. Assuming a more patient demeanor, she gave the snarling prisoner an exacting appraisal before tipping her head in respect. "Very clever, Mr. Seven. I must confess, I can't even begin to place that language." She waited until Seven's indecipherable outburst ran its course and the caged man fell silent once more. "Don't think that you've won so easily, however." She smiled in anticipation of Seven's ultimate capitulation. "A true scientist never abandons an experiment after just one failure."

She glanced at Williams. "There's a filled hypodermic syringe in my right coat pocket," Kaur informed her lackey. "Retrieve it and inject the contents of the syringe into the subject's arm." She continued to press the mug against her prisoner's lips. "I want to give the formidable Mr. Seven a booster shot of the serum."

"Is that safe?" Williams asked nervously, fumbling to fulfill her instructions. He plucked the hypo from Kaur's spotless lab coat, then removed the rubber cap over the needle.

"I don't know," she confessed. "That's one of the things I want to find out." She kept her intense, analytical gaze on Seven's face as Williams injected a fresh dose of the serum into Seven's exposed elbow. "Remind me to get a tissue sample later, regardless of the serum's effect. I definitely want to take a close look at this subject's DNA."

Seven welcomed the sharp sting of the needle as it threaded his vein; it distracted him momentarily from the constant psychic pressure to answer Kaur's questions. Then the needle withdrew, leaving behind an all-too-familiar burning sensation, and the grueling inter-rogation resumed.

"Who are you?" the director cross-examined him once more. Within minutes, Seven could feel the con-centrated neurotransmitter agitating his brain cells all over again, adding a horrible new keenness and inten-sity to what was already an overpowering compulsion. "Who sent you?" Kaur asked forcefully, and he felt the muscles in his jaw loosen to a dangerous degree. His tongue rose against his palate, poised to speak the in-stant he parted his lips. "And no speaking in tongues this time. I want English. Only English."

"[My name—]" He tried to bypass Kaur's new re-strictions, but the harsh Klingon words caught in his throat. He grasped for other, even more alien vocabu-laries, yet the strange, unearthly words would not stick to his tongue. In desperation, he tried falling back once more on the ancient wisdom of the sages of Vulcan: *My mind is, my mind is, my mind is—what?* He could not re-member the rest of the mantra. The pounding in his head was too loud. All he could hear were the ques-tions, echoing loudly within his skull, and the answers that could no longer be restrained.

"My name is Gary Seven," he began.

"Here we are," Takagi declared grandly, reminding Roberta somewhat of a carnival barker. "The spiritual, if not actually the geographical, heart of Chrysalis. Get ready to see what the whole project is really all about."

World domination? Roberta speculated, hoping that wasn't the case. A pair of turquoise steel doors stood before her, concealing the next stop on her tour of Chrysalis. Before Takagi could lead her past the mysterious doors, however, an indignant and altogether too familiar meow interrupted her sight-seeing expedition/reconnaissance mission. "Oh, great," Roberta muttered as she spun around to see, just as she expected, a twelve-pound, four-legged busybody horning in on her undercover snooping.

"What the devil?" Takagi exclaimed. He stared through his spectacles at the furry black feline on the floor behind them. "How did your cat get here?"

"Just misses me, I guess," Roberta answered dryly, glaring daggers at Isis, who didn't look at all bothered by the human woman's baleful gaze. *What's the matter?* Roberta thought testily. *Wasn't I spying fast enough for you?* Isis had scolded her mercilessly for sleeping in this morning, and then protested vocally when Roberta left her behind in their room. *I don't blame her for being anxious about Seven. I'm worried, too. But she's not helping by being a pest.*

"But what's she doing here?" Takagi asked, still flummoxed by the cat's surprise appearance. "How did she get out of your room?"

Roberta shrugged. "Trust me, she has an amazing talent for turning up where she's not invited." None too gently, she scooped up Isis, who clambered just as roughly onto her shoulder. *Guess she's along for the ride now,* Roberta thought, wincing as the cat dug in with her claws. To change the subject, she tilted her head toward the waiting turquoise doors. "So, you going to show me what you've got here?"

Takagi eyed the cat uncertainly, then threw up his hands in resignation. "Okay, I suppose there's no harm bringing little Isis along on this part of the tour. It's not like there's anything delicate or dangerous inside."

"Just the heart of Chrysalis," Roberta teased.

"Exactly," he grinned, going back into carnival-barker mode. Stepping forward, he pressed a plastic button alongside the double doors. They slid open in front of her, and Takagi gestured for her to step inside. Perched alertly atop Roberta's left shoulder, Isis peered ahead intently.

The noise hit her at once, before her eyes even had a chance to take in what lay beyond the obviously sound-proof doors. The babble of a dozen high-pitched voices produced a cacophonous battering ram of sound that came as quite a change from the calm, focused atmosphere of the reactor control room. Roberta was only momentarily disoriented, though, instantly recognizing the carefree and discordant clamor of small children at play.

The heart of Chrysalis turned out to be a spacious classroom/playroom populated by the same pack of toddlers she had spotted earlier. In typically Indian style, there were no chairs or desks, but rather a generous assortment of mats and pillows for the children to work and play upon. At least a dozen kids were present, supervised by a trio of adult caretakers, who circulated among the kids, offering advice and encouragement. The class was admirably integrated, Roberta noted, including children of various races and ethnicities. Each child appeared to be working independently on a project of his or her own, under the gentle supervision of the soft-spoken and smiling instructors. Roberta heard several different languages, from Hindi to Esperanto, being spoken. Her translator pendant could decipher any or all of the various dialects, of course, but the din of competing voices pretty much reduced the bulk of the chatter to white noise.

At first, the scene looked like a typical nursery

school or kindergarten, albeit more international than most. But as her gaze zeroed in on the individual children and their activities, Roberta's eyes widened and her jaw dropped open in astonishment.

Nearby, only a few feet away from the entrance where Roberta now stood, a tiny little Japanese girl, who couldn't have been more than three years old, was painting a flawless re-creation of the Mona Lisa with her watercolors. What's more, she appeared to be doing so from memory. Next to her, a slim blond boy was busy scribbling quadratic equations all over a mounted blackboard, while a distinctly intimidated-looking tutor struggled to keep up. Two more children squatted upon a paint-stained Persian carpet, meticulously constructing a miniature Taj Mahal out of Legos without any visible set of instructions. Nearby a cute little girl with red hair and freckles sang an aria from *La Bohème* (flawlessly) while jumping rope at the same time.

I don't believe this, Roberta thought. It was one thing to theorize about building smarter kids through creative biochemistry, but confronting a whole room of such supertots was a whole different mind trip. *When I was that age,* she thought, aghast and embarrassed, *I felt like a whiz kid if I could get all the way through the alphabet without screwing up!*

Remembering the handsome little Indian boy she had made eye contact with the day before, Roberta glanced around the playroom. She quickly spotted him sitting in a lotus position upon the floor, his nose buried in a large hardcover book that was much too thick to be either *Curious George* or *Green Eggs and Ham.* She squinted to make out the title of the book, and gulped audibly when she saw that it was Dante's *Divine Comedy*—in the original Italian, no less!

"Ohmigosh," she blurted out, still not quite believing what she was witnessing. Her eyes sought out Takagi's for confirmation. "Please, please, tell me this is the advanced class."

Takagi chuckled, enjoying her thunderstruck reaction. "They're *all* advanced classes," he informed her.

"All?" A tremor crept into her voice as the full implications of Takagi's response sank in. "There are more?"

"A few hundred," he stated chirpily. "Chrysalis is packed with educational facilities like this. It meant a bit more construction, naturally, but the smaller groupings allow for more individualized attention and instruction. Besides," he added, giving Roberta a friendly wink, "it's easier to monitor our progress if we can track each new batch of kids separately."

Let's hear it for quality control, Roberta thought sarcastically. Despite his affable manner, Takagi suddenly sounded a bit more cold-blooded and clinical than she was comfortable with. These were kids he was talking about, not lab projects. Happy, healthy kids.

Maybe even extra-healthy kids, for that matter. Surveying the entire classroom, she observed that every one of the children appeared to be perfectly fit, lacking any obvious handicaps or birth defects. Nobody was wearing glasses or needed braces on their teeth. None of the kids were too skinny, or sickly, or overweight, or coping with a mild case of the sniffles. *I bet they don't even have any cavities,* she thought, both appalled and envious. She couldn't quite bring herself to complain that the toddlers were *too* perfect—how could anyone object to insuring a child's good health?—but there was something unnervingly weird about the class's eerily uniform physical fitness.

Noting Takagi's and Roberta's arrival, one of the adult instructors, a thirtyish woman with severe features and frosty blond hair tied neatly in a bun, detached herself from the little genius she was assisting and approached the front entrance. "Hello, Walter," she said warmly. Alert blue eyes regarded Roberta with curiosity. "Who's your friend?"

"A new addition to the project," he replied, introducing "Dr. Veronica Neary" to the other woman, a highly trained educator and child psychologist named Maggie Erickson, who, according to Takagi, had once written a much-talked-about doctoral thesis on the care and education of extremely gifted children. "I couldn't wait to show Ronnie just how impressive our kids are."

"I can't blame you," Erickson said, her lack of an accent (as far as Roberta was concerned) branding her as another American. "At the risk of tooting our own horn, we're working wonders here. Not only are these children intellectually advanced, but their physical development is vastly superior to any ordinary child. They have fifty percent more lung capacity, for example, as well as a significantly improved cardiac system." She smiled sincerely, clearly delighted at the opportunity to show off her precious prodigies. "Come, let me introduce you to one of our star pupils."

With the proud instructor leading the way, the three adults navigated across the busy playroom, taking care not to step on any of the children's scarily ambitious works-in-progress. Roberta still got a little freaked out every time she peeked down to see, for instance, a three-year-old child putting together a five-hundred-piece jigsaw puzzle in less than ten seconds, and with his eyes closed to boot. A few seconds later, she caught a different toddler examining her closely, then realized that the tiny little tyke, who was barely more than a baby, had already sculpted a perfect likeness of Roberta in Play-Doh. *That looks more like me than I do!* she realized in amazement, even as the pint-sized Michelangelo put the finishing touches to Roberta's portrait. The way-too-youthful sculptor eyed her creation critically, only to spot some subtle defect invisible to Roberta, who felt a definite chill tiptoe down her vertebrae as the child cheerfully squashed her miniature masterpiece and started over again. *So much for immortality,* Roberta quipped to herself in a doomed attempt to overcome her growing uneasiness.

The little sculptor wasn't the only child who looked up at Roberta as she passed, but none of them appeared at all alarmed by the stranger in their midst. Many of them smiled appreciatively at the sight of the sleek black cat riding upon Roberta's shoulder. Had shyness or timidity been excised from their genetic makeup, she wondered, or had the children of Chrysalis simply been raised in an exceptionally secure and unthreatening environment? The latter was a much less scary explanation.

She was not too surprised when Dr. Erickson's prize pupil turned out to be Roberta's friend, the inquisitive Indian boy from the day before. Even in a roomful of budding geniuses, this boy stood out by virtue of a unique charisma all his own. *He's going to be really something when he grows up,* Roberta mused, unsure if that was a good thing or not. *What kind of impact could he have on the world?*

Erickson introduced Roberta to the boy. "We call him 'Noon' for short," she added, before addressing the child again. "Noon, Dr. Neary is very interested in learning more about you and the other children."

"Call me Ronnie," Roberta insisted. She knelt down on the carpet so she could converse with Noon at his own level. What with his deceptively childish age and appearance, she had to resist the temptation to speak to him in baby talk. "Hi. I guess you speak English pretty well."

"I speak English, Arabic, Hindi, Punjabi, Mandarin, French, German, Spanish, and Japanese," he stated matter-of-factly. The boy's poise and unselfconscious dignity would have been comical in a child his age, like a toddler trying on his parents' oversized clothes, except that somehow this particular munchkin could pull it off. He wasn't just playing at acting grown-up, Roberta intuited; he really was that confident and unafraid. *I wonder,* she thought: *Is this what Gary Seven was like as a kid?*

"How's your book?" she asked, still somewhat taken aback by the tyke's choice of reading material.

"Intriguing," he answered with a certain sober gravity. "The *Inferno* is the most entertaining part, naturally, although I prefer *Paradise Lost.*" His serious dark eyes stared boldly back at Roberta, unintimidated by the age difference between them. "Have you read Milton?"

"Er, just the Cliffs Notes version," she confessed. Once again, she noted Noon's unmistakable familial resemblance to Sarina Kaur. *I guess a little old-fashioned heredity survived all that high-tech genetic tinkering,* she surmised. *Kind of reassuring in a way.* She felt better knowing that Noon was not entirely a product of artificially manufactured DNA.

Isis took advantage of Roberta's kneeling posture to drop lightly onto the carpet between Roberta and Noon. She stretched luxuriously, digging her claws into the rug as she extended her spine and tail as far as they could go. Glossy black fur stood out sharply amid the bright, cheery colors of the classroom.

"Is she yours?" Noon asked, exhibiting an encouragingly childlike interest in the cat. Isis flirted with him shamelessly, purring and rubbing her head against his leg. He responded by gently stroking the cat's head with his pudgy little hand. "What's her name?"

"She's sort of mine, I guess," Roberta answered, slightly startled by the cat's sudden sociability; her temperamental feline cohort was usually more standoffish than this. "And her name is Isis."

"Like the Egyptian goddess?" asked the frighteningly well read four-year-old. Observing his playful interaction with the cat, the rest of the children hurried over to join in the fun, rapidly turning Isis into a one-cat petting zoo. Surprisingly, the cat seemed to bask in the attention, even lifting her head so that eager little fingers could more readily scratch the fur beneath her chin. *I always knew you were just a spoiled tramp at heart,* Roberta thought snidely, standing up and stepping back from the growing throng around Isis.

She also let out a sigh of relief. More than anything else, the children's enthusiastic response to Isis convinced her that these kids, no matter how stupendously smart and talented, were not, in fact, refugees from the Village of the Damned. She made a mental note to remind Gary Seven, assuming she ever made contact with him again, that these tots were more than just an unexpected complication in the Aegis's grand agenda for humanity's progress; these were innocent kids who deserved to be treated as such, no matter what Seven decided to do about Chrysalis.

"Looks like your furry friend is quite a hit with the children," Dr. Erickson commented. Isis had virtually disappeared from view, buried beneath a crowd of excited toddlers jostling each other for the privilege of petting their feline visitor.

"Well, I wouldn't exactly call us friends," Roberta muttered, then turned to apologize to Erickson and the other instructors. "Sorry to disrupt your class this way."

"No problem," Erickson insisted. "The children have been working hard on their individual projects; they're entitled to a break." She removed a small notebook from her jacket pocket and scribbled a few notes on the children's behavior. "As a matter of fact, we've been planning to introduce some pets into their environment, in order to encourage their ability to empathize with genetically inferior life-forms."

Like the rest of humanity? Roberta translated, biting down the first cutting remark that came to mind. Was there no aspect of these children's lives, she wondered silently, that wasn't designed to serve some quasi-scientific purpose or protocol? "That sounds like an excellent idea," she said diplomatically.

"Thank you," Erickson replied. "Early studies strongly indicate that—"

The American teacher's incipient dissertation was cut off abruptly by shrill cries of alarm from the nearby children, who began hurriedly backing away from the site of the impromptu kitty lovefest. At first, Roberta feared that Isis had run out of patience and scratched or bit someone, but she rapidly realized that this was a far more grievous situation. These were seriously frightened kids, with genuine tears of terror and distress streaming down their cheeks. They frantically scrambled away to the far corners of the classroom, until the only children who remained were Noon himself, holding on to Isis protectively, and a single little girl sprawled on her back upon the floor, her small limbs twitching convulsively.

With a start, Roberta recognized the underage sculptor who had so painstakingly re-created Roberta in Play-Doh only minutes before. Now that same artistic prodigy looked to be caught in the throes of some sort of epileptic fit. Glazed violet eyes stared wildly at nothing in particular, their pupils dilated alarmingly. Saliva frothed at the corners of her tiny mouth, while her entire body twitched violently, as though being jolted repeatedly by a powerful electric current.

"Blast it!" Erickson swore loudly, then immediately dropped onto the floor beside the stricken child. "Help me hold her still!" she cried out to Roberta as she swiftly inserted her fingers into the little girl's mouth to keep her from swallowing her own tongue. "Get the sedative—hurry!" she shouted to the other two instructors, who also went into emergency mode. Grabbing on to the little sculptor's flailing legs with both hands, Roberta got the clear impression that the staff of the classroom had coped with this sort of crisis before.

Her suspicions were instantly confirmed when she heard Erickson mutter to herself in passable Hindi. "Dammit, not again!" she cursed, unaware that Roberta's peace-symbol pendant provided the visiting newcomer with a literally simultaneous translation. Roberta held on tightly to the epileptic child's ankles and pretended not to be listening.

While one of the other instructors tended to the rest of the children, doing her best to calm them down,

the remaining tutor—a dark-skinned African man—
joined them alongside the spasming toddler. He
smoothly and efficiently slid a hypodermic needle into
her arm. Roberta had no idea what kind of potion the
hypo held, but it clearly did the trick; seconds later
she was relieved to feel the taut muscles in the little
girl's legs relax at last. The child's breathing settled
and her eyelids drooped shut as she slipped into a
drugged, narcotic state.

The male instructor spoke to Erickson in Hindi, in a
clear attempt to exclude Roberta from the discussion.
"I was afraid of this," he said gravely. "The medication
isn't working; the neurological aberration is too severe.
She should be transferred to the Developmental Deviations Unit as soon as she recovers."

Erickson nodded reluctantly, gently letting go of the
victim's tongue. Roberta noted deep bite marks above
the woman's knuckles. "I was hoping that wouldn't be
necessary," the female teacher stated with obvious sad-
ness, "but you're right, these fits aren't getting any better." She sucked on her wounded fingers before
delivering her final verdict on the disposition of the
child. "What a waste. She's so talented otherwise."

Feigning incomprehension, Roberta didn't like
what she was hearing. The Developmental Deviations
Unit? *Sounds to me like Chrysalis's genetic assembly line isn't
a hundred percent foolproof just yet,* she guessed. *But what
exactly do they do with the rejects? And do I want to find
out?*

A gentle hand took hold of her upper arm and tried
to tug her up and away from the comatose child.
"C'mon, Ronnie," Takagi urged her. "We should probably get out of here. Let's give Dr. Erickson and her col-

leagues some space to handle this little emergency."

Roberta had almost forgotten Takagi was present at all. "But what was that all about?" she demanded urgently, slowly rising to her feet to interrogate her tour guide. "What happened to that little girl?"

"I'm not sure," he stammered nervously. "I'm a biochemist, not a pediatrician." He kept tugging on her arm, trying to escort her to the exit. "There's nothing to worry about, though. Maggie and the others know what they're doing, trust me."

That's getting harder and harder, she thought grimly, but now was probably not the time to stage a major confrontation, not before she found out what had happened to Gary Seven. "Okay," she assented grudgingly. "Let me get my cat."

Alone of all the superchildren, only Noon had not fled screaming away from their convulsing classmate. Even now, he stood calmly by, stroking Isis's furry head as he silently contemplated his unconscious playmate. His stern, unreadable expression offered no clue as to what was going through his genetically enhanced mind. *Is he just braver and more stoic than the other children,* Roberta pondered, as she quietly retrieved Isis from Noon's arms, *or simply more inhuman and unfeeling?*

She wished she knew.

CHAPTER FOURTEEN

"WHO ARE YOU?" SARINA KAUR ASKED THE MYSTERIous Mr. Seven. "Who sent you?"

Scientific curiosity mingled with more pragmatic security concerns as she observed the caged American spy. Part of her almost hoped that he could keep on resisting the serum, just to see what the ultimate limits of his endurance were, but she was also growing impatient to extract some much-needed answers from the man in the cage.

Who was this Gary Seven, and how had he become aware of Chrysalis's existence, despite their strenuous efforts to conceal the entire project from the outside world? What had inspired him to investigate their New York connection in the first place, and for whom? The CIA? The KGB? Interpol? There were too many distressing possibilities, and not enough hard information to point her in the right direction.

This was simply unacceptable. *We've come too far, worked too hard*, she thought passionately, *to have the project compromised by unknown adversaries.*

Williams hovered nervously behind her as she kept her attention focused on her captive. Seven's shirt was stained with perspiration and spilled tea, and he leaned weakly against the bars of his cage. A day's worth of stubble encrusted his face, which was locked in a fixed grimace as he struggled to keep his jaws clenched shut. Seven's willpower was phenomenal, she conceded, but he *had* to crack soon; no one could resist two full dosages of the serum. It was physiologically impossible.

Who are you? she speculated, fascinated by the man's superhuman resistance, despite the threat it posed to both the project and her peace of mind. Whoever he represented, he clearly had considerable resources at his disposal; a cursory examination of his so-called pen had indicated a degree of technological sophistication that quite possibly exceeded even Chrysalis's capabilities, while his psychological discipline suggested advanced training and possibly even posthypnotic conditioning.

He really was almost more interesting as a test subject than as a spy or potential saboteur. *If I didn't know better,* she mused, *I'd swear he was genetically engineered himself.* But that was ridiculous; Seven was over thirty at least, which meant he would have to have been conceived in the forties, which was absurd. Watson and Crick hadn't even cracked the double helix back then. No one on Earth had been even close to engineering one-celled organisms, let alone enhanced human beings.

No one on Earth . . . Intrigued and baffled by Seven's unaccountable endurance, she began to flirt with more exotic explanations. Could Seven's unique qualities possibly be extraterrestrial in origin? She had heard

whispers about an alien spacecraft that the United
States military had supposedly captured back in 1947,
at a place called Roswell. Rumor had it the alien technology was still being studied at a top-secret installation somewhere in Nevada. An outlandish proposition
to be sure, but her contacts in the U.S. intelligence apparatus had assured her that there was indeed some
truth to the rumors.

Could it be? she wondered, keeping a tight grip on the
back of the prisoner's head, so that he couldn't possibly
look away from her. Had the impossible Mr. Seven
been created and dispatched by American scientists at
Area 51, or did he come from someplace even farther
away, possibly another solar system? The very thought
made her heart pound with excitement. What wouldn't
she give to get her hands on some genuinely extraterrestrial DNA? Who knew what revolutionary secrets
such a genome might hold?

Tell me who you are, she thought urgently, staring hun-
grily at the glazed eyes and gritted teeth of the puzzle
that called himself Gary Seven. Her free hand squeezed
the handle of a porcelain teacup so tightly that she
risked snapping it in two. Jaw muscles twitched beneath
the drawn skin of her drugged captive, giving him a
grotesque facial tic. *Speak to me,* her eyes demanded. *Tell
me where you came from. I* have *to know!*

Finally, at long last, Seven seemed to succumb to fatigue and the neurotransmitter's irresistible compulsion. His jaw sagged open and a parched whisper
escaped his lips. "My name is Gary Seven," he began.

"Good Lord!" Williams exclaimed. He leaped off his
stool and onto his feet. "And about time, too! I thought
he was never to going to crack."

"Quiet!" she admonished him brusquely. With Seven's voice little more than a hoarse croak, the last thing she needed was Williams's babbling in her ears. "Go on," she entreated Seven. "Tell me more."

His lips and tongue seemed the only part of him that was still alive. The rest of him hung limply from the handcuffs around his wrists, his arms suspended above his head. "My name'sss Gary Sseven," he slurred, so faintly that Kaur had to strain to make out what he was saying, "Ssupervissor 194, pressently asssigned to the planet Earthh, late twentieth century. Missshhion: to prevent the human rasse from desstroying itself during the mosst critical juncture in its hissstory. . . ."

Kaur couldn't believe what she was hearing. Suddenly, her wildest imaginings were coming true. If neither she nor Seven were deluded, then Chrysalis stood on the verge of implementing evolutionary developments even more significant than she conceived of before. Visions of human-alien hybrids, embodying the finest traits of two completely different sentient species, fired her imagination. "Where do you come from?" she cross-examined Seven. "Where?"

She held her breath as the crucial information dribbled out of Seven with excruciating slowness, one word at a time. "Cloaked planet, light-yearss away, located in Ssystem Zeta-Gamma-Five-Three-Ssev—"

"Wait until you see our new gel-transfer hybridization unit," Takagi promised, in a clumsy attempt to avoid discussing that ugly and alarming incident in the classroom. He escorted Roberta briskly down a long hallway, obviously trying to put as much distance as possible between Roberta and the scene of the disturbance. "After we drop Isis back in your room, we can go check out some of the labs on Level Five. We're still waiting for some spare parts from America," he babbled nervously, "but then we'll really be able to move into high gear."

At the moment, however, Roberta couldn't even pretend to be interested in Chrysalis's spiffy new jelly-whatsit. "Hold on a minute," she protested, digging in her heels right in the middle of the wide corridor. A three-wheeled scooter bearing a couple of jumpsuited technicians zipped past Roberta and her jittery tour guide, on its way to another part of the vast underground complex. "What was that all about," she demanded, "back at that day-care center for juvenile geniuses? What happened to that little girl?"

At first, Takagi avoided making eye contact with her, studiously contemplating the tops of his sneakers instead, but he soon realized that there was no getting around this conversation. "That wasn't supposed to be part of the tour," he explained, somewhat unnecessarily, "but I'm sure it wasn't really as serious as it looked."

"That kid had a full grand mal seizure, Walter," Roberta challenged him, just as she figured any other intelligent person would under these circumstances. "What gives? I thought these supertykes were supposed to be perfect."

"They are!" he insisted hastily. His chin bobbed forward, propelled by the vehemence of his rebuttal. "It's just that, well, sometimes the genetic resequencing produces some unexpected side effects. Viktor thinks it has something to do with the accelerated formation of the critical neural pathways, which may affect protein synthesis in ways we don't entirely understand just yet, but so far—"

Roberta cut off the lecture before Takagi could stray too far from the big picture. "What sort of side effects are we talking about here?" she pressed him. "And how often do you run into this little problem?"

"Er, I'm not sure of the exact ratio," Takagi waffled, "but I'm sure we'll isolate the key causal factors eventually. We're learning more and more with each new batch of kids, so it's only a matter of time before we can account for every variable."

And how many defective children get churned out, Roberta wondered solemnly, *while you're working things out by trial and error?* Once again, ghastly pictures of limbless thalidomide babies flashed across her mind.

Takagi mustered a weak smile as he tried his best to put a positive spin on the situation. "If you're really interested, maybe you can convince Dr. Kaur to let you tackle that project yourself. Who knows, you might be just the person to get to the bottom of this particular challenge."

Roberta knew that wasn't going to happen, but she decided to feign scientific curiosity in the hope of getting Takagi to open up even more. "Hmmm, that does sound intriguing," she said thoughtfully. "But you still haven't told me exactly what kind of side effects you're getting. Is it just epileptic seizures?"

"Oh, most of the time, it's not anything so dramatic," he assured her fulsomely. "Just some minor personality disorders and/or neurological glitches: autism, hyperactivity, possibly a tendency toward schizophrenia. . . . There's nothing wrong with the basic process, though," he asserted. "Even with these rare—repeat *rare*—complications, as frustrating as they can be, every one of our kids is still physically and intellectually superior to ordinary children."

Oh, great! Roberta thought privately. *A whole generation of emotionally disturbed super men and women!* She was starting to understand why Chrysalis had Gary Seven so worried. *And just when I'd begun to think that Seven had misjudged Takagi and the others....*

"I see," she said in a noncommittal tone. Deciding to push her luck, she looked Takagi squarely in the eye and declared, with as much conviction as she could amass, "I think I need to see the Developmental Deviations Unit next."

"What? How do you know—" Her request definitely threw Takagi for a loop. Surprise was written all over his face, and he gulped loudly before coming up with a reply. "That is, I'm not sure what you mean."

"I understand Hindi," Roberta informed him bluntly. She realized she was sacrificing a strategic advantage by divulging this fact, but figured it was worth it to get a firsthand look at Chrysalis's dirty little secret. "I want to see the Developmental Deviations Unit. Now."

Takagi looked extremely uneasy about this prospect. "I'm not sure that's such a good idea," he hedged. "Are you sure you don't need a break first?" He offered this feeble alternative so hopefully that it was almost painful to watch. "There's a pretty good cafeteria on Level Three. Maybe we should go there before we hit anyplace else?"

Roberta's stomach rumbled treacherously, reminding her that it was past lunchtime already, but she stood by her guns. "No more stalling, Walter, unless there's something you're really trying to hide."

"Of course not!" His denial came out shriller than intended, and he chewed nervously on his bottom lip, looking more and more flustered. He shrugged and flashed Roberta a sheepish grin, in a vain attempt to postpone the inevitable. "It's just that, well, maybe we should check with Dr. Kaur first?"

In a contest of wills, the affable and ingratiating young scientist didn't stand a chance, not against a woman who'd been known to hold her own against time-traveling Starfleet officers. *Isis hardly has a monopoly on stubbornness,* Roberta thought, knowing that Takagi was bound to cave if she just kept the pressure up. "Look, you're supposed to show me around, right? How am I supposed to feel like a full-fledged member of the Chrysalis team if you're excluding me from vital data already?" She stared back at him resolutely, her arms crossed upon her chest, making it clear she wasn't going to budge an inch until she got what she wanted. "For pete's sakes, Walter, I'm a scientist, not a tourist. You don't need to give me the cleaned-up, rose-colored version of the project."

"Okay, okay," he surrendered at last. "I don't suppose you want to take your cat home first?" Roberta just scowled at him in silence. "No, I didn't think so." Frowning, his head drooping miserably, the cowed biochemist changed course at the very next intersection, leading Roberta down yet another lengthy corridor past a series of numbered doorways. Unlike the attractively decorated reception areas where she had met with Sarina Kaur, this section of Chrysalis rapidly took on a more utilitarian, institutional feel: stark white walls, scuffed floor tiles, and closed gray doors with small glass windows installed at eye level. "There's an elevator just around the corner," Takagi promised as Roberta shuffled after him, Isis draped over her shoulder.

Suddenly, just when Roberta thought she had the situation under control, the bored and seemingly boneless cat upon her shoulder came to life. Letting out a high-pitched yowl right next to the young woman's unprotected left ear, Isis squirmed free of her human partner's grasp and launched herself off Roberta with enough force to send the cat soaring into the air and onto the floor several feet behind the two startled humans. Isis hit the ground running, making kitty tracks down the hallway.

"Hey!" Roberta cried out indignantly. The recoil of Isis's explosive exit had left painful scratches in her shoulder, but she was more worried about the cat's unexpected behavior, not to mention Takagi's reaction to the animal's headlong flight. *What in the world has possessed that gosh-darned cat this time?* she wondered frantically as she took off in pursuit of her uncommunicative feline accomplice, taking only a second to give Takagi an embarrassed shrug and abashed expression before racing after Isis. "Wait a second! Come back here, you infuriating feline freak!" she hollered even as she heard Takagi's sneakers pounding the floor behind her. *I swear,* she fumed, *that cat loves to make me look stupid!*

If Isis heard Roberta's cries, the cat (as usual) paid them no heed. Reaching an intersection at the opposite end of the corridor, she made an almost mathematically exact ninety-degree turn to the right. Trying futilely to catch up with the running cat, Roberta watched a sinuous black tail disappear around the corner, heading for only Isis knew where. *That tears it,* Roberta vowed angrily, heart pounding, legs pumping. *I don't care what Seven says. That purring prima donna is getting a leash.*

"Don't let her get away!" Takagi shouted as he struggled to keep up with her. He sounded more agitated than Roberta would have liked, no doubt envisioning the berserk animal getting into one of the labs and ruining some vital and extraordinarily delicate experiment. She could hear him breathing hard, and guessed that this was probably more physical exercise than the nerdy scientist had undergone in years.

Roberta, who was in a lot better shape, thanks to an exceptionally strenuous lifestyle, quickly left Takagi far behind. She rounded the corner at top speed, gaining steadily on Isis, who appeared to be heading for a closed gray door at the far end of this new corridor. "No way," Roberta muttered under her breath. "You're not getting away from me this time." Her outstretched arms reached out for the fleeing feline, ready to yank Isis back by her tail if necessary, but not before Isis slammed her front paws against the door hard enough to sending it swinging inward. The determined cat disappeared into the room beyond, with Roberta chasing so close behind her that she barged through the open portal before the door had a chance to swing back into place.

Roberta skidded to a stop just inside the room Isis had invaded. "Omigosh!" she gasped out loud, transfixed by what she discovered on the other side of the seemingly innocuous door.

She had found Gary Seven at last: locked inside a cage like an animal at the zoo. He looked like hell, too, and far from his usual immaculate appearance. His disordered hair fell over his eyes, while his shirt and trousers were rumpled and soaked with sweat. There was blood on his lips and an alarming brown stain on his shirtfront. He squatted inside the cage, sagging against the metal bars with both arms stretched uncomfortably over his head. Stunned by the shocking sight, it took Roberta a moment or two to realize that his wrists were handcuffed to the cage.

Seven was alone in the cell, but not in the room, which Roberta now saw was stocked with a wide variety of caged animals, including a full-grown tiger, which growled and bared its fangs menacingly. Sarina Kaur knelt outside the cage, along with three guards and a dumpy-looking, middle-aged man Roberta had never seen before. They all stared at Roberta in surprise, obviously caught off guard by her abrupt arrival. Kaur dropped a ceramic mug, which shattered upon the concrete floor. The tiger's snarls were joined by the clamor of yapping dogs and shrieking apes, excited by the sight and smell of Isis and her human pursuer. The din raised by the animals rapidly reached ear-punishing proportions.

Under the circumstances, Roberta felt free to act almost as thunderstruck as she felt. "What in the world?" she exclaimed, a hand over her mouth in horror. "I don't understand."

Two of the guards stepped forward, looking as though they intended to escort her physically from the premises, but Kaur waved them back with a curt gesture. The startled director regained her composure with impressive speed. "I'm sorry you had to see this, Dr. Neary," she said coolly, rising up from her kneeling position beside the cage. Despite her unruffled demeanor, Roberta heard a definite edge of frustration in Kaur's voice. *What exactly did I interrupt just now?* Roberta wondered.

Isis, standing her ground defiantly on the floor between the two women, hissed angrily at Kaur. The cat's ebony hackles bristled all along her spine, so that she looked nearly as ferocious as the irate tiger caged only a few feet away. Moving quickly, before the justifiably enraged feline could blow their cover for good, Roberta darted forward and snatched Isis up off the floor. She held on to the tense pussycat as firmly as she could while stammering awkwardly. "Um, I was looking for my cat," she explained.

"So I see," Kaur said dryly. Her companion, the pudgy white guy, looked Roberta over dubiously.

"But who is that man?" she protested in a suitably appalled fashion. In her arms, Isis gave up trying to escape Roberta's grip and contented herself with merely glaring at Kaur instead. "What are you doing to him?"

"This *spy*," Kaur began, emphasizing the epithet, "attempted to infiltrate Chrysalis, for purposes we are now striving to determine." She gestured around her, calling Roberta's attention to the veritable menagerie of lab animals on display. "As you can see from our surroundings, we're hardly in the habit of holding human beings against their will. This veterinary storage area is the closest thing Chrysalis has to an actual prison, I assure you."

Kaur raised her voice, so as to be heard over the squawking menagerie, but neither her nor Roberta's words elicited any response from the caged prisoner, whose head remained drooped and silent, his chin resting mutely upon his chest. Roberta hoped that her consistently crafty boss was only pretending not to acknowledge her presence, for the sake of the mission, and that he was not really as wiped out as he appeared, but it was impossible to tell for sure. *I haven't seen him look this bad,* she thought, *since that time his life force got sucked into the Fourth Dimension.*

She fingered the servo in her pocket, strongly tempted to try to liberate Seven right there and then. The odds were against her, though. Three guards, Kaur, the Brit; even counting on a little assistance from Isis, she was still outnumbered nearly three to one. With surprise on her side, she might be able to zap one, maybe two, of the guards before Kaur and the others realized what was happening, but somebody was bound to disarm her before she could tranquilize the whole crew, meaning she would have blown her cover for nothing. *Now is no time to get servo-happy,* she concluded reluctantly, hating to leave Seven in such an awful state for at least a little while more, but not seeing any other alternative. *I'm good, but I'm no Quick Draw McGraw.*

Behind Roberta, the door swung open once more, admitting a disheveled Takagi. "Did you catch it?" he blurted, panting, only to shut up in a jiffy once his gaping eyes absorbed the bizarre tableau he had just intruded upon. "Dr. Kaur!" he ventured a moment later, once he got over his initial dumbfoundment. "I'm sorry, I never intended—"

"That's all right, Walter," Kaur interrupted. "We'll speak of this later." She glanced back at the mute and pathetic specimen in the cage and sighed regretfully. "I must say, though: your timing could not have been worse."

Watching the embarrassed and out-of-breath scientist, Roberta wondered once more what exactly Kaur had been up to before she'd burst onto the scene, then tried to assess just how taken aback Takagi was by the ghastly scene Isis had led them to. Was he genuinely shaken by Seven's harsh treatment, or merely appalled that Ronnie Neary had accidentally stumbled onto the truth? *What did he know and when did he know it?* she thought. *To borrow an ever-so-topical phrase.*

She wished she could be sure that the friendly Takagi had been kept in the dark about Seven's imprisonment and obvious abuse, but knew that she had to assume the worst. If nothing else, Takagi's arrival meant that she was now even more outnumbered than before. "How long has he been a captive here?" she asked Kaur, looking anxiously at her supervisor's slumped figure.

"A day at most," Kaur insisted soothingly. "In fact, we suspect he stowed away on the very same jet that brought you to India."

"He must have done so," the other scientist said, revealing an upper-crust British accent. "How else could he have gotten from New York to Delhi in so short a time?"

Guess you've never heard of the Blue Smoke Express, Roberta thought. After all she had seen at Chrysalis, it came as a comfort to recall that she and Seven still had a technological edge over all these assembled mad geniuses. "New York?" she asked innocently.

"Nothing you need to worry about," Kaur answered, deflecting her query. "What's important is that our uninvited visitor has clearly gone to great lengths to penetrate our security." She took Roberta gently by the arm and attempted to guide the younger woman toward the exit to the storeroom. "I know that what you've seen appears quite barbaric and upsetting, but you must understand that it is also absolutely necessary. There are forces in the world that would readily undo everything we've accomplished, and, more importantly, everything we hope to achieve, so we have no choice but to defend ourselves against spies and saboteurs like this man." She looked back at Seven, more in sorrow than in anger, before returning her attention to Roberta. "To surpass Nature, Veronica, one must sometimes be as ruthless as Nature. This is a cogent truth that you will come to understand as you become more familiar with our work."

Roberta was appalled to see both Takagi and the English scientist nodding in agreement. "I don't know," she said, feigning uncertainty while resisting Kaur's efforts to ease her out of the room. *I need to play this scene carefully,* she realized, striving to strike the perfect balance between conscience and complicity: *protest too little about Kaur's draconian methods and the shrewd director might get suspicious, object too much and I might end up in the cage with Seven.* "You can't just turn him over to the authorities, I guess," Roberta equivocated in what she prayed was a convincing manner, "but what's going to happen to him in the long run?"

Kaur did not answer the question directly. "Don't worry," she told Roberta. "Our guest is bound to cooperate with us eventually. One way or another."

CHAPTER FIFTEEN

THE PERSONAL QUARTERS CHRYSALIS HAD PROVIDED for Roberta were cozy enough. Peach-colored walls brightened the room, while fresh flower blossoms, no doubt garnered from some well-lit subterranean garden, floated in a porcelain dish upon the bedstand, which looked hand-carved from rich brown teak. The very comfortable bed had been neatly made in her absence, suggesting that the project employed maids as well as Nobel Prize-winning geneticists. In short, it was a nice place to visit, but Roberta wasn't planning on staying much longer.

Having been dropped off by Takagi only minutes before, at the conclusion of her somewhat overly eventful tour of Chrysalis, she planned to sneak back and rescue Seven as soon as the coast was clear. With any luck, Kaur and her bodyguards would have moved on as well, improving Roberta's odds of a successful raid. That was a fairly big *if*, she realized, but, hey, she had to do something. *No way am I leaving Gary in that cage one minute longer than necessary.*

Pacing restlessly across the sheets of the queen-sized bed, Isis squawked impatiently at Roberta, who guessed that the cat was just as anxious as she was to spring Seven from his hellish-looking confinement. "Yes, yes, I hear you, Isis," Roberta declaimed for the benefit of any-one who was listening. After what went on in Rome, she wouldn't put it past Chrysalis to have bugged her quar-ters again. "I know you want Mommy to play with you right now, but Mommy wants to take a shower first."

The southern wall of the combined bedroom and living area was entirely covered by a large glass mirror. The reflective surface made the compact room appear more spacious, but Roberta suspected that the mirror might also provide a one-way window through which she could be covertly observed by security-conscious guards. She had been careful the night before not to do anything at all suspicious in view of the mirror, confining her failed attempts to contact Seven to the (she hoped!) privacy of the shower stall, while also discreetly calling the glass-covered wall to Isis's attention ("Don't you look pretty, kitty!") so that the cat would not alert the bad guys by, say, turning into an excessively slinky-looking biped when she thought no one was looking.

Slipping out to rescue Seven, however, was going to take a little more effort. Stepping into the adjacent bathroom, Roberta moved rapidly from the sink to the shower, turning on all of the hot-water spigots as far as they would go, while casually singing to herself to allay suspicion. She kept the bathroom door wide open, and periodically tossed extra items of clothing into the liv-ing room to make it appear that she was undressing. She got halfway through the chorus of "Crocodile Rock" before, as planned, the steaming torrents fogged up every mirror in the place, including the big one between her and the exit.

Leaving the shower running, Roberta took advantage of the mirror's "accidental" obscurement by snatching Isis up off the bed and darting for the door. She quickly slipped into the hall outside, grateful that nobody at Chrysalis had been paranoid enough to lock her in her quarters. She looked up and down the corridor, but saw no indication that her departure had been observed by anyone who might raise a fuss.

Ready or not, here we come! Clutching Isis to her chest, Roberta marched swiftly down the hall. Having taken care to memorize the route between her quarters and the smelly menagerie where Seven was being held captive, she now retraced her steps as hurriedly as she could without looking too out-of-place or alarming.

Okay, she thought, reviewing her plan as it hastily came together in her mind. *Get to the storeroom, zap the guards, and 'port us all back to the Big Apple to consider our next move.* She had already logged Chrysalis's geographical coordinates into her servo's memory, so they could always take the Blue Smoke Express back to the complex whenever they felt like it. *We've learned enough for this go-round,* she decided. *Time to get the heck out of here.*

The corridors of Chrysalis were fairly busy this afternoon, and Roberta passed several groups of technicians and lab workers going about their business as she traversed the intricate warren of tunnels, catwalks, and elevators. She feigned a confident and casual manner, as though she belonged here as much as anyone else, which seemed to work well enough; her unfamiliar face elicited a few curious glances, but nobody looked inclined to raise an alarm, an indication, perhaps, of how much faith the average worker had in Chrysalis's tight security and assiduously maintained anonymity. *Guess they all just assume that I wouldn't be here unless I was invited,* she surmised. Which was more or less the case.

The cat in her arms made her a bit more conspicuous than she would have liked, but Roberta knew that Seven would never forgive her if she left Isis back with the luggage, even though the cat's glittering collar held a microscopic homing device. Besides, as much as she hated to admit it, the demanding feline came in handy occasionally. Considering the circumstances, namely that she was on her own, deep in enemy territory, attempting to outwit a score of scientific geniuses and their hired army, Roberta figured she could use all the help she could get.

But that didn't mean she had to like it.

"It's no good," Williams pronounced. "He's out cold."

Damn! Sarina Kaur regarded Gary Seven's limp corpus with an acute sense of frustration. She had come so close to extracting their prisoner's seemingly extraterrestrial secrets, only to be interrupted by that idiotic American and her cat. Now Seven appeared to have dropped into a comatose state that left him incapable of answering all the questions she was aching to ask him. *Dr. Neary had better be a damn fine scientist,* Kaur thought irritably, *after all the trouble she's caused.*

"Can't you revive him?" she asked.

"Hah!" Williams snorted bitterly. He crouched on the floor outside Seven's cage, flashing the beam of a penlight into the prisoner's unresponsive eyes, whose lids he lifted sequentially. He then checked Seven's pulse one more time before letting go of the insensate captive's wrist, leaving it to dangle lifelessly from its shackles. "After a double dose of that blasted neuro-transmitter, I wouldn't be surprised if his gray matter's completely fried." He rose to his feet, wiping his hands of any responsibility for the prisoner's dire condition. "Looks to me like we've got a vegetable to dispose of."

"That doesn't make any sense," Kaur protested, overlooking the Englishman's increasingly insubordinate attitude. "The serum has never produced that sort of effect before." Then again, she reflected, no one had ever resisted the drug for so long, let alone required a second injection. Had the strain of resisting the serum's compulsion indeed caused irreparable neuro-logical harm, or had Seven's apparent surrender eventually triggered some manner of deep-rooted mental block? It was possible, she speculated, that the intruder's prolonged unconsciousness was a last-ditch defense mechanism against the most intense and overpowering of interrogations. Such a precaution was theoretically possible; in fact, Kaur had once looked into the feasibility of hypnotically installing similar blocks in the minds of the key Chrysalis personnel, before rejecting the technique as unreliable given the current limits of psychological conditioning. *But perhaps Mr. Seven knows a few tricks modern practitioners do not?*

"Well, it may not make sense," Williams said, "but one thing's for sure: You're not getting anything out of this poor sod anytime soon." He yawned loudly, while massaging the sore muscles at the back of his neck. "Frankly, Madame Director, we're wasting our time here, and I, for one, could use a break."

Sadly, Kaur conceded that Williams had a point. She

herself had many other pressing duties to attend to, while the enigmatic Mr. Seven was undeniably dead to the world, at least for the present. *Perhaps we can try reviving him again later,* she considered, *after his mind and body have had the opportunity to recover from their mutual ordeal.*

"Very well," she informed Williams. "You're dismissed for now." She turned her attention to the guard in charge of the storeroom. "Bhajan, please keep a close eye on the prisoner. Summon me immediately if there is any change in his condition."

"Yes, Director," the burly Sikh agreed.

Williams wasted no time exiting the storeroom-cum-jailhouse, but Kaur lingered a few moments more, reluctant to leave the captive behind while so many of his secrets remained unplumbed. Her personal bodyguards waited patiently as she toyed absently with the pen-shaped instrument she had confiscated from Seven earlier. *Was there alien technology employed in its construction?* It occurred to her that, should Gary Seven never recover from his current vegetative state, this small artifact might prove to be the only tangible evidence of his unearthly origins, that and whatever knowledge might be gleaned from his DNA and eventual postmortem.

She inspected the instrument more closely, impressed by the persuasive simplicity of its camouflage; the device certainly looked like just an ordinary writing utensil. Keeping the point of the weapon carefully aimed away from her, she tinkered with its controls, which appeared to be activated by twisting the outer casing of the pen to various gradations. Suddenly, she discovered that it could be twisted in more than one direction as well, resulting in a gentle click followed by a far more audible electronic beep.

Hmm, she thought, intrigued. *What have we here?*

By her own reckoning, Roberta was two-thirds of the way back to the animal storeroom when the servo in her pocket beeped for her attention. *Hey!* she thought jubilantly, her spirits lifted immeasurably by the unexpected sound of the servo's hail. *Seven must have sprung himself from behind bars.* She suddenly felt foolish for having underestimated him after all these years. *Guess he was just playing possum after all.*

Isis climbed onto Roberta's shoulder, freeing the young woman's hands. Glancing around quickly to make sure no one was watching, Roberta retrieved the servo from her pocket and activated its reply function. "Hello, Seven? Boy, am I glad to hear from you!" The situation was obviously far too urgent to waste time with silly code names. "Isis and I are en route to your last known location. Please advise."

An unnervingly long silence followed, broken finally by the last voice Roberta expected. "Dr. Neary?" asked the Indian-accented tones of Dr. Sarina Kaur. "Is that you?" A cold, sardonic amusement, lacking any trace of warmth or good will, crept into the scientist's voice. "What an extremely . . . revelatory . . . development. I look forward to meeting with you again, Dr. Neary, and as soon as possible."

Roberta could feel the blood rushing from her face to her toes. *Uh-oh.* She switched off the servo with record-breaking speed, but the damage had already been done. *The jig is up,* she realized with a gulp. The time for complicated cover stories and clever dissembling was over; *nothing left now but the running and the shooting and the gratuitous violence.* She set her servo on tranquilize, as Isis leaped from Roberta's shoulder onto the floor. *Let's just hope that Chrysalis hasn't genetically improved its guards' marksmanship.*

She took a deep breath, pausing to let the adrenaline kick in, then took off down the corridor at top speed. Isis sped along beside her, her paws barely touching the polished tile floor. With luck, Roberta prayed, they could still spring Gary Seven before Kaur could call in reinforcements, assuming they got to the storeroom first. "C'mon, c'mon," she urged herself on, running so hard that she could hear her heart pounding in her chest. Alert eyes scanned the corridors and doorways ahead, looking out for trouble. She knew she'd just hit the top of Chrysalis's Most Wanted list.

Startled lab workers gasped in surprise as the unidentified blond woman, accompanied by a speeding black cat, came sprinting down the hallways. "Coming through!" she hollered, forcing clumps of shocked Chrysalis technicians to scatter out of her way.

So far, so good, Roberta thought. At the moment, the inhabitants of the top-secret lab were too confused and off-balance to even try to detain her, but these were just the civilians; trained security forces were undoubtedly on their way. By now, someone had surely found the empty shower back at her cozy underground hotel room, just as Kaur must have guessed where she and Isis would almost certainly be heading. *Hang on, Seven,* she thought desperately. She counted down doorways and detours as she rushed by them in a blur. *We're almost there.*

No such luck. Just as she approached a metal stairway she remembered from before, two teams of guards converged from opposite directions, blocking her way to the stairs. "Halt!" the lead guard called out, flaunting an automatic pistol. Four additional guards displayed gray steel batons that reminded Roberta uncomfortably of cattle prods. "You are ordered to surrender to our custody immediately."

"Sorry, no can do," she muttered, targeting the gun-wielding guard with her servo even as she struggled to keep her own forward momentum from carrying her straight into the guards' midst. An electronic hum resonated across the gap between Roberta and her adversary, and the lead guard's belligerent stance relaxed dramatically. His stern, forbidding scowl gave way to a goofy grin and a dreamy expression as the muzzle of his firearm drooped toward the floor. His baffled cohorts looked on in puzzlement as their senior officer let go of his pistol, then stretched out on the floor for a nap. Loud snores replaced the harsh commands the guard had emitted only seconds before.

Roberta, on the other hand, did not pause to inspect the effects of her tranquilizer beam on the hired soldier. She was too busy reversing direction and taking off back the way she had come. Isis was way ahead of her, leading Roberta on an improvised detour through the bowels of Chrysalis. Boots pounded on tile behind her as the rest of the security team resumed its pursuit. "Stop! Surrender at once!" they shouted, in at least three different languages and dialects.

They might as well have been speaking in Martian for all that Roberta intended to obey their commands. The race to rescue Seven had turned into a chase, with herself the primary quarry. *Shades of Berlin,* she thought, remembering the tumultuous and exhausting mission that had first launched her and Seven on the investigation that had eventually led her to this hidden stronghold, deep beneath the surface of the Indian desert. *How come I always end up running from gun-toting goons?*

Keeping her head low, she spotted a small cluster of scientists milling about in an airy underground atrium, complete with a spewing marble fountain sculpted in the shape of a dolphin leaping above chiseled waves. Many of the white-jacketed workers appeared to be enjoying a late-afternoon cigarette, safely distant from the volatile chemicals back in their respective labs.

"Over there!" Roberta hollered to Isis, before plunging into the throng of stunned researchers. She barreled through the crowd at top speed, hoping to discourage her irate pursuers from opening fire, but her plan backfired when the onrushing guards called out to the civilians surrounding Roberta. "Stop her!" their angry voices demanded. "Don't let her get away!"

A few brave scientists grabbed on to Roberta, hoping to hold her long enough for the security team to catch up with the apparent fugitive. "Hey, watch the hands!" Roberta objected indignantly.

Luckily for her, a couple of overeager lab jockeys were hardly a match for her hard-earned martial-arts expertise. She flipped one over her shoulder onto his back, while jabbing her elbow into another guy's sizable gut. For a second, she thought she was free and clear, and started to race ahead once more, only to discover that yet another techie, more determined and/or foolhardy than the rest, had what felt like a death grip on her hair. She winced, her eyes watering, as he pulled mercilessly on her roots, until Isis doubled back and bit the clinging creep in the ankle. "Ow!" he yowled, letting go of her hair and hopping away on one foot.

Roberta made tracks before anybody else felt inspired to play catch-the-fugitive. "Thanks for the assist," she murmured to Isis as they broke away from the crowd and veered toward a blessedly less populated corridor. Isis mewed a curt acknowledgment.

So much for losing myself in Chrysalis's teeming employment pool, she realized, resolving to keep away from any and all of Kaur's loyal personnel from now on. A moment of inspiration struck her and she spun around, adjusting the setting on her servo, until the elegant marble fountain came within her sights.

ZAP! The sculpted dolphin exploded upon impact with a beam of invisible force, producing a geyser of unchecked water that sprayed wildly into the air, flooding the once-tranquil atrium. Shrieks of surprise from drenched technicians mixed with angry curses as Roberta turned her back on her torrential handiwork and ran down the nearest convenient tunnel. *Gee,* she thought ingenuously, grinning at her own brilliant improvisation, *I guess the monsoon came early this year.*

"That should slow them down a little," she muttered to herself, grateful for a momentary respite. Her legs were already sore from running so hard, and she was, she realized, panting like Bobby Riggs after Billie Jean King whipped his butt on the tennis court. She was running out of steam, she knew, but that ought to be okay. *Just need to put a little more distance between me and the bad guys,* she promised her fatigued legs and lungs. *Then I can look for a quiet corner to 'port out of.*

It was a cardinal rule of Gary Seven's, observed in all but the most extreme of instances, never to transport in front of witnesses, lest they expose primitive twentieth-century minds to the futuristic reality of matter-transmission technology. Scooting down a deserted-looking side corridor, Roberta scanned ahead, looking for a phone booth or a closet or any place where she and Isis could 'port away without fear of being observed by passersby. *Why is there never an abandoned bomb shelter around when you need one?*

"Dr. Neary! Ronnie! Stop!"

A pair of figures stepped out in front of her, cutting her off as they called out her alias. Roberta almost tranquilized them with her servo, then realized that the men before her were none other than Takagi and Dr. Lozinak. "Don't move!" she warned them, holding them at bay with a fountain pen, which must have looked vaguely ridiculous. "I'm serious. Trust me, this is more than just a pen."

"We *did* trust you, Veronica," Lozinak said pointedly. His ancient eyes held bottomless reservoirs of sorrow and resignation as he leaned wearily upon his wooden cane. "That is why this is such a disappointment."

Roberta felt a stab of guilt. "Look, my name's not Veronica," she explained, as if that somehow justified her deception. "You have no idea who I really am."

"Apparently," Lozinak reproached her, eliciting another pang from her conscience.

"I can't believe this!" Takagi exclaimed, visibly agitated. His face was flushed and his hands fluttered erratically. "How can you do something like this?"

Tension suffused the air-conditioned atmosphere of the subterranean tunnel. How very different this confrontation was, she thought, from that convivial dinner in Rome only a few days before. *That seems like weeks ago now.* "Sorry, guys," she said in as tough and hard-boiled a tone as she could manage, doing her best to harden her heart in the best double-agent tradition. Would Modesty Blaise have any qualms about hoodwinking a pair of mad scientists? *Heck, no!* Roberta scolded herself, but she still had trouble looking Viktor Lozinak in the eyes.

"It's nothing personal," she insisted. Isis mewed impatiently, rubbing her head against Roberta's leg to get her attention. The cat had the right idea, she realized; she didn't have time for this. "Step aside," she instructed the two scientists, gesturing toward the left with her free hand. "With any luck, you'll never lay eyes on me again."

"No," Lozinak said firmly. He limped forward, clutching his cane like a weapon. "Whoever you are, I cannot permit you to endanger our work. The future of humanity is at stake. Everything else, our own small confidences and betrayals, do not amount to—what is the phrase?—a peak of peas."

"Hill of beans," Roberta corrected automatically. Behind her, from not very far away, she heard bootsteps and shouting. The sounds of pursuit, drawing nearer. "Please, Viktor, get out of the way." She glanced quickly over her shoulder, not seeing any troops yet, but knowing they were on the way. Isis's squawking grew more insistent. "Now is not the time to get all kamikaze on me." She waved the servo like a talisman, but it failed to ward off the old man's steady approach. "Don't make me do this."

Cane in hand, Lozinak advanced on Roberta. The boots and shouting sounded much closer now. Isis was practically turning herself inside out trying to get Roberta on the move again, but the human woman still hesitated, her fingers on the servo's concealed controls.

"To stop Chrysalis you must stop me first," Lozinak

informed her solemnly. He raised his cane, perhaps intending to knock the servo from her hand.

You crazy old man, she thought sadly. The servo hummed once and Lozinak collapsed toward the floor, his cane still clutched in his bony fist. Roberta spared a precious second to ease the elderly scientist's descent, then stood up quickly to confront Takagi.

The younger man stared aghast at his fallen mentor, then looked at Roberta with shock and disbelief written all over his crestfallen face. He took a single step forward and opened his mouth to speak.

"Don't!" she cut him off decisively. She gave him a warning look that might have stopped a rampaging cybernaut in its tracks. Takagi got the message; nodding meekly, he shut his mouth and stepped back against the wall while she hurried by. Roberta reached the intersection at the end of the tunnel, then looked back at Takagi. "One more thing, Walter. If anything happens to me, make sure my cat is okay."

Takagi nodded once more.

Just a little insurance, she thought.

"Halt! Stop or we'll shoot!" A pair of guards appeared at the opposite end of the tunnel. They raised their weapons to fire, but Roberta and Isis had already fled around the corner, trying to keep out of sight of their relentless trackers. Roberta zigzagged through a maze of identical-looking tunnels, changing direction at random in hopes of shaking the determined guards.

This was harder than it sounded. No matter how fast she ran, or how wildly she detoured, she could still hear the persistent clatter and clamor of the security troopers in the distance, never less than a few turns behind her.

"ATTENTION!" a loudspeaker suddenly boomed overhead, adding to her anxiety. Roberta recognized the familiar cadences of Sarina Kaur. "INTRUDER ALERT! BE ON THE LOOKOUT FOR A BLOND-HAIRED AMERICAN FEMALE, APPROXIMATE-LY TWENTY YEARS IN AGE. SHE IS BELIEVED ARMED AND DANGEROUS. REPORT ALL SIGHTINGS TO SECURITY IMMEDIATELY!"

Okay, things are getting seriously out of hand, Roberta thought as Kaur repeated the announcement in Hindi and Japanese. The hunt was heating up almost as fast as she was running down. Adrenaline could only carry her so far, she knew; her legs already felt like they weighed a hundred pounds each, and her breaths were coming harder and harder. The indefatigable guards weren't giving her a moment's rest, never mind a chance to call up the Blue Smoke Express. *Gotta keep on going,* she coached herself on. *Just a little bit longer.*

Her flight soon led her to an out-of-the-way sector of Chrysalis that she didn't believe she had ever visited before. The lonely corridor was conspicuously de-serted, while the bare concrete walls were devoid of any color or ornamentation. *Definitely off the beaten track,* she concluded. *Just what I need, maybe.* She could hear the guards gaining on her, and realized with horror that she might have reached a dead end.

The barren hallway led to a single unmarked door at the far end of the tunnel. There was absolutely no indi-cation of what lay beyond, but Roberta didn't exactly have a choice. Through the door was the only way to go.

She tried the door, swearing under her breath when she found it locked. That slowed her for merely a mo-ment, though, as she zapped the lock with her servo, then turned the knob again, finding it much more cooperative this time around. *Better than a Swiss Army knife,* she thought approvingly of her handy, all-purpose, alien gadget, smiling at this small success. She hurriedly shut the door behind her as she dashed through the now-open portal, looking back momentarily to make sure she didn't close the door on Isis's sinuous black tail. *Please,* she thought, *let there be nobody in sight.*

Instead she found herself the focus of many small, wide eyes. "Ohmigosh," she murmured.

At first, Roberta thought she had simply stumbled onto another classroom full of bright, genetically engineered superchildren, just like the one she had visited before. Very quickly, however, she realized, with a sinking heart, that this was a very different assortment of kids.

The walls of the chamber were padded and covered with incomprehensible graffiti. Cushioning the walls was an obvious necessity, given that one child—a little boy with strangely leonine features—was busy pounding his mutated forehead against the wall repeatedly, with no one present making any serious effort to restrain him. A few children shrieked hysterically at Roberta's abrupt arrival, but just as many kids paid no attention to her at all, staring autistically into space, or engrossed in one-sided conversations with themselves, often in bizarre private tongues that even Roberta's automatic translator couldn't make sense of. One little Asian girl, who looked about five years old, rocked back and forth on her knees as she carried on a singsong chanting that seemed to incorporate fragments of several different languages, while a pale, gnomish child, whose cheek twitched uncontrollably, kept counting his own toes over and over with a frightening degree of concentration. He looked up from his task just long enough to register Roberta's existence, then went back to counting with renewed intensity. Nearby, a small boy with dark black bangs copied everything the toe-counting child did, facial tics included. "Mr. Eygor!" a nearby tattletale cried out. "Jarod is copying people again. Make him stop! Make him stop now!"

Elsewhere in the crowded classroom, an industrious toddler scribbled on the walls with a thick black crayon. Roberta couldn't make head nor tail of his jagged scrawlings, which, in places, resembled mathematical equations, Egyptian hieroglyphics, obscene stick figures, or some warped combination thereof. Just looking at the markings, which were scribbled over several previous generations of graffiti, frequently spilling out onto the thickly cushioned floor, made Roberta feel vaguely queasy. A few feet away, another child, not content to write upon the walls or floor, adorned his own arms and legs with intricate swirls and curlicues. Out of context, her avid self-decoration would have been cute, perhaps, but surrounded by so much other peculiar behavior on the part of her classmates, it was difficult not to see even this harmless pastime as evidence of a deeper and more pathological disorder.

Appalled and dismayed by what she saw, Roberta's heart nearly broke completely when she spotted the little epileptic sculptor from the earlier class, now sobbing forlornly in a corner of the room, clearly frightened and distressed by her unsettling new classmates and surroundings. "Let me guess," Roberta said bitterly, her eyes stinging with angry tears. "This would be the Developmental Deviations Unit."

In marked contrast to Chrysalis's stated preference

for smaller classes and personalized instruction, there was only one instructor present, keeping watch over at least two dozen dysfunctional children. More like an attendant, really, since Roberta didn't get the impression that much actual instruction was going on. The sole adult in attendance—a squat, hunched man with sallow skin, awful posture, bushy black brows, and two large, oddly protuberant eyes—rose up quickly from behind a cheap, plywood-and-aluminum desk, a dog-eared paperback novel dropping from his fingers. He didn't look like a rocket scientist or world-class educator; Roberta guessed that baby-sitting Chrysalis's failed experiments was hardly one of the project's most eagerly sought-after jobs. *No wonder they stuck this room way off in the middle of nowhere,* she realized, *so that the rest of the team wouldn't have to be reminded of their occasional setbacks.*

"Freeze, buster!" she warned him, holding her servo like a revolver. "You heard the announcement. I'm armed and dangerous."

Her declaration provoked more screams of terror from some of the more alert children, but Eygor obligingly raised his hands above his head, taking her implied threat just as seriously as she hoped. Roberta scanned the room, looking for any sign of an alarm or security camera. She was tempted to put the creepy, bug-eyed attendant to sleep, then 'port out in front of the children. *These kids are so messed up,* she thought, *who's going to believe them if they say I disappeared into thin air—or even a glowing blue cloud?*

"Hello, *bonjour,* hello!" A surprisingly strong little hand tugged on her skirt, and she looked down to see a cherubic little boy, maybe five years old, staring up at her with eyes that positively shone with excitement and enthusiasm. His entire body, in fact, vibrated with barely contained energy, as if he'd just consumed a year's worth of Cap'n Crunch in one sitting. "Whoareyou? Wheredoyoucomefrom? MynameisOliver." He pelted her with questions, speaking so fast the words literally ran together. "I'veneverseenyoubefore. What'syourname? Whatdidyoubringme? I'mthesmartestonehere. CanIhaveyourpen?"

"Er, pleased to meet you," Roberta answered distractedly, trying to keep one eye on the attendant while continuing her search for hidden cameras. The last thing she wanted to do was let Kaur and her fanatical associates capture the Blue Smoke Express on film. Her ability to transport was an ace in the hole that Roberta didn't feel like giving away just yet, especially with Seven still a prisoner of Chrysalis. *When I come back for him,* she vowed, *you're not going to see me coming.*

Oliver wasn't brushed off so easily. "MynameisOliver. What'syours?" He tugged on her skirt so hard that she had to grab on to the top of the garment with her free hand to keep it from being yanked down to her knees. "Whoareyou? Whyareyouhere?"

"My name's Veronica," she lied, mostly out of habit.

"Whatdidyoubringme? CanIhaveyourpen?"

"Er, not right now," Roberta temporized. Between Oliver's insistent craving for attention, plus the more frightened children crying and wailing in the background, she was finding it hard to concentrate on the vital business of making a clean escape. Isis hissed menacingly at Oliver, and Roberta deftly inserted herself between the boy and the annoyed cat, in hopes of shielding the hyper youngster from Isis's ever ready claws and teeth. "How 'bout we shake instead?"

She offered Oliver her hand, which he grabbed on to with unexpected force. *Ouch,* Roberta winced as the motor-mouthed little terror squeezed her hand harder than a two-hundred-pound quarterback with something to prove. *Must be that genetically enhanced muscular development,* she deduced. *Lucky me.*

"Givemeyourpen!" he demanded, bouncing up and down at the end of Roberta's arm. She tried to pull her hand free, but Oliver held on to it like a vise. He started grabbing at her other arm, trying to snatch the servo away. "Giveittome! Giveme! Giveme!"

"Oliver! Stop it! Let go of me!" The excited child tightened his grip, squeezing her trapped hand so tightly that she could feel the bones grinding together. For the first time, she realized she was in actual physical danger from the berserk supertyke. Oliver kicked her savagely in the shin, staggering her, but she still couldn't bring herself to strike back at the little boy. *It's not his fault,* she thought, torn between panic and compassion. *He's emotionally disturbed!*

She held the servo above her head, out of Oliver's reach. The tip of the weapon pointed uselessly at the ceiling, but, ignoring the pressure crushing her other hand, she struggled to turn the servo around with her fingers, a test of digital dexterity she could have gladly done without. *If I can just do this,* she thought desperately, *without dropping the darn thing or zapping myself by mistake . . . !*

Then Oliver jumped for her upraised arm, sinking his teeth into her biceps. Roberta cried out in pain, feeling his jaws bite down on her even through the fabric of her lab coat, and the servo flew from her fingers, landed several feet away among a gang of children, who instantly started fighting each other for possession of the shiny silver prize. "No, no, no!" Oliver shouted, letting go of Roberta to chase after the escaped servo. Roberta yanked her injured left hand back, shaking it hard to restore the circulation to her fingers. Nothing felt permanently broken, but it had been a close call. She looked quickly for Isis, half-wondering why the combative feline had not come to her defense. Then she saw that Isis had another crisis to deal with: taking advantage of Roberta's predicament, Eygor had lowered his hands to reach for a button beneath his desk. Isis sprang at the slouching man like a miniature panther, but she was too late. An alarm sounded and a metal grille descended from the ceiling, sealing off the exit.

Trapped! Roberta stared bleakly at the riot of thrashing children that had swallowed up the servo, along with her ability to transport herself and Isis to safety. High-pitched screams and angry yelling joined with the blaring alarm to produce a nearly unbearable volume of noise that just made it harder to think clearly. She approached the kicking and clawing children warily, uncertain of how to safely separate the kids, let alone retrieve her servo. She glanced at the only other adult present, the hunched, pop-eyed attendant, hoping he might intervene to halt the violence, only to see him gaping at the ceiling with an apprehensive expression on his homely face.

Her gaze followed his upward where she was shocked to spy tendrils of thick white gas pouring into the classroom from vents in the ceiling. *This is not good,* she thought, instinctively taking a deep breath and holding it. Alas, her quick reflex bought her only enough time to wonder whether every chamber in Chrysalis came equipped with knockout gas, for reasons of internal security, or if this was just an emergency measure installed just in case the Developmentally Deviant kids got out of control.

If nothing else, the gas attack served to quiet the brutal skirmish that had broken out over possession of the servo. Trying hard not to breathe, Roberta watched as, one by one, the brawling children, along with the rest of their behaviorally impaired classmates, succumbed to the narcotic effect of the billowing white fumes. She couldn't help noticing how angelic, how touchingly *normal*, Chrysalis's misfit children looked when they slept.

She rushed forward, gently pulling the children's collapsed bodies off each other as she searched frantically for her servo. The kids' inert forms were dead weight, which left her struggling against gravity as well as time. *If I can just find it in time,* she thought desperately, *I can still 'port us out of here!*

But such furious exertion only used up her last breath faster. Cheeks bulging with exhaled carbon dioxide, she caught one brief, frustrating glimpse of metallic silver, poking out from beneath a pile of slumbering toddlers, before she burst out gasping, sucking in lungfuls of tainted air that sent her head spinning and turned her legs into overcooked spaghetti. She tried to focus her increasingly fuzzy vision, which fell helplessly upon an indistinct black blur atop the attendant's desk.

Isis was already out cold by the time Roberta's world went completely dark.

CHAPTER SIXTEEN

"YOU KNOW, WHEN YOU THINK ABOUT IT, SHE CAUSED more confusion than actual harm." Walter Takagi tugged uncomfortably on the collar of his T-shirt as he and Dr. Kaur contemplated the gassed form of the woman he knew as Dr. Veronica Neary, prostrate upon the padded floor of the Developmental Deviations Unit. All around them, teams of security guards and child-care specialists tended to the unfortunate children who, with their caretaker, had been gassed along with Ronnie. *Like these poor, defective kids didn't have enough problems,* he thought sourly. "Ultimately, the project was only compromised, not irreparably damaged."

"That's small comfort, Walter," Kaur said soberly. The director of Chrysalis watched the unconscious children being carted away to the infirmary, a discontented expression upon her refined features. "After years of secrecy and meticulous preparation, we have now been infiltrated by two spies in nearly as many days, one of whom we actively welcomed into our ranks." A slippered foot tapped impatiently against the floor, hinting at the degree of anxiety at work behind Kaur's composed exterior. "A most unsettling turn of affairs."

Takagi gulped nervously. He had heard rumors about what happened to those who violated Chrysalis's acute code of secrecy. *Like that American, Singer, who disappeared without explanation while I was in Rome*, he remembered. *Nobody even mentions him anymore.*

"I take full responsibility," he offered, secretly hoping that his willingness to own up to his mistake would count in his favor, perhaps mitigating whatever harsh disciplinary action Kaur had in mind. "She fooled me completely."

"So it seems," Kaur agreed. Takagi waited for the axe to fall, resolving to face his punishment with as much dignity as he could muster. Grisly visions of seppuku, lifted mostly from old samurai movies he saw as a kid, slashed their way across his imagination. To his surprise, however, Kaur merely sighed and gave him a thin, rueful smile. "Unfortunately, Dr. Lozinak and I were equally taken in. Nor can you be blamed for the unwelcome advent of Mr. Seven. Clearly, our essential security was breached at some earlier point, perhaps via our New York operation." She scowled thoughtfully. "I think it best that we declare a moratorium on recruiting new talent into Chrysalis until we get to the bottom of these incursions, and perhaps beyond."

"Absolutely!" Takagi responded hastily. An overwhelming sense of relief coursed through his body, rendering him almost light-headed. *Looks like I'm not dead meat after all!* "That's a very good idea, of course."

About a meter away, the guards hefted the last of the imperfect children off the floor. A glint of silver caught his eye, and he recognized the slim, metallic pen that Ronnie had used to put Dr. Lozinak to sleep. Judging from the alert expression that suddenly leaped into Kaur's eyes, she had spotted the suspicious device as well.

Without waiting for one of her bodyguards to retrieve the disguised weapon, she pounced on the pen herself. Lifting it from the floor, where it had lain hidden beneath the bodies of the narcotized toddlers, she held it up to the light, inspecting it carefully from every direction. "Of course," she murmured intensely, her eyes narrowing in anger, "I knew there had to be a connection."

Before Takagi's baffled eyes, she fished an identical pen out of the pocket of her lab coat. She held them side by side in front of her, then collected them both in her fist and forcefully thrust them both back into her pocket. "It appears that Mr. Seven and Dr. Neary, or whatever their real names are, are supplied by the same unknown agency," she explained curtly.

Takagi was tempted to ask for more details, but decided, upon rapid consideration, not to push his luck. *Best to keep a low profile for a while,* he resolved, as much as he was dying to find out more about who this Gary Seven character was, *until this whole fiasco has time to fade in people's memories. Assuming it ever does.* Times like this, he couldn't help wondering if he wouldn't have been better off sticking with his comfortable teaching gig in Osaka.

Sprawled upon the cushioned and graffiti-covered floor of the DDU, Ronnie stirred fitfully, coughing hoarsely before dropping back into drug-induced slumber. Despite everything, Takagi was glad to see that she was recovering from the potent anesthetic gas used to subdue her. Kaur nodded at her personal bodyguards, and the two Sikhs took hold of Ronnie by her wrists and ankles, lifting her from the floor. "What would you have done with her?" the senior guard inquired.

Kaur stared at Ronnie as she would at a particularly virulent strain of bacteria. "Put her in with her partner," she said harshly. "I'll deal with them both soon enough."

Another guard, a survivor of the recently overthrown right-wing regime in Portugal, lifted a limp clump of glossy black fur off the caretaker's desk. "What about the cat?" he asked brusquely.

"I couldn't care less about the blasted cat," Kaur snapped, her patience clearly nearing its limits. Exasperated, she clenched her fists and unleashed some of her pent-up frustration on the unlucky guard. "Adopt it. Eat it. Dissect it. Do whatever you wish with the miserable creature."

Takagi couldn't help recalling Ronnie's final words to him, seconds before she fled the scene of her ill-fated confrontation with Dr. Lozinak. *"If anything happens to me, make sure my cat is okay."* Experiencing distinctly mixed feelings, he watched Kaur's guards carry Ronnie's supine body out of the depressing confines of the DDU. He took a deep breath, knowing he was going to regret this, and stepped forward. "I'll take the cat," he said.

"Is that so?" Kaur fixed a quizzical gaze on Takagi, looking like she wasn't sure whether to be amused or annoyed. "And what in the world are you going to do with it, Walter?"

Takagi squirmed beneath the director's radioactive

surveillance. He could feel himself losing every bit of credibility that he had somehow, miraculously, managed to hang on to. "Um, I thought maybe I'd donate the cat to the kids in Lot Epsilon." Kaur continued to regard him dubiously, and Takagi groped for a plausible rationale. "They were quite taken with the animal earlier today, when, er, 'Dr. Neary' and I dropped in on the class. Noon seemed particularly fond of it."

"Noon? Really?" Just as he'd prayed, Kaur's forbidding attitude appeared to soften fractionally at the mention of her brilliant and multitalented progeny. She shrugged and nodded to the Portuguese guard. "Fine. Give the cat to the children." A trace of venom crept back into her voice. "The duplicitous Dr. Neary might as well make some small contribution to the project, despite her best efforts to betray us."

Takagi gratefully took the flaccid, inanimate pet from the smirking guard, then scurried out of the classroom before Dr. Kaur had a chance to change her mind.

I hope Ronnie appreciates this, he thought peevishly. *Whatever happens to her.*

Squawks, chirps, barks, and yelps roused Roberta from a drugged, dreamless sleep. At first, she thought it was just Isis, being a pest as usual. "Go away, you stupid cat," she muttered, trying to brush away the nonexistent feline. Slowly she realized, however, that not even Isis could sound like an entire menagerie. *Uh-oh,* she thought, a more discouraging scenario presenting itself to her mind.

With considerable effort, she forced her eyes open, only to find herself lying upon a bed of straw, one cheek pressed against the dry fibers. The light immediately hurt her eyes and set her head throbbing. *I feel hungover,* she realized, *but how come?* She didn't remember drinking to excess, or even drinking anything at all. *Oh yeah, the gas,* she recalled. Unpleasant flashbacks to the shocking injustice of the Developmental Deviations Unit, and of the noxious white fumes filling her lungs, flooded Roberta's memory, bringing her more or less up to speed, or at least until her present rude awakening.

Her first attempt to sit up was a complete flop. The minute she lifted her head from the straw, a wave of dizziness hit her and she had to retreat back to a horizontal position. *Too fast,* she concluded groggily, *no good.* She took it much more slowly the next attempt, gradually rising onto her knees. The dizziness washed over her again, but she was ready for it this time; her head reeling, she closed her eyes and waited for the queasiness to pass.

All right, she thought, after a few rocky moments. *That's better.* Cautiously, she opened her eyes again, confirming what she already suspected: she was back with Gary Seven and the lab animals again, but this time on the wrong side of the prison bars.

In fact, she was stuck in the same cage as Seven, who, to her dismay, looked exactly as she'd last seen him. He hung, silent and all but lifeless, from the handcuffs that shackled his raw, reddened wrists to the bars of the cage. A single guard, posted outside the cage, watched both prisoners warily, one hand resting upon the grip of his holstered pistol.

At the moment, Roberta paid little attention to the guard. "Gary?" she addressed her fellow inmate. Despite six years spent saving the world together, she had never felt comfortable calling him by his first name. Sometimes it slipped out, though, especially at moments like this. "Gary? Can you hear me?"

His silence unnerved her. Something was seriously wrong here. She'd seen Seven unconscious before, but seldom for long; as she knew from experience, he had five times more stamina and endurance than your typical twentieth-century human.

Unlike Seven with his cuffs, Roberta was free to move about the cage. Bracing herself against the nausea she experienced whenever she moved too fast, she crawled over to where Seven's immobile body drooped. Craning her neck so that she could see his face, she tried urgently to bring him back to the world of the living.

"Gary? It's me, Ro—" She glanced sideways at the watchful guard. "It's Agent 368. Can you hear me? Are you okay?" She slapped his face gently, then again with enough force to sting. Despite her efforts, Seven's chin continued to rest upon his chest. His sealed eyelids didn't so much as flutter. "C'mon, Gary, wake up! Give me a sign you're still in there."

Roberta's heart sank. Seven was more than simply out cold; this was like some sort of trance or coma, and she had no idea how to snap him out of it. Attempting to check his vital signs, she had to strain to detect any pulse or heartbeat at all. *The last time I felt a pulse this weak,* she recalled, *the guy turned out to be Undead.*

Not exactly an encouraging sign.

She shot an angry glance at the solitary guard, whose mute indifference to Seven's wretched state infuriated her. "Don't just stand there!" she shouted at him. Instinctively, she searched her pockets for her servo, only to find it missing. "I know you have plenty of doctors here. The best in the world, probably. Why don't you call someone? This man needs medical attention!"

For a moment, she thought her tirade had produced results. Keeping careful watch over Roberta, the uncommunicative guard walked over to a videophone mounted on the wall by the exit. *About time,* she thought, assuming the sentry was, however belatedly, calling a doctor for Seven.

Such hopes were crushed, though, when the stern, immaculate face of Sarina Kaur appeared upon the video screen. "The woman is awake, Director," the guard reported gruffly.

"And the man?" Kaur inquired.

The guard shook his head. "Still silent as death."

Kaur sighed in disappointment. "I see." Roberta tried not to take it personally as Kaur apparently decided to make do with Roberta instead. "Thank you for informing me, Bhajan. I will be there shortly."

No need to hurry on my account, Roberta thought. The formidable director of Chrysalis was no Florence Nightingale, that was for sure. Roberta awaited her next meeting with Kaur with extreme apprehension. *Why do I suspect that we're not going to share a lovely Indian lunch this time around?*

CHAPTER SEVENTEEN

"THEY SAY A CAT MAY LOOK ON A KING. IS THAT WHY you watch me so attentively?"

Only four years old, young Noon already knew he was destined for greatness. His mother had told him so frequently, and she was the director of the entire project. His genes made him stronger and smarter than ordinary children, and even among his similarly gifted classmates, Noon stood out as someone special. His mother said he had genuine "leadership potential," and she should know; she had engineered him herself.

No wonder the sleek black cat had gravitated toward him as soon as Dr. Takagi had dropped the animal off at the classroom, explaining that the cat's owner, Dr. Neary, was currently indisposed and could not look after her pet. Noon had immediately taken custody of the cat, and was now supervising her inspection by the other children, who had lined up to pet the kitty in his arms. "Be gentle. Don't frighten her," he admonished an obviously excited little boy named Joaquin, although, to be honest, this cat did not act at all afraid. Instead she purred contentedly, enjoying the attention, as she carefully observed Noon and his playmates. The cat's unruffled demeanor reminded the well-read toddler of yet another archaic quotation, this one attributed to Montaigne: *"When I play with my cat, who knows if I am not a pastime to her more than she is to me?"*

How true! Noon considered, stroking the cat's velvety head. Dr. Neary had called her pet Isis, he recalled. An appropriately regal name, in his opinion.

Dr. Erickson stood behind Noon, watching the children take turns welcoming Isis. The cat's arrival had completely disrupted the day's educational activities, but neither Dr. Erickson nor the other instructors had objected too heartily; Noon suspected that they hoped all the commotion over the cat would help the class forget about what had happened to Shirin earlier that afternoon. So far, he noted, their strategy seemed to be working.

Not that Noon himself had really forgotten about the way the little girl had been removed from the class, after having another of her scary fits. He felt bad for Shirin, whom he assumed he would never see again, but there was nothing anyone could do about it; his mother had explained to him once that a certain amount of experimental error was unavoidable, and because of that a few unlucky children had mental or physical defects that could not be corrected. It wasn't fair, he understood, to force these poor, damaged kids to stay in the same class as perfect children like himself; in the long run, Shirin would be happier with the other inferior kids. *Maybe someone should give the flawed children a kitten, too*, he thought generously. *I'll bet that would cheer them up.*

"You know, class," Dr. Erickson began, attempting to turn the children's fascination with Isis into a learning experience, "in the outside world, where things are much more primitive and unfortunate than they are here, there are many boys and girls who can't even come near a cat because of allergies."

"What are allergies?" asked Suzette Ling, who was much more interested in math and machines than books. Noon rolled his eyes; he had read all about allergies months ago.

"Allergies are a genetic defect," their teacher explained, "that cause people to become sick whenever they're exposed to some common material, like fur or flowers. In fact, to tell you the truth, I'm intensely allergic to peppermint. I get a sore throat and a rash every time I take a bite of anything peppermint." A few of the children gasped in horror, but Dr. Erickson gave them a reassuring smile. "You children are very lucky. You've all been carefully designed to have no allergies at all, so you can eat and touch most everything without getting sick. Any questions?"

Suzette's hand shot up like the rockets she loved to design. "What does 'sick' mean?"

The five-o'clock bell interrupted what Noon considered a long and rather unnecessary lecture on the history of human infirmity. He already knew that ordinary people were a lot more fragile than he and his classmates were, even if this salient fact had somehow escaped the attention of Suzette and some of the other kids. "Their food actually comes back up their throats and out of their mouths?" Liam MacPherson asked, appalled and intrigued by the grotesque notion of regurgitation. "They can't help it?"

"Well, no," Dr. Erickson admitted, "although now is

probably not the best time to go into that." She clapped her hands together to get everyone's attention. "No more classwork for today. Everyone line up by the exit so we can get to the dining hall in a prompt and efficient manner."

The children closest to Noon crowded forward to stroke their feline visitor a few more times before leaving the classroom. He clasped the cat protectively against his chest as he looked hopefully at Dr. Erickson. "Can I take her with me to the dining hall?" he asked.

The instructor gave the matter a moment's thought, then shook her head. "Probably not a very sanitary idea," she pronounced, inspiring an eruption of groans and pleas from the class. "Tell you what, though. If you're all very well behaved at supper tonight, then *maybe* I'll let the cat stay with you in the dormitory tonight. Maybe."

Noon knew this was the best they were likely to get, so he reluctantly placed Isis back onto the floor and joined the other children by the exit. Dr. Erickson flicked off the lights as she and her partners escorted the children out of classroom and into the hall, leaving the cat behind.

They marched down the tunnel in single file, with Noon uncharacteristically last in line. He looked back over his shoulder wistfully, hoping Isis would be okay. His stomach growled, anticipating dinner, and he wondered if the cat was hungry as well. *Maybe I should save her part of my supper,* he mused, then remembered that he still had a leg of tandoori chicken, left over from lunch, stuck in his pocket, neatly wrapped inside a napkin. *That's perfect!*

In his imagination Isis was already ravenous, and he couldn't wait to feed her. Breaking away from the line of children as stealthily as he could, Noon doubled back toward the classroom, arriving at the entrance mere moments after he left. He threw open the door, chicken leg in hand, only to freeze upon the threshold, taken aback by the unexpected sight before him.

The cat was gone, but standing in the center of the classroom, not far from where he had left Isis, was an exotic-looking woman that Noon was sure he had never seen before.

Tall and slender, with lustrous long black hair, she was dressed, rather immodestly, in a revealing two-piece ensemble that was far from standard attire at Chrysalis, especially for grown-ups. Two black velvet hairpieces, shaped like the ears of a cat, adorned her scalp, while a very familiar silver collar glittered around her pale, alabaster neck. Noon recognized the collar instantly, just as he knew at once the amused, aloof expression in the woman's golden, almond-shaped eyes.

"Isis?"

The woman merely smiled back at him as she removed a spare lab coat from the teachers' closet, pulling it on over her skimpy black garments. The twin cat ears disappeared into a pocket of the jacket, while a tissue lifted from a box on the floor wiped away most of the woman's strikingly exotic makeup. Transfixed and confused by Isis's miraculous transformation, Noon stood by speechlessly as the impossible stranger patted him softly on the head, much as he had petted the cat earlier, and languidly plucked the chicken leg from his unresisting fingers. "But . . . how did you . . . ?"

he stammered, finding it unusually hard to craft a coherent response.

The cat-woman held a finger before her lips, bidding him to hush. The astounded child couldn't help noticing that her darkly painted nail curved to a sharp point, like a cat's claw. He nodded meekly as she slipped out the door, leaving him alone in the empty classroom.

"Isis," he whispered in wonder. Like the goddess. Could it be that the cat really was the Egyptian deity in disguise, or something even rarer and more mysterious?

For once in his young life, Noon didn't know what to believe.

Isis walked by herself down the corridors of Chrysalis. Clad in the borrowed lab coat, which was considerably less snug and comfortable than her usual ebony pelt, she stalked the maze of tunnels, sniffing the air as she nibbled delicately on the spicy chicken leg. The scent of her prey lingered in the sterile atmosphere of the underground complex, so she knew exactly where she was going and why.

It being the dinner hour, the halls were suitably ill populated, much as Isis had anticipated. The occasional stray passersby glanced at her curiously, but the disguised cat-woman roamed with such ease and confidence that few doubted that she belonged here as much as they did themselves. She resisted a strong temptation to smirk at the two-legged monkeys' general gullibility, but it wasn't easy.

She had traveled thus for less than ten minutes before her nose alerted her to the approach of her prey. Purring in anticipation, she deposited the chicken bones, now thoroughly stripped of meat, into a convenient trash receptacle before circling around to come up on the prey from behind. This was proving even easier than she had anticipated; how nice of Dr. Kaur to come this way.

Padding stealthily upon the scuffed tile floors, Isis heard Kaur and her ever-present bodyguards even before she spotted them striding down the tunnel in front of her. If Isis recalled the layout of the complex correctly, and there was no reason at all to imagine that she didn't, then the three humans were heading directly for the room where Seven was caged. Isis could smell the impatience and barely suppressed rage emanating from the Indian woman's pores. Clearly, Isis had tracked her down just in time.

The humans were in a hurry, too, so she had to quicken her pace to creep up on them, even as they remained oblivious of her pantherish approach. Anger filled her, and she bared her gleaming incisors at the memory of Seven locked away in that cage, like some primitive life-form. Isis had spent too much time in cages herself lately, posing as the Silly Blonde's pet, which only heightened her seething resentment at the way Seven had been treated. Even in this clumsy humanoid shape, every muscle was poised and ready, primed for the pounce.

Moving more quickly than any Terran ever could, she struck out at the left-hand bodyguard first. Skilled fingers found the nerve cluster at the base of the man's neck, rendering the ambushed human unconscious before either Kaur or the remaining guard realized what was transpiring. The second guard let out a savage bellow as his colleague crumpled to the floor, but his lumbering attempt to retaliate was no match for Isis's feline swiftness. A scissor-kick to the man's throat, followed by a proficient karate chop to the side of his bull-like neck, dropped him beside his fallen comrade.

"What—?" Kaur looked understandably startled. Both her guards had been neutralized almost before she registered that she was under attack. She spun around in amazement, only to be confronted by two unconscious bodyguards and the unarmed woman who had defeated them so effortlessly. "Who—who are you?" she blurted, fear and confusion written all over her face.

Isis smiled maliciously, her eyes agleam with the thrill of the hunt. She sniffed the air experimentally, then slashed out at Kaur with an open hand.

Kaur flinched and gasped with alarm, but Isis's claws sliced through only the fabric of the director's lab coat, spilling out the contents of one pocket onto the floor. Her eyes widened further when she spotted the two servos rolling across the tiles. "No!"

Realizing the alien weapons were her only defense, Kaur dived for the servos, but Isis's superlative reflexes were too fast for her. The cat-woman deftly kicked the small silver cylinders out of Kaur's reach, then tweaked the human woman's nerve clusters as expertly as she had the first guard's. Her eyes rolling backward into her head, Sarina Kaur collapsed next to her vanquished protectors.

Isis smiled with satisfaction, sparing only a moment to admire her handiwork before recovering the wayward servos. The devices shone prettily in the light, but Isis refused to let herself be distracted by the devices' enticing silver luster; there was too much else left to do.

Hearing strangers approaching from several corridors away, Isis used one of the servos to transport both Kaur and her guards into the nearest empty storeroom. With any luck, their sleeping bodies would not be found for some time.

Sniffing the air once more, Isis let her nose lead her toward Seven and the Other One. Her one regret was that there hadn't been more time to play with her prey before disposing of them.

Maybe later. . . .

CHAPTER EIGHTEEN

THE KNOCK ON THE DOOR SURPRISED ROBERTA. SHE knew Sarina Kaur was on the way, but she never imagined that the magisterial director would feel obliged to knock before entering the animal storeroom. Then again, someone had probably decided to keep the door locked after she and Isis had barged in unannounced earlier. *That's what I would have done,* she decided.

Certainly, the guard acted as though he was expecting the knock. Keeping one eye on Roberta, who was still securely ensconced inside her cage, he glanced through the small rectangular window in the door to the hallway. A puzzled grunt escaped his lips as he apparently failed to see the face he'd anticipated. Cautiously placing a hand on the grip of his handgun, he unlocked the door and opened it a crack.

A second later, he slid slowly onto the floor, a dopey grin visible beneath the bushy black whiskers of his beard. Roberta sprang to her feet inside the cage, gripping the bars in excitement. She recognized the effects of a tranquilizer beam when she saw them, so she was not at all surprised to see Isis, in her annoyingly attractive human guise, step inside and close the door behind her. A servo was gripped in the cat-woman's lethally manicured fingers. *Thank goodness!* Roberta thought, relieved by Isis's timely arrival.

Not that she was about to let her feline rival know how much she appreciated this rescue; Isis was insufferable enough already. "About time you got here, Your Slinkiness," Roberta groused. "Hurry and get me out of here. There's something wrong with Seven."

The alien woman ignored Roberta's remarks, as was her habit. Roberta strongly suspected that Isis *could* speak, but preferred not to, at least not when Roberta was listening. *Fine,* the caged woman thought. *Just so she lets me out of this zoo.* "C'mon! We need to get Seven to a doctor!"

But Roberta was not the only one noisily calling out to Isis. Perhaps sensing her unearthly nature, the other animals reacted strongly to the cat-woman's presence, squeaking and hooting and yelping and barking. The tiger roared either a greeting or a challenge; Roberta could not tell the difference, but feared the primeval uproar would attract additional guards. *It sounds like Noah's Ark in here,* she thought anxiously, *and I don't mean the Bill Cosby routine.*

She needn't have worried. With a single emphatic hiss, Isis silenced the raging menagerie, who ceased their bestial racket. Roberta had to admire the way Isis cowed her four-legged peers, even if there was something distinctly creepy about it. *What can these dumb animals tell about her that I can't?*

Stepping over the body of the tranquilized guard, Isis rushed over to the cage and knelt down beside the comatose Seven. Before Roberta could even ask Isis what she was up to, the cat-woman thrust her busy hands through the bars of the cage, yanking open Seven's collar with both hands, then jabbing his breastbone with the knuckles of one hand. "Hey!" Roberta objected, alarmed by Isis's rough ministrations. "What are you doing?"

Isis did not reply, but Roberta's startled queries were answered by a hoarse cough from Seven himself. He blinked once and lifted his head from his chest, looking about with a somewhat dazed expression. He shook his head roughly, as though to clear his mind of cobwebs, then surveyed the situation with a far more focused gaze. Alert gray eyes shifted from Roberta to Isis and back again. "I see that everyone is accounted for," he remarked dryly, "but I'm afraid I don't recall convening this meeting."

"Gary! You're back!" Relief flooded Roberta. "Thank God! I thought you'd gone all Rip Van Winkle on me. I tried and tried to rouse you, but nothing worked. I was afraid that—"

"I appreciate your concern, Ms. Lincoln," Seven interrupted, "but now is not the time for lengthy emotional displays." He looked automatically at his shackled wrist, only to recall that his watch had been removed. "How long was I out?"

Roberta had been stripped of her timepiece as well, but she could make a safe guess. "It must be five, six P.M. Saturday," she estimated. Despite her jubilation at Seven's hasty recovery, she couldn't just accept this new development without explanation. "But what was the matter with you?" she demanded. "You had me scared to death."

"My apologies," he replied. "My brain and body went into deep shutdown mode to prevent me from revealing any of the Aegis's most crucial secrets." He stood up slowly, his wrists still cuffed to the bars of the cage. A wince betrayed his discomfort as stiff muscles were called back into service. "It's a conditioned response, triggered by only the most grueling of interrogations." Beads of sweat dotted his brow, suggesting that Seven had not yet fully recovered from his long ordeal. "A similar state can be attained by the most skilled yogis of your own era. Fortunately, Isis possesses the knowledge and skills to return me to full consciousness."

Roberta noticed a small bruise forming on Seven's chest, exactly where Isis had jabbed him so sharply. She didn't know whether to be reassured or ticked off by Seven's explanation, but a note of aggravation definitely crept into her tone. "Well, you might have let me in on the trick," she protested. "What if Julie Newmar here hadn't been able to pussyfoot her way back to this place?"

Isis hmmphed indignantly, giving Roberta a distinctly condescending look, but Gary Seven simply raised an eyebrow as he asked her skeptically, "And would you have been able to resist the temptation to snap me out of my cataleptic state prematurely, while we were still in the hands of the opposition?"

"Maybe," Roberta answered tentatively. To be honest, she wasn't sure how long she could endure seeing Seven so seemingly close to death. "I think."

"In any event, your point is well taken," Seven stated in a conciliatory fashion. Isis wrinkled her nose dubiously, clearly unconvinced of any need to appease Roberta. "Perhaps we can discuss training you in the proper manipulation of pressure points—some other time. At the moment, we have more urgent business to attend to." He tugged on his handcuffs, rattling the sturdy chain between them. "Isis, if you please?"

The servo hummed for a fraction of a second, and the steel links connecting the cuffs disintegrated instantly. Seven lowered his arms, for the first time in who knew how long, grimacing briefly as he flexed his fingers experimentally, insuring that everything was still in working order. A moment later, the servo hummed again, and the lock holding the cage door shut fell with a clang onto the concrete floor.

"Thank you, Isis," Seven said as he emerged from his former place of captivity. Isis handed the pair of servos over to Seven, who obligingly returned one of them to Roberta. The blond woman glanced down for a moment to brush some clinging straw off her tweed skirt, but when she looked up again, Isis's human incarnation had vanished, replaced by an alert black cat, standing smugly atop the crumpled fabric of a discarded lab coat. Isis mewed insistently, urging Roberta to hurry.

"I'm coming, I'm coming!" the human woman exclaimed, stepping out of the cage and slamming the iron door shut behind her. In the next cage over, the restless tiger growled at the commotion, swiping his paw at Roberta, who took pains to stay safely out of the big cat's reach. *Just what I need,* she thought irritably. *Another feline pain in the butt.*

Seven took a moment to adjust his rumpled clothing, straightening up his appearance as much as was possible under the circumstances. His jacket had gone missing, and his plain white shirt was stained with sweat. Scowling, he rubbed the thick layer of stubble carpeting his lower jaw, no doubt wishing he had time to shave. Roberta knew how much he disliked disorder, in himself as much as anything else.

He quickly got down to business, however. "Now then," he addressed them crisply. "Tell me everything you've learned about the Chrysalis Project." Roberta and Isis both answered immediately, the cat's mewing competing with Roberta's hasty recitation of her adventures. Seven held up his hand to halt the cross-species clamoring. "You first," he specified, looking at Roberta.

"This is just as bad as I feared," Seven declared after quickly debriefing both Roberta and Isis. Roberta, naturally, hadn't understood a word of the other agent's feline vocalizations, but Seven appeared to glean useful information from the cat's vociferous mews and squawks. "Never mind Kaur's killer bacteria, for the moment. Chrysalis needs to be shut down immediately, just to stop them from producing any more genetically enhanced children." His expression was as grim and troubled as Roberta could ever remember seeing it. "As is, the superhuman prodigies they've already created constitute a potentially destabilizing element at this critical juncture in human history."

"Er, we're not going to have to . . . do something bad . . . to the kids, are we?" Roberta asked anxiously. She couldn't imagine that Seven would seriously consider exterminating dozens of innocent children just because they messed up the Aegis's timetable for humanity, but he didn't look at all happy to find out that Kaur and her scientists had already begotten several batches of scarily smart superkids. *Me*, she thought, *I'm just freaked out to find out that Kaur really is planning to let loose some sort of global epidemic. Does Walter know about that part of her plan? Does Lozinak?*

"It's not their fault that their parents souped up their DNA," she pointed out, trying to stay focused on the fate of Noon and the other children.

Seven shook his head. "We are not butchers," he reassured her. "The existence of a certain quantity of genengineered children is simply a challenge that we will have to cope with in the years to come. But we can make certain that this foolhardy project ceases immediately, and that the children are removed from the fanatical influence and ideology of Kaur and her associates." A hint of genuine animosity crept into his voice at the mention of Kaur and her vision for the future. "The last thing we need right now is Chrysalis encouraging these children to see themselves as apart from—and above—the mass of humanity."

Roberta breathed a sigh of relief, glad to know that the welfare of the Chrysalis kids was at least a factor in Seven's calculations. "So what do we do now?" she asked.

"That nuclear reactor you mentioned sounds like the most effective means of ridding the world of both this installation and Kaur's mutated bacteria," Seven announced. "If I can activate its self-destruct procedure, Kaur and the others will have no choice but to abandon Chrysalis and its entire infrastructure."

Roberta gulped, remembering the concrete silo housing the underground fission reactor. "A nuclear explosion? Isn't that a bit, well, extreme?"

"Trust me, Ms. Lincoln," Seven said gravely. "Extreme measures are called for to eliminate the dire threat Chrysalis poses to the future safety of this planet. Fortunately, this facility's remote location works to our advantage; for better or for worse, underground nuclear tests are a fact of life in this era. One more will make very little difference in the grand scheme of things."

He rubbed his chafed wrists, still red and raw from the cruel grip of the shackles. "I only wish there were a surefire way to eliminate all knowledge of Kaur's custom-made bacteria. Unfortunately, scientific knowledge, once discovered, is harder to eradicate than any physical installation; there's no telling how many of Kaur's people know the exact genetic sequence for the bacteria, or how many copies of the recipe exist elsewhere on the planet." Seven wasted little time lamenting what could not be altered, preferring, as usual, to focus on the task at hand. "At least the atomic blast will destroy Kaur's ability to manufacture the bacteria in mass quantities, as well as incinerating whatever stockpiles may already exist."

"Okay, if you say so," Roberta assented. The notion of intentionally setting off a nuclear explosion, even in the middle of the desert, still gave her the heebie-jeebies, but she had learned to trust Seven in this kind of thing; heck, the first time she met him he had caused an orbital weapons platform to detonate only 104 miles above the Earth, and that had turned out okay. What was one more mushroom cloud between friends? "What do you want me to do?"

"Your job is to make sure that every child in this complex is transported to safety before the explosion. I'll try to give the adults sufficient time to evacuate, but those children are our first priority." He raised an inquiring eyebrow. "I assume you've entered the geographical coordinates for this location into your servo?"

Roberta nodded. The servo was capable of using Earth's magnetic force lines to determine its exact position anywhere on the planet. "First chance I got."

"Good," Seven acknowledged. "I want you and Isis to return to New York immediately. Once you've given the Beta 5 the correct coordinates, it should be able to zoom in on Chrysalis with its long-range sensors. You can use the computer to transport the children en masse to a secure location."

"Got it," she confirmed, making a mental note not to forget the unfortunate kids in the Developmental Deviations Unit. "How about that kids' academy in Puyallup?" she suggested. "We've placed orphans there before. They should be able to look after the kids, at least for a while."

"An excellent idea," Seven stated, nodding soberly. He clearly realized this was only a temporary solution at best. "We can deal with the children's ultimate disposition later on, after we've insured that there will be no more problem children created here."

Isis mewed forcefully, prompting Seven to glance at the caged animals surrounding them. "Thank you, Isis," he said. "I had overlooked these other life-forms." He turned toward Roberta once more. "After you've removed the children from jeopardy, please transport these animals away from the impending explosion." He paused briefly to consider the matter before coming up with the ideal solution. "The Sariska Nature Preserve is located elsewhere in Rajasthan. Our striped friend," he added, indicating the nearby tiger, "should feel quite at home there, along with the rest of these creatures."

"Will do," Roberta agreed readily; her stint in the cage gave her a little extra empathy with the penned lab animals, who just happened to be at the wrong place at the worst possible time. She picked up Isis and got ready to go. "Is there anything else I need to—"

The door slammed open, cutting Roberta off in mid sentence. "Freeze!" Carlos ordered as the gigantic Cuban enforcer burst through the door brandishing a blue-steel Beretta. He glowered venomously at Roberta, ugly scratch marks still defacing his cheek. "Drop your weapons—and don't even think about siccing that *gato cabrón* on me!"

Isis hissed ferociously, but wisely stayed put in Roberta's arms. *Yikes!* the human woman thought. *What's* he *doing here?* Her brain worked overtime, trying to figure out what crummy twist of fate had brought Carlos along to spoil their plans. *Was he looking for Dr. Kaur,* she wondered, *or just coming to gloat over my captivity?*

Whatever the reason, the sneering ape-man looked all too happy to have caught her and Seven right in the middle of their jailbreak. "I knew you were trouble," he snarled at Roberta, "right from the beginning. I told the doctors they were fools to trust you!"

You know, she thought, *that "gloating" scenario is sounding more and more plausible. . . .* She scanned the storeroom out of the corners of her eyes, looking for something she could use to turn the tables on Carlos. Seven's servo now lay at his feet, while her own servo rested uselessly in her pocket, where she couldn't possibly pull it out before Carlos could shoot one or both of them. *I don't believe this!* she thought indignantly. *We were almost out of here.*

Carlos glanced down contemptuously at the tranquilized guard on the floor. "What did you do to him?" he demanded. Keeping both Roberta and Seven in his sights, he regarded the now-empty cage with hostile, suspicious eyes. "Where is the director? What have you done with her?"

You'd be better off asking Isis, Roberta thought. She wasn't clear on the details, but she knew that the catwoman had to have retrieved their servos *somehow.* "I have no idea," she insisted, more or less truthfully. "Dr. Kaur hasn't been here for hours."

"Liar!" Carlos accused her. "She was on her way here, I know that." He waved his gun in front of her. "Tell me now, *gringa.* Where is she?"

Seven cleared his throat, distracting Carlos. "What's that?" the gunman asked. "You want to say something, spy?"

Ignoring Carlos, Seven made eye contact with Roberta, then glanced quickly down at the floor by the mutated Cuban's feet. Roberta followed Seven's gaze downward, where she saw that one of thug's polished black shoes rested on the corner of Isis's discarded lab coat. *Aha!* Roberta thought, maintaining her best poker face. As discreetly as possible, she started to wrap the opposite end of the coat around the heel of her sensible white pump. *Just keep looking away for a sec,* she urged Carlos with her (sadly nonexistent) psychic powers.

"I'm talking to you, spy!" Carlos taunted Seven. *You see what I had to deal with in Rome?* Roberta thought, now that Seven was getting a firsthand taste of Carlos's dubious people skills. "I want answers and I want them now."

"I have nothing to say to you," Seven stated firmly, undeterred by the loaded gun in the angry bodyguard's grasp. Seven's icy composure, even at gunpoint, reminded Roberta of all the times he had faced down berserk supercomputers. "Perhaps you should contact your superiors for further instructions."

Carlos spat at the floor in front of Seven, his clawed, simian face a mask of frustrated belligerence, but Roberta saw his baleful black eyes drift in the direction of the videophone on the wall. While hardly likely to credit Seven with the suggestion, Carlos must have realized that reinforcements might, in fact, be a good idea. "Stay where you are!" he ordered and stepped toward the videophone, which just happened to bring his foot down even more squarely on the spilled white fabric of the lab coat.

Roberta waited until Carlos reached for the phone, then yanked her foot back with all her strength, pulling the coat out from beneath him. "Wha—!" he exclaimed as he stumbled backward, temporarily thrown off-balance. Seven took advantage of the ape-man's instability to dart forward and strike Carlos on the wrist, freeing the Beretta from his grip. Cursing in Spanish, Carlos slammed shoulder-first into the wall, almost toppling over entirely before regaining his footing—only to discover his gun now in the steady grip of Gary Seven.

"Please remain where you are," Seven informed him coldly. The muzzle of the Beretta held Carlos securely in its sights. "It's not my preferred mode of self-defense, but I assure you that I am perfectly capable of operating this primitive firearm."

Growling furiously, Carlos raised his hands and backed up against the wall. Seven knelt to retrieve his servo, then aimed the slender silver cylinder at Carlos as well, clearly intending to tranquilize the bellicose Cuban in an admirably humane and civilized fashion.

"Wait!" Roberta blurted. "Let me." Dropping Isis roughly onto the floor, she rushed across the room toward Carlos. Seven might have expected her to employ her own servo, but instead Roberta clenched her fist and delivered a solid left hook to the thug's protruding jaw. Carlos gasped in pain, his eyes bugging out as blood leaked from a split lip. Roberta smiled in satisfaction as she stepped back from the battered bodyguard, her knuckles smarting. "Okay," she told Seven. "*Now* you can zap him."

A moment later, Carlos crumpled onto the floor beside the guard Isis had pacified earlier. "Hardly an enlightened response to aggressive behavior," Seven observed archly.

Roberta shrugged defiantly. "So I'm an unevolved twentieth-century Earthling," she said, unrepentant in the extreme. "Sue me."

To her surprise, Isis purred in approval. *How 'bout that?* Roberta thought. *We actually agree on something for once.*

Perhaps knowing he was outnumbered, Seven let the matter pass. "You had better depart before another troublesome assailant arrives," he advised her. "I'll head for the reactor."

She couldn't help noticing that, despite his determined demeanor, Seven still looked considerably the worse for wear. Purple shadows sagged beneath his eyes, which were red and bloodshot. Fatigue and responsibility dragged down his shoulders, adding an uncharacteristic stoop to his usually impeccable posture.

His cheeks were gray and bloodless, and his hands trembled subtly but perceptibly. Roberta even thought she saw white hairs in his scalp that she didn't remember from before. *What did Kaur do to him?* she fretted, not sure she wanted to know.

"Are you sure you're up for this?" she asked him worriedly. "Maybe we should all just 'port back to NYC, then come back here after you've had a chance to recover."

Seven shook his head solemnly. "Kaur knows her secrets have been exposed. We can't risk her tightening security, or relocating the children to another site." Through sheer force of will, he brought his shaking frame back under control. "It has to be done today— before another strand of DNA can be twisted into something more dangerous than you can possibly realize. I only wish we could have stopped Chrysalis years ago, before it came to this. . . ."

You and me both, Roberta thought.

CHAPTER NINETEEN

ONLY A FEW STRAY WISPS OF LUMINOUS BLUE MIST still floated over the tranquilized goons as Seven exited the animal storeroom for what he expected would be for good. First, though, he disconnected the videophone above the fallen guards, just in case they roused themselves prematurely. He considered fusing the door shut behind him, then realized that he could hardly lock anyone up inside a structure that he intended to condemn to thermonuclear destruction. Even the subhuman Cuban operative, whom both Isis and Roberta appeared to dislike so, deserved a chance to evacuate the premises with the rest of the project's personnel.

Seven warily scanned the corridor outside the storeroom. In theory, Roberta and Isis were already back in Manhattan by now, fulfilling their end of the operation. *I'm on my own now,* he acknowledged resolutely. This was just as well; the obliteration of Chrysalis was too important to trust to any less-experienced agent, no matter how resourceful or enterprising she might be.

What's that Terran expression again? If you want a job done right. . . .

Isis's borrowed lab coat was a few sizes too small for him, but it would have to make do; ill-fitting camouflage was better than none at all. He rubbed his stubbly chin once more, hoping that his unshaven appearance would not attract unwelcome attention. Holding on tightly to his servo, concealed within a pocket of the overly snug white jacket, he marched rapidly down the sterile tunnel, looking for the nearest stairwell. According to Roberta, the nuclear reactor occupied the lowest sublevel of the complex, and he preferred taking the stairs over an elevator, the latter being far too reminiscent of a cell for his liking. *I'm not about to get trapped inside an enclosed space,* he resolved, *not if I can help it.*

His decision proved a wise one; Seven was less than fifty yards away from the storeroom when an alarm blared loudly overhead: "ATTENTION! INTRUDER ALERT! BE ON THE LOOKOUT FOR THREE UNAUTHORIZED VISITORS: A DARK-HAIRED FEMALE, A BLOND AMERICAN WOMAN, AND A TALL, BROWN-HAIRED, AMERICAN MALE. THE INTRUDERS ARE ARMED AND EXTREMELY DANGEROUS. REPORT ALL SIGHTINGS TO SECURITY IMMEDIATELY. REPEAT: REPORT ANY SUSPICIOUS INDIVIDUALS AT ONCE. THIS IS A MATTER OF THE GRAVEST IMPORTANCE."

Seven frowned, but wasted little mental or physical energy lamenting this unfortunate turn of events. *We've been lucky so far,* he realized, *but exposure was inevitable.* Either someone had discovered the sleeping bodies in the storeroom, he speculated, or else Kaur and her bodyguards had finally recovered from Isis's ambush. *Most likely the latter,* he guessed. In any event, his task had just become significantly more challenging.

He quickened his pace as the alert repeated itself in several languages, its essential message remaining the same. Seven drew some amusement from the fact that two of the described intruders—Isis and Roberta— were already well beyond Kaur's grasp. With any luck, the project's security force would squander a portion of their efforts searching fruitlessly for the two female operatives. Not to mention a missing black cat.

Seven's own good fortune ran out at the very next intersection, where he abruptly ran across a mixed group of technicians and scientists, all excitedly discussing the upsetting alarm echoing through the corridors of the underground complex. "Another intruder?" a German biochemist (whom Seven recognized from his missing persons list) exclaimed anxiously, gesticulating wildly with his hands. "What the devil is going on? If we're in any sort of danger, we ought to be better informed!"

Casually slipping his servo out of his pocket, Seven maintained a steady pace toward the knot of confused and agitated personnel. Perhaps he could still bluff his way past the clustered men and women? From what Roberta and Isis had told him, Chrysalis's staff was populous enough that strangers were not immediately identifiable; both women had managed to traverse the project's sprawling maze of tunnels without too much interference.

But that was before repeated alerts had put everyone's nerves on edge. "Hey!" the discontented German called out as Seven attempted to pass by. His meaty hand clamped down tightly on Seven's upper arm. "Who are you? I've never seen you before!"

A few of the assembled civilians backed away from Seven apprehensively, but, unfortunately, a couple of braver souls joined the German in detaining Seven, taking up hostile postures in front and behind the outnumbered secret agent. "The name's Kirk," he improvised. "James T. Kirk. From the Developmental Deviations Unit."

"The DDU, huh?" the German repeated skeptically, citing the only department Seven actually knew by name. "How come I've never heard of you?" He tightened his grip on Seven's arm, while the other men closed in on the suspected intruder. "Let me see your ID."

"Yeah!" another scientist seconded, brute anger thickening his voice. He shoved Seven harshly from behind. "Make him show his ID!"

So much for going incognito, Seven thought, sighing deeply. Obviously, he was not going to be able to talk his way out of this confrontation. *Very well.*

"Let me show you," he began meekly, feigning cooperation. Without warning, he fired the servo in his hand straight into the German's torso. The biochemist's tenacious fingers went as limp as the rest of his body, so that only a gentle push was required to send him toppling backward as his startled associates clambered to break his fall. At the same time, Seven elbowed the ill-tempered individual behind him, jolting the wind from the man's lungs. Seven spun around and fired again, turning the shove-happy scientist into a sagging mass of tranquilized bliss.

Seven thought he was free and clear until two strong arms suddenly seized him from behind, squeezing his arms against his sides. "Drop that—whatever it is!" an anxious voice commanded shrilly. Its Brooklyn accent seemed incongruous at this remote location. "Somebody call security—pronto!"

That last suggestion provoked a scowl from Seven. *This is taking too long,* he appraised. He needed to exit this scene before *real* opposition arrived. Even in his present debilitated state, his training and physical conditioning made him more than a match for a mob of overexcited scientists and maintenance workers. He was much more concerned about Kaur's predominately Sikh security force; the ancient brotherhood of the Sikhs had been famous for their military prowess and discipline since at least the seventeenth century, and had frequently formed the backbone of the subcontinent's defense forces. *Those guardians will not be so easily overcome.*

Taking a deep breath, he marshaled his parahuman strength, throwing off his captor's amateurish hold with a single concerted effort. He twisted around at the waist, ready to subdue the third man with a tranquilizing burst from his servo, but instead discovered that such measures were not required; at the first sign of serious resistance, the frightened scientist fled in retreat, joining his fellow workers as they ran from the manifestly dangerous intruder in their midst. Seven heard the rapid-fire pounding of their footsteps echoing through the corridors ahead, just as he also registered, alas, their frantic cries for help.

His cover well and truly blown, Seven dashed down the right-hand tunnel, opposite the direction in which the panicked scientists had retreated. He was surprised to find that the brief tussle, which had lasted less than a minute or two, had actually left him short of breath. *I must be in worse shape than I thought,* he concluded grudgingly. *Fatigue and dehydration have taken their toll.*

A map of the complex, conveniently inscribed on the wall, provided a welcome supplement to Roberta's fragmentary directions. Panting heavily, his chest heaving with every breath, Seven took a moment to memorize the schematic. According to the map, there was an exit less than fifty yards away that led directly to the catwalks overlooking the wide central shaft around which the rest of Chrysalis fanned out. Seven recalled observing those same catwalks when he first descended into Chrysalis via the hidden elevator from the ruined Rajput fortress above. He would be uncomfortably exposed on the open catwalks, he realized uneasily, but they appeared to be the shortest route available to the complex's lower levels. *I'll have to chance it,* he decided.

"Halt! Stay where you are!" a deep voice shouted in strongly accented English. Seven turned his head to see a pack of security officers heading straight for him. Almost a dozen men ran on foot ahead of two more guards riding a compact motorized vehicle designed for cruising Chrysalis's many tunnels. Most of the men appeared to be Sikhs, but Seven spotted a couple of European and Asian individuals running alongside the bearded and turbaned Indian guardsmen. "Put your hands up and surrender!" the leader of the unit barked loudly.

Rather than complying with the officer's demands, Seven swiftly raised his servo and fired into the oncoming troopers. With expert aim, he targeted the guard behind the wheel of the small, three-wheeled scooter. The driver immediately collapsed over the steering column, causing the vehicle to veer wildly out of control. The soldiers on foot were forced to scatter and scurry for safety, momentarily abandoning their pursuit of Seven, as they broke ranks in a chaotic attempt to avoid the runaway scooter. The guard in the passenger seat struggled to grab hold of the steering wheel, but the dead weight of his comrade's listless body obstructed the passenger's frantic efforts to regain control of the transport. "Watch out!" he shrieked in Punjabi.

Seven spared only an instant to observe the guards' momentary disarray. The cramped corridors, he knew, would prevent the two-man scooter from accelerating to a genuinely life-threatening velocity; at most, the driver and his passenger would merely be stunned when the vehicle inevitably slammed into one of the tunnel walls. *Whenever possible,* he reminded himself, *keep enemy casualties to a minimum.*

In the meantime, he meant to make the most of his reprieve, sprinting down the empty hallway at full speed, occasionally firing back over his shoulder at his pursuers. Tranquilized guards dropped like crunchblossoms on Equinox IV, while their cohorts ducked for cover. The most persistent guards, however, undaunted by invisible beams or the wayward scooter, began firing back at Seven, the sound of gunshots ringing throughout the lengthy tunnel. Seven bent over as he ran, presenting as small a target as he could. Bullets whizzed past him, raising miniature clouds of dust and debris wherever they perforated the walls and floor of the tunnel. Seven knew that, no matter how distracted and rushed the marksmen, he couldn't evade the blistering hail of lead for long.

Clearly visible ahead, the promised exit beckoned to him, offering a much-needed escape route. He propelled himself forward with all his strength, relying on adrenaline to compensate, in part, for the weakness brought on by his long captivity. His lungs burned, and Earth's gravity felt as though it had increased by several orders of magnitude over just the last few minutes. A bullet chipped out a corner of the wall only a few inches from his head, spraying the right half of his face with powdered plaster. *Almost there,* he spurred his aching legs, keeping his gaze fixed immovably on the exit sign. *Just a few more feet ...!*

With his peripheral vision, he glimpsed a cherry-red fire alarm mounted to the wall on his right. Playing a hunch, he turned quickly and fired a thermal discharge at the ceiling. Not enough to ignite a serious blaze, naturally, but sufficient to activate any overhead sprinklers that might be lurking out of sight.

A piercing siren greeted his efforts, followed by an immediate torrent of water spraying down from concealed jets in the ceiling. Angry curses competed with the siren as the pursuing security guards, already rattled by the amuck scooter, slid and slipped on the suddenly soaking floor tiles. The artificial (and entirely unnecessary) downpour also interfered with their marksmanship, granting Seven the grace period he needed to reach the once-distant exit. *Good to know Kaur and her architects practiced responsible fire safety,* he mused wryly, *but how could they not, with future generations of superhumanity at risk?*

The exit door was locked, possibly because of the security alert, but Seven slammed his shoulder against the barricade, breaking the lock. Escaping both the shrillness of the siren and the drenching spray of the sprinklers, he found himself upon the wrought-iron catwalk, several flights of stairs above the ground floor. Leaning heavily on a safety rail, painted a drab industrial green, he looked out over the enormous vertical shaft penetrating the hub of Chrysalis; after numerous hours spent in cramped cages and interlocking tunnels, it was startling to encounter so much open space. Elevator cables dangled from on high, extending through a circular gap in the floor to the sublevels below. *That's where I need to go,* Seven thought, taking an instant to assimilate the breathtaking view from his lofty vantage point. A butterfly design adorned the ground floor at least five levels below, adding a decorative touch to the vast excavation. *Too bad*, he reflected grimly, *that this man-made chrysalis is more likely to disgorge dangerous wasps than any delicately ornamental lepidoptera, and in swarms that may well consume Earth's fragile hopes for peace.*

The network of steel balconies and catwalks erected up and down the wide circumference of the great shaft looked oddly unpeopled at present; Seven guessed that the majority of the project's population were staying put in their own quarters and laboratories until the current security crisis was resolved. Only multiple teams of security guards prowled the catwalk and the ground floor below, leaving no sector of Chrysalis unexplored in their hunt for the intruders. Seven briefly regretted that he was wearing a scientist's white coat and not a security guard's blue uniform; with more guards than civilians on the prowl, he stood out like a sore thumb.

A sore, tired thumb, to be exact. Winded from the chase, he craved a few more seconds to catch his breath, but he knew he couldn't afford to rest for even another heartbeat. The sprinklers would not slow his dogged pursuers for long, and already additional teams of guardsmen were spotting him upon the catwalk. On the other side of the mammoth shaft, roughly a quarter of a mile away, a bearded guard shouted and pointed at Seven with the muzzle of his gun. More heads turned in his direction, both upon the sprawling catwalks and from the floor below. Behind Seven, through the ruptured doorway, he heard the splashing and yelling of his original hunters, drawing nearer by the moment. *No time to linger,* he realized, brushing the powdered debris off his face. *Best to present a moving target.*

Despite the fatigue poisons building up in the muscles of his too-weary legs, Seven started down the iron stairway leading to the lower levels of the catwalk. He took the dull green steps two at a time, grabbing on to the cool metal handrails to swing forward onto the next balcony-like landing. His heels slammed into the solidly-mounted grillework so hard that he could feel the vibration all the way up his legs. *At least it's downhill all the way,* he thought, *until I get to that reactor.*

No sooner had he reached the first of the lower platforms than the original security team arrived at the doorway he had smashed his way through only moments before. Seven was ready for them; aiming his servo back the way he had come, he disintegrated the landing outside the door, cutting the guardsmen off (he hoped) from the lower levels. The iron platform glowed briefly, suffused with incandescent energy, before vanishing entirely, reduced to a cascade of free-floating atoms.

But the landing's instantaneous disappearance did not discourage his hunters entirely. To Seven's dismay, one of the guards tried to jump from the brink of the newly created abyss to the landing where Seven now stood; Seven watched in horror as the determined trooper fell short of his goal, instead plummeting hundreds of feet to the ground floor of the shaft, where his lifeless body came to rest upon the attractive blue-and-white tiles. His colleagues on the ground flocked to his splattered remains, but Seven knew they were too late to provide any medical attention or spiritual comfort. No ordinary mortal could survive that plunge.

Seven profoundly regretted the man's death, but declined to accept full responsibility for the tragedy. *I can't protect every Homo sapiens from his own recklessness,* he thought sadly. *Saving the mass of humanity is difficult enough.*

Having learned a deadly lesson from their comrade's fatal mistake, the surviving members of the security team clung tightly to the doorframe as they fired their guns at Seven, who struggled to keep one step ahead of the merciless fusillade. Bullets ricocheted off the metal steps and handrails, throwing sparks in every direction. The sharp reports of the gunshots drowned out the excited and irate cries of guardsmen both near and far.

More trouble rushed toward Seven from below. Glancing down through the grillework beneath his feet, Seven spied a second security team hurrying up the steps to intercept him. Within seconds they were only a level or two below him, and eating up the remaining distance at a furious clip. The barrage of gunfire from the upper doorway slowed dramatically as the elevated snipers held their fire, reluctant to catch their own forces in their fire. *A small silver lining,* Seven noted gratefully, *to an otherwise dire situation.*

"Get him!" the guards called to each other. Multiple sets of boots stomped up the iron stairways, climbing toward the exposed intruder. "Don't let him get away!"

Having literally burned his bridges behind him, Seven realized he couldn't turn back even if he wanted to. With a fresh pack of Sikh guardsmen closing on him, Seven directed the servo's disintegration beam on the stairs and landing directly beneath him, halting the climbing guards' upward progress. Two levels below, the uniformed men backed away apprehensively, wary of Seven's obviously formidable weapon. Little did they know that he'd turn the ray on himself before obliterating any undeserving human beings. *They're just foot soldiers, doing their job,* Seven realized. *Unfortunately, that job just happens to interfere with mine.*

His tactic had bought a few more seconds, but left him effectively stranded on a steel platform several dozen feet above the floor. It also made him vulnerable to a crossfire between the two teams of security guards. *Not a very tenable position,* Seven concluded, searching his surroundings for a viable alternative. His cool, analytical gaze fell upon the dangling elevator cables, stretching from the desert floor high above them to unseen sublevels of the immense underground complex. The cables were approximately four hundred yards away from the edge of the steel landing, a considerable jump, even for him. A hundred feet below, the pool of blood spreading from the body of the fallen guard tellingly illustrated the terminal consequences of failing to make the jump. It was a long way down indeed.

"Nothing else to do," Seven muttered. A quick blast from his servo disintegrated the guardrail separating him from the empty space between the ledge and the cables. Placing the weapon in his pants pocket, he hastily shucked off the confining white lab coat and wrapped the fabric over the palms of his hands, so that a ribbon of white cloth linked his hands like shackles. He backed up against the wall of the shaft, to give himself as much of a running start as possible—little more than a yard's worth—then ran toward the edge of the landing, asking his already overtaxed legs for one more Olympics-caliber feat.

His feet left the safety and support of the ledge and Seven hurled himself into the gap, his hands stretched out in front of him. Forward momentum carried his fragile human frame toward the hanging cables even as gravity pulled him down, causing him to descend toward the floor in a long, sloping arch. Startled onlookers gasped in astonishment at the intruder's death-defying dive even as Seven focused entirely on the potentially lifesaving elevator cables. A self-generated wind blew against his face, but he kept his eyes open until, maybe sixty feet above the floor, he came within reach of the cables. Hands swaddled in protective cloth grabbed on to one of the thick steel cords, abruptly arresting his descent. The impact of his sudden stop nearly yanked his arms from their sockets, but he held on to the greasy cables through the fabric of the lab coat, swinging precariously for a few seconds before catching on to the cable with his ankles as well.

Made it! Despite the extremely unfinished nature of his mission, he allowed himself a moment of elation. *That was a riskier stunt than I usually like to pull,* he admitted. Good thing Isis wasn't around to see him taking chances like that; he'd never hear the end of it. *From now on, I'm inclined to leave the death-defying leaps to Evel Knievel.*

Using the now-greasy lab coat to control his descent, and protect his hands from friction, he slid down the elevator cable toward the hole in the floor. Caught by surprise, the guardsmen let him slide most of the way unopposed, realizing only too late what he was up to. Bullets rang against the floor tiles in a last-minute attempt to target Seven before he dropped out of sight. The would-be saboteur felt very relieved that Kaur had not yet had a chance a raise a generation of marksmen with genetically perfect aim.

Ducking his head, Seven rode the cable down through the center of the floor's ornate butterfly logo. The din of gunfire grew more distant as the elevator shaft continued through at least four feet of solid concrete, eventually emerging from the ceiling of a large, starkly unadorned cement bunker. A single elevator car rested at the bottom of the shaft, going mercifully unused at the moment. Seven waited until he was only ten feet or so above the roof of the elevator before letting go of the cable and dropping onto the top of the car.

The minute he hit the elevator, he dived onto all fours and rolled swiftly to one side. He was just in time; one level above, the frustrated guards had finally thought to fire their weapons straight down the elevator shaft. Multiple gunshots shredded the top of the elevator, but Seven had already hopped onto the cement floor beside the elevator car. He pressed the nearby Up button, sending the punctured elevator back up the shaft, effectively stopping any of the guards from mimicking his rapid descent down the cable—at least for a few minutes.

He looked around quickly. According to both Roberta and the map in the corridor, the nuclear generator was located on this level of the complex, a prediction confirmed by the large painted warnings on the wall in front of him:

CAUTION! ATOMIC POWER STATION
NO UNAUTHORIZED PERSONNEL PERMITTED!

The warnings were printed in English, Hindi, Punjabi, and Chinese, and accompanied by a bright yellow rendering of the universal sign for nuclear radiation. Even more daunting were the two armed guards flanking what appeared to be the only entrance to the power station.

"Halt!" one of the guards commanded Seven, raising his rifle as he stepped between Seven and a lowered steel door. "Identify yourself!"

Seven knew he couldn't outdraw both armed guards with his servo—his reflexes weren't *that* fast—so he clicked the transport function of the servo instead, summoning a cloud of roiling, luminous plasma that appeared from nowhere between Seven and the guards, shielding him from their view. Alarmed by the shimmering smoke screen, both guards fired randomly into the fog, not realizing that their bullets dematerialized the moment they entered the plasma, instantly converted into pure energy. Both guards discharged a full clip of ammo in a vain attempt to shoot the intruder on the other side of the glowing cloud; Seven used the sound of their weapons to target first one guard, then the other, with the servo he quickly drew from his pocket. The tranquilizer beam, not being composed of matter, passed through the plasma unobstructed, silencing both gunmen within seconds.

Seven canceled the transporter command, banishing the unnatural mist back to subspace, then hurried forward through the last blue wisps to the sealed entrance to the reactor. The subdued guards were slumped on both sides of the lowered steel door, dozing contentedly. Seven methodically searched the pockets of the nearest guard, quickly turning up an electronic passkey, which he inserted into a slot next to the door. "Open sesame," he muttered, reflecting a thorough grounding in Terran folklore and literature.

Hidden motors thrummed as the door began to slide upward, receding into a slot in the ceiling. Seven did not wait for the barrier to disappear entirely, ducking beneath the door the minute there was enough room to squeeze under. "No one move!" he ordered, announcing his arrival to the startled technicians in the control room. He held the servo in an overtly threatening manner. "As recent announcements confirm, I am indeed armed and dangerous."

The half-dozen technicians present backed away from the entrance nervously, most of them abandoning their posts at the control. A single techie, however, risked Seven's wrath by slapping his palm down on a large red button, triggering an immediate alarm. Seven swiftly turned the servo's beam on the security-conscious offender, causing that individual to droop in his seat, but the damage had already been done. Sirens blared overhead, no doubt alerting all of Chrysalis of his incursion into the reactor's control room.

Seven sighed, but shrugged his shoulders. *No matter,* he thought. *Kaur and her security forces were bound to guess my intentions eventually, especially after seeing me slide down that cable to this level.* He gestured with his servo, forcing the remainder of the technicians to line up against the back of the room, in front of the startlingly old-fashioned computers with their refrigerator-sized housings and large, rotating spindles. "All right," he instructed the cowed techies. "I want you all to leave here as quickly as possible, taking that gentleman with you," he added, nodding at the tranquilized whistle-blower, now slumped over his control panel. Seven's gaze zeroed in on one particular technician, who struck him as older and most likely to be in charge. "Except you," he specified, singling out his chosen candidate: a lanky European, whose security badge identified him as Ryan Johnson, Chief Engineer. "I need to talk to you."

The other technicians needed no further encouragement to make themselves scarce, abandoning the control room in record time. Seven waited for the last two engineers to depart, carrying their droopy colleague between them, then used his stolen passkey to bring the metal door crashing back down. The control panel next to the door was rudimentary in design, at least to Seven's standards, so it took him only a moment to reprogram the locking mechanism, effectively sealing the control room off from the security teams that were probably arriving on the scene at this very minute. *They'll need an acetylene torch to get through this door,* he thought approvingly. *That should give me all the time I need.*

"Sorry about the delay," he said to his sole remaining hostage. "Thank you for waiting." He walked between the rows of consoles, quickly familiarizing himself with the layout. The fundamentally crude and antiquated nature of the controls made his current task easier, but appalled him nonetheless. He glanced out the wide Plexiglas window at the huge concrete silo housing the reaction chamber itself and shuddered accordingly. *I can't believe that the people of this era think they can play with nuclear fission so haphazardly. At the rate mankind's building these slipshod power generators, they're sure to stumble into a serious meltdown or two within a decade.* "How do I initiate the self-destruct procedure?" he asked Johnson.

"What?" The man's weathered face went pale. "You can't be serious!"

"I've seldom been more serious," Seven assured him. "If you don't assist me, I will have to attempt to initiate an explosive chain reaction on my own, with possibly less control over the timing of the resulting conflagration than I might have otherwise. It's up to you, Mr. Johnson. Do you want to give Chrysalis's entire population a chance to evacuate, or shall I just start fooling around with the controls?" He strolled toward the nearest console, laying a hand upon a complicated array of switches, gauges, and knobs. "I'm guessing these regulate high-pressure coolant infusion. Shall we see if I've figured them out correctly?"

Johnson's Adam's apple bobbed like a vacuum buoy in a cosmic storm. "But it's impossible," he gulped. Terrified eyes tracked the progress of Seven's fingers as they roamed over the control panel. "I couldn't help you even if I wanted to. Only the director can order the detonation sequence."

Naturally, Seven thought. Not that Sarina Kaur really worried too much about the accidental release of one of her handcrafted bacteria; this entire self-destruct option was no doubt a concession to the safety concerns of project engineers who were unaware of Kaur's genocidal ambitions.

His eyes narrowed. "Show me," he insisted.

A hissing sound, coming from overhead, interrupted his interrogation of the chief engineer. Johnson peered upward, with a look of definite relief upon his face. Recalling Roberta's account of her own capture, Seven was not surprised to see thick white fumes entering the control room via the ceiling. *Apparently the Developmental Deviations Unit is not the only section of Chrysalis so equipped,* he concluded.

Placing his hand over his mouth and nostrils, he aimed his servo at the corners of the Plexiglas window occupying most of the southern wall of the chamber. He set the beam on Disintegrate, then proceeded to dissolve the molecular bonds holding the massive sheet of transparent plastic in its frame, so that a single shove sent it falling onto the concrete pavement one level below the control room.

Seven heard it clatter when it hit the cement floor. Fresh air rapidly entered the once-sealed chamber, even as the knockout gas dissipated into the vast open space surrounding the reactor silo. The roar of the turbines penetrated the formerly soundproofed control room, adding to the humming and clicking supplied by the computers and other apparatus.

Seven coughed to clear the last of the invasive fumes from his lungs. "Now then, Mr. Johnson," he reminded the chief engineer, "I believe you were about to show me to how to destroy Chrysalis."

Wide eyes staring where the unbreakable window used to be, Johnson nodded weakly, and led Seven to a console located directly in front of the now-empty windowframe. He sat down in front of a microphone and switched the mike on. "Activate Emergency Self-Destruct Sequence," he said, swallowing hard.

Voice-activated controls in 1974? Seven was impressed; Kaur had clearly harnessed the best efforts of some of the planet's top minds in the fulfillment of her ambitious design. *What a shame,* he thought, *that so much genius and creativity was spent on such a dangerous endeavor.*

A fresh onslaught of bullets suddenly zipped past Seven's head to slam into the ceiling behind him. Obviously, the guards on the level below were taking advantage of the Plexiglas window's disappearance. The barrage of gunfire, angling upward from the floor some fifty feet below, forced Seven to crouch down behind a sheltering console. "Are they out of their minds?" a distraught Johnson asked frantically. "What if they hit something important, costing us our control over the reactor?"

"Please remain calm, Mr. Johnson," Seven urged him, keeping the business end of his servo aimed at the back of the man's neck. Despite the coolness of the air-conditioning, sweat soaked the engineer's collar. He started to hyperventilate. Seven hoped that Johnson's middle-aged heart was up to the strain of trying to trigger a nuclear explosion while under fire. "Continue the procedure."

As quickly as it had begun, the scorching eruption of bullets trailed off, as cooler minds presumably recognized the considerable hazards of shooting up the reactor's control room. Johnson's breathing calmed a bit once the gunfire quieted, but his hands still trembled as he gripped the coiled throat of the microphone. "Repeat: Activate Emergency Self-Destruct Sequence. Control Room Authority: Johnson-slash-zeta."

Computers whirred and tractor-fed printers clacked away as the automated controls processed Johnson's request. "Control Room Authority accepted," a faceless voice intoned from a built-in loudspeaker. The computerized response lacked any trace of personality, quite unlike the acerbic tone Seven expected from his own Beta 5 computer. "Executive Authorization Required."

Johnson brought his mouth away from the microphone and whispered to Seven, who crouched beside him. "This is the part I told you about. Only the director can give the final command; the computer's programmed to respond to her voice alone."

"That won't be a problem," Seven whispered back, gesturing for Johnson to step aside. Seven sat down before the mike and massaged his throat, recalling the unique inflections and cadences of Sarina Kaur's speech. *If nothing else,* he reflected with a trace of bitterness, *I had opportunity enough to listen to her.*

Prompted by Seven, Johnson scribbled down the required command on the back of a green-and-white computer printout. Seven nodded and read the message out loud—in flawless mimicry of Kaur's own voice. "Executive Authorization granted: Kaur-slash-zeta-zeta."

"Emergency Self-Destruct Sequence confirmed," the mechanical voice acknowledged soullessly. "Please input timing sequence."

Next to the microphone was a digital display panel controlled by a ten-digit numerical keyboard. Flashing red numerals, currently set at 00:00:00, presumedly counted off the seconds and minutes and hours before the self-destruct sequence was completed. "Quickly," Seven demanded of Johnson, "how much time do you need to evacuate the entire Chrysalis installation?" He subjected the rattled engineer to a probing stare that tolerated neither evasion or deceit. "You must have had drills. Tell me the truth. How much time?"

"Twenty minutes," Johnson stammered. "Maybe thirty without any warning." He looked longingly at the sealed door to the control room, perhaps wondering how or if he would be able evacuate the doomed underground complex. "There are emergency, high-capacity elevators to the surface, and fully fueled desert transports hidden in the old fort."

"An admirable degree of preparation," Seven commented, genuinely thankful for Kaur's foresight; knowing that the misguided, but not necessarily evil, scientists and staff of Chrysalis had a viable escape plan eased his conscience concerning the atomic conflagration ahead. *Too bad the secret of the flesh-eating bacteria is likely to escape as well,* he thought, *but there's nothing that can be done about that now;* that particular genie was already effectively out of the bottle. Playing it safe, Seven keyed a thirty-minute countdown into the control panel, then had Johnson show him how to access the public-address system.

"Your attention please," he announced to all of Chrysalis. On the digital display panel, the countdown proceeded, a second at a time. It now read 00:29:16. "This is the intruder your leaders warned you of. I have taken control of the nuclear reactor station and initiated the emergency self-destruct sequence. You have thirty minutes to evacuate Chrysalis before this entire installation is destroyed. This is not a drill. This is not a hoax. You have thirty minutes to flee, starting now."

Fortunately, he considered, *all the previous disturbances created by Roberta, Isis, and myself will have already put the entire population on alert, which should help speed the evacua-*

tion. He looked at the glowing red numerals on the annunciator panel. 00:28:45.

Rising quickly from his seat at the console, Seven
crossed the control room to a fire-safety station near
the entrance. He smashed a sheet of protective glass
with his elbow, then pulled out a length of coiled fire
hose. He tossed the nozzle of the hose through the gap
where the picture window had been. The nozzle plum-
meted from sight, dragging several yards of hose behind it. Confused shouts rose from the floor of the
turbine room as the metal tip of the hose hit the cement pavement.

"You can go now, Mr. Johnson," Seven said, gesturing
toward the gray hose snaking across the floor. It wasn't
the most graceful way for the former hostage to exit
the control room, but it would suffice. Seven, on the
other hand, knew he had to stay until the very last moment, to insure that no one—specifically Sarina Kaur—
could override or cancel the self-destruct procedure.

"Don't shoot! It's me! Don't shoot!" Johnson yelled
to the guards below, as he scurried over to the edge of
the open window. With as much speed as his middle-
aged frame could muster, he awkwardly grabbed on to
the unspooled hose, tugged on it briefly to reassure
himself that it would support his weight, then dropped
over the ledge. "Don't shoot!"

Seven had the control room to himself now. He
looked at the illuminated red display. 00:27:16.

Twenty-seven minutes to go.

CHAPTER TWENTY

811 EAST 68TH STREET, APT. 12-B
NEW YORK CITY
UNITED STATES OF AMERICA
MAY 18, 1974

ALTHOUGH DINNERTIME IN INDIA, IT WAS SEVEN-THIRTY in the morning in New York. Roberta knew that the transporter lag would catch up with her eventually, but right now she was too busy to even try to reset her circadian rhythms. Depositing Isis onto Gary Seven's desk, she quickly paged the Beta 5 computer. "Computer on!"

Like the revolving secret door in an old haunted-house movie, shelves of mostly decorative books automatically rotated into the wall, replaced by the wall-sized computer interface. A circular monitor, about two feet in diameter, telescoped out from the reflective black panel centered in the matte-gray casing of the Beta 5, just above the protruding control panel. Prismatic waves of color cycled across the cosmic radiation gauge above the round viewscreen, while, to the immediate left of the monitor, flashing, multicolored strips of light appeared and disappeared at right angles to each other, charting the mental activity of the Beta 5's artificial intelligence. "Computer on," the super-computer responded. With every syllable, the blinking lights reconfigured themselves.

"Process incoming data," Roberta addressed the machine hastily. She aimed the twin antennae of her servo at the receptor site on the control panel and clicked the Transmit function; in theory, this should have transferred Chrysalis's exact geographical coordinates directly into the computer's memory, although Roberta always found the whole process somewhat magical. "I need you to scan that location right away!"

"Authorization required to conduct scan." The computer's feminine, electronic-sounding voice held a distinctly snippy tone that Roberta knew only too well. "Please identify yourself."

"You know who I am!" she blurted, seething with impatience. No matter what it was asked, the Beta 5 always made it sound as if Roberta was interrupting something far more important than, say, the fate of the planet. "We don't have time for this," she protested. She glanced at her wrist, then recalled that her watch had been confiscated by the guards at Chrysalis. Watch or no watch, though, she could feel vital seconds ticking away. "Just do what I told you!"

"Please identify yourself," the Beta 5 insisted, the embodiment of cybernetic stubbornness.

Roberta clenched her fists at her sides, nearly snapping her servo in two. "Roberta Lincoln. Agent 368." Her foot tapped irritably upon the orange shag carpet. "Satisfied?"

"Beginning scan," the computer allowed smugly. A

color image appeared on the viewer, depicting the lonely Rajput fortress at sunset. Violet shadows crept down the pitted sandstone walls of the fortress.

That's better, Roberta thought. *Now we're getting somewhere.* She hoped that some remnant of the gorgeous ruins would survive the underground explosion. "Deeper," she instructed the Beta 5. "Beneath the surface."

"Affirmative. Exceiver circuits tapping into existing surveillance system." Multiple views of Chrysalis's interior flashed upon the viewer, one after another, providing Roberta with glimpses of the complex's many labs and corridors. "Please narrow parameters."

Roberta nodded thoughtfully. *First the kids,* she remembered. *Then the animals.* "Prepare for remote transportation. Lock on to all humanoid life-forms . . . oh, one hundred pounds or less." *That should cover every toddler,* she thought confidently. *I sure didn't see any freakishly huge children in the DDU, and that's gotta be where any amazing colossal kids would've ended up.*

"Scanning," the Beta 5 reported. A moment later, a series of images flashed upon the monitor, one after another, presenting views of several different assortments of small children. Nearly all of the kids were sitting up in bed, looking alarmed and/or half-awake as they looked about in confusion. Rows of bunkbeds hinted at some sort of dormitory arrangements. Roberta didn't need to hear the warning sirens to know that Seven had thrown all of Chrysalis into chaos, right on schedule. "Transporter matrix locked on two hundred sixty-four life-forms."

Roberta whistled appreciatively at the sheer number of superchildren residing in the underground installation. Even working together, she and Seven would never have been able to transport so many children directly from the Chrysalis—there was a limit to how much you could accomplish with just a servo or two—but such a massive operation was well within the capabilities of the Beta 5. *Thank goodness for good old-fashioned alien know-how,* she thought, *attitude or no attitude.*

Staring at the hijacked images on the monitor, she gulped as a view of the Developmentally Deviant kids cycled onto the screen. "Computer, maintain surveillance of this site," she instructed quickly, feeling an urgent need to take a closer look at this particular dormitory. Even now, a few of the "imperfect" children appeared oblivious of the crisis going on around them; Roberta saw the little counting boy, his cheek twitching like crazy, calmly enumerating his toes, while most of his fellow misfits reacted fearfully to the commotion. Tears streamed down the cheeks of those children who were aware enough of their surroundings to be frightened. One scared child pulled all her sheets over her head in a desperate attempt to escape from the alarms, while the boy whose face resembled a lion's shredded his pillow with what looked like claws, adding a blizzard of feathers to the chaotic scene.

Disturbed once more by the DDU kids' varied afflictions, Roberta looked away from the screen. "Continue cycle of images," she told the Beta 5, feeling a lump in her throat. The view on the screen shifted to another location, and Roberta's gaze, returning to the monitor, promptly zeroed in on another familiar face, the one belonging to her little friend Noon. Dr. Kaur's remarkable offspring was, no surprise, coping with the crisis much more stoically than you'd expect of a child his age. Barefoot and in pajamas, he stood quietly on the carpeted floor between matching rows of bunks, with an alert yet pensive expression on his deceptively childlike face. He looked more intrigued than distressed by the unusual goings-on, and curious about what was going to happen next. A shudder ran through Roberta's spine as the small Indian boy stared directly at the security camera in the ceiling; for a heartbeat, she felt like his striking black eyes were looking right back at her.

Don't be silly, she scolded herself. *He's probably just wondering what his caretakers are up to.* Despite Noon's unnatural grace under pressure, Roberta was nevertheless appalled that Sarina Kaur was not there to comfort or care for him in this emergency. *He's her own son,* Roberta thought indignantly. *Where the heck is she?*

"Transporter matrix locked in," the Beta 5 reminded her pointedly. "Please specify destination of selected life-forms."

Tearing her gaze away from the eightfold images of confused and panicky children, Roberta hurriedly keyed in the coordinates for their associate's safe house in Puyallup. Even though she knew that what she was doing was necessary, especially with Seven intent on Chrysalis's utter destruction, she couldn't help feeling like a kidnapper. "Engage transporter," she ordered the computer.

Indicator lights blinked on and off upon the polished black face of the Beta 5. Above the monitor, the cosmic radiation gauge glowed like the aurora borealis.

Isis squawked rudely from the desktop nearby.

"Yeah, yeah," Roberta replied, knowing exactly what the gosh-darned cat was nagging her about. "Don't worry. I won't forget the tiger."

CHAPTER TWENTY-ONE

**CHRYSALIS BASE
INDIA**

"ATTENTION. TWENTY-FIVE MINUTES TO ATOMIC sterilization."

The automated warning echoed through every level of Chrysalis, spurring Maggie Erickson onward as she dashed for the children's dormitories. *I can't believe this is happening,* she thought fearfully, her heart pounding in her chest as she ran down the hall, passing equally desperate men and women rushing about on their own urgent missions. She gaped in amazement at the frenzied activity and distraught expressions she saw all around her. *How?* she wondered in disbelief. How had the well-ordered, scientifically structured routine of Chrysalis been transformed into this mad, unscheduled exodus?

It had all happened so quickly. She had been in one of the staff cafeterias, having coffee with her colleague and fiancé, Dr. Everett Walsh, when, all of a sudden, that bizarre and terrifying announcement had come over the PA system. Some stranger, informing them that Chrysalis was doomed, and that they had less than half an hour to evacuate the entire complex. *It's completely insane!* she thought.

Yet here she was, racing to see to her students, while the automated countdown provided a chilling confirmation of the intruder's ghastly prediction. Everett ran beside her, looking just as stunned and bewildered as everyone else.

Granted, they had all planned and drilled for just such an emergency situation, but Maggie had never really expected to ever have to actually evacuate Chrysalis. Not after all the precautions they'd taken to keep the very existence of the project concealed from the world.

The two instructors arrived at Children's Dormitory #5 within minutes. The swing-shift caretaker, Jessica McGivney, had already started getting the pajama-clad toddlers ready to leave, rousing them from bed and helping them into slippers and robes. Maggie offered a silent prayer of thanks to the gods of smaller class sizes, grateful that she was only personally responsible for the safety of Lot Epsilon, a grouping of no more than fifteen students. *Twenty-five minutes,* she thought. That should be just enough time to herd all the children to the nearest emergency exit.

"All right," she said loudly, clapping her hands together to get the children's attention. "Everyone be quiet and listen closely." She paused long enough for the chatter and general hubbub to die down, except for some mild sobs and sniffles, which Jessica and Everett attended to as best they could. "Everything is going to be okay," Maggie assured her underage audience, "but you need to do exactly as we practiced. Please line up by the door, quickly but calmly. Remember, no pushing."

To her relief, the children complied readily, with only minimal jostling and disarray. As usual, Noon was first in line, a position uncontested by any of the other toddlers. *He has a natural talent for leadership,* she noted, *just like his mother.* Noon's presence in Lot Epsilon only added to Maggie's acute sense of responsibility. *The director would never forgive me if anything happened to her boy.*

The very thought sent a shudder down her spine.

"Very good," she praised the class, forcing that nightmarish scenario out of her mind. Pride brought a small smile to her face as she watched the toddlers follow her directions to the letter; she doubted if any ordinary four-year-olds, conceived via a random shuffling of genes and chromosomes, could have coped even half so well with an emergency of this nature. "Now then," she instructed, opening the door to the corridor outside, "I want you to follow me as quickly as you can." She looked over the children's mussed and uncombed heads to her fellow caretakers. "Jessica, Everett, watch the rear of the line to make sure we don't lose any stragglers."

Before she could step through the door, however, something bizarre happened. From out of nowhere, a strange blue fog filled the dormitory, glowing like radioactive waste. For a few heart-stopping seconds, Maggie felt sure that the self-destructing reactor below them had released its blazing atomic venom prematurely. *Time's up,* she thought despairingly. *We're dead.*

But when the luminous mist did not scald the flesh from her bones, she realized that instant incineration was not in the offing. Nor did the strange fog assault her lungs, the way an enemy gas attack would. She was alive, she could breathe, she was still conscious; she just didn't know what was happening. All she felt was a peculiar tingling sensation all over her body, like static electricity. *What is this?* she worried, cringing instinctively from the touch of the mist. *I don't understand.*

The blue fog spread rapidly, growing thicker and more opaque by the second. Within moments, the mist completely hid the children and the other adults from view. "Maggie?" Everett called from deep within the swirling, incandescent fog, his voice almost lost amid the frightened cries and questions of the confused and disoriented children. She heard dozens of tiny slippers stampede upon the carpet as the neatly ordered line of toddlers broke apart into utter bedlam. "Maggie!" Everett shouted again. "Where are you?"

"Over here!" she yelled back. Desperate to save at least one of her precious charges, she reached into the fog and grabbed on to Noon. Thankfully, her prize student had not yet scattered like his classmates. *How brave!* she thought. *How superior!* She clutched Noon tightly against her waist, almost smothering him. "Don't be scared!" she exclaimed fervently. "I have you."

"I am *not* afraid," the boy insisted, his pride wounded. His diminutive frame maintained a tense, ready posture, neither pulling away nor yielding to Maggie's embrace. "But we should leave here. Now."

Yes! Maggie thought. *Of course!* She could come back for the other children later, or Everett and Jessica could take care of them. First, she had to get Noon to safety, and away from this insane, unnatural fog.

Then, just as she reached her decision, she felt Noon

literally *dissolving* within her grasp. His very flesh and bones seemed to melt away, becoming as insubstantial as the mist surrounding them. "No!" she shrieked in anguish, trying to hold on to him with all her might, but the evaporating child slipped like vapor through her fingers, leaving her empty-handed and alone. "Noon!" she screamed, so hard it left her throat raw, but it was too late. The little boy was gone.

The mysterious fog departed with him, dispersing as swiftly and inexplicably as it had come, leaving the three adults standing, baffled and aghast, in an empty dormitory. It was not only Noon who had disappeared into the mist, Maggie saw. All the children were missing. "Where are they?" Jessica asked stridently, her hands clutching her skull in horror. Her shocked face was white as the chalk they sometimes used in class. "Where have they gone? Where?"

Maggie knew just how the other woman felt. Panic and hysteria clawed at her sanity. How could a roomful of children just vanish like that? It was like magic—black magic—but Maggie had never believed in magic. *I'm a psychologist, dammit,* she thought, trying hard not to fall apart. This was like something out of some horrible fairy tale. The Pied Piper maybe, spiriting away the beloved children of Hamelin. . . .

"Twenty minutes to atomic sterilization."

So dumbfounded was Maggie by the children's miraculous disappearance that it took a few seconds for the full urgency of the automated warning to sink in. *Sterilization—hah!* she thought bitterly. She knew that was just a feeble euphemism for a full-scale nuclear explosion. *And why not? With the children gone, what is there left to save?*

Everett tugged on her arm. "Maggie, we need to hurry." Jessica fled the abandoned dormitory as Everett pleaded with his fiancée. "There's no choice, Maggie. We have to go."

"But the children . . ." she murmured. Her eyes searched the corners of the bunk-filled chamber, not yet accepting that so many toddlers could just vanish like that. Only empty beds met her hopeless gaze. "Lot Epsilon?"

"They're gone, Maggie. I don't know how, but they're gone." He glanced anxiously at the clock over the door, counting down the moments to Chrysalis's thermonuclear demise. "Please, we have to hurry!"

Reluctantly, Maggie looked away from the vacant dormitory, letting the other teacher drag her out of the children's quarters and into the hallway, where they joined a pell-mell rush to safety. Everett was right, she realized; there was nothing else to do. Chrysalis had become Hamelin, and the glorious future they had worked so hard to bring about had somehow been snatched away by forces unknown. She could only hope that, wherever Noon and his classmates had gone, they were someplace very far from the radioactive inferno Chrysalis was about to become.

I should have killed that smug American bastard when I had the chance! Donald Archibald Williams raged as he keyed his security code into the electronic lock guarding the top-secret germ-warfare labs on Level Four. His ruddy face was flushed and sweating, and his frantic sprint from his quarters, where he had been enjoying a much-needed snooze, had left him panting and short of breath. The blaring emergency sirens wreaked havoc with his migraine, sending agonizing pulsations through his temples with every clangorous repetition of the alarm. *I knew he was trouble the minute I saw him.*

He cursed Sarina Kaur as well, for dragging him into this bloody project in the first place. Not that he'd had much choice in the matter; having uncovered his own legally dubious efforts at human cloning, along with its unfortunate casualties, Kaur had all too easily blackmailed him into joining Chrysalis. Now, with the entire insane enterprise seemingly crashing down all around him, he couldn't help wondering if he wouldn't have been better off facing the music in the first place.

A loud hiss escaped from inside the lab as the airtight metal door unsealed itself. Only three individuals in Chrysalis had access to the facilities on Level Four: Kaur, Lozinak, and himself. Now, with his future suddenly thrown into uncertainty, Williams intended to take advantage of that privileged status to secure a crucial bit of insurance to help him weather whatever storms might lie ahead. *Nothing like a unique, new bioweapon to use as a bargaining chip,* he thought, formulating desperate new plans on the run. *The Russians are bound to be interested in Kaur's pet bacteria, and maybe the Americans as well. . . .*

"Attention. Twenty-two minutes to atomic sterilization," the PA system announced, continuing its inexorable countdown. Acutely aware that time was rapidly ticking away, Williams ignored the protective biohazard suits hanging inside the entrance to Level Four, hurrying on to the inner chambers of the laboratory. Empty steel vats, waiting for the vast quantities of peptone that had just arrived from America, rested between aisles of sterile white tiles and plastic tubing. Williams glanced nervously over his shoulder, half-expecting to be surprised by either Seven or Sarina Kaur, arriving just in time to catch him in the act. He wasn't sure who he was most afraid of confronting. Kaur, most likely; as far as he knew, Seven had never ordered the cold-blooded execution of any of his subordinates.

Another set of airlocks stood between him and the object of his impromptu shopping expedition. Sweaty fingers pounded a frustratingly long numerical sequence into a mounted keypad, and he waited impatiently for the lock to verify his security clearance. He yanked hard on the gleaming chrome door handle the minute he heard the welcome hiss of escaping air, and hurriedly entered the earthquake-proof chamber beyond.

Strictly off-limits to all but Kaur and her most trusted associates, the cool, air-conditioned metal vault contained only a locked filing cabinet and a refrigerator hooked up to its own emergency generator. William attacked the filing cabinet first, hastily unlocking the top drawer and rifling through an assortment of tightly packed hanging folders. An adhesive label reading "Carn-Strep—gen.18.7" identified the specific file he required. *Yes!* he thought avidly. *Just what I was looking for.*

Enclosed was the exact genetic sequence for the latest generation of Sarina Kaur's carnivorous streptococcus. With this recipe, he knew, and the proper facilities, anyone with sufficient know-how and desire would be able to re-create the fearsome flesh-eating bacteria, and perhaps even improve on it. For himself, Williams only wanted to use the formula to buy himself a comfortable retirement somewhere far from the reach of anyone who might come looking for him. The West Indies, maybe, or South America.

He glanced quickly at the nearby refrigerator, containing actual samples of the modified Strep A bacteria. He briefly considered snatching a carefully sealed specimen of the vicious microorganism, for added insurance, but promptly decided against it. Transporting a living sample of the bug, even in an unbreakable plastic container, would be just too nerve-racking, particularly given the uncertain exodus ahead.

"No need to get greedy," he muttered. The formula for the disease was more than enough. He pocketed a folded piece of paper bearing the relevant genetic sequence, then looked toward the exit. His head throbbed miserably.

"Attention. Twenty-one minutes to atomic sterilization."

Time to go, he realized. In a moment of perverse defiance, he tugged open the door of the refrigeration unit, exposing the vulnerable bacteria inside to room temperature, not to mention the coming nuclear holocaust. *Take that, you blackmailing witch,* he thought. *Let your microscopic little monsters go up in flames with the rest of this wretched place!*

Carrying a stolen recipe for a biological nightmare, along with half-cooked plans for the future, Williams rushed out of Level Four in search of safety—and whatever else fate had in store for him.

CHAPTER TWENTY-TWO

00:19:51

LESS THAN TWENTY MINUTES TO GO, SEVEN NOTED FROM his seat at the control panel. He studied the various gauges on display, carefully monitoring the self-destructive process unfolding within the concrete reactor silo. According to the instrumentation, temperatures within the reactor core were rapidly approaching two thousand degrees Celsius, while the chain reaction building inside the silo would soon pass the point of no return, as the uranium fuel rods melted into a single critical mass. Seven intended to stay at the reactor controls until the very last minute, just in case Sarina Kaur and her followers attempted to abort the coming explosion.

As he familiarized himself with Chrysalis's primary source of energy, he had to admire, in a perverse fashion, the manner in which the reactor had been expressly designed to provide a spectacular funeral pyre for the project, had circumstances so required. Ordinarily, the breakdown of this sort of primitive pressurized-water reactor would only result in a catastrophic meltdown, not a full-scale nuclear explosion, but the Chrysalis reactor was different; as far as he could tell from the schematics on display in the control room, the processed uranium at this reactor's core had deliberately been arranged in precisely the right quantity and configuration to guarantee an atomic explosion deep beneath the desolate sands of the Great Thar Desert.

"Typical," Seven muttered under his breath. The reactor's insidious design seemed emblematic of the project's overall approach: the latest in cutting-edge technology inextricably wed to an overwhelming potential for disaster. *The sooner the whole endeavor is obliterated,* he resolved, *the better.*

"Fifteen minutes to atomic sterilization."

The recorded announcement confirmed the digital readout before him. Seven prayed that Chrysalis's numerous inhabitants had heeded the previous warnings, and that they were already on their way to safety. He worried less about the fate of the project's blameless superchildren; Roberta and Isis, he knew, could be trusted to carry out that end of the mission. If only the larger problem caused by the children's very existence could be dealt with so easily . . . !

A blinking red annunciator light alerted Seven to a worrisome buildup of hydrogen gas within the reactor core. While insufficient to halt the chain reaction itself, the excess hydrogen could cause preliminary explosions inside the concrete silo, explosions that might pose some danger to Seven himself. *Best to keep an eye on that,* he determined, at least until it was time for him to transport out of the doomed complex, roughly ten minutes from now.

To his surprise, however, an explosion came not from the enormous cement cylinder beyond the open window, but from the sealed metal door at the far end of the control room. The powerful blast literally blew the heavy metal gate inward and out of the doorframe, while the accompanying shock wave knocked Seven out of his seat and onto the floor. Billowing clouds of black smoke permeated the control room, making his eyes sting, and the acrid scent of crude plastic explosives assailed his nostrils. *What in the Aegis's name . . . ?* he thought, his ears ringing from the thundering detonation.

Dazed, he lifted his battered head from the floor just in time to witness Dr. Sarina Kaur come striding through the hazy fumes into the control room. She held a Walther PPK pistol in her hand and a determined expression on her face. Behind her, as the smoke quickly cleared, Seven glimpsed the now-open doorway, through which he spotted the elevator and foyer beyond. Kaur carefully stepped around the scorched and crumpled remains of the fallen gate as she aimed the muzzle of her weapon at the stunned and defenseless man upon the floor. "Please don't get up, Mr. Seven," she instructed him, her icy tone belying the blazing hatred in her dark eyes. "And keep your hands where I can see them; we don't want another demonstration of your singularly efficacious penmanship."

His servo tucked away in his pocket, Seven avoided any sudden moves, not wanting to provoke Kaur to further violence. "Listen to me," he beseeched her hoarsely. Lingering traces of smoke irritated his throat as he spoke. "You have to believe me, this is for the best."

"Silence!" Kaur barked. She was without her ubiquitous Sikh bodyguards, whom Seven assumed she must have given leave to evacuate with the rest of Chrysalis's personnel. He found it hard to reconcile that concern for her people with the ruthlessness which he knew, from firsthand experience, she was capable of, but then, he recalled acidly, twentieth-century humans, no matter how brilliant, still tended to divide the world into Us and Them, with only the former worthy of concern. *I wonder if Kaur's all-star team of geniuses managed to eliminate that trait from the human genome?* he mused. *Somehow I doubt it.*

Keeping her gun pointed at Seven, Kaur hurried to the control panel Seven had just vacated. Without bothering to right the toppled chair next to the console, she flicked a switch on the control panel and leaned toward the attached microphone. "Abort Emergency Self-Destruct Sequence," she commanded emphatically. "Executive Authority Kaur-slash-alpha-alpha."

Was it still possible to halt the chain reaction? Seven honestly wasn't sure, and, judging from the worried expression on the director's face, neither was Sarina Kaur. How could anyone make reliable predictions about such an archaic and unstable piece of atomic engineering?

"Attempting to abort emergency self-destruct sequence," the computer reported. *Easier said than done, apparently,* Seven noted, as Kaur stared uneasily at the gauges before her. Seven himself couldn't see the displays from his position on the floor, but he guessed that the data was not encouraging. "We need to get out of here," he told Kaur sincerely. "Please believe me, if not for yourself, then for the child you carry. Let me up and I can get us both to safety."

"Quiet!" Kaur snapped at him, punctuating her command with a gunshot that burrowed a hole in the floor in front of Seven. The gravid geneticist frantically worked the controls of the reactor, trying to undo the irreversible.

"Ten minutes until atomic sterilization."

All of Kaur's attention was focused on the reactor controls. *Now is my chance,* Seven realized. Mobilizing his bruised and aching muscles for one more superhuman feat, the extraterrestrial operative sprang to his feet and hurled himself out the empty windowframe looking out over the turbine chamber. "No!" Kaur shouted angrily, squeezing the trigger of her Walther PPK, but she succeeded only in chipping out more fragments of the control-room floor.

Seven fell fifty feet to the level below. The impact when he hit the ground jarred his bones, but he absorbed the blow as best he could by tucking his limbs against his torso and rolling as he landed, then used his momentum to end up standing upright upon the asphalt floor of the turbine room. He found himself not far from the base of the massive containment silo. Iron scaffolding circled the gigantic concrete cylinder, then stretched out over the nearby turbines, which seemed to roar even more deafeningly as the reactor core overheated, sending a torrent of hot steam through the power-generating turbines. Seven wondered how much longer the immense turbines would be able to withstand the strain.

"Attempting to abort emergency self-destruct sequence," the loudspeakers announced over the churning din of the turbines. "Ten minutes and holding."

Damn, Seven thought. Kaur had succeeded in arresting the chain reaction, if not yet reversing it entirely. In
his mind, he visualized the carbon-alloy control rods
sliding back into place between the partially melted
uranium fuel rods, preventing the radioactive ore from
attaining critical mass. *I can't let that happen,* he vowed,
hurriedly climbing the scaffolding between the silo and
the turbines. *I have to make sure that reactor blows, no matter what happens to Kaur and myself.*

Ideally, of course, he would just transport the control
rods out of the reactor core, but the intense amount of
radiation generated at the core, not to mention the
dense, reinforced shielding, made such an operation
problematic. Seven's eyes narrowed shrewdly as he contemplated the massive pipes carrying much-needed
coolant into the containment silo. Fortunately, there was
more than one way to cook a reactor.

Setting the servo for a wide-angle beam, he targeted
a stretch of pipe less than twenty feet away. The dense
metal conduit, painted a dull green, dissolved beneath
the influence of the disintegration beam, spilling a cascade of radioactive H_2O onto the floor of the vast
chamber. Even located upon the scaffolding, several
feet above the flood, Seven winced at the thought of
what the invisible roentgens were surely doing to his
own cellular structure. *I'll have to give myself a couple of
strong antiradiation pills,* he realized, *provided I make it
back to Manhattan at all.*

He watched with grim satisfaction as the reactor's
precious coolant gushed onto the floor. Without
freshly chilled water to carry away the awesome heat
being produced by the near-meltdown, the tempera-

ture of the reactor core would inevitably build toward its ultimate apocalyptic demise, despite Kaur's futile attempts to bring the feverish reactor back under control. He didn't need X-ray eyes to picture the coolant draining away from the reactor, exposing ever more of the volatile fuel rods. *Defuse that disaster if you can,* he silently challenged Kaur, *but I don't envy the odds against you.*

"Unable to abort emergency self-destruct sequence," the robotic voice confirmed. "Nine minutes to atomic sterilization."

Within seconds, the mighty turbines ground noisily to a halt, literally running out of steam. Seven felt the scaffolding quiver beneath his feet as the powerful engines struggled unsuccessfully to keep running. Grabbing a safety rail to steady himself, he wrapped his fingers tightly around the vibrating metal. "Kaur!" he shouted, his hoarse voice finally audible now that the turbines had quieted. "It's time to go. Let me help you escape!"

While reluctant to reveal too many of his secrets to Sarina Kaur, Seven realized that the only way left to save the ambitious scientist was to transport her to a less hazardous location. But would the fanatical director cooperate with this last-ditch emergency measure?

A barrage of gunfire suggested otherwise, the harsh report of Kaur's gun echoing eerily in the suddenly silent turbine room. "Never!" she declared furiously, looking down at Seven from the brink of the control room, her pregnant form framed by the borders of the missing picture window. "I'm not going anywhere—and neither are you!"

Seven ducked behind the curve of the silo, which

shielded him from Kaur's deadly bullets. He didn't want to think about what the unchecked radiation was doing to the woman's unborn child. "Don't be insane, Dr. Kaur," he called out. Cautiously extending his servo beyond the concrete barrier of the silo, he tried to get a lock on Kaur, but the surging radiation made it impossible to get a reliable reading on the woman from this far away. She would have to let him get closer to her before he could 'port both of them to safety, a scenario that was looking increasingly unlikely. "Chrysalis is doomed," he yelled, still hoping he could reason with Kaur before it was too late. "There's nothing else you can do, and we're running out of time!"

"Reactor core approaching critical mass," the loudspeaker announced, as though seconding Seven's impassioned appeal to Kaur's sanity. "Five minutes to atomic sterilization."

Seven hoped the computer's warning would prove more persuasive than his own disregarded words. Would Kaur's instinct for self-preservation win out over her desire for vengeance? He prayed that her remarkable brain would come to its senses in time. "Listen to me!" he shouted urgently. "You don't have to die here!"

Kaur laughed bitterly, holding her smoking Walther before her. "Are you familiar with the concept of *jauhar,* Mr. Seven? It's a venerable Rajput tradition, practiced for centuries in fortresses such as the one above us. Faced with certain defeat, the women and children would set themselves on fire rather than surrender to the enemy." She fired the pistol at the concrete silo until she ran out of bullets, then carelessly tossed the weapon into the churning radioactive flood below the window ledge. "Perhaps the old ways are best after all. . . ."

Seven placed his palm against the wall of the containment silo, feeling a definite tremor in the thick concrete wall. The hydrogen gas, he remembered, building up within the core, ready to ignite. The scaffolding shuddered alarmingly beneath the soles of his shoes, while a spidery network of cracks spread across the face of the silo. "One minute to atomic sterilization."

No more time, he realized despairingly, even as an early, prenuclear explosion, deep within the reactor's interior, jolted the scaffolding, throwing Seven roughly against a safety rail. Grunting in pain as his bruised ribs were hammered again, he clicked his servo.

The glowing blue fog preceded the mushroom cloud by seconds.

CHAPTER TWENTY-THREE

811 EAST 68TH STREET
NEW YORK CITY
UNITED STATES OF AMERICA
MAY 19, 1974

"THE GOVERNMENT OF INDIA," WALTER CRONKITE intoned solemnly upon the viewscreen of the Beta 5, "has confirmed that an underground nuclear test, the first in their nation's history, occurred yesterday beneath the deserts of Rajasthan. Prime Minister Indira Gandhi insists that the test was merely 'a peaceful nuclear explosion experiment,' and that her regime has no intention of developing offensive nuclear weapons. Neighboring nations, however, most notably China and Pakistan, have reacted with alarm and suspicion. . . ."

"Lower audio transmission," Gary Seven instructed the computer, having apparently heard enough. He sat behind his marble and mahogany desk, his chin resting pensively upon his cradled fingers. Purple smudges persisted beneath his eyes, and his lean face was even gaunter than usual, yet his gaze was clear and alert. He had not yet fully recovered from his ordeal in India, but Roberta thought he was already looking more like his old self. *I guess the Aegis really knew what they were doing,* she thought, *when they bred Seven and his ancestors for endurance.*

"So," she asked from the couch, where she was enjoying the relaxed aftermath of another successful mission, "do you think that people are going to actually buy that cover story?"

"Why shouldn't they?" Seven replied. "Sadly, rampant nuclear proliferation is a hallmark of this era. More importantly, it is in the best interests of all concerned, including those in the Indian government with connections to the Chrysalis Project, that the truth remain a closely guarded secret."

"What about Lozinak and the others?" she asked. "Won't they try to rebuild somewhere else?" She liked to think that Viktor, Walter, and their well-intentioned but misguided colleagues had survived the fiery subterranean cataclysm (except for Sarina Kaur, of course), but she didn't want to have to shut them down again a few years from now. As far as she was concerned, Dr. Veronica Neary, that celebrated geneticist, had spliced her last piece of DNA.

"That is unlikely to be a problem," Seven assured her. Isis, looking happy to be home, strolled across the desktop before hopping lightly onto the carpet. "I intend to report the activities and locations of the key conspirators to our contacts in their respective governments, which should be able to keep the guilty scientists under surveillance from now on. That should be enough to keep them from setting up shop again. In addition, I believe I can arrange for the U.S. National

Academy of Sciences to call for a moratorium on all genetic engineering, at least temporarily." A look of profound regret passed over his face. "Without the inspiration and leadership of Sarina Kaur, I suspect that Chrysalis has been extinguished forever."

His hopeful prediction was tainted by one lingering worry. "I only wish I knew who, if anyone, ended up with the genetic sequence for Kaur's mutated streptococcus." His fingers drummed unhappily upon the polished obsidian desktop. "According to Kaur, the most advanced version of the germ was not yet rapidly contagious, but I fear we'll have to keep our eyes out for outbreaks of flesh-eating bacteria in the decades to come."

"And the kids?" Roberta asked worriedly. Even though she had successfully transported every one of the supertoddlers away from Chrysalis before it exploded, she couldn't help fretting about the children's futures. *In a way, I'm responsible for them now.*

"That poses a genuine dilemma," Seven conceded. "We can hardly report their identities to the authorities; despite their ominous potential, they cannot be held accountable for their own creation." He sighed wearily, and slumped back into his leather chair. "The best we can do is scatter the project's children via responsible child-placement organizations throughout the world and hope for the best. Perhaps by separating the children, and by removing them from Kaur's corrupting influence, we can minimize their impact on humanity's future history."

"You really think so?" To be honest, she'd been more concerned about the kids themselves than their effect on the world, but she supposed Seven had a point. Even as munchkins, the Chrysalis kids had been pretty darn impressive; heaven only knew what they'd be like once they grew up.

"I wish I could be more certain," Seven said gravely. The apprehension in his voice caught Roberta's attention; it wasn't often that Gary Seven admitted to uncertainty. "The only alternative, however, is unacceptable."

Roberta knew what he meant. Despite his covert efforts to push humanity in the right direction, Seven drew the line at outright assassination. *And thank goodness for that!* she thought.

"We should definitely keep an eye on the children, of course," Seven added, clearly thinking ahead. "Particularly that little Indian boy you mentioned, the son of Sarina Kaur. The genetically enhanced offspring of Kaur is not someone we can afford to ignore." Leaning forward, he scribbled a note to himself on a piece of blank stationery. "What was his name again?"

"Noon," Roberta answered. The boy's dark, intelligent eyes gazed up from the depths of her memory, holding the promise—or the threat—of the man he would someday become. A chill ran through her, despite the pleasant springtime weather. "Short for Khan Noonien Singh."

CHANDIGARH
THE PUNJAB, INDIA
SEVERAL WEEKS LATER . . .

Lightning flashed to the south, heralding the coming monsoon. A book upon his lap, Noon sat on the roof terrace of his new home, staring up at the cloudless blue sky above him. Fragrant basil plants and leafy ferns sprouted from polished brass urns placed strategically around the rooftop, transforming the terrace into an open-air garden. A mosaic of white and blue china decorated the floor of the terrace, reflecting the late-afternoon sunshine.

If he was honest with himself, Noon had to admit that, after growing up underground, he still found the wide-open sky rather intimidating. Unlike the comforting security of Chrysalis, the soaring heavens made him feel exposed and all too vulnerable, both to the elements and to the unpredictable whims of fate. The latter, he had learned only too recently, could strike without warning, overturning one's entire existence. (Sometimes in the evening, right before he fell asleep, he imagined he could still hear the warning sirens blaring, the way they had the night his life changed forever.)

Unwilling to surrender to either fate or fear, however, he'd resolved to confront any trace of agoraphobia by spending as much time as possible up on the roof, in defiance of both his qualms and the oppressive summer heat. *Nothing in this new world will get the better of me,* the boy vowed, sweating beneath the sun. *Not even myself.*

He still missed his mother, of course, not to mention his teachers and classmates, but he was adapting to his changed circumstances, just as any truly superior being would. His new foster parents, distant relations of his deceased mother, were kind enough, and capable of providing him with a comfortable home environment. Prabhot Singh worked as a civil engineer for the city, while his wife Sharan illustrated children's books. Childless themselves, they doted on the newly orphaned Noon, marveling at his obvious talent, strength, and precociousness. Neither Prabhot nor Sharan were his intellectual equals, naturally, but the challenge of exploring a brand-new world, as well as the Singhs' admirably well equipped library, were providing him with sufficient mental stimulation, at least for the time being.

Noon lowered his gaze to the thick hardcover book spread open upon his lap. Certainly, he couldn't complain about his current reading material. *The Life of Alexander the Great* was an engrossing tale, made all the more thrilling by Noon's knowledge that all of it was absolutely true. Caught up in its inspiring account of conquest and glory, the young boy flipped the pages eagerly, temporarily abandoning modern-day Chandigarh for the bloodstained battlefields of ancient Greece and Persia. He saw himself, with Alexander, at the head of a mighty army, conquering city after city, nation after nation. Thebes fell, and Tyre, Jerusalem, and Babylon, until the entire ancient world, all the way to the eternally flowing Indus, surrendered to the power and destiny of a single indomitable will. Noon's heart, stronger and more resilient than any ordinary child's, beat in unison with the bygone war drums sounding in his brain, while visions of empire filled his imagination. . . .

Thunder rolled, and dark clouds gathered on the horizon, as the monsoon drew ever nearer.

CHAPTER TWENTY-FOUR

STARDATE 7004.1

"CAPTAIN, WE ARE APPROACHING SYCORAX."

Spock's voice, emerging from the intercom in Kirk's quarters, roused the captain from his historical research. *So soon?* he thought. It felt as though he had just begun delving into the *Enterprise*'s extensive database, but, no, upon reflection, he realized that a full three Earth days had passed. "Understood," he replied promptly, rising from his desk and switching off the computer terminal. "I'm on my way."

Although present-day responsibilities now demanded his attention, the events of the distant past lingered in his mind, following him through the ship's corridors all the way to the nearest turbolift. *So that's how it all began,* he mused. *I don't envy the decision that Gary Seven and Roberta faced back in 1974.* There was no way, of course, that Seven could have known for certain how dangerous Khan and his fellow supermen would become, but, even if he had, what else could he have done? How do you protect the future from the threat posed by innocent children?

Definitely a dilemma to keep in mind when dealing with the Paragon Colony, he resolved. The turbolift came to a stop and Kirk stepped out onto the bridge, where he saw that McCoy had already joined Spock and the others. The Vulcan first officer surrendered the captain's chair to Kirk and took his accustomed place at the science station. "As you can see," he informed Kirk, "Sycorax is now within visual range."

On the viewscreen, a solitary planet spun slowly against a backdrop of star-studded darkness. Swirling clouds, dirty yellow in hue, blanketed the approaching sphere, concealing the planet's terrain from sight, while periodic flashes of intense electrical activity lit up the churning clouds from within. Kirk looked in vain for any visible sign of habitation. "Not exactly the most inviting world I've ever seen," he commented out loud.

"Indeed," Spock acknowledged. The light from his scanner cast deep blue shadows on his refined Vulcan features. "Long-range sensors indicate that Sycorax is a Class-K planet, roughly comparable to Venus in Earth's own solar system. The atmosphere consists primarily of carbon dioxide, with gaseous sulfuric acid providing a heavy layer of cloud cover at an altitude of approximately fifty to sixty meters. Wind velocity in the upper atmosphere exceeds three hundred and fifty kilometers per hour. The temperature at the surface can surpass four hundred and sixty degrees centigrade, while the atmospheric pressure is approximately ninety-one point four times that of Earth at sea level, and equivalent to the pressure half a mile below the surface of the

Pacific Ocean. Gravity is point eight-seven-three standard, and the planet itself is composed primarily of nickel-iron and various silicates. Hardened lava plains cover seventy-five point eight percent of the surface, with the rest of the terrain taken up by a variety of craters, mountains, and plateaus. Sensors detect no indigenous life-forms. . . ."

"Thank you, Mr. Spock," Kirk interrupted. He rested his chin on his knuckles as he contemplated the fog-wreathed planet. "I get the idea. Sycorax is not exactly the local garden spot."

"It makes Siberia sound like a resort town on the Black Sea," Ensign Chekov observed from his post at the navigation console, to the captain's right.

"Hell of place to start a colony," McCoy groused. The doctor stood behind the central command area, leaning against the cherry-red safety rail. "Let alone a genetically engineered utopia."

"Perhaps they had their reasons, Doctor," Spock stated. "Certainly, the Federation has established colonies on less hospitable worlds, when there was sufficient incentive to do so."

"But what sort of incentive could possibly induce people to spend over a hundred years in such a lifeless hellhole?" McCoy argued, not willing to concede the point to Spock.

Kirk decided to head off any long debate. "I guess we'll find out soon enough, Bones," he said. "Mr. Sulu, place us in orbit around the planet. Lieutenant Uhura, see if you can hail the colony."

Sulu and Uhura carried out his orders with their customary speed and efficiency. Within minutes, the communications officer had made contact with the planet on the viewscreen. "I have the regent of the colony for you, Captain," she reported.

"Thank you, Lieutenant." Kirk nodded toward the main viewer. "Onscreen."

Sycorax's stormy, amber countenance was replaced by the head and shoulders of an attractive Asian woman, possibly in her mid-sixties. Shrewd black eyes examined Kirk from a round, benign-seeming face framed by short white curls and bangs. *At least she doesn't look like Khan,* Kirk thought, then introduced himself.

"Welcome to our system," the woman responded warmly. "I'm Masako Clarke, current regent of the Paragon Colony. Thank you for answering our invitation."

"Thank you for having us," Kirk said diplomatically. "My officers and I are looking forward to learning more about your society. When would be a convenient time for us to beam down a landing party?"

Clarke gave the matter a moment's thought, then smiled out from the screen. "Well, it's late afternoon here. Why don't you give me an hour or so to prepare a proper reception, then come down whenever you're ready. I'm afraid, though, that I'm going to have to ask you to take a shuttlecraft instead of using your transporters. The colony is protected by a permanent forcefield, for reasons which I can explain more fully during our meetings. I hope that's not too much of an inconvenience."

"Not at all," Kirk assured her. Piloting a shuttlecraft through the planet's turbulent atmosphere was going to mean a bit of a bumpy ride, but it wasn't anything the shuttle's own deflector shields couldn't handle. "A shuttle it is. I'll see you in an hour then, Regent Clarke."

"Please," she insisted. "Call me Masako."

Less than sixty minutes later, the landing party assembled in the shuttlebay. For this initial encounter, Kirk had chosen to keep the mission's personnel down to the minimum: just himself, McCoy, and a single security officer, discreetly armed with a compact Type-1 phaser. Kirk himself took the pilot's seat in the *Columbus-2*, while the security officer, Lieutenant Seth Lerner, occupied the copilot's chair. Muttering under his breath, McCoy strapped himself into the seat directly behind Kirk. "An awful lot of trouble," the doctor complained, "just to hear a sales pitch for genetic engineering."

Kirk fired up the shuttle's impulse engines, then used the ship's communicator to contact Spock on the bridge. "Last chance, Spock," he joked over the carrier wave. "Are you sure you don't want to come along?"

"Perhaps on some later occasion," Spock's voice replied. Kirk could easily visualize the Vulcan's cool, thoughtful expression as he explained his reasoning. "As far as we know, the inhabitants of the Paragon Colony have spent over a century attempting to perfect the human genome, so it is not implausible that they might be disturbed, or perhaps even offended, by the presence of a human/Vulcan hybrid." Spock's dispassionate tone suggested that he was not at all personally offended by any hypothetical prejudices on the part of the Paragon colonists. "Until you and Dr. McCoy have determined otherwise, it seems more politic for me to remain aboard the ship at this moment in time."

"An admirably prudent course of action, Mr. Spock." As ever, Kirk was unable to find fault with Spock's analysis. "Good to know I'm leaving the ship in such responsible hands."

"I would be appalled if you had any thoughts to the contrary," Spock answered. "May you a have successful meeting with the regent and her associates."

"Will do," the captain said. He checked the control panel to make sure that the shuttlecraft was sealed and fully pressurized. "Preparing for takeoff. Kirk out."

"About time," McCoy grumbled behind him. "Let's get this over with."

"Why, Bones," Kirk teased the irascible physician, "I thought you preferred old-fashioned vehicles to transporter beams?"

McCoy snorted disparagingly. "Not when it involves flying into a thunderstorm the size of a continent! If man were meant to travel through that kind of toxic tempest, we'd have evolved on Venus instead."

Kirk noticed that Lieutenant Lerner was starting to look a bit uneasy. The security officer was relatively new to the *Enterprise*, having recently transferred from the *U.S.S. Forge*. "Don't let the doctor's Cassandra act get to you, crewman," he advised. "His general attitude is only slightly less ominous than his bedside manner."

"Says the man who can talk a supercomputer into committing suicide," McCoy retorted, eliciting an amused grin from Kirk.

"Touché, Doctor." Kirk waited until the shuttlebay was fully depressurized, then watched as the clamshell doors slid open in front of the shuttlecraft, providing access to the airless void outside the *Enterprise*. He pulled back on the throttle, and the shuttle lifted off from the launchpad, cruising slowly toward the open archway and out into space. Artificial gravity kept the landing party comfortably secured in their seats.

Once clear of the larger spacecraft, Kirk immediately set course for Sycorax. The hostile, cloud-covered planet looked considerably larger and more forbidding from the cockpit of the *Columbus* than it had from the *Enterprise*'s more spacious bridge.

At full impulse, it took them less than five minutes to enter the planet's atmosphere. The transition was like going from a clear summer night into the heart of a hurricane. Cyclonic winds buffeted the shuttle, shaking Kirk and his companions in their seats. Lightning flashed all around them, presaging titanic bursts of thunder that could be heard even through the shuttle's insulated bulkheads. Flying droplets of sulfuric acid pelted *Columbus*'s duranium hull, although the ship's deflectors protected the outer ceramic plating from the acid's corrosive effect. Struggling with the controls, Kirk and Lerner worked in tandem to keep the shuttle on a steady downward trajectory. Even with their forward lights on full power, Kirk and his copilot were unable to see beyond the smoggy yellow haze through which they descended. Kirk had to navigate from instrumentation alone, keeping a watchful eye on the astrogator as he followed a homing signal provided by the colony. A bolt of lightning struck *Columbus,* rocking the shuttle so hard that McCoy gasped out loud. "I knew this was a bad idea," he said.

"Only a few more meters," Kirk promised him. As they neared the surface, the temperature outside the shuttle increased dramatically, boiling away the billowing clouds of acid rain so that the atmosphere gradually cleared, improving visibility. Kirk could now glimpse a cracked, arid landscape through the last retreating wisps of vapor. Vast basaltic plains, occasionally pitted with gigantic craters, stretched for countless kilometers between rocky mountain ranges totally devoid of snow or vegetation. Waning sunlight, filtered through the dense, yellow-white cloud cover, gave the lifeless wasteland a dull beige tint. *Spock certainly didn't exaggerate Sycorax's desolate nature,* Kirk concluded. *Hard to imagine anyone would want to settle down here for good.*

"Atmospheric pressure approaching eight thousand kilopascals," Lerner reported. McCoy whistled appreciatively; that was enough pressure to crush a humanoid body many times over. "And rising."

Kirk nodded, not too worried yet. He had plenty of faith in Starfleet engineering. Perspiration glistened upon his brow as some of the blistering heat outside penetrated the shuttle's bulkheads. "Structural integrity holding?"

"Yes, sir," the security officer reported.

"Very good, Mr. Lerner. Let me know if there's any change." Despite his confidence in the shuttle's construction, Kirk knew that the sooner they reached their destination, the better. Peering through the cockpit windshield at the barren terrain below, Kirk spotted something rising in the middle of an empty plain directly ahead of them. Its smooth lines and perfect symmetry clearly advertised its artificial nature. "Look, right ahead. That must be the colony."

The man-made structure appeared to expand in size as the shuttlecraft descended toward it. The Paragon Colony turned out to be enclosed in a large domed biosphere, approximately fifty kilometers in diameter and apparently built atop an immense crater in the planet's scorched and splintered surface. The dome was a pale translucent green, constructed seamlessly from a substance Kirk couldn't immediately identify. *Some variety of transparent aluminum?* he speculated. A sparkling, bluish aura hinted at the existence of the forcefield defending the dome from the planet's unforgiving environment.

A tractor beam soon locked on to the shuttle, and Kirk surrendered control of the vessel to operators within the colony. Automated doors opened near the base of the dome, and the tractor beam smoothly guided the shuttle through a dock-sized airlock and into a large interior hangar. Reduced to sight-seeing for the moment, Kirk glanced around the cavernous landing bay, spotting a wide assortment of vehicles parked within the hangar. Ranging from small scout ships to massive cargo haulers, the heavily reinforced transports appeared durable enough to explore and endure the intense heat and pressure outside the dome.

Columbus shuddered momentarily as its stabilizers and landing pads touched down on the floor of the hangar. Behind Kirk, McCoy expelled an audible sigh of relief. "Don't go kissing the ground once you're out of the shuttle, Doctor," Kirk cautioned him. "You might give our hosts the wrong idea."

External sensors indicated that it was safe to exit the shuttlecraft, so Kirk unsealed the main doors and stepped out onto the floor outside. Sycorax's gravity, slightly weaker than Earth standard, added a little extra bounce to his step. The air was cool and comfortable compared with the overheated interior of the shuttle. McCoy and Lerner exited *Columbus* behind him, just in time to greet the delegation sent to meet them.

Masako Clarke led a party of maybe a dozen men and women, who crossed the hangar on their way to the shuttle. Kirk couldn't help noticing that, at first glance, the colonists appeared uniformly trim and attractive; even the older citizens, silver-haired though they might be, looked healthy and fit. Clearly, infirmity, obesity, baldness, even simple homeliness had been purged from the colony's gene pool. *Poor Bones,* Kirk thought, recalling the doctor's somewhat lived-in features. *He must look like Quasimodo to them.*

"Welcome to Sycorax, Captain, gentlemen." Along with the rest of the delegation, Regent Clarke wore a skintight, one-piece bodysuit that could become standard apparel only on a world where everyone had a flawless physique. "Let me introduce you to a few of my senior staff," she said, gesturing toward the individuals to her immediate left and right, respectively. "This is Aaron Rosenberg, chairman of the Committee for Genetic Development." The dignitary in question, an athletic-looking older man with short brown hair, bowed politely at Kirk and the others. "And this is Karen Jones, the head of our Engineering and Infrastructure Department." Another perfect physical specimen, this one with unblemished mahogany skin and an elegantly coifed crown of snowy white hair. "I'm afraid," the regent continued, "that we've been cut off from the rest of the galaxy so long that we don't actually have any sort of diplomatic corps, but perhaps that's something we can remedy in the weeks to come."

"You seem to be handling the diplomacy perfectly well all on your own," Kirk complimented Clarke, then introduced McCoy and Lerner. The good doctor, Kirk was glad to note, offered their hosts nothing but down-home Southern charm and graciousness, despite his personal reservations about the colony and their mission. "You'd never guess that you don't receive visitors every day."

Clarke accepted Kirk's praise humbly. "In all honesty," she admitted, "I have had a bit of practice recently." The welcoming committee behind her began to part down the middle as those at the rear of the party worked their way toward the Starfleet officers. Kirk's eyes widened in amazement and he heard McCoy gasp as well. "What the—?" Lerner blurted involuntarily, his hand instinctively reaching for his phaser.

Three Klingon soldiers, in full uniform, joined the regent at the front of the delegation. The leader of the Klingons, his hands resting arrogantly upon his hips, smiled coldly at Kirk. Gray eyes held a glint of wicked amusement.

"Permit me to introduce our *other* guests," Clarke stated amicably. "I believe you already know Captain Koloth."

CHAPTER TWENTY-FIVE

"My dear Captain Kirk! How delightful to see you again!"

Koloth greeted his old adversary with mock hospitality. With his arched black eyebrows, widow's peak, and neatly trimmed goatee, the urbane Klingon commander was arguably even more satanic-looking than Spock. His silver-and-black military uniform glittered beneath the glare of the hangar's overhead lights. Two lieutenants, whom Kirk thought he recognized from that incident at Deep Space Station K-7, flanked Koloth, glaring at the Starfleet officers with unconcealed hatred and contempt.

"Captain?" Lerner asked, his hand on his phaser. He sounded ready to give the Klingons a fight if that's what they wanted. Kirk admired his spirit, but questioned the timing.

"Stand down, Lieutenant," he instructed, as his brain raced to catch up with this unexpected (and unwelcome) turn of events. Klingons? On Sycorax? What did this mean? "I must admit," he said to Koloth, "it's a . . . surprise . . . to see you here as well."

Masako Clarke stepped between the rival starship captains. Although she maintained a scrupulously neutral demeanor, Kirk could tell that the regent was conscious of the tensions between the two parties. "The Klingon Empire," she explained, "has also expressed an interest in, well, absorbing our colony into their alliance."

"I see," Kirk said skeptically. He was only too aware that, where the Klingons were concerned, "alliance" was merely a euphemism for out-and-out conquest and tyranny. He suspected that the regent knew this, too. *So why invite the Klingons here?* he wondered. *Unless she had no other choice?*

"We feel it is in the best interests of the Paragon Colony to accept the protection of the Klingon Empire," Koloth stated in a deceptively agreeable manner. Kirk knew better than to take his peaceful pose at face value.

"Protection?" he asked, recognizing a veiled threat when he heard one. "Protection from whom, exactly?"

Koloth flashed Kirk a devilish grin. "The galaxy is full of dangers, as I'm sure I don't need to remind you, Captain." Lean and lanky by Klingon standards, the enemy commander had always struck Kirk as more of a schemer than a warrior, but Kirk felt certain that Koloth could be lethal if crossed; you couldn't rise to captain in the Klingon military without getting your hands bloody now and then. "I am here to convince the regent that only the Klingon Empire can truly guarantee her colony's safety."

"Safety, my left foot!" McCoy growled acerbically. "Talk about putting the foxes in charge of the henhouse!"

"That will be all, Doctor," Kirk said, shushing

McCoy's overly candid remarks. He agreed with the sentiments, but now was not the time or the place; Kirk wanted to get a better sense of the situation before proceeding to open confrontation. "Remember, we're guests here." The *Enterprise*'s captain eyed Koloth suspiciously. "So what does your empire get, in exchange for your vaunted 'protection'?" He gave that last word an unmistakably sarcastic spin. "Sycorax is too out-of-the-way to be of strategic value."

"Ah, but their scientific expertise far exceeds the value of their remote location!" Koloth observed enthusiastically. "Our intelligence informs us that the geneticists bred here are second to none in their knowledge of advanced genetic-engineering techniques." He looked the regent and her staff over appraisingly, as though registering their obvious physical perfection. "The Empire would welcome adding their technological expertise to our own."

"I'll bet you would!" McCoy exclaimed, only slightly less acidly than before. "I don't imagine your leaders would have any qualms about applying genetic engineering to your own people."

One of Koloth's lieutenants, a younger Klingon with a thick head of tangled brown hair, laughed derisively. "Only Earthers would devise a means to create a race of conquerors—then forbid its use!" He sneered at McCoy and the other humans. "Weaklings."

Koloth made no effort to curb his subordinate's intemperate remarks. He merely gestured toward the young Klingon instead. "You remember my second-in-command, Korax?"

"Yes," Kirk said dryly. "I believe he once compared me to a Denebian slime devil." Kirk had not actually been present at the time, but the insult, along with several equally unflattering comparisons, had been dutifully recorded in Scotty's report on the incident, which had provoked a full-fledged brawl between various members of Kirk's and Koloth's crews. Judging from the smirk currently residing on the Klingon's swarthy face, Korax had not repented of his role in that unsanctioned free-for-all, nor of his strenuous efforts to slander Kirk. *Remind me to thank Scotty for pounding his face in,* the captain thought to himself.

"Ancient history!" Koloth insisted, dismissing the entire episode. "We mustn't bore our hosts with our dusty old war stories. After all, there's important diplomatic business to attend to, is there not?"

"Yes," Masako Clarke assented. "Of course." Without being obvious about it, she appeared anxious to get this tense encounter over with. "Naturally, we intend to give the Klingons' proposal all due consideration, but before taking such a momentous step, it seemed wise to consult the Federation as well, especially since our original gene pool is derived from Earth's human population."

"Human genes, hmmph!" Korax grunted. "Klingon DNA makes Earther seed look like worthless chaff." The third Klingon soldier, a hulking bald warrior whose face was scarred by an old, untreated disruptor burn, snickered in agreement.

"Be that as it may," Clarke stated tactfully, "I would certainly like the opportunity, Captain Kirk, to discuss this matter with you more fully sometime soon. In private."

Koloth frowned, but Kirk thought he grasped the bare essentials of the situation. Obviously, Clarke did not feel free to refuse the Klingons' dubious "protection" outright, yet entertained hopes of joining the Federation instead. The Klingon threat, he guessed, was probably what prompted the Paragon Colony to contact the Federation in the first place.

"By all means," he assured the regent. "I'm anxious to sit down with you whenever's convenient."

"As am I," Koloth insisted. "I'm sure I can be equally as persuasive as the good captain here."

"We'll see about that," Kirk said boldly. He was about to remind Koloth of just who had come out on top at K-7 when his communicator beeped urgently. A message from Spock, no doubt. "Excuse me," he apologized, stepping away from Clarke, Koloth, and the rest of the delegation. A deft flick of his wrist lifted the protective lid of the handheld communicator. "Kirk here. What's happening?"

Spock wasted no time getting to the point. "A Klingon battle cruiser, class D7, has revealed itself in orbit around Sycorax. Previously, it had hidden from our sensors by keeping the planet between itself and the *Enterprise,* but apparently the Klingons no longer consider stealth necessary." Spock's voice was grave as he conveyed the news to Kirk. "Logic suggests, Captain, that the Klingon Empire has designs upon the Paragon Colony and its unique scientific resources."

Out of the corner of his eye, Kirk saw Koloth watching him smugly, almost certainly aware of what was transpiring in orbit, hundreds of kilometers overhead. "Tell me about it," Kirk said.

CHAPTER TWENTY-SIX

NAI SARAK BAZAAR
DELHI, INDIA
NOVEMBER 1, 1984

MONSOON SEASON WAS OVER, BUT ANOTHER STORM was brewing. Fourteen years old, Khan Noonien Singh could feel the tension in the air as he sifted through the used books piled high in one of the many stalls lining the crowded market street. It was only ten in the morning, but the bazaar was already crammed with shoppers, vendors, beggars, and tourists. Dozens of voices haggled over jewelry, books, fabric, sweetmeats, and other items, competing with the blaring horns of taxis and bicycle-rickshaws as the vehicles inched through swarming crowds and impossibly jammed traffic, belching their exhaust into the smoggy city air. Crippled beggars, baby-clutching young mothers, and impoverished elders pleaded for bread or rupees, while dirty, barefoot children scurried to shine shoes and pick pockets. Banners advertising fantastic bargains were strung over the narrow alley like laundry, above countless signs and billboards, mostly in English. The spicy scent of cardamom, tumeric, and ginger teased Noon's nostrils. Shrill pop tunes, playing loudly from transistor radios and the doorways of various shops, assailed his ears. Stray dogs and sacred cattle wandered through the litter-strewn street, adding to the crush and congestion.

All of this was normal enough, routine even, but there was something different about today. Beneath the usual hustle and clamor, Noon sensed darker impulses at work. He heard an edge in the market's collective voice, and an almost palpable mood of anger and apprehension, building steadily all around him. Even the beggars seemed distracted and worried, targeting the tourists without their customary zeal and histrionics. The owner of the bookstall eyed Noon suspiciously, scowling as the turbaned teenager handled his wares. *Perhaps going shopping today was a mistake,* Khan thought. Was it just his imagination, or did he really feel the gaze of hostile eyes upon him, prickling the skin at the back of his neck?

Yesterday, only slightly more than twenty-four hours ago, India's controversial prime minister, Indira Gandhi, had been assassinated in her garden by her own Sikh bodyguards, who had reportedly filled her body with over thirty bullets. The killing had been in retaliation for Mrs. Gandhi's military assault on Sikhism's holiest site, the Golden Temple in Amritsar. Thousands had been killed in the attack, and a library of sacred scriptures incinerated, and Noon feared that the sectarian bloodshed had only begun.

His friends back at the university, where he was

working toward a doctorate in engineering, had cautioned the young prodigy not to leave the campus this morning, given the heated emotions raised by the prime minister's murder, yet Noon had never been one to let fear determine his actions. Now, however, he began to wonder if his pride had overcome his judgment. He stroked his cheek thoughtfully; although his first beard was just beginning to come in, his sparsely whiskered face, along with his turban and steel wristband, clearly identified him as a Sikh, albeit one barely grown.

An unexpected odor attracted his attention. Amid the omnipresent reek of spices and smog, was that smoke he smelled? He sniffed cautiously. Yes, something was definitely burning nearby. Had a building caught fire? He looked up and down the busy street, but all he could see was the constant press of bustling humanity. Straining his ears, he heard angry shouts coming from the direction of the smoky aroma, followed by screams and the sound of breaking glass. *What's happening?* he wondered with concern, his heartbeat quickening as every nerve ending in his body screamed at the approach of danger. *What is burning?*

Without warning, the book merchant snatched a dog-eared history text out of Noon's hands. "Get out of here, you filthy Sikh," the man barked at Noon, spittle flying from his lips. His eyes burned with murderous hatred. "Get away from my books!"

Caught off guard by the ferocity of the vendor's bile, Noon stepped backward into the street. *How dare he speak to me like that?* he thought, ire rapidly overtaking surprise. Without meaning to, he jostled a passing pedestrian, who shoved him back roughly. "Watch where you're going, you murdering dog!" the other man said, then spit at Noon's feet. "You've got your nerve, showing your ugly face today!"

An angry retort sprang to Noon's lips, but he held his tongue, suddenly very aware of the wrath-filled eyes that glared at him from every direction. Noon's hand went instinctively to the silver-plated dagger tucked in his belt. Until today he had only carried the brightly-polished kirpan for tradition's sake; never before had he needed it for self-defense. He hesitated to draw the blade, though, lest that provoke the mob further. "Leave me alone," he warned. His adolescent voice cracked, undermining his show of defiance. "I mean you no harm."

But it was already too late to avoid violence. The smell of burning timbers grew stronger and Noon glimpsed tendrils of ash and smoke rising above the sales banners festooning the buildings less than a block away. He heard gunshots, and the horror-stricken cries of men and women, as the angry shouting drew nearer. "Blood for blood!" roared many raging voices, sending a shiver down Noon's spine. Although he had lived a fairly sheltered life since his mother's death so many years ago, he knew a riot when he heard one. "Death to all Sikhs!"

The crowd surrounding Noon took up the cry. "Blood for blood!" Women grabbed their children and hurried for safety while their menfolk surged toward the outnumbered teenager. Brahmans and beggars, old men and grinning youths, joined the gang threatening Noon, hurling jeers and obscenities. *Very well,* he resolved, unsheathing his blade. *They will find that I am far more than I appear.*

"Stay back!" he shouted, waving the knife before him

to carve out a swath of empty space between him and the mob. His eyes narrowed shrewdly as he waited for his foes to make their move.

He did not have to wait long. A man charged at Noon from behind, trapping the youth in a crushing bear hug that pinned Noon's arms to his sides. But the man had not counted on the teen's enhanced muscle density; Noon effortlessly broke free from the larger man's clasp, then rammed his elbow into the attacker's gut. The resulting grunt of pain was music to Noon's ears, and he savored his easy victory. *That will teach these rabble,* he thought, *to accost a superior being!*

Then a rock struck him soundly in the face, bruising his cheek. "Got him!" someone yelled and the crowd laughed raucously. More missiles followed: rocks, bottles, books, cans, even fist-sized pieces of dung snatched up from the trash-covered street. Jagged stones and broken glass pelted his body, and he staggered upon the pavement, trying to shield his face with his hands. Pain struck from all around, smashing into his back, his shoulders, his ribs. Something wet and sticky leaked from a cut above his eye, and he tasted blood on his lips. "Get him!" the bloodthirsty crowd screamed. "Kill the dirty Sikh!"

As much as it galled his soul, Noon realized he had to flee for his life. The mob was out of control, and there were simply too many of them to defeat all by himself. *A wounded lion can be torn apart by jackals,* he thought, rationalizing his retreat as he barreled through the human net surrounding him, tossing grown men aside like bags of flour. His knife gripped between his teeth, he ran headlong through the bazaar, dodging traffic and shrieking tourists. *They should have known better than to venture into the streets today,* Noon thought, feeling little sympathy for the hysterical sightseers. *As should have I.*

As he sprinted, adrenaline fueling his athletic legs, he saw with horror that he was not the only victim of today's furor. The hate-crazed mob was taking vengeance on every Sikh in sight, while setting fire to any shops or stalls that might conceivably belong to a Sikh. The air was soon thick with smoke and the sickening smell of burning flesh. Racing north up Nai Sarak, he saw a gray-bearded taxi-wallah dragged from his cab, then doused with kerosene and set aflame. Khan wanted to strike back, to defend his innocent kinsmen, but there was nothing that a single youth, even one such as he, could do against the insane conflagration erupting in the streets. *Someday,* he vowed, choking back tears of rage, *I will put an end to such madness.*

But where could he run to now? Old Delhi, as this sector of the city was called, was a maze of narrow alleys and overpopulated markets, but, no matter how swiftly he raced, he could not outrun the riot, which was spreading even faster than the blazing inferno it had spawned. Vengeful fingers grabbed at Noon as he ran, tearing the fabric of his dung-spattered Nehru jacket and unraveling his turban, so that his uncut black hair streamed behind him. Hateful insults and profanities chased after the fleeing teenager, while rocks and bottles continued to bounce off his bruised back and shoulders. Overturned cars and trucks, flames licking their exposed underbellies, blocked his way, but Noon leaped around and over any obstacles, only to find more mayhem directly in his path. Looters ransacked Sikh businesses and homes, before setting them to the torch.

I must get away, Noon thought, his lungs laboring to keep up with the extreme demands placed on them by his desperate flight. But where was safety to be found? The university was too far away, in a newer part of town. There was no chance of getting there alive and intact, but he knew he had to find refuge as soon as possible. Even his superhuman strength and stamina had its limits, while the homicidal bloodlust of the crowd appeared boundless. Already the aching muscles in his legs were slowing down.

Scouring his brain, he recalled a *gurudwara,* a Sikh temple, on Chandni Chowk, maybe half a dozen blocks away. Would such a site provide sanctuary, he wondered, or merely serve as an even greater target for the rioters' wrath? Possibly the latter, he feared, but there was also a police station on the same street, only a few doors down from the temple. Perhaps the police could provide the *gurudwara* with some measure of protection, even in the face of total chaos and anarchy?

It was a slim chance, but the best one that presented itself. He paused momentarily to get his bearings, using his knife to fend off any looters who might want to spill more Sikh blood. "Keep away from me!" he threatened, slashing the air with his blade. His voice, mercifully, did not crack this time. "Leave me alone, or I swear I shall kill you all!"

Through the smoke and haze, he spotted the gleaming minarets of Jama Masid, the largest mosque in India, rising southwest of where he now stood. That meant Chandni Chowk, the market district's main thoroughfare, was straight ahead, to the north. *So be it,* he resolved, his course set. Before he could resume his flight, however, a drenching splash of liquid struck him in the face, soaking his head, hair, and shoulders. The oily fluid stung his eyes, while harsh fumes filled his nostrils. *No!* he thought, realizing with horror that he had been doused with kerosene.

The cold hand of fear clutched his heart. Noon considered himself braver than most, but even he shuddered at the thought of being burned alive. Vivid memories of the taxi-wallah's ghastly fate raced through his mind as he blinked and sputtered, the taste of kerosene drowning his tongue. The scratchy sound of a match being struck sent a thrill of terror through his body. A fiery death, he realized, was only seconds away.

Without thinking, he turned toward the sound, spitting a mouthful of kerosene at the burning match. An orange-yellow flash rewarded his desperate effort, followed by an anguished, masculine scream. Through blurry, tearing eyes, Noon barely discerned a panicked figure, one arm ablaze, flailing wildly only a few paces away. Noon threw himself backward, away from the burning man, fearing that a stray spark would set him on fire, too.

Half-blinded by the kerosene in his eyes, he darted up the alley, clearing a path with frantic slashes of his dagger. Most of the time the blade met only empty air; sometimes it did not. The reek of the kerosene soaking his hair and garments added new urgency to his death-defying run for safety. Only speed and agility could save him now; one match, one spark, would be enough to light his funeral pyre. Paying no heed to the protests of his exhausted legs, he cannonballed through the riot-racked bazaars, his vision clearing as he blinked the last of the kerosene from his eyes. Shocking evidence of the ongoing massacre littered the dusty pavement before him. Dead bodies, many charred and smoking, lay upon the ground in contorted positions of agony, joining splintered wood and broken glass from dozens of vandalized shops and stalls. Expensive silks and saris, dyed every color of the rainbow, were strewn carelessly about, soaking up the blood and kerosene that collected in scattered pools like the aftermath of a heavy rain. Noon had to watch his step as he ran, to avoid tripping over a blackened corpse or slipping upon a spreading crimson puddle.

As he ran, the fleeing teenager hastily shed his fuel-drenched jacket and shirt, exposing a chest more muscular than any fourteen-year-old was entitled to. The stench of the kerosene still clung to his hair and skin, however, marking him as a likely candidate for immolation. "Get him!" frenzied voices called after him. "Burn the stinking Sikh!"

Could he make it to the temple before his maddened pursuers could carry out their incendiary threat? Noon's questing eyes searched the cramped, cluttered street before him. His knife gashed the back of a looter who did not get out of the way fast enough, slicing through both fabric and flesh. *Almost there,* Noon promised himself. Chandni Chowk could not be far away now.

Swinging his bloodstained kirpan like a machete, he hacked through the chaos of the riot, leaping over fallen bodies and veering away from any hint of an open flame. Then, just as he began to feel more confident about his chances for survival, he saw something that stopped him in his tracks.

A deserted bus lay on its side across the width of the bazaar, its burnt-out husk still smoldering volcanically. Smoking tires suffused the smoggy air with an added smell of burning rubber. Worse still, the ruined vehicle rested directly in Noon's path, blocking his escape route. *No!* he cursed angrily. *It's not fair!*

He looked back over his shoulder to see a gang of rioters gaining on him. "Burn the Sikh bastard!" a furious voice shouted. "Blood for blood!" Many of the men carried torches made from broken timbers and looted textiles. "Death to the murderers!"

Noon briefly contemplated climbing the toppled bus, but quickly realized that was impossible. There were too many small fires still burning upon the torched vehicle to risk scaling its scorched and smoking remains. *I might as well light the match myself,* he concluded bitterly. Vigorously looking for an alternative means of escape, he scanned the bazaar from left to right, hoping some small, forgotten side street might offer the detour he so critically needed. All he found, though, were the shattered windows and desecrated facades of burning buildings. Smoke and flames escaped from the upper window of the tailor's shop to his right, while a peculiar blue mist, perhaps caused by some kind of natural gas leak, seeped from the store's ground-floor entrance, whose battered door hung crookedly from a single set of hinges. Terrified screams and barbaric shouting came from the Sikh-owned clothing store to his left. A sari-clad mannequin lay on the ground beneath a torn banner extolling low, low prices. The mannequin's painted eyes and docile expression offered Noon neither hope nor sympathy.

He had reached a dead end, then. *Fine,* he thought proudly. *Let this be my last battlefield.* Turning to face the onrushing mob, the curved silver blade of his kirpan held out in front of him, Noon spared a moment to worry about his foster parents in Chandigarh; he prayed that they were safely distant from the virulent fever consuming Old Delhi. Then he turned his full attention on his torch-wielding tormentors, grimly determined to slay as many of his foes as he could before the flames made of him a human sacrifice. "Lay on!" he whispered, quoting *Macbeth,* "and damned be him who first cries 'Hold, enough!' "

But before the murderous gang caught up with him, an unexpected voice called out. "Noon! Khan Noonien Singh! Over here!" Surprise complicating his resolution to meet a heroic death, Noon glanced to the right, where he saw a pale-skinned stranger standing in the doorway of the pillaged tailor's shop, that same odd blue mist wafting around the newcomer's ankles. He was a lean man, dressed in a dark blue suit of Western style. Another hapless tourist caught up in Delhi's heated religious strife? But then how did he know Noon by name? Where had he come from? "Hurry!" the stranger urged, speaking English with an American accent. "There's no time to explain, but you have to trust me!"

A hurled Coke bottle hit Noon in the chin, tearing a fresh gash beneath his already swollen lips. "Get him!" a young Indian man shouted. With a shock, Noon realized that the shouter, whose face was flushed and distorted by bloodthirsty mania, was one of his fellow students at the university. "Blood for blood!" his one-time classmate shrieked, snatching up another shard of broken glass from the street. "Kill the Sikh!"

A thrown torch spun toward Noon, trailing sparks like a comet. Anticipating its trajectory, Noon jumped to one side, but the tossed firebrand still struck the pavement dangerously close to his feet. He looked in confusion and desperation at the stranger in the doorway. The blue mist now seemed to fill the entire entrance of the plundered shop. "Hurry!" the man called again. "You have to trust me!"

Trust the stranger, when he couldn't even trust another colleague from school? Noon found the entire situation incomprehensible, but what other option did he have. Keeping a tight grip on the handle of his kirpan, now baptized in blood, he flung himself toward the fog-shrouded doorway and into the unknown.

CHAPTER TWENTY-SEVEN

NOON EMERGED FROM THE SHOWER, HAVING RINSED the last traces of kerosene from his hair and body. The bruises and numerous small cuts that marked his face and frame were harder to shed, but he knew that his injuries could have easily been very much worse. He found fresh clothes and first-aid supplies waiting for him, including a brown bathrobe that fit him perfectly. He had encountered so many oddities and impossibilities in the last hour or so that this latest unlikely occurrence piqued his curiosity only a smidgen more. *Who are these people?* he wondered. *And what is their interest in me?*

Although grateful for his miraculous rescue, which had almost certainly delivered him from an agonizing death, he remained on guard, mentally and physically. The mysteries accumulating around him were too bizarre and unsettling to accept at face value; he was relieved to see his dagger and wristband, obligingly wiped free of blood and soot, sitting atop the bathroom counter along with a change of clothes. The solid weight of the blade comforted him as he thrust it securely beneath the belt of his robe.

Toweled, dried, bandaged where necessary, and suitably armed, he rejoined his anonymous savior in the office outside the bathroom. The nondescript furnishings offered few clues to his new location, although he noted that all the titles upon the bookshelf appeared to be printed in English. Encyclopedias, mostly, plus a few other routine reference works. His gaze drifted involuntarily to the heavy steel vault from which he had exited that cool, luminescent fog. His skin tingled in remembrance of the peculiar, static-like sensation he'd experienced within the strange blue haze. Now, however, the vault looked empty except for a couple of metal shelves, nor did Noon see any obvious exit connecting the vault with the streets of Old Delhi. *Perhaps a secret door?* he speculated. He strained his ears, but he could no longer hear the frenzied shouts and screams of the riot.

"Good morning, Noon Singh," the nameless American greeted him. He was seated behind a marble-topped desk upon which various folders and documents were scattered. A translucent green cube served as a paperweight, holding assorted papers in place. "I trust you're feeling a good deal less flammable now."

"Yes, thank you." Noon declined to take a seat on the nearby couch or plush chair, preferring to stand, his arms crossed upon his chest. *Enough pleasantries,* he thought, deciding to cut straight to the heart of his concerns. "Who are you and where have you brought me?"

"Reasonable questions," the man conceded, "although you may find some of the answers difficult to accept." He was, Noon saw upon closer inspection, a middle-aged Caucasian of maybe forty to fifty years. Streaks of gray lightened his brown hair at his temples. "My name is Gary Seven, and, although we have never met, I know a great deal about you."

"How—?" Noon began, only to be interrupted by a knock on the door. His muscles tensed instinctively, fearing the mob had caught up with him at last.

Instead a woman's voice called from the other side of the door. "Is everyone decent in there?" she asked in a distinctly nonthreatening manner. "I have coffee."

"Thank you, Roberta," Seven answered, his casual tone implying that Noon had nothing to fear from the newcomer. "Please come in and meet our guest."

The door swung open, and a blond woman entered, bearing a tray and three coffee mugs. To his surprise, she wore what appeared to be a NASA flight suit. She offered one cup to Seven, who accepted it with a grateful smile, then crossed the room to where Noon was standing. She winced visibly at the sight of his bruised and bandaged face, but offered him a sympathetic smile along with the coffee. "Help yourself," she instructed him. Like Seven, she spoke English with an American accent.

A sleek black cat followed the woman into the office, only to disappear behind Seven's desk. The sight of the cat jogged a memory deep in the recesses of Noon's past, but he could not immediately place the source of the familiarity. A small portion of his mind fiddled with the puzzle, while the bulk of his attention stayed focused on the here and now.

He stared in confusion at the woman's incongruous outfit. A cloth patch depicting the space shuttle was affixed to one side of her zippered, navy-blue flight suit,

while an embroidered NASA nametag identified her as
SALLY RIDE. *The American astronaut?* he wondered, utterly baffled. What was she doing in Delhi, and why
did Seven call her Roberta?

"Oh, don't mind the costume," she said, apparently
noting his puzzled expression. "I came here straight
from the Halloween Parade in the Village. As you can
see, I was going as Sally Ride, the first American
woman in space." She winked at Seven, sharing a private joke. "As far as anyone knows."

Village? Parade? The woman's explanation left him
scarcely less confused. What village was she talking
about?

"This is my associate, Ms. Roberta Lincoln," Seven
elaborated. Unlike his female companion, he did not
appear to be indulging in any sort of holiday masquer-
ade. "She is also very familiar with your case."

Noon took a mug from the tray, warily sniffing its
contents. He preferred *chai*, actually, but had been introduced to black coffee by American students at the
university. He sipped the beverage carefully, finding it
both hot and soothing.

"Hello, Noon," Roberta Lincoln said, taking a few
steps back from Noon. She eyed him somewhat nervously. "I don't know if you remember me or not."

Did he? Noon examined the woman's face. She was
younger than Seven, perhaps in her mid-thirties, but
there was something disturbingly familiar about her.
His mind scrolled backward through the years, seeking
to place her rosy cheeks and bluish-green eyes. Not in
Delhi, he concluded, nor Chandigarh, but somewhere
else, long ago and far away. . . .

An ancient memory, long forgotten, surged up from

the past. "Chrysalis," he uttered, eyes wide. "You were at Chrysalis, beneath the desert."

"That's right," she said. A sober expression replaced her welcoming smile. She walked slowly to an end table, where she put down her tray, before looking at Noon again. Her own coffee cup was clutched between her palms, and she held it close to her chest, as if to dispel a sudden chill. "You were just a toddler then. I'm surprised you remember."

"I never forget a face," he informed her, while his heart and soul struggled to cope with the powerful emotions conjured up by the woman's revelation. *So many years ago . . . !* His childhood at Chrysalis, his mother's beaming face and proud expression, that final, panicky evacuation and abrupt dislocation—they were like a distant dream to him now, a prior existence he could scarcely recall. "Did—did you know my mother?" he asked.

"Briefly," Roberta answered, her eyes evading his.

"I was there as well," Seven said, "although, as I stated, we never met." He took a sip of coffee before continuing. "What's important is that Roberta and I are fully cognizant of the special circumstances surrounding your birth, and of your own unique potential. Which is why," he explained, "we have been keeping a careful eye on you for the last ten years."

"I'll say!" Roberta seconded, slumping onto a fuzzy orange couch opposite Seven's desk. "The papers all claimed that what's-her-name in England, Louise Brown, was the world's first test-tube baby, but we know better, don't we?" A look of sincere relief passed over her face. "Thank goodness that Seven heard about those riots in Delhi. We could have lost you for good!"

Seven humbly accepted the woman's gushing praise. "Fortunately, I have been monitoring the political situation in India for several weeks." He glanced down at the papers on his desk. "You may be interested to know, Noon Singh, that Rajiv Gandhi, Mrs. Gandhi's son, has been sworn in as the new prime minister."

Noon nodded. Seven's news came as no surprise; it was well known that Indira was grooming her oldest son as her successor. His gaze fell upon the white push-button phone atop Seven's desk. "I should call my parents," he stated, "make certain they are safe."

"I believe they are unharmed," Seven assured him. "The worst of the rioting is in the capital, not Chandigarh. But you can certainly contact your family shortly. First, though, permit me to explain a bit further about where you are and who we are."

Khan nodded. He had to admit he was curious to hear more. Was Seven merely an American intelligence agent of some sort, and this place a top-secret CIA safe house in the heart of Old Delhi, or could it be that the Chrysalis Project, for which his visionary mother had given her life, was not really dead at all? His foster mother and father had always discouraged any discussion of the project, hinting ominously that unnamed personages in the government would strike him down—just as they had his unfortunate mother—if he let his secret slip. Nonetheless, he had always known, deep down in his heart, that he had been born to serve some special destiny, that his innate superiority, both mental and physical, meant that he must ultimately make his mark on history, just like Alexander and Caesar and Ashoka. Perhaps, at last, that golden destiny was finally beginning?

"Go on," he said.

"Ms. Lincoln and I represent a private organization, unaffiliated with any of the major superpowers, that keeps a watchful eye on world events. We also attempt, discreetly, to encourage humanity's difficult journey toward peace and progress." Seven gestured at the assortment of folders and documents fanned out upon his desk. Craning his neck to take a peek at the scattered papers, Noon identified reports on famine in Ethiopia, the U.S. presidential campaign, and an unexplained explosion at a Soviet military base in Severomorsk.

"As you can see," Seven continued, noting the teenager's inquisitive gaze, "this is something of a full-time job. Fortunately, Roberta and I have access to technology that is not yet available to the rest of the world. It was just such technology that allowed me to remove you from the chaos in Delhi, transporting you here instead."

"Which is where?" Noon inquired, growing impatient with Seven's cryptic remarks. He wanted to know just how safe he was from the violence outside, and if and how he could leave this place when he chose.

"Are you quite sure you don't want to sit down first?" the older man asked, indicating the unoccupied chair just as his cat reappeared from somewhere behind the desk. The glossy black animal leaped onto the desktop, then settled down to watch Noon through gleaming yellow eyes. If he didn't know better, Noon would have thought that the cat was intent on observing their visitor's reaction to Seven's words.

Another long-forgotten memory surfaced, of an elegant black cat, much like this one, who was also, impossibly, a beautiful woman. This was clearly a childish fancy, however, born of an overactive imagination and the stress and confusion of that final night at Chrysalis. *Strange,* Noon mused, *how vividly the whimsical fabrications of our infancy can linger in the mind, even long after we have outgrown them.*

"No, thank you," he said stiffly, rejecting the chair Seven had offered him. "Please tell me where I am."

"Fair enough," Seven granted. His craggy face maintained a scrupulously neutral expression. "You are in New York City, Noon Singh, in the United States."

"What!" Noon exploded. Anger flared in his heart. "That's absurd! We spent less than five minutes in that tunnel of yours," he challenged Seven, pointing at the empty steel vault. "Do you think I'm a fool? What sort of game are you playing?"

Seven looked unfazed by the young man's fury, while his cat watched Noon with obvious amusement. "Perhaps you should see for yourself," Seven said calmly.

Noon was seldom at a loss for words, but now his jaw hung open mutely as he gaped in thunderstruck amazement at the view from the roof of Seven's building.

Where he had expected to see the familiar contours of Old Delhi, perhaps in flames, he saw instead the glittering spectacle of Manhattan at night. Among the towering skyscrapers and fabled concrete canyons, he spotted landmarks recognizable from countless American films and TV programs: Central Park, the Empire State Building, the Chrysler Building. Horns honked and sirens blared in the busy streets below, while the autumn air seemed cleaner and much colder than Delhi's overheated smog. *This is impossible!* he thought, astounded and confused, but how could he deny the evidence of his own senses?

Equally bewildering was the cloudy night sky spread out above him, whose crescent moon cast an erratic glow upon the not entirely sleeping city. It had been not even noon when the riots broke out in the bazaar, catching him in those bloody convulsions, yet now the moon was high in the sky and the sun nowhere in sight. "What time is it?" he asked out loud, unnerved at the loss of so many unaccounted-for hours.

Seven, standing nearby upon the roof, consulted his wristwatch. "Quarter to noon in Delhi, one-fifteen in the morning in New York."

"In other words, way past my bedtime," Roberta yawned. "Coffee or no coffee." In contrast, the cat, winding between Seven's legs, looked wide awake.

Noon could not tear his gaze away from the nocturnal cityscape surrounding him. To the west, the leafy shadows of Central Park provided an oasis of darkness amid the incandescent lights of the city; to the east, moonlight rippled upon the murky waters of a wide river. Despite the lateness of the hour, bizarrely costumed pedestrians—clad as vampires, gypsies, Ghostbusters, and other imaginary creatures—still wandered the city streets below, celebrating a far more peaceful Halloween than India had known.

How is this possible? he wondered, his powerful mind battling to make sense of what had happened to him. Had he been drugged, perhaps? Rendered unconscious by that unearthly blue vapor, then shipped halfway around the world before waking here? That struck him as highly implausible, but what other rational explanation was there?

None, he realized. Even as he knew intuitively that

Seven had not lied to him. Somehow, through some astounding means completely unknown to modern science, he had been whisked from Delhi to Manhattan in a matter of moments. He turned away from the ledge, toward Seven and his companions, questions burning upon his face even through the bruises and the scabs. "How?" he asked, the engineer in him intrigued by the very notion. "Matter transmission?"

"Something like that," Seven confirmed. "Although I'm afraid that the world is not yet ready for the secret of this technology. And, I'm sorry, neither are you."

That's not fair, Khan thought angrily, frustrated by Seven's reticence. *He can't dangle this fantastic discovery in front of me, then hold back the crucial details about how it's accomplished!* Seven's tone, however, made it clear that he was not about to change his mind on the subject. For a long second, Noon toyed with the idea of trying to force the secret out of Seven or Roberta, but to do so, he realized, would be less than honorable. The man had, after all, saved his life. Reluctantly, Noon decided to respect Seven's decision—for now.

"What do you want of me?" he asked instead.

Seven appeared pleased that the teenager had not raised a fuss over the secret of matter transference. "At present, just your continued good health," he insisted. "It may be that at some later date, however, you might be in a position to aid us in our endeavors." His eyes locked on to the younger man, whom he spoke to with considerable gravity. "You're a remarkable person, Noon Singh, with much to offer the world. Perhaps, someday, we can help you fulfill that potential."

I see, Noon thought, flattered by Seven's well-informed assessment of his abilities. As much as he disliked being obliged to another person, he was also intrigued by the notion of joining Seven's covert campaign to build a better future. As today's carnage in Delhi proved beyond any doubt, mankind was grievously in need of order and security, of the sort only truly enlightened leadership could provide. He owed it to his country—and the world—to take bold action to bring modern humanity's suffering to an end. "I am in your debt," he told Seven solemnly. "And you have given me much to think about."

It took three days for the riots in Delhi and elsewhere in India to subside, and for some semblance of order to return. Finally, though, Seven judged it safe to send young Noon home via the transporter vault. Roberta, who had spent the last few days chaperoning him around New York and environs, was not entirely disappointed to see him go. *He's not a bad kid,* she thought, *but, boy, is he full of himself. Guess that's what happens when you're told from birth that you're superior to everyone else.* She waved good-bye to Noon as he stepped into the swirling azure mists of the transporter. *Let's hope he grows out of it.*

She and Seven watched as the blue fog dissipated into nothingness, taking the bruised teenager with them. Seven adjusted the controls upon his desk (which were disguised as a set of pens), and the vault's heavy steel door sealed itself automatically. Isis, looking bored, concentrated on washing her paws.

"Well, that went smoothly enough," Roberta commented, leaning against Seven's desk in her ripped cotton T-shirt, stonewashed jeans, and running shoes. "Especially considering we killed his mother."

"She chose her own fate," Seven reminded Roberta. His somber tone declared that he had hardly forgotten Sarina Kaur's tragic fate. "It's her son's destiny that concerns me now."

Roberta fiddled with the straps of her new Sony Walkman. "You seriously thinking of recruiting him?" She wasn't exactly sure how she felt about that; although Seven had contacts and informants throughout the globe (and beyond), Roberta was the only agent privy to all his out-of-this world secrets. She was used to this being a two-person (okay, two persons and a self-important feline) operation. "He's only a teenager."

"Which means he may still be young enough to influence in a positive manner," Seven pointed out. His thoughtful eyes gazed past Roberta into space, as though peering into the future. Sometimes Roberta wondered how much her space-born supervisor really knew about the years to come. "I may want to test Noon further, see if that formidable will and intellect can be harnessed to a cause greater than his own ambition. Married to restraint and compassion, his talents could indeed make him a very valuable agent."

"I suppose," Roberta said. She still couldn't believe that Seven had actually broken his own rule by allowing Noon to find out about the transporter. Granted, it would have been hard to explain his instant exit from Old Delhi otherwise; Noon was no fool. "What about all those other superkids?"

Seven frowned, his gaze returning to the present. He pulled out the bottom drawer of his desk and removed a thick folder, bulging with reports and psychological profiles. Bound together with rubber bands, the folder landed atop his desk with a heavy thud.

"Unfortunately, Noon, for all his arrogance, is the most psychologically well adjusted of his peers. The other children of Chrysalis, although undeniably gifted in their own ways, are all too emotionally unstable to be trusted with any of our secrets." Seven leafed slowly through his files, shaking his head glumly. "Many will self-destruct," he predicted, "while a paltry few may fade into obscurity, making little impact on history. The rest, I fear, will be keeping us busy through the millennium."

"Oh," Roberta said, dismayed at the prospect of another decade-plus of playing bodyguard to the entire planet. The twenty-first century seemed very far away, and Seven wasn't getting any younger. *Neither am I*, she thought, *no matter how much jogging and aerobics I do.* Her eyes sought out the silver in Seven's hair, as well as the deepening worry lines upon his face.

Maybe we do need some new blood after all.

CHAPTER TWENTY-EIGHT

THE PARAGON COLONY
SYCORAX
STARDATE 7004.1

KIRK LOOKED AWAY FROM THE VIEWER, TAKING A break from his historical research. He wished he could go back in time to warn Seven about Khan, but that was impossible; the danger to the timeline was simply too severe. Unfortunately, the Eugenics Wars were something that human history had to live with.

Rubbing tired eyes, he rose from the workstation the Paragon Colony had provided for him. To avoid too many hazardous flights through Sycorax's turbulent atmosphere, Kirk had decided to keep the landing party on the planet until their business here was concluded. The guest quarters they had been stowed in, at least until Regent Clarke managed to shake off Koloth and his Klingon cronies, were clean and comfortable, but Kirk was glad that he had brought along a copy of the *Enterprise*'s files on Khan, Gary Seven, and their seem-

ingly intertwined destinies. If nothing else, it gave him
something productive to do while he cooled his heels
waiting for his next audience with the regent.

He glanced around the VIP suite, which was only
slightly larger than his own personal quarters on the
Enterprise. Unlike the sleek, streamlined steel decor of a
starship, however, accommodations within the Paragon
Colony had a much more organic ambience. Now that
he noticed it, he was struck by the realization that almost everything in sight, both the furnishings and the
suite itself, appeared to be constructed from biologically generated materials. The floors were hardwood,
maybe oak or teak, while the walls were adorned with
varnished walnut panels. Knobs, switches, and faucets
were made of polished bone or ivory, and the ceiling
shone with a natural bioluminescence, reminding Kirk
of the glow-in-the-dark mouse that Roberta Lincoln
had witnessed in Rome, nearly three hundred years
ago. Silk and cotton sheets covered a bouncy sponge
mattress, while even the workstation at which he'd
been sitting looked to have been carved from some
form of petrified coral. Kirk had to search hard to find
anything metallic or plastic. Maybe the internal components of the computer station . . . ?

Makes sense, he realized. The founders of the Paragon
Colony specialized in the biological sciences, just as
their spiritual forebears at Chrysalis had, so it only
stood to reason that their architecture and technology
had developed along those lines. *I wonder where their scientific know-how has surpassed the Federation's over the last
hundred years, and in what departments they might have
fallen behind?*

A mild knock on the pinewood door interrupted his

speculations. Kirk pressed an ivory switch and the door slid open automatically, revealing a young, somewhat nervous-looking aide in an olive bodysuit. "The regent is ready to see you now," the colonist informed him.

Kirk and McCoy met with Masako Clarke on a high balcony overlooking the colony. Sunlight filtered through the great green dome, giving everything a slightly chartreuse tint. "My apologies for the delay, gentlemen. Captain Koloth was in no hurry to leave me alone with you."

"You don't say," McCoy muttered. Unlike the scene at the landing bay, with its sizable delegation of colonists and Klingons, attendance at this meeting had been restricted to a bare minimum. The regent was accompanied only by a single secretary, and Gregor Lozin, a stern-faced older man whom she introduced as the chairman of the committee in charge of the colony's internal security. Kirk's own security officer, Lieutenant Lerner, was posted outside the regent's office, along with two of Lozin's own men.

"An impressive-looking colony," Kirk told Clarke, admiring the view from the balcony. Miles of buildings, gardens, and hydroponic farms stretched to the outer boundaries of the dome. Kirk saw dozens of men, women, and children going about their daily lives in a well-ordered and peaceful fashion. An underground monorail system, he had been told, connected every individual wedge of the circular colony, cutting down on traffic upon the surface. "I have to ask, though: Why choose such an inhospitable planet to settle down on?"

Clarke gave Kirk a pained smile. "Good question," she conceded, not at all offended by Kirk's harsh description of her adopted world. "To be honest, our founders originally intended to colonize Miranda, the third planet in this system. Miranda is a Class-M world, without any indigenous sentients or hostile life-forms, which made it seem ideal for colonization. Unfortunately, early unmanned surveys of the planet failed to note that Miranda's only moon had an unstable orbit. By the time our grandparents' ship, an old Daedalus-class freighter, reached its destination, Miranda's moon was orbiting dangerously close to the planet's Roche limit, causing massive tectonic shifts, tidal waves, and cataclysmic volcanic activity throughout the entire planet. Our early pioneers even recorded tides of solid matter on Miranda's surface, causing daily fluctuations of ten centimeters or more."

"Good lord!" McCoy reacted. "That sounds wildly unstable, not to mention unsafe."

"Exactly." Clarke sighed in sympathy with the frustrated pioneers. "To make matters worse, our founders did not have the option of searching elsewhere for a more suitable world. Their supplies of dilithium and other resources were all but depleted. It was too late to turn back, so they had no choice but to look around and select the next-best planet in the system." She lifted her gaze toward the dome arching high overhead, protecting them from the fierce heat and pressure outside. "That turned out to be Sycorax."

Kirk nodded, recalling similar stories from the early days of interstellar exploration. Colonizing alien worlds was always a risky, uncertain endeavor. "I have to admire your founders' ingenuity and perseverance," he told Clarke sincerely. "Making a home here, building a working colony, could not have been easy."

"No it wasn't," Clarke confirmed, "especially when you consider that the first generation of pioneers had not been genetically enhanced, unlike their heirs." The very idea seemed inconceivable to her. "I often marvel that ordinary human beings, with merely baseline DNA, could have accomplished all that they did."

There was something distinctly condescending—not to mention, Khan-like—about the way the regent talked about her "merely" human forebears, but Kirk decided to let the comment pass, for diplomacy's sake. For the first time in years, however, he found himself wondering how Khan and his own band of superhuman colonists were faring on that harsh frontier world in the Mutara Sector. If the original Paragon settlers had managed to survive—and ultimately thrive—on a Class-K planet such as Sycorax, what might Khan and his people have built on Ceti Alpha V? *Knowing Khan, he's probably carved out an empire already.*

Perhaps to change the subject, McCoy looked upward at the verdant dome cresting high above their heads. "What's with the greenness?" he asked. "I feel like I'm in the Emerald City of Oz, or maybe in an undersea city on Celadon Prime."

"The dome is one of our proudest accomplishments, Doctor," Clarke said, clearly delighted to expound further. "Believe it or not, the dome is a living organism, genetically designed by some of our top scientists. It's chlorophyll-based, meaning that it can convert Sycorax's diffuse sunlight directly into energy the dome can employ for its own use and maintenance. In addition, it also absorbs carbon dioxide from the atmosphere outside, converting it into oxygen. At present, most of that oxygen is consumed by the colony's population, but enough is released back into the outer environment that, over centuries, the dome's own respiration should help terraform the planet."

"A living biosphere," McCoy uttered, sounding genuinely impressed. "That's astounding!"

"We think so," Clarke said proudly. "The dome also has roots extending deep beneath the planet's surface, absorbing vital minerals, nutrients, and even fresh water from underground reserves." She watched the faces of her guests, gauging their reactions to her revelations concerning the dome. "It's completely adapted to its environment."

"What about the forcefield?" Kirk asked. "Is that to reinforce the dome against the extreme atmospheric pressure?" He still remembered the strain that Sycorax's crushing air density had placed on the shuttlecraft's hull and shields.

"In part," Clarke admitted, "but the deflector screens also serve a more important purpose, namely shielding our own carefully constructed DNA from ultraviolet light, cosmic radiation, or anything else that might trigger random mutations." She frowned momentarily at the thought, then shrugged her shoulders. "Obviously, after devoting generations to refining and perfecting our genetic heritage, we can hardly leave ourselves vulnerable to unpredictable factors beyond our control."

"But random, unplanned mutations are how all living species evolve," McCoy objected. "By eliminating chance, you take yourselves out of the elementary process of natural selection." His dour tone and expression made it clear where he stood on the subject. "You're risking total genetic stagnation."

With an expansive sweep of her arm, the regent invoked the prosperous colony below. "We're far from stagnating, Doctor," she chuckled. "In fact, we've evolved more in two generations than *Homo sapiens* has in two hundred thousand years. Natural evolution has too high a failure rate; as a physician, you must be aware of all that can go wrong when chromosomes mutate." She turned toward Kirk, directing her argument at the highest-ranking Starfleet representative present. "Just how long, Captain, do you think it would take for something like our dome to evolve naturally?"

Kirk saw where she was going with her query. "Several hundred millennia, I imagine."

"We created the dome, from test tube to final organism, in less than a century," Clarke bragged on her people's behalf. She gave Kirk a calculating and meaningful look. "Naturally, we'd be happy to share the exact genetic sequence for the dome with your scientists should we be accepted into the Federation."

That's quite an inducement, Kirk thought, but was it enough to overlook the colony's genetic experimentation on humans? The Chrysalis Project had no doubt had its breakthroughs as well, but its ultimate legacy was still the Eugenics Wars.

"For now, though, I think you've said enough," Gregor Lozin cautioned the regent. His harsh tone, and disapproving demeanor, provided a striking contrast to Clarke's personable manner. "We should not share all our secrets with these strangers before we are certain that it's indeed in our best interests to do so."

"Captain Kirk and Dr. McCoy are more honored guests than strangers," Clarke admonished Lozin. "But perhaps we should get down to business. . . ."

The discussion moved indoors, where Clarke seated herself behind a solid coral desk. Kirk and McCoy each claimed an oak chair padded with organic sponge, while Lozin paced restlessly about the regent's private office. Clarke's secretary occupied a corner chair, typing notes into a personal datapad.

"As you may have gathered," the regent began, "Chairman Lozin has his own reservations about allying ourselves with the Federation. Perhaps he should elaborate a bit."

"Thank you, Regent," Lozin said brusquely. "No offense, gentlemen, but I am scarcely alone in my concerns about surrendering our colony to Federation hegemony." He stood stiffly beside the regent's coral desk, his posture practically trumpeting his wary and intractable nature. "This colony has managed for decades without the involvement of outside powers. Indeed, it can truly be said that we have prospered in defiance of the Federation's antiquated and irrational strictures on human genengineering. Some of us have not forgotten that it was precisely the Federation's ridiculous prejudices and superstitions that drove our founders out of UFP-controlled space a century ago. And, judging from Dr. McCoy's remarks, the Federation hasn't changed its attitude much since then."

Kirk wondered briefly if Lozin could possibly be descended from the late Viktor Lozinak, one of the guiding lights of the old Chrysalis Project. It was certainly possible, he theorized, that Lozinak could have passed on his dream of a genetically engineered society to his descendants, along with a healthy dose of paranoia where outside forces were concerned.

"Strict controls on the alteration of human DNA are

hardly ridiculous," Kirk replied. "The more I learn about the Eugenics Wars that nearly destroyed humanity, the more I appreciate the dangers—as well as the potential advantages—of what you're doing here."

"You see," Lozin challenged Clarke. Resting his palms on the desktop, he thrust his scowling face at the regent. "I told you that the Federation is still not ready for us. Their minds are still bogged down in the mistakes of the distant past, rather than open to a new and revolutionary vision of tomorrow." He stepped away from the desk, casting a critical eye on the seated Starfleet officers. "We should never have invited them here."

"You know, for a genetically engineered utopia," Kirk observed with a trace of humor in his voice, "you seem to have a surprising amount of disagreement going on." He softened his remarks by smiling good-naturedly. "Perhaps you haven't transcended ordinary human nature as much as you believe?"

Clarke shook her head. "To the contrary, Captain. A certain, specified degree of opposing temperaments and opinions has been deliberately worked into the fabric of our society, in order to achieve a healthy balance of viewpoints." She nodded at her more conservative colleague. "My friend Chairman Lozin is simply fulfilling the function he was expressly designed to serve."

"Sort of a genetically engineered Loyal Opposition," McCoy translated, sounding both intrigued and scandalized.

"Exactly," Clarke stated. "Just as my DNA has been carefully tailored to help me perform an executive role in our society." She once again directed her words to Kirk. "You see, Captain, we're far from the out-of-control genetic tyrants that caused so much trouble back in the bad old days of the twentieth century. We're no threat to the Federation, and we may just be its future."

"I still think this is a mistake," Lozin protested, raising his voice as he grew even more insistent. Heavy brows converged above his nose as the angry furrows in his forehead deepened. "Both the Federation—and the Klingons—can only contaminate the advanced society we've worked so hard to create. They're random variables, capable of completely undermining all our efforts and precautions."

"The Klingons were not exactly invited," Clarke reminded him pointedly. "Despite Captain Koloth's pretense at civility, we face the very real possibility of an armed invasion." Her face took on a grim expression as she leaned forward to look Kirk in the eye. "Let me be perfectly frank with you, Captain. Despite some isolationist tendencies, we're no fools. We know who and what the Klingons are. Given a choice, we would much rather throw in our lot with the Federation. But, and please do not misunderstand me, if the Federation is unwilling to accept us, then we will have no choice but to join forces with the Klingon Empire, on the best terms that we can negotiate." She paused to let the full implications of her ultimatum sink in. "That would be bad news for us, but possibly even worse news for the Federation. Do I make myself clear?"

"Absolutely," Kirk said, frowning. The prospect of genetically enhanced Klingons overrunning the galaxy was as troubling as the possibility of another round of Eugenics Wars. Maybe even more so.

CHAPTER TWENTY-NINE

DA VINCI RESEARCH BASE
SOUTH MAGNETIC POLE
ANTARCTICA
DECEMBER 2, 1984

THE FROZEN WASTELAND WAS COLDER THAN RURA
Penthe, Gary Seven observed. Transporting into the
antarctic wasteland was like traveling back in time to
Earth's Ice Age, something Seven personally hoped
never to do again. He half-expected to see a herd of
woolly mammoths lumbering across the barren polar
icescape. *Good thing Isis is in Moscow with Roberta,* he reflected. *With or without fur, she wouldn't find this frigid environment very appealing.*

Even now, at the height of the antarctic summer,
when the endless white snow reflected the glare of a
never-setting sun, the temperature outdoors was still
many degrees below zero. A fierce, flaying wind blew
against him; Seven could feel the biting chill of the
wind even through several layers of nylon insulation

and heat-trapping undergarments. A greasy black unguent protected his exposed cheeks from frostbite, but the ongoing blizzard severely reduced visibility. He estimated that he couldn't see more than three hundred feet ahead, tops. Beneath his parka, his fifty-two-year-old body shivered involuntarily, a survival mechanism designed to generate heat. Despite the discomfort, he was grateful for every painful sensation. In an environment like this, it was when you *stopped* feeling the cold, when a deadening numbness set in, that you really had to worry.

The fur-lined hood of his parka obscured his peripheral vision, so he had to turn his head in order to check on his partner on this mission. Like himself, Noon Singh wore heavy arctic gear, as well as protective goggles to avoid snow blindness. "Are you all right, Mr. Singh?" Seven asked, his breath misting before his lips. This wintry climate was a far cry from the sweltering Indian heat that the young man was accustomed to. "How are you doing?"

Noon had to raise his voice to be heard over the howling wind. "I am quite well," he insisted, clearly determined not to show any sign of weakness, despite the telltale chattering of his teeth. "Where is this laboratory you spoke of?"

Less than two hours ago, Seven had surprised Noon in the Indian city of Bhopal, where the young student had been visiting friends during the annual Sikh festival of Nanak Jayanti. Seven had finally chosen to call in the favor that the gifted teenager owed him. His intentions in doing so were twofold. For one thing, this seemed like a good mission on which to test the youth. For another, he needed backup on this operation, and Noon's genetically enhanced stamina made him better equipped to cope with the inhospitable antarctic climate than either Roberta or Isis, both of whom were, in any event, otherwise engaged. The two female operatives were busy monitoring the situation in Moscow, where Communist leader Konstantin Cherenko was rumored to be near death. Seven had high hopes for one of Cherenko's potential successors, a man named Gorbachev, but only if the reform-minded Russian apparatchik managed to survive the Kremlin's bitter internal power struggles. Roberta and Isis were there to insure that he did.

Which left him and Noon to cope with the crisis at hand. Seven used his servo to confirm that their destination lay to the south, roughly five minutes away by foot. The wand's sensors locked in on the nuclear generator powering the top-secret American science station, providing him with a guidepost to navigate by.

A frown cracked the frozen grease upon Seven's face. Given the immense difficulty of transporting conventional fuel across the snowbound wastes, atomic energy was the only practical way to provide Da Vinci Base with heat and power; nevertheless, it was hard not to be reminded of Sarina Kaur's tragic last moments, especially with her orphaned son standing only a few feet away. *Noon Singh will have a much more promising future,* Seven vowed, *if I have anything to say about it.*

Seven shoved the memory aside. "This way," he said, pointing a gloved finger in the direction indicated by his servo. Leaning forward against the wind, their faces turned downward to shield them from the stinging gusts, the two men trudged through the turbulent snowstorm, their insulated boots sinking deep into crystalline snowdrifts that crunched beneath their steady tread. Seven knew that the snow was merely the upper layer of an immense ice sheet that stretched nearly two miles beneath them, weighing heavily upon the buried continent below. Nearly ninety percent of the world's ice was tied up in the antarctic icecap, or so the Beta 5 had informed him earlier. He had to admire the determination and perseverance of the men and women who had established a scientific outpost here at the coldest and most isolated place on Earth. *Too bad,* he thought, *that their work is so dangerous to the peace and safety of the entire planet.*

Noon's vision turned out to be just as superb as the rest of his physical attributes. "Look!" he called out, spotting their target even before Seven did.

The older man hurried to catch up with Noon, then squinted through his goggles at the view ahead of them. Peering down from a slight incline, he saw a grouping of prefabricated metal huts, probably connected by scaffolded passageways beneath the snow. A small, thousand-kilowatt nuclear power plant was installed at the outer perimeter of the camp, while a large satellite dish had been mounted atop the central hut. Two large Sno-Cat tractors were parked outside the base, and the falling snow had not yet covered the lengthy runway and landing field that the tractors had carved into the dense polar ice sheet. A single helicopter rested unmanned upon the landing field, wisely sitting out the present blizzard. Not one human figure could be seen moving about outside the heated metal huts; in this sort of weather, one braved the elements only when it was absolutely necessary, and for the shortest amount of time possible.

Seven nodded approvingly. One good thing about the severity of the climate: there were no guards posted outside the central laboratory. After all, they were hundreds of miles away from the nearest human habitation. Who in their right minds would come snooping around the South Pole?

Just me and my potential protégé, he thought wryly. "Careful," he warned Noon, placing a restraining hand upon the teenager's shoulder when he started to hurry forward. "Look over there."

Despite its remote location, Da Vinci Base was not entirely unguarded. Security cameras were mounted at regular intervals all around the camp, scanning the surrounding snowscape with unblinking electronic eyes. Noon nodded, acknowledging that he had now spotted the cameras as well.

Fortunately, the blowing snow flurries limited the usefulness of the spycams. Seven estimated that he and Noon were still safely outside the range of the watchful mechanical sentinels, which gave him sufficient time and privacy to take suitable countermeasures against the ring of cameras.

His knee crunched through the frozen crust as he knelt in the snow just beyond the cameras' view. His gloved hands shaped the fallen snow while he swiftly calculated the angles of reflection between the camera lenses, his own snow sculptures, and the fixed antarctic sun above. Noon stood by, watching intently, as Seven used the palm of his glove to polish the surface of two precisely positioned cairns of snow.

When he was done, the frozen heaps reflected the blinding glare of the sun directly at the lenses of the two nearest security cameras, rendering them effectively snowblind. *Perfect,* Seven thought with satisfaction, rising to his feet once more. Granted, he could have disabled the cameras directly via his servo, but that might have alerted those within the base that an intruder was at work. Better to simulate the natural phenomenon of a south polar "whiteout" instead, rather than risk exposure this early in their mission. "Okay," he informed Noon, now that the blinded cameras were no longer a concern. "Let's go."

Moving swiftly but silently, they snuck toward the unsuspecting base. Seven suspected that the central hut, the one with the satellite dish atop its roof, was the nerve center of the base, but he used his servo to confirm that the building in question was indeed drawing upon more of the station's electrical power supply than any of the other huts. He indicated as much to Noon, gesturing toward the center hut. *That's where we'll find our target,* he thought, *assuming my information is correct.*

Officially, Da Vinci Base did not exist. That there was indeed an outpost here, unknown to most authorities, added considerable credence to the rumors he had heard about the experiment being conducted here. *And here I was hoping that Guinan had been mistaken this time around,* he admitted privately. He should have known better; the expatriate El-Aurian was nothing if not a reliable source.

The shrieking wind conveniently concealed the sound of their approach as the two men slipped between the camp's outlying buildings, watching warily for more security cameras as they crept toward the main laboratory. Seven noted that Noon had already drawn the modified servo that he had provided the Indian youth with. Unlike the multipurpose nature of Seven's own standard servo, Noon's device was capable of only two discreet functions: a mild tranquilizer beam and, in the event of an emergency, a preprogrammed escape command that would automatically transport the young man back to a secluded alley in Bhopal. This particular instrument, Seven recalled, had once belonged to Roberta, who had disparagingly referred to it as the "training wheels" version before graduating to possession of her own fully-functional servo.

Seven saw that the deliberately nonlethal weapon was gripped tightly between Noon's fingers. *Good thing he's wearing gloves,* Seven observed wryly. Otherwise the subzero temperature would have caused the young man's flesh to stick to the cold steel casing of the servo.

For the same reason, neither of them could safely place an ear up against the prefab metal walls of the center hut. Seven tried to detect the number of human life-forms currently inhabiting the structure, but the extreme contrast between the freezing outdoors and the laboratory's heated interior made any thermal readings highly suspect. There could be anywhere from one to a dozen people inside the lab at this moment.

Very well, he resolved. *We'll just have to rely on the element of surprise.*

They quickly located the front entrance of the hut. A handmade sign crookedly nailed over the rusty metal door read HOLE HQ—NO SPIES ALLOWED. Seven called the sign to Noon's attention, eliciting a rare grin from the usually stoic and self-important youth. *Good to know he has a sense of humor,* Seven noted; *that's an important sign of a well-adjusted personality.* So far the fledgling operative had performed well on this assignment; then again, Seven conceded, the mission had barely begun.

While Noon stood at attention, servo in hand, Seven tried the doorknob, which turned out to be unlocked. More evidence, or so it seemed, that their secluded and remarkably inaccessible locale had lulled the base's personnel into a false sense of security, making Seven's current operation all the easier. *Let's hope our luck continues to hold out,* he thought.

Noiselessly signaling Noon to get ready, Seven took a deep breath, then kicked open the door. "Nobody move!" he shouted, bursting into the laboratory and wielding his servo like a gun. To demonstrate its efficacy, he fired an invisible beam at the ceiling, disintegrating layers of foam insulation and steel to form a circular hole, roughly six inches in diameter, in the roof of the hut, through which the wind and snow immediately invaded the building's shelter. Deftly (and inconspicuously) switching the servo's setting back to Tranquilize, he aimed his weapon at the startled denizens of the lab. "Everyone stay where they are!" he ordered. "Please cooperate. No one will be harmed."

Disregarding Seven's suggestion, a uniformed soldier pulled his gun. Seven would have promptly neutralized the threat, but Noon beat him to the punch, rushing into the lab after Seven and, without even breaking his stride, immobilizing the armed guard with a tranquilizer beam. *Excellent work,* Seven judged, impressed by both Noon's aim and his reflexes. The young man definitely had the makings of a first-class agent.

With their twin servos drawn, the two intruders held a small assortment of scientists and soldiers at bay. A quick scan of the laboratory revealed that there were slightly under a half-dozen people present, mostly technicians, although Seven quickly located one more armed security guard on the scene. He instructed Noon to disarm the remaining soldier even as worried and befuddled scientists watched the first soldier slump to the floor, a blissful smile upon his face. "Don't worry, he'll be fine," Seven informed the apprehensive hostages.

This sort of commando raid was less subtle than Seven's usual methods, but, under the circumstances, that couldn't be helped; a top-secret military base at the South Pole did not exactly lend itself to more covert infiltration. Thankfully, the hoods, goggles, and greasy facial masks that he and Noon wore effectively concealed their identities, eliminating the need for any further disguise.

Although frigid winds now entered the laboratory through both the punctured roof and open doorway, Seven was intensely conscious of how much warmer the room was than the refrigerated environment outside. Already he was sweating heavily beneath his parka. He shifted position to place himself directly below the gap in the ceiling. The falling snow and icy wind offered some relief from the heat, but he was still extremely overdressed for the occasion. *Too bad we couldn't transport directly into this building,* he thought, *but there were too many unknown variables.*

Massive computer banks covered nearly every wall of the antarctic laboratory. Seven chose to ignore the hardware for the moment, while he concentrated on his reluctant hostages. He searched the faces of the assembled scientists and technicians, looking for the specific individual whom he knew to be in charge of Da Vinci Base's hazardous experiments. His eyes quickly located the person he wanted: a fit-looking older man, in his late forties, with neatly trimmed silver hair and cool, intelligent eyes. An olive-green turtleneck sweater kept him warm, along with his trousers and boots. Unlike many of his younger colleagues, he did not look overly anxious or alarmed by Seven's surprise visit to the remote outpost; instead he watched the invaders attentively, waiting cautiously to see how the drama unfolded. *Not an excitable individual,* Seven concluded. *Good. That should make matters less complicated.*

He approached the elder scientist, who neither flinched from Seven's gaze nor attempted to hide behind his frightened staff. "Dr. Wilson Evergreen, I presume," Seven stated calmly. The silver-haired man nodded, confirming his identity. "We have much to talk about, Doctor," Seven continued, "but first"—a sweep of his hand encompassed the rest of the hostages—"is there somewhere nearby where these people can be kept safe and warm?"

Evergreen called Seven's attention to a staircase at the rear of the lab, leading downward. "A tunnel connects the lower level of this structure with the adjacent huts," he explained in a flat mid-Atlantic accent, which struck Seven as subtly but distinctly artificial. He couldn't place Evergreen's origins, though; the renowned scientist had done too good a job of burying his linguistic roots beneath a deliberately neutral diction. *I wonder what he's trying to hide?* Seven wondered. "There is a heated storage facility, approximately fifty yards to the east, that should suit your purposes."

"Very good," Seven agreed. The fewer witnesses to his discussion with Evergreen, the better, but he could hardly expose these innocent bystanders to the glacial weather outdoors. "Agent Singh," he instructed, "please escort these ladies and gentlemen to the storage area Dr. Evergreen described." Given that "Singh" was the Indian equivalent of "Smith," he saw no harm in addressing the young man by name. "Make sure that they are all properly 'calmed,' then return here promptly."

"Understood," Noon acknowledged, aware that Seven wanted him to tranquilize the rest of the hostages once they were securely stowed away. Keeping his servo pointed at the whispering bystanders, he herded them down the stairs and out of sight, leaving only Evergreen and the pacified soldier behind. Seven put his business with the elder scientist on hold until the departing hostages' footsteps faded from hearing.

"There," Evergreen said brusquely. He held a mug of steaming coffee in one hand and a pocket calculator in the other. "My staff and that guard are gone. What do you want from me?"

"I'm interested in your work, Doctor," Seven replied. The heat of the parka was becoming unbearable, but he needed Noon to return before he could risk fumbling with his outer garments. "I found your articles on artificial weather engineering quite ahead of their time, at least until you mysteriously fell silent over two years ago."

"My work is classified these days," Evergreen said, "as you are obviously aware." He eyed Seven appraisingly, no doubt trying to gauge the intruder's motives and potential for violence. "How much do you already know?"

"I know about the hole in Earth's ozone layer," Seven declared confidently, noting the startled expression in Evergreen's clear blue eyes, "located directly above us. I also know that you intend to do something about that hole, something involving a so-called weather satellite which the space shuttle *Discovery* placed in a geostationary orbit above the South Pole less than two months ago."

Evergreen looked surprised by the extent of Seven's knowledge. "How?" he asked, sounding more intrigued than dismayed. "The very existence of the hole hasn't even been made public yet."

"I have my sources," Seven said cryptically. There was no reason Evergreen—or Noon either, for that matter—needed to know that a wise and benevolent alien had chosen, for her own reasons, to live among Earth's human population. He respected Guinan's privacy, just as he did her advice.

Rapid footsteps upon the stairs presaged Noon's return. "The prisoners are taken care of," he reported proudly. His hood had slipped off his head, revealing a greased face gleaming with perspiration. "The soldier attempted to surprise me," he declared, raising a clenched fist, "but his strength was no match for mine."

Seven thought Noon sounded a little too enthusiastic about his victory, but, then again, he was only fourteen. *Time enough to teach him humility and restraint later on,* he decided. *Preferably not in the middle of a vital mission.* "Fine," he commented. "Why don't you close the door, for Dr. Evergreen's sake, then shed that heavy parka?"

"With pleasure!" Noon announced, crossing the wooden floor of the laboratory with astonishing speed. He slammed the painted red door shut, cutting off the howling antarctic wind, and hurriedly wriggled out of his parka, which he let fall carelessly to the floor. He lowered his goggles as well, counting on the black grease to obscure his less than celebrated features.

"That's better! I was suffocating in that monstrous jacket."

His triumphant tussle with the guard had definitely elevated Noon's spirits. *Something to watch out for,* Seven thought with concern. *We wouldn't want him to develop a taste for physical violence.* He frowned at the ceremonial silver dagger tucked into Noon's belt, visible now that the young man had shucked his outdoor gear. Seven disapproved of the weapon's presence on this mission, but knew that male Sikhs were required by their faith to carry such blades at all times. Granted, Noon didn't strike Seven as overly religious, yet he could hardly ask the young man to disregard the centuries-old traditions of his people—at least not without good reason.

"I'm glad you're more comfortable," he stated, removing his own goggles. "Now cover the doctor while I dispose of my own excess layers."

Evergreen sipped thoughtfully from his coffee while Seven efficiently discarded his parka. Overheated limbs gratefully welcomed their sudden lack of confinement. "I assume you appreciate the significance of the hole?" Evergreen challenged him, fiddling with his calculator as he did so.

Seven knew exactly what the hole meant. "It's alarming proof that humanity's widespread use of chlorofluorocarbons is having a serious effect on Earth's upper atmosphere. Furthermore—"

A moan from the tranquilized guard interrupted Seven, who glanced quickly at the prone figure to make certain that the guard was not reviving prematurely. Noon's servo, he recalled, was locked at a very low setting; still, the pacified soldier should have remained insensate for another half hour or so. *Probably a false alarm,* Seven guessed, even as Noon turned toward the guard as well.

Evergreen took advantage of the distraction to hurl the contents of his coffee cup at Seven's face, while simultaneously pointing his handheld calculator at Noon. Bizarrely, a dart fired explosively from the top of the calculator, trailing a thin metal wire behind it. The missile struck the surprised teenager in the shoulder, causing him to jerk suddenly, as though receiving a powerful electric shock. His servo flew from his twitching fingers, landing on the floor several yards away. A wordless cry of pain and anger erupted from Noon's lips.

At the same time, Seven staggered backward, caught off guard by the splash of hot coffee in his face. The greasy ointment on his face protected him from any serious burns, but the shock left him momentarily vulnerable to further attacks. Seizing his opportunity, Evergreen tossed aside his exotically equipped calculator and closed the distance between them, cracking Seven on the side of the head with the empty coffee mug, then grabbing on to Seven's wrist with unexpected strength. Blinking and sputtering, Seven struggled to hang on to his servo even as Evergreen shoved Seven's trigger arm up and away from his own body. "I don't know who you are," the scientist boasted, his face only inches away from Seven's, "but you'd be surprised how many spies and assassins have tried to get the better of me!" With his free hand, he slugged Seven viciously in the kidneys. "I've outlasted them all."

Wincing in pain at Evergreen's repeated blows,

Seven grappled with the renowned researcher, who was clearly no stranger to hand-to-hand combat. *Blast it!* he thought, cursing himself for his carelessness. *The whole mission is falling apart.* But how was he supposed to have known that a respected scientist, stationed thousands of miles from any possible threat, would be carrying a concealed taser weapon?

Ironically, it now appeared that the nameless guard, whose ill-timed utterance had distracted Seven in the first place, had merely been talking in his sleep. Peering over Evergreen's shoulder, the last of the coffee trickling away from his eyes, Seven saw the tranquilized soldier contentedly roll over and slip back to dreamland. *And thank the Aegis for small favors,* he thought, blocking one of Evergreen's left-handed punches to his midsection. *I'm having enough trouble with the man the soldier was supposed to be guarding!*

Evergreen was proving to be a formidable opponent, but Seven's superior strength, produced by generations of selective breeding on an alien world, gradually began to prevail. Recovering from the older man's earlier attacks, Seven succeeded in grabbing on to the scientist's free hand, even as they continued to wrestle for control of the servo. Seven's weapon arm slowly lowered, pushing back against Evergreen's strenuous resistance, while the combative older man stumbled backward involuntarily, losing ground. Seven did not want to have to render Evergreen unconscious with the servo—he still needed to confront the man regarding his potentially destabilizing experiment—but realized that might be the only way to subdue the resourceful scientist. His thumb hovered above the servo's touch-sensitive controls. "We don't need to battle like this, Doctor," he tried to convince his opponent. "I just want to—"

His urgent appeal to reason was drowned out by a vengeful war cry from Noon. "Villainous cur!" Rotating both himself and his foe clockwise, so that he saw the quaking teenager over Evergreen's shoulder, Seven watched as Noon violently yanked the electrified dart from his shoulder, then reached for his knife, his face contorted by murderous rage. "You'll pay for that, old man!"

"Noon! No!" Seven shouted, horrified at the disaster he saw unfolding before his eyes. "Don't!"

But he was too late. The furious youth hurled the unsheathed blade with all his superhuman strength and accuracy. Seven felt the impact of the dagger as it struck Evergreen squarely in the back. The stabbed researcher stiffened abruptly and fell against Seven, who hastily grabbed on to the man's body to keep him from falling. Bright arterial blood trickled from Evergreen's lips while his eyes widened in shock. He tried to speak, but only a faint gurgle emerged from his throat. Seven watched in agony and dismay as the brilliant scientist took his last, dying breaths. *This can't be happening!* he thought.

As gently as he could, he lowered Evergreen's body to the floor, laying him carefully on his side. The gleaming silver handle of Noon's dagger, buried in the man's back all the way up to its hilt, was the center of a spreading crimson stain soaking through Evergreen's thick woolen sweater. A hasty inspection of the injury confirmed Seven's worst fears—the wound was clearly mortal. Although Noon had missed, barely, his target's spine, the dagger had instantly pierced Evergreen's heart from behind. He was beyond saving.

Sickened and appalled, Seven put away his servo and plucked the bloodstained knife from between Evergreen's shoulder blades. He mournfully contemplated the fatal weapon, then rose from the murdered man's side to face the young warrior he had so foolishly brought to the South Pole. "What have you done?"

To his credit, Noon himself looked a bit shaken by what had just occurred. Now that his deadly fury had claimed its victim, he stared at Evergreen's lifeless body with the aghast expression of someone who had obviously never killed a man before. "Is he . . . ?" he asked Seven hesitantly.

"Yes." Seven massaged his forehead, smearing the oily grease above his brow. *Now what do I do?* he pondered hopelessly. An icy chill even more numbing than Antarctica's glacial deep-freeze radiated outward from his heart. *About the mission* and *Noon?* "He's dead."

Panic flickered briefly in the young Sikh's brown eyes, only to be quickly replaced by a look of cold defiance. His expression hardened, along with the rest of his body language, as Noon's adolescent pride overcame whatever guilt he might have felt. "He struck the first blow," the youth asserted boldly, crossing his arms atop his broad chest. Spotting the discarded taser-calculator on the floor, he strode toward the offending weapon, then crushed it beneath the heel of his boot. "He chose his fate." He shrugged his shoulders with as much worldly indifference as a fourteen-year-old could muster. "Such are the fortunes of war."

"This wasn't a war!" Seven said sharply. "Our mission is to *prevent* wars, not create still more needless bloodshed." Despite his stern tone, he blamed himself more than Noon. *I should have never brought him on such a pre-*

carious mission. He is too young, too violent. Evergreen's blood dripped down the length of the silver blade, turning the hilt wet and sticky within Seven's grasp, and staining his own fingers scarlet. *This is an unmitigated catastrophe. For all of us.*

Noon stubbornly refused to admit any error or regret. "You were under attack. I removed the threat." Leaving behind the smashed remains of Evergreen's well-armed calculator, he crossed the floor to retrieve his fallen servo. "You should be grateful, not indignant."

I could have handled Evergreen myself, Seven thought bitterly, *and without killing him!* "There were other ways," he began, hoping that, at the very least, he could still somehow force Noon to confront the magnitude of what had transpired. "There are *always* alternatives to murder. . . ."

A harsh, choking cough from the floor startled Seven, cutting him off abruptly. He looked down in amazement to see Evergreen stirring restlessly upon the wooden timbers. The stricken man was pale and gasping, his face grimacing in pain, but he was clearly, impossibly alive. Moreover, he appeared to be recovering from what should have been a fatal injury at an incredibly accelerated rate. Even the flow of blood had evidently halted from the gash in his back, judging from the way the crimson stain had stopped spreading. The sound of his laboring lungs echoed within the confines of the arctic lab, defying probability with every sharp intake of breath.

"You said he was dead!" Noon accused, his rebellious pose collapsing in the face of Evergreen's astounding resurrection. The teenager stared at the quaking target of his wrath, his blackened face torn between astonishment and relief.

He should be relieved, Seven thought, grateful that at least some part of Noon was glad to see his victim return to life. *That wound would have killed even Noon or myself instantly; there was no way an ordinary human being could have survived. Unless. . . .*

When Evergreen, still trembling and gasping, attempted to lift his body from the floor, Seven was so taken aback by the sheer unlikeliness of this event that he almost forgot to offer the injured man any assistance. At the last minute, he remembered to lend Evergreen a hand, carefully helping the man back onto his feet. The scientist groaned loudly, taking a second to regain his balance, then reached back over his shoulder, groping for the site of his injury. "Where?" he mumbled, looking genuinely surprised to find the knife missing. Spotting the blood-smeared weapon in Seven's hand, he cautiously backed away from his recent opponent, then cast a wary glance at Noon, who stood several yards away, himself more than a little confused. "Damn," Evergreen muttered gloomily. He acted more like a criminal caught in the act than a man who had just escaped death by the thinnest of margins.

"You needn't fear us," Seven insisted. "No one is going to attack you again." He dropped the dagger onto the floor, then gave it a kick in Noon's direction. He raised his hands slowly to show that he was no longer armed. "What happened was a mistake."

"One hell of a mistake," Evergreen grunted, scowling at Seven while rubbing his palms together to restore his circulation. Already the color was coming back into his face, rendering him remarkably hale and hearty for a man who had just been stabbed in the heart. "I suppose you're wondering why I'm still alive."

Seven had his suspicions. "You're an immortal, aren't you?"

Now it was Evergreen's turn to look surprised. His head jerked backwards as he stared at Seven with startled eyes. "How the devil do you know that?"

"It's the only logical explanation," Seven replied. Although it was incalculably rare, he had encountered this unique human mutation before. "I assume your injured flesh has already regenerated?"

"Something like that," admitted Evergreen, whose name, Seven now presumed, was something of a private joke. "If there's a way to kill me for good, I haven't found it yet."

"No!" Noon blurted. He held his dagger at his side, unwilling to sheathe his knife despite its failure to inflict any lasting harm on Evergreen. "This is a trick! It's not possible."

"Yes, it is," Seven corrected him brusquely, "and put away that barbaric weapon right now." He returned his attention to Evergreen, who now regarded Seven with open curiosity and respect. "If I may ask, Doctor, exactly how old are you?"

Evergreen shrugged, apparently seeing no point in further pretense. "I was born in Mesopotamia over six thousand years ago," he divulged, "and have survived much more than your young accomplice's knack for knife-throwing. I've lived many lives, as Solomon, Alexander, Methuselah, and others. Believe me, the unmoving sun above us would be setting before I finished listing all my past identities and accomplishments." He chuckled dryly. "Consider yourselves privileged, gentlemen. You're in the presence of living history."

So it seems, Seven reflected. The only other possible explanation, that Evergreen was some manner of extraterrestrial entity, was even less probable; Seven tried hard to keep track of any alien visitations to this era (although the Q had occasionally been known to slip beneath his radar). The shattered remnants of the ageless scientist's highly unusual pocket calculator caught Seven's eye and he nudged the broken bits of plastic with the toe of his boot. "For a man immune to mortal injury, you come surprisingly well armed."

Evergreen snorted acerbically. "One does not live through six millennia of human history, much of it bloody, without learning to be prepared to defend oneself at all times. Paranoia, I fear, is a natural consequence of long acquaintance with mankind." He sighed at the mess Noon had made of his ingeniously concealed taser weapon. "Besides, I'm an inveterate tinkerer. Well, at least since the Renaissance."

Seven wondered what else the man now known as Evergreen might have invented over the last sixty centuries. "I wish I had more time to inquire as to your personal history, Dr. Evergreen. As one deeply concerned with the future of humanity, I would value your perspective on the past." Despite his and Roberta's occasional forays into time travel, there was still much of Earth's tumultuous history that defied reason and comprehension. "Nevertheless, I must return to the matter at hand." Stern gray eyes surveyed the computers and control panels lining the walls around them. "I confess that I am puzzled to find you, with all your accumulated experience, engaged in such a reckless endeavor. If nothing else, surely you are aware that military activities in Antarctica are expressly forbidden by international treaty?"

"Military?" Offended by the very suggestion, Evergreen turned away from Seven to contemplate a control panel composed of numerous switches, buttons, and gauges. "To the contrary, sir, my work here is expressly designed to rescue mankind from its own foolhardiness. Rampant abuse of CFCs, in aerosol sprays and such, is literally eating away at Earth's protective ozone layer; in fact, close to three percent of the world's ozone has disappeared in the last five years alone. If nothing is done, the increased ultraviolet radiation will drastically increase skin-cancer rates, kill the vital phytoplanktons at the base of the marine food chain, and even accelerate global warming."

Seven appreciated the scientist's foresight and concern, but had little time to listen to lectures on rudimentary atmospheric maintenance. "I am fully aware of the 'greenhouse effect' and its implications, Doctor. I am concerned that your cure may be just as dangerous as the crisis you hope to avert."

"Nonsense," Evergreen asserted testily. "My solution is elegance itself." He gestured at the generous array of computers and apparatus surrounding them. "By manipulating Earth's own magnetic field, via a geostationary satellite secretly launched into orbit by the space shuttle *Discovery*, I hope to use the Van Allen radiation belt surrounding the planet to convert free oxygen into ozone, thus repairing the damage done to our atmosphere." He glanced upward, beyond the ceiling. "If I can close the hole directly above us, as I have every reason to believe I can, then humanity will have the means to undo the hurt done by our chemical carelessness."

"All very well and good, Doctor," Seven conceded, "but let me ask you this: Couldn't the same technology be used to *create* holes in the ozone layer, say above an enemy nation?"

Evergreen scratched his chin, looking disturbed by the suggestion. "It's possible, I suppose, but surely no one in their right mind would. . . ." His voice trailed off as the dire implications of such a scenario sank in.

"Would what, Dr. Evergreen?" Seven asked, pressing his point home. "Want to inflict an ecological catastrophe—including pandemic cancer, blindness, famine, et cetera—upon another country? Or, at the very least, desire the ability to threaten as much?" He subjected the immortal scientist to a penetrating stare. "After six thousand years, you must be aware of the human capacity for warfare—through every means possible."

"But that's not what this experiment is all about!" Evergreen protested, more than a little defensively. "Why, our funding comes straight from the Environmental Protection Agency and the National Institute of Science. We have nothing to do with the Pentagon." He glanced over at the slumbering soldier. "Well, aside from a reasonable need for security, that is."

Seven could tell that, despite the scientist's very vocal objections, he was getting through to Evergreen. *Too bad I can't tell him what ozone-depleting weapons did to the Vyyoxi homeworld,* he reflected somberly, *or how the Zakpro managed to completely wreck their environment.* Stratospheric warfare had proved disastrous on every planet where it had been pursued, so Seven had no intention of letting humanity head down that road, not if it could possibly be avoided.

"I'm afraid I have to disillusion you further, Doctor."

Seven retrieved a floppy disk from one of the inner pockets of his insulated nylon vest and handed it to Evergreen. "As you can see, not only does the majority of your funding come, albeit indirectly, from the United States Defense Department, but military applications of your technology are already being developed and analyzed by top Pentagon strategists."

Looking more and more unhappy, Evergreen inserted the disk into a nearby PC and began scrolling through the documents displayed on the monitor. His expression darkened as he skimmed the various classified reports and memos Seven had, with varying degrees of difficulty, extracted from the shadowy recesses of the military-industrial complex. "Those bastards," Evergreen muttered angrily, the phosphor glow of the screen casting mauve shadows upon his remarkably well preserved face. "Those lying, two-faced—"

His heartfelt stream of invective ended with an ancient Mesopotamian obscenity. Or so Seven assumed; his briefing on Terran cultures and history, although extensive, was not quite *that* comprehensive.

Finally, after several minutes, Evergreen looked up from the monitor. "I don't suppose," he said morosely, "that there's any possibility these are masterfully done forgeries?"

Seven shook his head. "If necessary, I can provide you with additional evidence regarding the provenance of these documents, but I trust that won't be necessary. You strike me as perceptive enough to recognize the truth when you see it, no matter how distressing."

"You want proof?" Noon said, intruding into the discussion. He pointed the tip of his dagger, whose blade still glistened redly, at the insensate guard. "Let me wake him up. I can get the truth from him."

A cruel glint in his dark eyes left no doubt as to his intentions, much to Seven's dismay. Now the youth wanted to beat or torture a helpless prisoner for information? Seven wasn't sure what horrified him most: Noon's unfeeling ruthlessness, or his own failure to spot this aspect of his protégé's character earlier on. *Is this something he inherited from his Machiavellian mother,* Seven wondered mournfully, *or a response to nearly being burned alive a few months ago?*

If the former, then perhaps Sarina Kaur was having the last laugh after all, with her son's callousness proving a disheartening testament to the power of genetics. A deadly arrogance, it seemed, was coded into his very DNA.

Evergreen forestalled Noon's brutal intentions before Seven had a chance to reprimand the Indian youth. "That won't be necessary, young man," the ageless scientist said, his voice suffused with resignation along with profound regret. His head drooped in front of the PC, his fingers massaging his brow as he cradled his skull upon his hands. "How could I have been so naive?" he asked himself accusingly. "I suppose I wanted to think that mankind had advanced beyond such things, that we were truly on the verge of a more peaceful, more enlightened era."

"Soon," Seven assured him, "but not right away." He looked askance at the high-tech hardware filling the metal hut. "And weapons like this will only postpone, perhaps for centuries, the fulfillment of humanity's bright promise."

Evergreen shrugged fatalistically. "Well, I've waited

six millennia for utopia; I suppose I can wait a while longer." He rose slowly from his seat before the PC, suddenly seeming to feel the full weight of his myriad years and identities. A melancholy tone entered his voice. "The longer I live, though, the more I sometimes want to withdraw from history altogether, sequester myself away on some remote island or planetoid, far away from the ceaseless Sturm und Drang of mortal men and women." He chuckled bleakly. "I suppose, after all I've seen and experienced, that it's something of a miracle that I haven't completely transformed into some flinty old misanthrope."

Seven sympathized with the immortal's acute disappointment. *If I sometimes grow impatient with the twentieth century's unsteady trek toward a new millennium,* he reflected, *how much more world-weary must be someone who has suffered through humanity's growing pains since the very beginning?* "Believe it or not, Dr. Evergreen, I have faith in the human race to evolve into a species—and a society—embodying their highest aspirations."

Stepping past Evergreen, he reclaimed the incriminating floppy disk and deleted the data from the scientist's PC. "But society is not ready for this technology, I'm sorry."

"I am as well," Evergreen said. "After I've repaired the hole above us, I will destroy all my files and fake my own death once again." He sighed gloomily, sounding more bored than dismayed at the prospect. "Lord knows I've 'died' enough times already. At this point, I have it down to an art."

"So I imagine," Seven stated, wondering how many different lifetimes and identities the immortal had lived through. *No wonder I couldn't pinpoint his origins.*

"Before you act to close the gap in the ozone layer, however, consider: Wouldn't it be wiser to leave the hole as it is, as a warning to humanity?"

"What?" Evergreen exclaimed, startled by Seven's suggestion. He stared at Seven in disbelief. "You can't be serious!"

"I am seldom otherwise," Seven insisted. Clearly, Evergreen required more persuasion. "The other problem with your technique, Doctor, besides its potential military applications, is that it provides the people of the world with little incentive to modify their environmentally careless behavior. You're offering the world a technological quick fix—a convenient Band-Aid of sorts—when what is really needed is a deeper, global awareness of the long-term impact of chemical pollution."

Reluctantly, Evergreen digested Seven's arguments. "I see your point; the hole would certainly serve as a cautionary example, should its existence become widely known." He grimaced, as though his admission had left a bad taste in his mouth. "I hate the idea, though, of leaving the sky so injured when it's within my ability to heal the wound."

"But repairing the hole would also prove, beyond any shadow of doubt, the efficacy of your technology," Seven pointed out, "which would almost surely spur an all-out effort, on behalf of your sponsors in the Defense Department, to re-create your work." He crumpled the floppy disk within his fist, then deliberately tore the primitive storage mechanism in half. "Better that your theories remain untested, at least as far as the world is concerned."

"You've thought this all out, haven't you?" Evergreen didn't bother to conceal the resentment in his voice.

"What would you do if I decided not to go along with this scenario?" He looked suspiciously at the knife-wielding young Sikh standing nearby. "Is that what *he's* here for?"

"Assassination is not my business," Seven assured the aggrieved scientist, who was certainly entitled to some hard feelings, given that Seven was forcing him to abandon the work of many years. "Had you not cooperated, I would have taken control of your apparatus to create a massive electronic pulse that would have temporarily disrupted electronic equipment throughout this entire continent, thus alerting every other scientific outpost in Antarctica to your unsanctioned experiments here. I would have also used this command center to order the satellite above us to self-destruct, thus putting you months, if not years, behind your original schedule."

Evergreen flinched at the prospect of destroying his specialized satellite, but Seven continued to outline his backup plan, if only to convince the skeptical genius of just how committed he was to his goal of calling off this perilous scientific endeavor. "With luck, the resulting international outcry would cause this entire project to be shut down indefinitely. Or, at the very least, I would have bought myself—and the world—time enough to pursue other means of defusing the threat posed by your discoveries."

Evergreen gaped at Seven, nonplussed. "*Who* are you anyway?" he asked with more amazement than the jaded immortal was probably accustomed to feeling. "Where did you come from?"

"That's a conversation for another day," Seven answered. Kneeling to search through the deep pockets of his discarded parka, he produced a handful of miniaturized explosive charges. "The point is that I would much rather secure your own assistance in this manner, rather than provoke an international incident. But we need to move quickly, before your tranquilized colleagues and guardians can interfere."

"Yes, I suppose you're right," Evergreen said, frowning. He looked wistfully around the south polar laboratory, knowing that he would never see this place again. *Or not for a century or two,* Seven corrected himself. Perhaps someday, when civilization was ready, the undying genius could return to Antarctica to finish his experiment.

Seven wanted to think so.

Less than forty-five minutes later, the three men watched from the safety of a snow-covered ridge as the metal hut containing Evergreen's one-of-a-kind apparatus imploded before their eyes, turning into a smoldering, smoking pit at the center of the top-secret outpost. Seven had carefully rigged his explosive charges to keep the destructive force of the detonation confined within the perimeter of the now-empty laboratory, thus preserving the rest of the buildings to serve as shelter for the base's personnel.

Mission accomplished, Seven thought, an icy wind carrying the smell of burning circuitry and insulation across the frozen barrens, *despite too many unpleasant surprises.* Their departure had been delayed only by Seven's insistence on personally transporting the tranquilized guard to a safer location within the base; after Noon's murderous attack on Evergreen, Seven was not about to delegate care of another hostage to the merciless young superman. Only an impossible stroke of luck, he realized, had kept this mission from resulting in a needless death. *I can hardly count on Noon's next victim to be unkillable as well.*

Sullen and silent, Noon stood in the snow a few yards away, pointedly keeping his distance from the two older men. The youth's pride was still smarting, apparently, from Seven's reprimands earlier. He had paid careful attention, however, to Seven's placement of the plastic explosives, something that his would-be mentor found more than a little troubling.

But now was not the time to fret about Noon's apparent aptitude for sabotage and warfare, not out in the open in subzero temperatures. "How many other copies of your research and designs exist?" Seven asked Evergreen, shouting over the wintry Antarctic gusts. Somewhere above them, he knew, a one-of-a-kind satellite had already plunged toward Earth, burning up in reentry. Evergreen himself had sent the self-destruct command to his orbiting panacea, only minutes before they had fled the sabotaged control room.

"Just the master copy, in my office in Los Alamos." Evergreen rubbed his gloved hands together vigorously, struggling to keep warm. "Like I've said, I've gotten paranoid in my own age. Over the years, too many greedy people have stolen the credit for my discoveries and inventions—don't get me started about Edison. These days, nobody sees my work until I'm good and ready to unveil it myself."

"Good," Seven acknowledged. That made containing the knowledge much easier. "We can get you to New Mexico before news of this incident reaches America, and long before anyone realizes you survived the explosion. After that, I'm more than willing to lend you whatever assistance you need to set up a new identity elsewhere."

"That won't be necessary," Evergreen stated. "I've already made all the necessary arrangements to start over again." He ruefully contemplated the cremated remains of one lifetime's work. "I just didn't think I'd be doing so quite so soon."

On that somber note, Seven proceeded to transport all three men out of the cold. Ordinarily, he went out of his way to avoid using matter transmission in front of civilians, but Da Vinci Base's remote location had left him very little choice. He felt he could trust Evergreen, however; the ageless scientist had too many secrets of his own to risk exposing Seven's. *We make an unusual trio,* he reflected, as the luminous blue mist enveloped them. *An immortal, a genetically engineered superman, and an enhanced human raised on another world.* Who would have ever thought that twentieth-century Earth could yield such unlikely allies?

What a shame, Seven thought, *that Noon proved so dangerous and unreliable.* He'd had the potential to become an excellent agent, maybe even a planetary supervisor someday. Was there any way to salvage the youth's tremendous promise—or were all his extraordinary gifts doomed to go to waste?

Or worse.

CHAPTER THIRTY

BHOPAL
CENTRAL INDIA
DECEMBER 3, 1984

IT WAS ONE-FIFTEEN IN THE MORNING BY THE TIME
Noon arrived, along with Gary Seven, in the moonlit
streets of Bhopal. The glowing fog dispersed, leaving the
sulking teenager and the older American in a murky alley
between two modern concrete apartment buildings. A
chilly breeze blew from the northwest, and Noon half-
regretted leaving his heavy parka behind at Seven's office, where they had dropped off Evergreen after their
adventure in Antarctica. Rats scurried around and within
the rusty metal Dumpsters hidden away in the alley. The
squeaking vermin struck Noon as uncommonly restless
and agitated, much to his annoyance.

"Quiet!" he barked, snatching up an empty soup can
from the alley floor and hurling it at the nearest cluster
of rats, which broke apart into a profusion of fleeing
gray bodies.

His return to India did little to soothe Noon's turbulent spirit, which still chafed at Seven's obvious disapproval. Even now, the meddlesome American regarded him with mournful eyes and a dour expression. Noon knew that Seven remained disappointed that he had hurled his dagger at Evergreen, no matter how justified he had been in retaliating against the scientist's treacherous taser attack. *How dare he judge me?* Noon thought angrily, glaring at Seven. *I knew what I was doing!*

The light from Hamidia Road, north of the alley, cast elongated shadows upon the dingy asphalt. Distant voices and footsteps sounded from several blocks away, which was peculiar given the lateness of the hour, but Noon's wounded pride took precedence over any curiosity he might have felt. "Well?" he challenged Seven, breaking an awkward silence. "Is that it? Did this misbegotten expedition discharge my debt to you, or was my performance too inadequate to serve as fit payment?"

Seven gazed at Noon, seemingly more in sorrow than in anger. "It wasn't your fault, Noon," he stated solemnly. "I should have never thrust you into such a combustible situation. You are too young, too apt to overreact."

If Seven thought he was helping Noon save face, then he clearly did not understand the aristocratic teen at all. "Do not patronize me, old man!" Noon snarled, Seven's condescending attitude only infuriating him more. "Do not blame me if you lack the will to fight your own battles."

Seven shook his head sadly. "I hope someday you realize, Noon, that life is much more than a combat to be won." He held out an open palm. "In the meantime, I'm afraid I have to ask for your servo back."

"Take it," Noon said defiantly, throwing the slender instrument at Seven's feet, where it skittered across the uneven black pavement. "It is a feeble weapon anyway, limited and halfhearted, much like its wielder."

His flawless vision rapidly adjusting to the murk of the alley, Noon watched Seven's face, hoping to see his insult strike home. Maddeningly, the mysterious American merely offered another bit of unwanted advice as he stooped to retrieve the discarded servo. "Beware of more powerful weapons, Noon. They often inflict as much damage to your soul as they do to your enemies."

Noon opened his mouth, intending to reject Seven's cryptic counsel, but the hubbub of voices in the background, growing ever louder and nearer, could now be recognized as loud, anguished screaming, shocking both men out of their tense verbal duel. "What—?" Seven asked, apprehension deepening the lines of his craggy face. "That's more than one person screaming. Many more."

On this, Noon had to agree. Straining his ears, even as he ran anxiously toward the unknown source of the tumult, he found himself unable to distinguish just how many men and women and children were shrieking in unmistakable pain and terror. For a single blood-chilling moment, his memory flashed back to the bloodthirsty riots in Delhi, only slightly more than a month ago, but, no, this was a different kind of madness, he could tell. The rising clamor of high-pitched human voices, steadily increasing in volume as it drew closer and closer, was not the sound of an angry mob; it was the many-throated cry of a city in mortal agony.

Something terrible has occurred, Noon realized at once. The soles of his boots pounded the pavement as he charged out of the alley into the broad, well-lighted thoroughfare that was Hamidia Road. "Noon!" Seven hollered after him, unable to keep up with the younger man's genetically engineered leg muscles. "Be careful!"

But Noon wasn't worried about himself, only his people. Eyes wide, his long dark hair streaming behind him, he ran headlong into a nightmare. Dozens of people came stampeding toward him, pursued by some horror whose nature Noon could not yet determine, but whose torturous effects were all too visible. A common sickness afflicted the distraught, disorganized crowd; crying, gasping, retching, they tried and failed to outrun whatever ailment was ravaging their defenseless bodies. Men and women in various stages of undress, seemingly driven from their homes and beds in the middle of the night, collapsed onto the street, only to be trampled to death by their panicking neighbors. Tears streamed down a cavalcade of tortured faces, as the fleeing victims clutched their throats and clawed at their eyes, rushing blindly down the road toward Noon. The wailing mob smelled of sweat and vomit and excrement, having lost control of their stomachs and bowels. *By my martyred mother,* Noon wondered, agog with horror, *what kind of plague strikes so quickly?*

A tide of reeking bodies slammed into Noon, almost carrying him away. Thinking quickly, he wrapped an arm around a sturdy lamppost and batted away the frantic refugees whose chaotic flight carried them too near him. "Stay back!" he commanded, gagging at the touch and smell of the befouled wretches jostling against him. "Don't touch me!"

The crowd parted around him as Noon clung to the lamppost with all his strength. Consumed by the necessity to know what had caused this pandemonium, he randomly grabbed one of the refugees by the arm, halting the man's breakneck dash for safety. He yanked his chosen informant, a bearded man wearing only a soiled bathrobe, around so that the stranger was forced to look Noon in the face. To his shock, Noon saw that the man's eyes had been blackened and blinded by some unknown agency. "What is it?" the anguished teen demanded. "What's happened?"

Desperate to get away, to elude the unnamed menace to the north, the man tried to break free, but could not escape Noon's powerful grip. "Let me go!" he yelled, tears gushing from sightless eyes. His voice gurgled wetly, as though his lungs were slowly filling with liquid. "Please, I don't want to die!"

The man was scared out of his mind, Noon realized, but by what? Still hanging on to the lamppost with his strong right arm, Noon longed for a spare hand with which to slap the man in the face, to snap him out of his hysterical state; instead he could only shake the man roughly before interrogating him again. "Speak to me—quickly!" he ordered. The incongruity of a fourteen-year-old boy bullying a grown man several years older than he was went unnoticed in the frenzied chaos threatening to engulf them. "What's happening? What started this panic?"

"I don't know!" the man protested, trying futilely to tug himself free. He swung at Noon's chin, connecting with his fist, but the indomitable youth shrugged off the blow, then retaliated by yanking on the man's arm hard enough to dislocate his shoulder. The man yelped in pain, his face contorting beneath his bushy black beard. "Stop, please! My arm!"

"Speak!" Noon gave the injured limb a vicious twist. He took no pleasure in hurting this unlucky stranger, but he craved answers and would do whatever was necessary to extract them from his unwilling captive. "Tell me now and you shall go free."

Wincing in agony, the man nodded and cradled his aching arm with his free hand. "Yes, yes! Of course!" he babbled, his watery eyes pleading for mercy. "It's something in the air! Poison! It killed my wife, my daughters . . . they died where they fell, coughing out their last breaths!" His entire body quaked at the memory. "For pity's sake, young sir, let me go!" Blackened eyes stared past Noon, into the north wind. "We have to go now, believe me! The poison—it's coming toward us even as we speak! Death is in the air!"

Satisfied that the man knew little more about the catastrophe, Noon expertly popped the dislocated arm back into its socket, then let go of him as promised. Sparing neither another word nor backward glance, the unfortunate man staggered away as quickly as he could, holding on tightly to his bad arm as he disappeared into the flood of scrambling refugees. Noon forgot the man just as swiftly, sifting instead through the particulars of the story he had just heard. *Poison in the air?*

Perhaps this was an enemy attack, he speculated, but his keen mind immediately cast doubt on that theory. Located at the heart of the subcontinent, Bhopal was hundreds of miles from the nearest border and, although the state capital, hardly a prime military target. Aside from the government bureaucracy, its principal industry was the old, and increasingly obsolete, pesticide factory at the outskirts of town. *Just north of here, in fact,* Khan recalled. An alarming possibility intruded into his mind, filling his soul with dread. *Oh, no! Not that . . . !*

Guessing the truth, but needing confirmation, he grabbed on to the lamppost with both hands and shinned up the iron post until he was several feet above the onrushing crowd. Peering north up the length of Hamidia Road, he saw thick white fumes blowing toward him, only four or five blocks away. The swirling mist was carried by the same icy wind that had chilled him ever since his arrival in the alley, and, through the fumes, he glimpsed a multitude of bodies littering the streets and sidewalks, some twitching and shuddering, others moving not at all. Fallen bodies were everywhere; he couldn't even begin to count the casualties.

Sirens blared overhead, too late for the blinded man's wife and daughters, and a police helicopter came flying over Hamidia Road, high above the throngs of scared and ailing civilians. "Warning! Poison gas is spreading!" the copter's loudspeakers bellowed over the heartrending cries of the frightened populace. Whirring propellers whipped up the air around Noon, but could do little to drive back the toxic cloud advancing southward. "Run! Run for your lives!"

Too little, too late, Noon thought bitterly, while yet admiring the courage and discipline of the police officers trying to spread the alarm. The suffocating white fumes crept forward, forcing the helicopter to climb higher to avoid being caught within the toxic cloud, even as Noon's worst fears cemented into certainty.

The chemical plant up north, he realized. Built decades ago by an American company, Union Carbide, to manufacture various forms of insecticide. Critics had been insisting for years that the outdated and run-down facility, housing many tons of toxic chemicals, was a disaster waiting to happen; as an engineering student, Noon had personally toured the plant in the past, and been appalled by its crude design and deteriorating condition, as well as by the slipshod conduct of its poorly trained employees. Corporate greed and inertia had kept the plant in operation, however.

Until tonight, when Bhopal's luck finally ran out.

Fools! Noon thought angrily, gripping the pole with both his hands and ankles. Who had allowed such an obvious hazard to fester all this time, upwind of a major population center? Even knowing what he did about the plant's defects and dangers, Noon was still taken aback by the scale of the catastrophe unfolding around him. At least four kilometers of densely packed slums and shantytowns, as well as a major railway station, he recalled, were crammed between the Union Carbide plant and this suburban district. *How many victims have there been already?* he wondered, envisioning the deadly fog as it swept through block after block of crowded neighborhoods, suffocating people in their sleep. *How many deaths?*

"Thousands," he estimated, his voice a whisper. Thousands would die—no, were doubtless dead already. He railed inwardly at the entrenched corruption and incompetence that had made this atrocity possible. *If I were in charge of the world,* he vowed, *such criminal carelessness would not be allowed.* A fierce resolve gripped him, that the world, overrun by imbeciles and charlatans, was careering out of control, sorely in need of a firm hand at the wheel. *Someone* needed to put this long-suffering planet to rights, and Noon could think of no one better suited to do so than himself. *Not if I ruled the world,* he corrected himself, fully understanding his true destiny at last.

When.

A voice from the street below intruded upon his lofty musings. "Noon!" Seven shouted, having fought his way through the tumult to catch up with the youth. Like Noon before him, he hung on to the bottom half of the lamppost to keep from being carried away by the panicked horde. "We have to get away from here!"

Was that all this colossal slaughter meant to Seven? Merely another daring mission to escape from? With a disdainful sneer, Noon dropped to the sidewalk below, his muscular legs easily absorbing the impact of his landing. "Leave me alone!" he snapped.

Twin antennae sprang from Seven's servo. He aimed the sensors at the approaching cloud, then scowled at the sequence of beeps the wand emitted. "That's methyl isocyanate," he informed Noon urgently. "Even you can't survive that."

Despite the youth's justifiable wrath, Seven's warning caught Noon's attention. He was quite familiar with MIC, a volatile and highly toxic compound that reacted violently with water. He could readily imagine what a cloud of gaseous MIC could do to a human being's eyes and lungs.

Even still, he was not yet ready to abandon Bhopal to its ghastly fate. "But all these people!" he objected, his adolescent voice cracking. "They're dying by the hundreds!"

"I know," Seven said grimly. The servo's antennae retracted and he hurriedly gave his all-purpose instrument a new set of coordinates. By now, the bulk of the fleeing crowd had moved on, leaving them alone on the sidewalk, amid the dead and the dying. Only a few paces away, in the middle of the street, an old woman in a bright yellow sari writhed upon the asphalt, drowning in her own fluids. She was only one of many dozens, unable to outrun the choking death that had come upon her in the night. "It's too late," Seven insisted, his face hardening into a stoic mask. "There's nothing we can do now."

A familiar blue fog began to form behind Seven, but Noon resisted stepping toward the shimmering portal. "My friends!" he reminded Seven, staring upward at the nearby apartment complex. His classmates from the university—Darshan, Rajiv, Zail, Maneka—were surely up there now, in a penthouse apartment belonging to Zail's older brother. "I can't just leave them!"

Seven followed Noon's gaze to the upper stories of the towering concrete building. "If they're high enough, your friends should be all right," he stated confidently, "provided they stay indoors and keep the windows closed." He looked north, toward the sprawling slums surrounding the city. "It's those who live closer to the earth, or without shelter at all, who will bear the brunt of this horrible accident."

His cold-blooded analysis of the situation fanned the flames blazing within Noon, but the brilliant teen could not refute Seven's assessment. In theory, his friends would likely survive, unlike the gasping masses impelled into the streets by the ever-expanding cloud of poison. Already, the first faint whiffs of the MIC threatened him and Seven, causing Noon's eyes and throat to burn. *This is it,* he realized. *My last chance to save myself.* He could either join the retreating mob in their panic-stricken flight from the gas—or take the preternatural avenue of escape offered by Gary Seven.

Misty white tendrils slithered down the sidewalk, licking at his ankles. Seven lingered at the periphery of a very different fog, one that glowed blue and radiant. "Noon!" he called out stridently, his face and figure growing indistinct within the numinous azure mist. "We can't wait any longer!"

He was right, damn him. Holding his breath, his eyes screwed tightly shut against the searing chemical fumes, Noon swallowed his pride and ran into the roiling cloud of plasma, his fists clenched in anger and frustration. He half-expected to collide with Seven inside the incandescent haze, but he encountered no resistance at all, the older man having apparently dematerialized mere instants before. Opening his eyes, Noon slowed to a trot within the opaque blue limbo Seven somehow used to flit hither and yon about the Earth. The transporter's electric tingle was pleasant compared to the caustic effects of the MIC. Tears leaked from the corners of his eyes, which still burned slightly, but the pain quickly faded, suggesting that no permanent damage had been done. *Not to me, that is.*

Many thousands in Bhopal could not say the same. Even the survivors, he expected, would bear the scars of this day for the rest of their lives, in the form of lasting illnesses and injuries, not to mention painful memories of loved ones lost. *Never again,* he decided, a look of unshakable determination upon his youthful face. *I shall not permit it.*

He kept walking forward until the mist began to thin. "Seven!" he cried out impatiently, desiring to waste no more time dealing with the crafty American's technological sleight-of-hand. There was too much to be done, there were too many injustices to be remedied. "Can you hear me, Seven? We must speak at once!"

As he stepped out of the tingling plasma, Noon expected to find himself back in Seven's offices in New York. Instead he had returned to his college dormitory in New Delhi, over six hundred kilometers north of Bhopal. The glowing fog evanesced rapidly, leaving the irate teenager and the older American in the center of Noon's private room, which was just as cluttered and cozy as he had left it. An electric typewriter and pocket calculator sat atop the heavy *sheshamwood* desk, next to piled textbooks and research papers. More books, ranging from advanced engineering texts to classics of Asian and Western literature, bulged from the inadequate bookshelves or accumulated in stacks upon the simple *dhurrie* carpet covering the floor. An ivory chess set, the pieces carved in martial poses, rested on a hand-carved *chowkie* stool, beside a smallish television set perched atop a heap of painted wooden milk cartons. Light mosquito netting covered the wrought-iron posts of his unmade bed, while the Nishan Sahib, the scarlet pennant of the Sikh people, adorned the monsoon-blue wall above his desk.

The familiar setting failed to quench his righteous fury at the inexcusably preventable disaster that had befallen Bhopal. "I suppose you expect me to thank you," he hissed venomously at Seven, "for rescuing me in the nick of time." He angrily kicked over the carved wooden stool bearing the chessboard, scattering pawns and bishops to the far corners of the room. "Never mind that, while we were playing spy games at the South Pole, my people were dying, gassed to death like rats being exterminated!"

He recalled the scurrying vermin he and Seven had encountered immediately upon their arrival in Bhopal. Small wonder the rodents had been so agitated in that dismal alley; they must have scented the fatal venom approaching on the wind. *Did those rats fare any better than their two-legged brethren?* he wondered morosely. *And why was there no advance warning alerting city dwellers of the accident at the plant?* There should have been time enough to raise some manner of alarm, if only to warn people to get indoors and close their windows. *More administrative incompetence,* he guessed, his blood boiling at the needless loss of life. *Simpletons! Half-wits!*

"I am very sorry," Seven volunteered, "that this disaster has struck your country." He stood stiffly at the back of the room, in front of a shelf crammed with used hardcovers and paperbacks. "It's a terrible thing."

His feeble condolences were not enough for Noon. "Then why couldn't you have averted it?" he accused Seven, turning savagely on the older man. "Why was a satellite over Antarctica more important than that ticking time bomb of a plant next to Bhopal?"

"I'm not omniscient," Seven stated quietly, taking no offense at Noon's harsh words. "There was no way of knowing that this was going to happen tonight."

"That plant was a menace that should have been shut down years ago!" Noon paced back and forth across the floor, unable to stand still. He hurled his heated reproaches at Seven like poison darts. "Everyone knew that! Why didn't you?"

"That's not my job," Seven answered, refusing, much to Noon's aggravation, to accept any complicity in the nightmare they had just exited. "What's happening in

Bhopal is a tragedy of horrendous, even historic, proportions, Noon, but it was only an industrial accident, not the start of a world war. My primary mission is to prevent mankind from destroying itself completely." He stepped toward Noon, raising his hands in a conciliatory gesture. "I can't solve all of Earth's social and economic problems. Nor should I. Those are for your own institutions—your own leaders and reformers—to grapple with as best they can. I'm sorry."

Noon could not believe his ears. "Accidents happen? Is that all you can say to me?" He heard shouting, and racing footsteps, outside the room, the dormitory jolting to life despite the lateness of the hour. *News of the disaster is spreading,* he surmised, none too surprised by this development. If bad news traveled quickly, then word of Bhopal's agonized convulsions must be crossing the country faster than a supersonic jet.

He strode across the room and switched on his small portable television set. It took less than a second to locate a special emergency bulletin, transmitted live from Bhopal. On the screen, thousands of injured victims mobbed a hospital emergency room, completely overwhelming the unprepared doctors and nurses. An ashen-faced reporter, clutching a microphone within his trembling fingers, informed viewers that equally horrific scenes were taking place at hospitals throughout the entire city. Preliminary estimates suggested that as many as twenty thousand people were in desperate need of medical attention, far more than Bhopal's overstressed emergency services could even begin to cope with. The camera lingered on row after row of choking and sobbing Indians stretched out on hastily erected cots outside the hospital. Many more, perhaps beyond help, were left to die on blankets and mats laid out in the parking lot, largely ignored by the frantic hospital workers madly running about, trying in vain to keep up with the tidal wave of poisoned refugees.

Noon lowered the volume on the television, content to let the hideous images speak for themselves. "This is more than just an 'accident,' " he spat at Seven. "This is an obscenity that should have *never* been allowed to occur. In a better world, a world under firm control, such abominable negligence would not be tolerated." He angrily slammed his fist into his open palm. "Least of all by the likes of you!"

"Perhaps," Seven offered by way of paltry consolation, "this tragedy will lead to positive steps to prevent future accidents of this nature. Increased safety standards. Greater awareness of the dangers of stockpiling dangerous chemicals near heavily populated areas. Stricter enforcement of whatever environmental statutes already exist." His dark suit, and pious platitudes, reminded Noon, unfavorably, of an undertaker. "It is a sad but universal principle that the most lasting lessons frequently come at the highest cost. It's small comfort now, I understand, but such disasters often spur enormous progress in the long run. I know; I've seen it happen before."

Noon would not let Seven shirk his responsibility so easily. "Do not lecture me, old man. I have seen the resources at your disposal, the astonishing technology at your command. You have the power to enforce your will anywhere in the world." He shook an accusing finger at the complacent, middle-aged spymaster. "And yet you let billions suffer while greedy corporations and weak, fallible, *inferior* men allow this planet to spin out of control. Men such as we, of superior intelligence and ability, have the power—the duty!—to bring order to the world!"

"There's a fine line between order and tyranny, Noon," Seven sermonized. "The human race cannot truly advance unless it is free to learn from its experiences, even those as heartbreaking as we now see in Bhopal. Civilization cannot be imposed on the world through force and coercion. It has to evolve naturally, over time." He placed the overturned chess set back on its stool and began carefully putting the tiny ivory soldiers back where they belonged. "Trust me on this, Noon. I know what I'm talking about."

Noon laughed mirthlessly. "Trust you? I did so once, and look what has become of my homeland!" On the television screen, silent aerial footage depicted city streets literally strewn with corpses. Noon clicked off the TV in disgust. "No, it is clear to me now that, despite all your impressive talk about making the world a better place, you lack the courage and conviction to do more than tinker with the status quo." He crossed his arms atop his muscular chest, striking a heroic pose before the crimson pennant on the wall. "The long-suffering people of this planet deserve more than your timid half-measures and insignificant course corrections. They require a genuine visionary, a leader who is strong enough to take the reins of command, and bold enough to guide mankind into a new golden age!"

Seven's dour expression grew more disapproving than ever, not that Noon cared anymore about the older man's opinion of him. "For your sake, and the world's," Seven intoned gravely, "I hope that this emotional outburst is just a reaction to today's traumas. The last thing Earth needs right now is an impetuous, would-be Caesar with messianic delusions." He activated his servo, summoning his distance-warping blue mist. "Farewell, Noon Singh. Perhaps we can speak again someday, when you are older and less overwrought."

"Do not call me that anymore," the youth said forcefully, making a momentous decision on the spur of the moment. "Noon" was child's name, and, after today, he was no longer a child. He had killed a man, only to see him rise up unscathed, and he had witnessed firsthand the murder, through unforgivable negligence and stupidity, of innumerable countrymen and their families. All this had changed him irrevocably, he realized with a sense of utter certainty. He was a man now, with a man's work ahead of him.

"Call me Khan," he said, claiming at last the exalted title his long-dead mother had prophetically bestowed upon him. It was a good name. A man's name.

A name for a conqueror.

CHAPTER THIRTY-ONE

NINETY MILES NORTH OF LAS VEGAS
NEVADA, USA
JULY 5, 1986

THE WHIRRING BLADES OF THE BLACK MILITARY HELI-copter, employing the latest stealth technology, made amazingly little noise as the top-secret aircraft carried Shannon O'Donnell through the warm summer night. The copter passed swiftly over the low mountain ridges below, which jutted upward from acres and acres of barren desert landscape. No artificial lights shone among the hills and plains below the chopper, suggesting that the bleak terrain was completely devoid of human habitation. The contrast with Vegas's gaudy neon excess, which Shannon had departed less than an hour ago, could not have been more striking. *Like going from Earth to the moon,* she thought. A trip she one day hoped to make for herself, assuming NASA accepted her application.

"Any idea what this is all about?" she asked the chopper pilot seated next to her. Thanks to the copter's special design features, she didn't need to raise her voice to be heard above the muted whisper of the spinning black rotors.

"Sorry, miss," the pilot replied. His khaki uniform bore no identifying badges or insignia. He kept his gaze fixed upon the infrared display mapping the rugged terrain ahead of them. The stealth aircraft flew without any visible headlights, navigating entirely by radar and infrared sensors. "All I know is that I was supposed to bring you back to the base, pronto."

Shannon sighed, none too surprised by the pilot's inability to satisfy her curiosity. Everything else at the base operated on a strictly need-to-know basis; why should this be any different? She couldn't help wondering, however, what was so urgent that the Powers That Be had sent a copter to fetch her back to the lab with all deliberate speed. *Has something happened to Dr. Carlson?* she worried. *I kept telling him that he smoked too much, especially for a man his age.*

The twenty-eight-year-old engineer had been attending an aeronautics conference in Vegas when she received a curt, cryptic summons to report back to the base immediately. With barely enough time to pack before the unmarked copter arrived to pick her up, she was still wearing the little black dress and high heels she had sported at the glitzy cocktail party she'd so hurriedly been spirited away from.

Feeling distinctly overdressed for this particular airborne excursion, and half-expecting the copter to turn into a pumpkin any second now, she tied her long red hair into a slightly more professional-looking bun. Her alert, intelligent face bore a distinctly apprehensive expression.

The nearly invisible aircraft descended silently toward a desert valley between a pair of moonlit hills. The infrared display revealed a runway and landing pad built into the dry, rocky bed of a long-vanished lake. A single metal hangar had been erected at one end of the runway, surrounded on three sides by a forbidding barbed-wire fence. Shannon looked past the hangar, at the weathered granite ridges at the base of the southwest hill. *Almost home,* she thought, anxious to find out the reason behind her hasty return. *I hope the doc is all right.*

A Jeep Cherokee was waiting for her at the landing pad, along with a driver wearing cammo fatigues and a holstered automatic pistol. The soldier helped her with her suitcase as she climbed out of the copter and scurried toward the Jeep, the wind from the spinning rotor blades threatening to undo her hastily constructed bun. Her driver whistled appreciatively at the sight of Shannon in her entirely incongruous party dress, but she was in too much of a hurry to be either amused or annoyed by the soldier's attentions. "Let's go," she tersely instructed him as he tossed her luggage into the back of the Jeep and climbed back into the driver's seat. Within minutes, they had left the ebony copter behind.

They headed straight for the southwest hill, the Jeep's headlights shining upon the perfectly graded dirt roadway before them. Cameras mounted on wooden posts kept watch over the lonely road and the surrounding wasteland, while radar dishes scanned the cloudless night sky for unauthorized aircraft. Patches of flowering yucca grew alongside the road, and, somewhere in the distance, a coyote howled at the moon. Shannon wondered how in the world the crooning canine had managed to penetrate the base's security.

As they approached the foot of the hill, their progress was blocked by a metal barrier lowered across the road. A machine-gun-toting soldier emerged from a concrete guardhouse next to the gate and asked to see Shannon's ID, which she promptly volunteered, just as she did every single time she hit this checkpoint on her way to work. Shining a flashlight in her face, the guard compared her features with the photo on her ID card before raising the barricade and waving the Jeep forward.

Although standard procedure, the stringent security measures felt more time-consuming than usual tonight, so impatient was Shannon to reach her final destination. She tapped her fingers restlessly against the dashboard as the Jeep's headlights fell upon a large hangar door built into the side of the mountain. An electric eye scanned the vehicle and its occupants, and the metal door rolled upward, well-greased gears making minimal clatter. The rising gate exposed a paved, man-made tunnel that led directly into the zealously guarded heart of what the United States government, when grudgingly forced to acknowledge this installation's existence, referred to simply as the "Groom Lake Facility."

Better known to the rest of the world as Area 51.

The Jeep parked deep inside the hollowed-out mountain, where yet another armed soldier appeared to escort Shannon the rest of the way. Not that she actually needed directions, of course; after so many months, the hardworking engineer guessed that she could probably find her way to the lab blindfolded, despite the maze of interconnected tunnels making up the underground complex, which was large enough to house numerous laboratories, mainframe computers, and storage facilities, including room for any number of experimental aircraft. Unlike, say, NASA, the clandestine projects at Area 51 seldom had to worry about budget crunches.

"Welcome back, Ms. O'Donnell," the guard said as he marched beside her down a long corridor lit by mounted fluorescent lights. Shannon was on good terms with this particular soldier, who had been stationed here for as long as she could remember.

"Thanks, Muck," she replied, her pace accelerating the nearer she got to her own designated corner of Area 51. Her high heels drummed rapidly upon the reinforced, earthquake-proof concrete floor. "Is the doc okay?"

Sergeant Steven Muckerheide didn't break stride as he answered her worried query. "As far as I know, yeah. Something's up, though. I hear the Navy got their hands on some whatchamacallit that has Doc Carlson and the other brainiacs all worked up." A carefree shrug conveyed that heavy-duty science was beyond the soldier's expertise. "You didn't hear that from me, of course."

"Absolutely," she assured him. "Thanks for the scoop."

Now that she knew nothing dreadful had befallen her boss, apprehension gave way to excitement, adding an extra spring to her step. She couldn't wait to find out just what sort of "whatchamacallit" Muck had alluded to. *Could it be?* she wondered breathlessly. *After all these years, had they made contact again?*

A brisk march brought her to the end of a corridor. Now only a gleaming steel door, guarded by an alert female soldier bearing an M16 assault rifle, stood between Shannon and the answers she craved. PROJECT F—AUTHORIZED PERSONNEL ONLY, read the large block letters printed on the face of the impregnable door. Shannon slid her laminated ID card into a slot next to the door handle, then waited for several interminable seconds as concealed lasers scanned her inside and out. A moment later, she heard the lock click, and the door slid open on lubricated grooves.

"See you later," she told Muck, who lacked the necessary clearance to go any farther. Instead her armed escort relieved the soldier at the doorway, taking a defensive position outside the lab entrance.

"Take care," he called out amiably as Shannon passed over the familiar threshold into the restricted laboratory. "Hope it's worth the rush."

Me, too, she thought. The steel door slid back into place with a muffled thunk, and she hurried past a short row of lockers and closets toward the working areas of the lab. "Doc?" she hollered, taking a second to put on a white lab coat over her black satin dress. "Are you there?"

An enthusiastic voice answered from the inner depths of the well-equipped laboratory. "Shannon? Is that you?" She instantly recognized the voice of her favorite mad scientist, Dr. Jeffrey Carlson. "Hurry! Come quickly. You have to see this!"

"Coming!" she shouted back, the back of her white coat flapping behind her. *This has to be big,* she realized, further energized by the remarkable exuberance in her boss's voice. *I've never heard him so excited before.*

She found the elderly scientist in Lab F-1, bent over a shining chrome counter. A fraying white lab coat was draped over his bony shoulders, blocking her view of whatever he was examining, while the smell of burning tobacco permeated the theoretically pristine atmosphere of the lab. Shannon sighed out of habit, hoping that her chain-smoking superior wasn't working with anything *too* flammable at the moment. *Amazing,* she thought, *how one of the brightest minds of the planet can't overcome a lifelong addiction to nicotine.*

"Ah, there you are," Carlson said, turning to greet her. The affable, sixtyish scientist had a high forehead that had only grown more prominent as his hairline receded to near nonexistence. Lively hazel eyes peered out from behind a pair of old-fashioned bifocals; despite his age, Carlson had retained more curiosity and idealism than many much younger researchers. A lit cigarette gripped between his fingers, he beckoned Shannon with a hasty gesture. "Take a look at these beauties!"

She joined him at the counter, where she discovered two curious artifacts, neither of which she could immediately identify. Each smaller than a shoebox, the objects were constructed of an odd black substance that seemed to possess qualities of both metal and plastic. Silver highlights added a bit of flair to the instruments' designs, suggesting that whoever—or whatever—had constructed the devices had taken aesthetic considerations into account. One of the objects vaguely resembled a pistol or welding tool, complete with a handgrip suitable for an adult human or humanoid, while the other was a compact, rectangular device the size and shape of a sixties-style transistor radio. The latter object also featured a digital display screen, currently unlit, as well as a variety of tiny switches and knobs. Shannon couldn't begin to guess what function the device was intended for. Maybe some sort of scanner or communications device?

"What are these?" she asked Carlson, running a gentle finger over the glossy black casings of both artifacts. They felt smooth and cool to the touch. "Where did they come from?"

Carlson's eyes gleamed as he brought her up to speed. "The Navy confiscated these objects from an unidentified intruder they caught snooping aboard the *U.S.S. Enterprise* about a week ago, at Alameda Naval Base in San Francisco. The intruder was injured, and later disappeared from Mercy Hospital under mysterious circumstances, but he left these devices behind. Navy Intelligence wasted a few days trying to figure them out on their own," he added with a derisive snort, "until somebody wised up and forwarded them on to us."

Shannon nodded, absorbing every detail of Carlson's explanation. The *Enterprise* was an aircraft carrier, she knew, but she still wasn't sure why an interrupted espionage attempt had her boss so excited. "What sort of intruder?" she asked. "I don't understand."

"A Russian, supposedly," the old scientist stated. "Named Pavel Chekov, according to his ID, but the CIA has no record of any Pavel Chekov entering the country, and the Soviets have vociferously denied any knowledge of his existence." Carlson sounded as though he had little reason to doubt the Russians' claims of innocence. "Naturally, various paranoid types are still convinced that this 'Chekov' was nothing more than an unusually slippery communist spy, but I have my doubts." He waved an outstretched hand over the unnamed objects on the counter. "If these devices are of Soviet invention, then the Reds are a lot farther ahead of us, technologically, than our friends in the Pentagon would like to think." He grinned at Shannon, revealing a mischievous smile regrettably stained by years of cigarette smoking. "Fortunately, I don't think that's the case."

She couldn't believe he was actually implying what she thought he was getting at. "You don't mean . . . you really think that this 'Chekov' might have been . . . ?" Even after all she had learned working on the project for the last couple years, she found it hard to say the words out loud.

"Not of this Earth? An extraterrestrial?" Carlson completed her sentence with a triumphant twinkle in his eye. "That's exactly what I think." He beamed at the unidentified objects like a kid who had just received the toys at the very top of his Christmas list. "As puzzling as they are, these artifacts bear a distinct resemblance to some of the equipment we salvaged at Roswell back in '47."

Shannon reacted with a sharp intake of breath. Until she'd come to work at Project F, about two years ago, she had always assumed that stories about UFOs and captured alien visitors were simply the stuff of tabloid headlines. Imagine her surprise when Doc Carlson informed her that he had personally met with and studied a party of sentient, extraterrestrial beings after an alien spacecraft crashed in New Mexico almost forty years ago. Although the unearthly creatures—who called themselves "Ferengi"—had escaped from captivity shortly thereafter, Dr. Jeffrey Carlson had devoted the rest of his career to studying everything he could find out about the aliens and their amazingly advanced technology.

"But surely," she protested, still unable to accept the enormity of what her boss was saying, "the Russian that was captured, Chekov, did not look like a Ferengi?" According to classified photos taken in '47, Earth's previous visitors had resembled hairless trolls, with grotesquely oversized ears and rodent-like features. It was hard to imagine how even the most paranoid Navy Intelligence officer could mistake a Ferengi for a Soviet spy.

"True," Carlson conceded, "but you're forgetting that the Roswell aliens, or at least one of them, were capable of changing their shape at will. I saw him do so with my own eyes, and so did Faith," he added, referring to his wife, now a retired Army nurse. "Why couldn't this Chekov actually have been a Ferengi in disguise?"

Good point, Shannon thought, gradually adjusting to the idea. Once you accepted the existence of shape-changing aliens from outer space, something she had come to terms with many moons ago, then it was certainly possible that one of them might have been visiting California last week. *But why?* she wondered. *For what purpose?*

She suddenly remembered a news report she had paid fleeting attention to a few days earlier, something about a prominent marine biologist who had vanished without a trace in San Francisco. *That would have been about the same time that this "Chekov" showed up at Alameda,* she realized. *Could there be a connection?* None of the woman's friends or coworkers had been able to explain her abrupt disappearance, and the police admitted to being baffled. Perhaps—*What was her name again? Gillian something?*—really had been abducted by aliens?

But what would the Ferengi want with a marine biologist? Shannon had no idea. According to Carlson, the original Roswell aliens had arrived on Earth by accident, or so they had insisted. Why had they, or others like them, returned at last, after so many years? "Are you sure," she asked Carlson, contemplating the newly arrived artifacts on the counter, "that these are Ferengi technology?"

"I think so," the doc said hesitantly. "There hasn't really been time to examine them properly just yet, and there's still a lot we don't know about what we saw in '47. After all, it's been almost forty years now, and we're still trying to figure out how Quark's ship and his other gadgets worked, based on sketches and photographs taken at the time." He smiled wanly. "Sometimes I feel like a caveman struggling to make sense of a microwave oven."

Shannon knew how he felt. Much of her own work at the project involved the seemingly impossible task of trying to reverse-engineer the Ferengi's spaceship with nothing to go on except forty-year-old notes and diagrams. She'd been at it for two years already, and success was nowhere in sight. Her slow progress frustrated Shannon, who had aspirations of being the first woman on Mars. Not even the *Challenger* disaster, earlier that year, had dampened her burning desire to make it into space; if anything, that tragic explosion had only heightened her determination to crack the puzzle of the long-departed Ferengi vessel. *Lord knows we need something better than the space shuttle if we're ever going to seriously explore the cosmos. . . .*

"And yet," Carlson continued, rapping his knuckles against the steel-like plastic (or plastic-like steel), "I'd bet my scandalously inadequate pension that this is the same sort of stuff that Quark's gear was made of." He stroked his chin thoughtfully as he regarded the objects in question. "The only thing that puzzles me, though, is that the design of these mechanisms strikes me as somehow less sophisticated than the apparatus we observed in '47. It's like their technology has regressed by a generation or so over the course of the last four decades, which is contrary to what you'd expect."

Shannon gently lifted the pistol-like device from the counter, her hand fitting comfortably around the grip. It was surprisingly lightweight. "Well, you know what they say: they just don't make them like they used to. Maybe that applies to extraterrestrial hardware as well." An even more far-out explanation occurred to her. "Or, who knows, maybe there's some sort of bizarre time-travel paradox at work here? *Back to the Future* and all that."

She was joking, naturally, but Carlson appeared to give the idea serious consideration. "You know, Shannon, that might well be the case." He watched her handle the alleged alien artifact. "Careful," he warned her, "the Navy spycatchers felt confident that the device you're holding is some kind of weapon, although so far no one's been able to make it work." His tone implied that maybe, where the U.S. military was concerned, this wasn't such a bad thing. "Before his accident, Chekov himself is supposed to have suggested that his weapon had been damaged by radiation from the *Enterprise*'s nuclear reactor." His gaze turned inward as he mulled over the possible implications of this claim. "You know, now that I think of it, Quark also had strong feelings about atomic energy. Maybe—"

A series of racking coughs interrupted his fervid

speculations. Shannon winced at the harsh, wet sounds coming from her mentor's much-abused lungs, and she watched in pain and sympathy as the explosive convulsions caused the old man's body to double over. Returning the "pistol" to the counter, she hurried over to help Carlson, snatching the cigarette from his palsied fingers with one deft motion, then guiding him over to a nearby stool where he could sit down.

It took a few moments, but the coughing jag eventually passed, and Carlson was able to catch his breath. "Sorry about that," he apologized meekly. "I guess I've been working too hard."

For the first time since returning to the lab, Shannon noticed that Carlson's face looked gaunter and more drawn than usual. The heavy black rims of his bifocals only partially concealed the purple shadows beneath his aged eyes. "Let me guess, you've been going strong for hours now, haven't you?"

Carlson shrugged dismissively. The flip side of his enormous enthusiasm for his work, Shannon knew, was that he often pushed himself too hard. "More or less," he admitted, "but can you blame me? This is the opportunity of a lifetime. Brand-new evidence of extraterrestrial intelligence! I couldn't take a break now if I wanted to."

He looked excited and worn-out at the same time. Shannon decided it was time to take a hard line; she cared too much for the sweet old scientist to let him trash his health like this. "Look, if you won't go home and get a good night's sleep, which is what you really need, then you should at least nap for a couple hours in your office. That's what I set up that cot for in the first place."

"If I wanted a nurse, I could have just stayed home with my wife," Carlson grumbled. He reached for his cigarette, but Shannon determinedly ground the noxious cancer stick into the bowl of a convenient ceramic crucible. "Dammit, I've been waiting forty years for another look at Ferengi technology."

"Then a few more hours won't make any difference," Shannon insisted. Adamant, she helped her exhausted boss back onto his feet and led him out of the lab toward his office a short walk away, in an adjoining block of compartments assigned to their project. Carlson muttered darkly the whole time, but reluctantly bowed to the inevitable. Deep down inside, the young woman suspected, her ingenious mentor knew she was right.

After making sure that Carlson had indeed stretched out on the portable cot that Shannon had installed in his office months ago, Shannon turned off all the lamps in his room, then slipped quietly out of the book-lined compartment. She lingered in the hall outside the door for several minutes, to make sure that Carlson was indeed taking it easy, and not sneaking up to work at his computer. Then her own curiosity won out, and she tiptoed back toward the main lab to take a closer look at the mysterious curios that had so intrigued her boss.

A tinted glass door sealed the lab off from the office area. Shannon was sure she remembered switching off the lights when she left the lab, but now she was surprised to see an eerie blue glow coming from the other side of the door. A wisp of sapphire mist seeped into the hall from beneath the door. *What the hell?* she thought. She sniffed the air, momentarily afraid that a discarded cigarette had accidentally started a fire in the lab, but she couldn't smell anything burning. Whatever that odorless blue vapor was, it wasn't smoke.

Instantly on guard, she crept closer to the closed lab entrance. Peering through the translucent glass, she glimpsed the silhouette of a humanoid figure moving across the lab. *An intruder—at Area 51?* That hardly seemed possible, unless maybe Chekov himself had somehow dropped by to reclaim his property. Who knew how Ferengi came and went? Could it be that a genuine space alien was only a few yards away?

On impulse, Shannon threw open the door and switched on the lights, surprising the intruder. The high-intensity white lights exposed a thoroughly human-looking woman caught in the act of searching the supply drawers beneath the metal counter. Tanned and blond, the woman looked to be in her late thirties, and wore a baggy, dark green sweater and black span- dex leggings. A stylish woven tote bag hung over her shoulder, and there was nothing alien at all about her wide-eyed expression of surprise and chagrin; she looked as sheepishly guilty as an underage teen caught sneaking into an R-rated movie. *That's no Ferengi,* Shan- non guessed intuitively, *and no "Pavel" either, not unless the aliens can change sex as well as shape.*

The stranger's hand still rested on the handle of a partially opened drawer, while her other hand gripped the black, rectangular "radio" captured from Chekov. The remaining artifact, the one that resembled a hand- gun, still rested on the polished steel counter, just be- yond the intruder's reach.

Thinking quickly, Shannon rushed forward and snatched up the suspected weapon. "Don't move!" she warned the older woman, aiming what she hoped was the business end of the "pistol" at the stranger. *Boy, am*

I going to feel stupid, she thought, *if I've got this thing pointed the wrong way!*

"Hold on! Let's not get carried away!" the other woman whispered urgently, without a trace of anything resembling a Russian accent. Her own arm jerked up suddenly, pointing the "radio" at Shannon. "You stay where you are, too!"

The young engineer wasn't sure whether to be disappointed or relieved that the mystery woman looked and acted so convincingly human. "That's no weapon," Shannon challenged the nameless intruder, nodding her head at the boxy, black instrument in the other woman's hand.

"Oh yeah?" Blushing embarrassment gave way to bravado as the honey-haired intruder held her ground, keeping her weapon aloft. Aquamarine eyes narrowed as the blonde squinted at Shannon like a gunslinger in an old Clint Eastwood movie. "Are you absolutely sure about that?"

Not exactly, Shannon thought, swallowing hard. The actual functions of both devices remained unknown. For all she knew, she was threatening a death ray with a pencil sharpener. *But if that's the case,* she thought hopefully, *then why hasn't Blondie already zapped me?*

"Who are you?" she demanded nervously. How had the intruder gotten past all the guards and security cameras anyway? Had the blonde done something to Sergeant Muckerheide, or was the friendly soldier still standing guard outside the lab, blissfully unaware of the Mexican standoff unfolding inside? Shannon was tempted to call out for assistance, but feared that the other woman would fire her weapon (?) if Shannon even tried to summon reinforcements. Besides, she recalled,

Muck couldn't even enter the lab if he heard her screaming for her life; he didn't have the clearance to get past the locked door. *How's that for irony?* she thought acerbically.

"Sssh!" the stranger cautioned Shannon, holding a finger before her lips. She wiggled her "radio" at Shannon for emphasis. "My name doesn't matter. The important thing is"—she let go of the drawer and pointed at Shannon's unproven firearm—"that doesn't belong to you."

"I don't see your initials on it," Shannon retorted, "whatever they might be." Her gaze darted around the tidy, well-equipped laboratory as she frantically considered her options. She could always shout for Doc Carlson, of course, but the last thing she wanted to do was place her boss in jeopardy as well. Instead, her eyes zeroed in on a white plastic phone mounted on the wall several feet away, next to a blackboard covered with arcane calculations and diagrams. *If I can just get a chance to call for help,* she thought, beginning to edge in that direction. "Besides, finders keepers."

But the radio-wielding blonde saw where Shannon was heading and moved to block her. "Look, you're a scientist, right?" the stranger asked hopefully. "So presumably you're a smart person. You must realize that civilization isn't ready for this kind of technology yet. You'd be jumping centuries ahead of humanity's current state of development; there's no way our psychology or social institutions could possibly keep up." The anonymous intruder certainly sounded earnest enough; imploring blue-green eyes reached out to Shannon without even a hint of guile or duplicity. "Just think what it would do to the balance of power if the Pentagon figured out how these sci-fi doohickeys work!"

"But this doesn't have to be about bigger and better weapons," Shannon insisted passionately. She and the doc had always been united in their commitment to do more than simply heighten the arms race. "That's what treaties and diplomacy are for. What about the peaceful applications of scientific progress? Like medical research, alternative energy sources, the space program . . . ?" The heartbreaking image of *Challenger* exploding in midair flashed once more before her mind's eye, causing her voice to catch in her throat. "If we can build better, more advanced spaceships, using just this sort of futuristic technology, then maybe no more astronauts will have to die like Christa McAuliffe and the others!"

The blond woman smiled sadly. "I understand what you're saying," she sympathized, "and I like the way you think. But you'll just have to trust me on this one, Red. Letting you people hold on to these gadgets is a worse idea than New Coke."

Without warning, she pressed a button on the "radio," which promptly emitted an electronic hum. Shannon flinched, in anticipation of being stunned or disintegrated, but the blond woman merely glanced down at the device's digital display and grinned triumphantly. "Sorry to break this to you, sister, but it looks to me like your ray gun is out of juice."

She blithely placed her own "weapon" in the handbag dangling from her shoulder, then lunged toward Shannon. The younger woman desperately squeezed something that felt like a trigger, but, just as the blonde had predicted, nothing happened. Her attacker confidently grabbed on to Shannon's arm, and, with some sort of practiced martial-arts move, put pressure on the startled lab worker's wrist, forcing her to let go of the pistol. "There!" the blonde said cheerfully, stepping back with her prize, which she tucked efficiently into the pocket of her sweater. "Now we're getting some-where."

Feeling the situation rapidly slipping out of her control, Shannon hesitated, uncertain whether to run for the phone or to try to physically wrestle the stolen artifacts away from the other woman. *I knew I should've taken that self-defense course at the gym!*

"Whoa there, Red," the blonde warned her, as if reading her mind. She removed a silver fountain pen from one of the fuzzy chartreuse leg warmers around her shins and pointed its tip at Shannon. "Believe it or not, I'm not bluffing this time. This little pen-thingie really is a weapon, sort of, so don't even think of going Rambo on me."

Glancing over her shoulder at a supply closet at the opposite side of the lab, she began backing away from Shannon. *I don't understand,* Shannon thought, unable to keep up with this bewildering chain of events. *Where does she think she can go? There's no way out of here except past all the guards!* Somehow, though, she knew that the nameless blonde was completely capable of slipping out of Area 51 as mysteriously as she had arrived, taking the two captured artifacts with her.

"Wait!" Shannon called out, more anxious than ever to plumb the secrets of the alien devices. "What if we promised to share the knowledge with the entire world, including our enemies? That way we could all benefit!"

The blonde paused, regarding Shannon with an intrigued expression. "I appreciate the sentiment," she said, shaking her head slowly, "but the world just can't risk that right now. Things are too delicate, geopolitically speaking." She looked Shannon over speculatively, as if appraising the young engineer according to some unspecified criteria. "But maybe we should talk again sometime. What's your name anyway?"

"Shannon," she answered uncertainly, hoping fervently that she wasn't signing up for her very own alien abduction, just like that missing marine biologist. "Shannon O'Donnell."

The blonde smiled. "Pleased to meet you, Shannon." From across the lab, she pointed her pen directly at the younger woman. "Don't worry, this won't hurt a bit."

Panic flared for an instant inside Shannon's pounding heart. Then the silver pen hummed loudly and all her worries went away.

At least for an hour or so.

CHAPTER THIRTY-TWO

RISING HIGH ABOVE THE KREMLIN'S RED BRICK WALLS, the clock tower chimed a revolutionary anthem as the clock struck seven. Colonel Anastasia Komananov of the KGB, Third Chief Directorate, quickened her step as she crossed Red Square toward the forbidding walled fortress that now served as the headquarters of the Soviet Union. Her double-breasted, steel-gray greatcoat was buttoned securely against the bitter cold of the evening. Gold stars, signifying her rank, glittered upon the collar of the heavy wool coat, and a slim black attaché case was chained securely to her wrist.

The wintry chill, extreme for October, had already driven both townspeople and tourists indoors, so that the square was largely deserted tonight. Komananov strode briskly across the wide expanse of white cobblestones, making swift progress toward her ultimate destination. Just ahead, on the far side of the square, the domed rotunda of the Russian Senate could be glimpsed above and beyond the crenelated red battlements of the Kremlin walls. Urgent business, vital to the continued existence of the Soviet Union, awaited Komananov within the Presidium building, next to the Senate, but first she had another stop to make.

A pyramid of stacked, cubiform blocks, Lenin's Tomb squatted in the shadow of the Kremlin, its red granite facade matching the stern walls looming behind it. Rows of neatly trimmed pine trees flanked the entrance to the mausoleum, which was also protected by an honor guard of uniformed soldiers, bearing AK-74 assault rifles. Above the doorway, large Cyrillic letters spelled out the surname of the Father of the Revolution.

By day, a long line of visitors, composed of both sincere pilgrims and curious sight-seers, usually stretched outside the Tomb, waiting for their turn to pay their respects to the deceased Soviet premier. Now, after closing time, only the stern-faced guards remained, standing stiffly at attention as Komananov approached. The colonel nodded curtly as the soldiers saluted her smartly and, without a word, let her pass. She did not need to express her intentions out loud; it was her habit, well known to the guards posted here, to meditate within the Tomb after the tourists had all departed. Although she was running slightly behind schedule this evening, having left KGB Headquarters, in nearby Lubyanka Square, several minutes later than she had intended, she judged it important that, tonight of all nights, she not deviate in the slightest manner from her accustomed routine, lest her actions attract unwanted attention.

I must do nothing suspicious, she cautioned herself silently, maintaining a solemn, inscrutable expression on her austerely attractive features. A pair of matching pearl earrings added a feminine touch to her otherwise intimidating aspect and apparel. *Not tonight, nor in the days to come.* Eyes the color of cloudless blue Siberian skies betrayed not a hint of the worries troubling her mind. *The operation* must *succeed,* she vowed. *The future of the Revolution depends on it.*

If all went as planned tonight, she would go down in history as one of the saviors of the Soviet Union, which was, if nothing else, certainly preferable to her other, more dubious claim to fame; to Anastasia Komananov's lasting embarrassment, she had already been immortalized in a trashy British spy novel written by a western agent of her acquaintance, who had retired from the field to pursue a more "literary" career. Fortune willing, her true accomplishments would soon eclipse those of her fictional counterpart—or so she fervently hoped.

Removing her fur-lined gray *ushanka* hat, she passed beneath the imposing granite portal into the dimly lit interior of the Tomb. Her footsteps echoed within the sepulchral atmosphere of the crypt as she walked down a couple of short, empty hallways until she came to the final resting place of the man who transformed Russia from a backward monarchy to a modern Communist state. Encased in glass, the mortal remains of Vladimir Ilyich Lenin lay in state upon an ornate bier of filigreed iron and crushed purple velvet, looking remarkably preserved for someone who had died over six decades ago. His balding pate rested upon a plush velvet pillow, while his skin, although a trifle waxy, retained the ruddy glow and hue of life. He looked as though he were merely sleeping, a serene expression upon his distinguished features, his arms resting comfortably at his side. Expert lighting cast a golden radiance over the scene, accenting the lifelike quality of the recumbent figure, who wore a conservative dark blue suit. Iron spears, their heads carefully crafted into the hammer and sickle emblems of the Soviet State, flanked the bier, symbolically standing watch over the great Bolshevik leader. Anastasia Komananov felt a surge of patriotism, and renewed resolve, as she contemplated the inspiring tableau before her.

Rumors persisted, of course, that all or part of the body on the bier was a clever forgery, that "Lenin" himself was nothing but a waxwork dummy, posing as an expertly embalmed corpse. Komananov had personally chosen never to probe too deeply into the subject. No doubt she could uncover the truth if she wished, given her extensive KGB connections, but the colonel preferred to believe that the body was genuine, especially at times like these, when her duty and devotion to the State were most severely tested.

Would Lenin have approved of tonight's drastic actions? *Most definitely,* Komananov assured herself emphatically, *once he understood all that was at stake.* Mikhail Gorbachev, the man currently at the helm of the Union of Soviet Socialist Republics, was a weakling and a traitor, who would almost certainly bring about the total ruin of the Soviet Union if he was not stopped. Komananov's hot Cossack blood boiled as she recalled the many ways in which their new general secretary had already undermined the safety and security of the nation: dropping the post of Minister of Defense from the inner circle of the Politburo, announcing a unilateral moratorium on nuclear testing, proposing recklessly sharp cutbacks in strategic weapons, and, incredibly, insanely, suggesting publicly that he might allow outsiders to conduct inspections of currently off-limits Soviet military installations, so that foreign operatives could check on Russia's compliance with the outrageous disarmament treaties that Gorbachev seemed all too eager to agree to!

The colonel glanced at her wristwatch. It was only ten after seven here in Moscow, which meant that the sun had not yet set in Iceland, where, even now, Gorbachev and his woolly-minded, liberal cronies were meeting with the American president to bargain away yet more of Mother Russia's military might. According to her informants within the Politburo, the general secretary seriously intended to discuss the *total elimination* of all strategic nuclear weapons with Reagan, that senile old warmonger. Along with his dangerously liberal internal policies, and his growing reluctance to press on with the war in Afghanistan, it was very clear that Gorbachev, seduced by his rising celebrity abroad, posed an unmistakable threat to everything that generations of heroic Communists had worked and sacrificed to build. *If Lenin knew what his deluded successor was up to,* Komananov felt quite certain, *he would rise up physically, wax or no wax, to squash Mikhail Sergeyevich once and for all!*

"Fear not, comrade," she whispered in Russian to the entombed Bolshevik, watching her words even in the privacy of the crypt. Her gloved fingers tightly gripped the handle of the black attaché case. "Tonight the Revolution is safe in my hands."

She turned to leave the crypt, only to be frozen in

place by the unexpected sound of a voice addressing her from behind. "And why is that, Colonel Komananov?"

The colonel's hat slipped from her fingers onto the floor. Spinning around in shock, she was stunned to see Lenin sitting up atop the bier, the transparent glass sarcophagus raised upon its side. Swinging his feet over the edge of the ornamented iron catafalque and onto the floor, the undead corpse stood up for the first time in sixty years and straightened his neatly pressed blue jacket. Piercing gray eyes, undeniably alive, locked on to Komananov, as though the fearsome figure already knew the deadly secrets closely guarded within her mind. "Well?" V. I. Lenin demanded imperiously. "How exactly do you intend to carry out your promise? And what is so special about tonight?"

For a few terrifying instants, a *frisson* of genuine superstitious fright coursed through the transfixed KGB officer, raising goose bumps beneath her austere brown army uniform. Eerie peasant folktales of vampires and ghouls and other unearthly revenants, planted deep in her mind during childhood, surged back into her thoughts like a bloodthirsty *vourdalak* bursting from its despoiled grave.

Then her intellect reasserted itself, and she realized in anger that she had been deceived. "Imposter!" she spat venomously at the tall, bearded figure, who looked disturbingly like every photo she had ever seen of Lenin. "How dare you desecrate the memory of Vladimir Ilyich!"

"My apologies, Colonel," the false Lenin replied. Although his Russian remained impeccable, he now spoke with an American accent, revealing his corrupt, capitalist origins. Stepping away from the bier, he drew a slender silver fountain pen from his suit pocket and aimed it menacingly at Komananov. With his spare hand, he peeled a rubber baldcap off the top of his skull, exposing a head of graying brown hair. "Rest assured that the spurious effigy on display here will be returned to its usual berth once our business is concluded." A fake red beard went the way of the rubber cap, but layers of waxy orange makeup still obscured the imposter's true features. "Knowing what I did of your habits, however, this appeared to be the mostly likely venue in which to secure a private interview with you."

Komananov was not impressed by the American's ingenuity or explanations. "Cheap theatrics!" she sneered disparagingly. "If you think that your morbid ploy gained you any sort of psychological advantage over me, you are profoundly mistaken." She warily eyed the polished silver wand holding her hostage. Its compact size did not trick her into underestimating the apparent weapon; KGB assassins, as she well knew, often fired deadly poison darts from mechanisms as small as or smaller than the American's fountain pen. "What do you want with me?" she asked defiantly.

Crossing the distance between them with a single stride, the disguised American pulled open her greatcoat and calmly frisked her for weapons, coming away with her loaded Makarov pistol. Satisfied that she had been effectively disarmed, he stepped back and regarded her soberly. "I have reason to believe, Colonel, that you and others in the military and intelligence hierarchies are plotting against Mr. Gorbachev, and may intend to take advantage of the summit meeting in Reykjavik to stage a governmental coup in his absence."

How does he know this? Komananov wondered anxiously. She silently cursed whoever had leaked even a hint of the operation to the Americans, and promised herself that, should she survive this encounter, she would track down the informer and see to it that they paid for their treachery. "I do not know what you are referring to," she stated flatly. "I am a faithful servant of both the State and the Party."

The American sighed wearily. "Please, Colonel, do not waste our time dissembling." He nodded at the attaché case gripped in her hand. "Kindly allow me to inspect the contents of your case."

"*Nyet*," she said. Under no circumstances would she allow the foreign agent to peruse the top-secret documents in her case. "It is locked," she informed him, rattling the sturdy chain binding the leather case to her wrist. "I do not have the key."

"A flimsy lie, Colonel," the American observed. "And hardly an issue in any case." The silver pen hummed briefly and an invisible beam of force snapped apart the chain midway between the case and her arm, causing Komananov to gasp out loud. The American adjusted the settings on his weapon, then fired at the case itself. To her dismay, the KGB officer heard the lock click open.

"No more obstructionist tactics, Colonel," the American instructed her. He gestured toward the sturdy catafalque that had previously held Lenin's body, or a reasonable facsimile thereof. "Please place the case down upon the top of the bier, then step away from the platform."

Despite the danger at hand, to both herself and, more important, the operation, Komananov had to admire the capabilities of the imposter's pen-shaped weapon. *A most versatile tool,* she thought enviously. *One I would be happy to add to my own arsenal.*

Reluctantly complying with the American's demands, she relinquished the briefcase, laying it flat upon the velvet cushions of the bier as instructed. "Hold on," he amended his directions, before she could back away from the catafalque. Twin antennae sprang from the sides of the silver pen and he quickly waved the device at the supine case, as though scanning it for hidden booby traps, while still keeping the colonel herself within range of the weapon. The pen beeped electronically three or four times, but apparently detected nothing amiss. Satisfied, the American nodded and gestured for Komananov to step aside, which she did quite unwillingly. *This is a disaster,* she despaired. *The entire operation could be in danger!*

As Komananov looked on in distress, her extreme anxiety hidden behind a stony, tight-lipped expression, the American lifted the lid of the unlocked attaché case and began inspecting the contents, rifling through sheaves of classified documents. What he found clearly shocked him. "By the Aegis," he murmured under his breath, his attention momentarily captured by the secrets contained in the top-secret papers, "this is worse than I imagined."

Komananov saw an opportunity. While the startled American spy was distracted, she reached up and brutally yanked the earring from her right ear, disregarding the jolt of pain from her torn lobe. She hurled the phony piece of jewelry onto the hard concrete floor, then averted her eyes as the earring exploded in a blinding explosion of high-intensity light. Even though she looked away, her arm thrown rapidly over her eyes, the incandescent flare burned at the periphery of her vision, causing blue spots to appear at the corners of her eyes.

Unprepared, the American was caught off guard by the flash. He staggered backward, clutching his eyes, effectively blinded for one full minute—just as Komananov had planned. Hearing him gasp in pain, she kicked backward at the sound. The cleats of her left boot slammed hard into the man's chest, knocking him back against the unyielding iron bier. He grunted loudly, the wind smacked out of him, but managed to hold on to his invaluable silver pen, which hummed as he fired blindly, missing Komananov, who ducked beneath the invisible beam to grab onto the man's trigger arm, twisting it roughly until the cunningly disguised weapon flew from his fingers, landing with a clatter a few meters away. *That's better,* Komananov thought, smirking in satisfaction. Now they were both unarmed.

Despite the gray in his hair, the American was surprisingly strong. He swung at her head with his free hand, but the well-trained KGB agent evaded the blow, then jabbed her knee into his unprotected abdomen, causing the man to double over in pain. Tears leaked from his watery gray eyes, which were still feeling the effects of the miniature flashbomb, making the orangish greasepaint on his cheeks streak and run. Clasping her hands together to form a double fist, she clubbed the back of his head with all her strength, driving him face first onto the floor. She then kicked him in the jaw for good measure. *Take that!* she thought vindictively, avenging her prior humiliation.

With astonishing fortitude, the battered imposter tried to climb up onto his knees, but the relentless colonel subdued him by kicking him viciously in the ribs with the steel-tipped toe of her boot. "Down!" she ordered the American as she plucked a pair of regulation army handcuffs from the pocket of her coat and chained his hands behind his back before reclaiming her trusty Makarov. "Do not move, American," she warned him, holding the gun to his head. Blood dripped from her ripped earlobe, which stung mercilessly; still, it was enormously satisfying to turn the tables on the arrogant Yankee who had possessed the gall and the temerity to impersonate a revered Russian hero. Keeping the muzzle of the Makarov steadily pointed at the American, she backed away from the prisoner, looking for his fallen weapon. *Our technicians and armorers will definitely want a look at that device,* she knew. *Now then, where did it go?*

The blue spots were already fading from her vision when she spotted the silver pen lying amid the shadows. "Excellent," she murmured, kneeling briefly to confiscate the weapon, which she tucked into her boot before reclaiming the stolen attaché case, which she carefully closed and locked once more. Holding on to the case by its handle, she marched across the crypt to her cuffed prisoner, whom she savagely yanked to his feet. "Out!" she ordered, prodding him in the back with the muzzle of her gun.

"You're making a terrible mistake, Colonel," the American blurted passionately, spitting a mouthful of blood and broken enamel onto the floor. "Gorbachev and his reforms are the best chance your generation has to halt this insane Cold War, reducing the risk of a catastrophic nuclear war!" He looked back over his shoulder, making what sounded like a sincere, last-ditch effort to sway her from her duty and her designs. "Never mind what happens to me," he sputtered, blood trickling from the corner of his mouth. "You can't let paranoia and misguided nationalism get in the way of world peace!"

"Quiet!" she demanded, pistol-whipping the back of the American's head to silence his ridiculous pleas. He sounded just as insane and foolishly idealistic as Mikhail Sergeyevich himself. It occurred to her, though, that she could hardly have the man sharing his all-too-valid suspicions with the uninformed soldiers in Red Square; what if someone actually listened to his accusations, before Gorbachev and his traitorous confederates were entirely eliminated?

I cannot take that chance, she realized. "Wait," she commanded her prisoner, temporarily halting his progress toward the exit. It was tempting to place a bullet in the man's skull, ending his unwanted interference forever, but, no, it was important to find out precisely whom the imposter was working for, and how much they knew about the all-important operation now in progress. *Just shut him up for now,* she decided, putting the precious attaché case down long enough to remove the man's blue silk necktie and use it as a gag to keep the American from speaking to anyone else. She tied the ends of the tie tightly behind the man's head, then checked to make certain that the knot was secure. *Yes, that will do.* "Keep going," she told the prisoner once more, jabbing her gun between his shoulders.

She propelled the American out of the Tomb into the clear, cold moonlight outside. The half-dozen soldiers posted at the entrance of the mausoleum reacted with understandable surprise as she escorted the captured spy at gunpoint down the steps of the Tomb to the weathered stone pavement below. "Lenin's Ghost!"

gasped one of the guards, not realizing how perversely appropriate that exclamation was.

Later, she reflected, there would have to be an investigation into just how the shameless imposter had managed to insinuate himself into the Tomb, as well as into what had become of Lenin's actual remains, real or otherwise. For now, however, she had much more pressing matters to attend to. She glanced down quickly at her wristwatch, chagrined to see that it was nearly 7:30 P.M., making it roughly late afternoon in Reykjavik. Time was passing swiftly and, according to plan, she needed to be in place within the Presidium, in the executive offices of the Supreme Soviet, when tonight's operation went into effect.

"*Yolki palki!*" she swore under her breath. The imposter in the Tomb had cost her precious time. As much as she longed to interrogate the prisoner fully, to find out precisely how much he knew about the planned coup d'etat, she could not spare a moment to extract his secrets now. The classified documents in her case weighed down her arm, reminding her of a higher duty. "Take this spy into custody," she commanded the guards, shoving the American toward the surrounding soldiers. "Escort him to Lubyanka on my orders, and have him confined there until I choose to question him. Leave his gag in place until then."

"*Da,* Colonel!" said the eager commander of the guards, rushing forward to grab the American by his collar. He shook the prisoner ungently, taking pains to demonstrate his contempt for an enemy of the State. "I will deliver him there myself!"

Before the heavyset soldier could carry out her orders, however, a peculiar whooshing noise cut through the icy night air. Komananov heard the sound of metal slicing into flesh and watched in surprise as the commander of the honor guard stiffened abruptly, then toppled face-forward onto the pavement. A flat steel hoop was embedded deep in the soldier's back, surrounded by a rapidly spreading red stain. Gleaming in the moonlight, the metallic ring was half-buried in the man's spine, so that it resembled a handle by which the prone body could be lifted like a piece of luggage. *What the devil?* the colonel wondered, shocked by the soldier's abrupt demise.

Whoosh! Before she or any of the other soldiers could react, another silver quoit came spinning through the air, striking a large, scowling soldier in the head. The guard instantly dropped to the ground; whether he was dead or merely unconscious, Komananov could not immediately tell. "Fyodor!" one of the guard's comrades cried out in alarm, rushing to the side of the fallen soldier. "Who did this?"

Clutching the grip of her Makarov, Komananov searched frantically for the source of the missiles. *There!* she thought, looking up at the top of Lenin's Tomb, where she spotted an unlikely figure striking a dramatic pose astride the uppermost block of the large granite pyramid. A muscular Indian or Pakistani youth, no more than sixteen years old at most, their turbaned assailant looked down at the colonel with yet another steel ring gripped in his right hand and five or six more threaded upon the bulging biceps of his left arm. Despite the chill autumn weather, the murderous youth wore only an embroidered cotton vest above his boots and trousers, with a strap or bandolier of some sort stretching diagonally across his broad chest and a silver metal band encircling his right wrist. His confident—

no, *arrogant*—stance betrayed no fear of the armed and angry soldiers below. "Behold! I teach you the Superman," he announced boldly, paraphrasing Nietzsche. "The lightning out of the dark cloud!"

Who? Komananov wondered, recognizing the grandiloquent declaration as the ravings of a decadent German philosopher, ably translated into Russian. Taking aim at the newcomer, she spared a second to glance over at the handcuffed American, now standing amid the fallen bodies of the ambushed soldiers. Was that recognition she saw in his eyes? The colonel felt convinced that Lenin's impersonator knew exactly who this bloodthirsty terrorist was, even as she vowed silently that this ill-timed and extremely inconvenient rescue attempt would not succeed. "Don't let the prisoner get away!" she shouted at the four remaining soldiers, then fired at the youth atop the pyramid. The blare of gunshots reverberated across Red Square as she held the trigger down, emptying an entire clip at the daring assassin.

But the youth's reflexes were almost superhumanly fast. Laughing insolently, he leaped out of the way of the fiery salvo, onto one of the lower tiers of the pyramid. Raising his right arm with remarkable speed, he expertly spun a silver hoop around his raised index finger, then sent it whizzing through the air at Komananov, who flinched involuntarily only seconds before the razor-sharp quoit sliced through the blue-steel muzzle of her Makarov, halting its destructive flight only centimeters from her own gloved knuckles. Shaken and frustrated, she hurled the now-useless pistol away from her. *Surely he couldn't have done that on purpose!* she hoped breathlessly, horrified by the uncanny accuracy of the terrorist's aim. *Could he?*

She recognized the flying ring now, her memory sparked by the youth's Indian appearance and attire. It was a *chakram*, the traditional weapon of India's famed Sikh warriors. But what was a teenage Sikh doing in the heart of Moscow, attempting to rescue a captured American spy? The possibility of a multinational intelligence operation, mobilized solely to counter the conspiracy against Gorbachev, sent shivers down her spine. How did these strangers find out about the operation? *Our security was foolproof!*

"Shoot him!" she ordered the surviving guards, who needed little encouragement to open fire on the cursed foreigner who had already struck down two of their comrades. Assault rifles unleashed their 5.45mm fury against the assassin's perch atop the pyramid, raising a deafening clamor and sending chips of red and black granite flying. Komananov winced at the damage done to the historic mausoleum, but monuments could be repaired; the safety and security of Russia's future took priority. She would have sacrificed almost anything to keep the devious American and his Indian accomplice from sabotaging the operation. Russia had to be rid of Gorbachev!

Driven backward by the ferocious hail of gunfire from the unleashed AK-74s, the murdering Sikh retreated into the shadows at the rear of the pyramid, ducking behind the massive granite blocks.

"Did you get him?" Komananov called out harshly, inwardly cursing the darkness that hid the assassin from her view. Her fingers held on tightly to the handle of her attaché case; she was determined not to part with it again. "Is he dead?" She signaled the soldiers to spread out around the bullet-scarred mausoleum, while keeping one eye on the American prisoner, who remained under guard by a single, acne-scarred, adolescent soldier, who gulped nervously as he clutched his rifle and looked about warily, no doubt fearing that spinning death would come winging out of the night at any moment, claiming him just as it had the first two victims of the Sikh's lethal *chakram*s.

Komananov dropped to her knees upon the pavement and attempted to wrestle a rifle of her own out from beneath the lifeless body of the dead commander. Unwilling to let go of the all-important attaché case, she awkwardly and one-handedly tugged on the barrel of the AK-74. Moonlight glinted off the *chakram* protruding between the man's shoulders, mocking her efforts even as the blood on the cobblestones stained her hands, coat, and trousers. The beefy corpse was literally dead weight, and a struggle to move.

Gunfire sounded from behind the Tomb, and the colonel looked up hopefully, praying fervently to no one in particular that one of the soldiers had finally managed to put a bullet into the maddeningly elusive young Sikh. "What's happening?" she shouted. "Did you get him? For hell's sake, someone tell me he's dead!"

A defiant war cry, in what sounded like Hindi or Punjabi, greeted the colonel's strident outcry. Her eyes tracked the sound to the very summit of the Tomb, where, after getting a running start across the crowning cube, the Indian youth leaped off the peak of the pyramid, landing on the Square below halfway between Komananov and the captured American. A flung *chakram* caught the soldier guarding the American in the throat, before he could fire a single shot, and the stricken guard dropped to the pavement, shredding his fingertips as he tugged uselessly at the sharpened steel ring wedged beneath his chin.

A muffled cry came from the gagged American, almost as if he was objecting to the ruthlessness of the Sikh's methods. To the colonel's amazement, the false Lenin suddenly snapped the chain linking his cuffs and dropped to check the slaughtered soldier's pulse before rising again and yanking off his gag with an angry gesture. "That's enough, Noon!" he shouted in English at the Indian youth. "No more deaths!"

Things were happening so quickly Komananov could barely keep up with events. Where had the defeated American found the strength to snap his shackles in two, and why was he railing against his determined rescuer? She watched in alarm as the older man armed himself with the butchered soldier's rifle.

"Over here! In the Square!" Komananov hollered hoarsely to the guards she had dispatched to circle the Tomb. Her knuckles whitened beneath her gloves as she tightened her grip on the attaché case and its incriminating contents. "Don't let them escape!"

Frustrated to the point of madness, she kept tugging on the rifle beneath the dead commander, but the inert corpse refused to budge. Responding to her cries, the three remaining guards came running from opposite sides of the Tomb, yet the American pinned down the soldier coming around the right corner of the mausoleum by laying down a relentless stream of automatic gunfire that forced the besieged guard to retreat back behind the bottom tier of the pyramid. That left only two more soldiers to converge on the Indian youth, who simultaneously charged toward Komananov, a savage glee shining in his eyes.

Looking directly into the face of the running Sikh, she was astonished to see that this "Noon" was every bit as young as she had first supposed, his scruffy black beard looking less than a year old. *He's just a boy,* she marveled. A boy who had already killed three trained Russian soldiers. Looking beyond his shockingly adolescent countenance, she noted unhappily that the young Sikh still had three more *chakram*s threaded upon his upper arm, plus a curved silver dagger thrust into his belt. *He's better armed than I am,* she realized. *Damn him!*

But instead of resorting to his fearsome quoits once more, Noon unstrapped another device from his back: what looked like a wagon wheel with heavy weights radiating out from the center of the wooden wheel. As the last two guards chased after the youth, unable to fire at him immediately for fear of hitting the colonel by mistake, the brawny Sikh lifted the ungainly contraption above his head and, grasping the spokes around the central hub, began spinning the wheel at enormous speed. The outer weights orbited the youth, providing a defensive cordon around him, as he charged toward one of the two guardsmen, who was trying to circle around to get between the terrorist and the colonel. The unlucky guard, perhaps transfixed by the bizarre spectacle presented by Noon, did not get out of the way fast enough, and the spinning weights clipped him in the head, sending him flying. Clobbered, the soldier hit the cobblestones hard and did not get up.

Unlike the fatally perplexed guardsman, Komananov recognized the exotic implement being employed by the Indian teenager, although she had never actually seen it used in combat before. It was a *chakar,* another traditional Sikh weapon. Intelligence briefings on arcane martial-arts techniques, however, hardly prepared her for the sight of a veteran soldier being laid low by a spinning wheel. *Who is this boy?* she wondered, aghast. *And for whom is he working?*

As the remaining guard slowed his pursuit, wary of being walloped in the head like his comrade, the Sikh turned to face him, taking care to keep both himself and the colonel in the soldier's line of fire. Muscular arms rippled as he arched his back and flung the entire *chakar* at the last guardsman. The massive wheel spun through the air like a flying saucer, or a *chakram,* its menacing weights whipping around the rotating hub. Under attack, the guard fired into the air, trying futilely to bring down the *chakar* in flight, only to dive hurriedly out of the way as the whirling missile crashed to earth exactly where he had been standing only seconds before.

Grinning wolfishly, the Indian youth paused for a heartbeat to savor the havoc he had wrought, then lunged again at Komananov with inhuman velocity. Abandoning her tussle with the recalcitrant cadaver and its infuriatingly inaccessible rifle, the distraught colonel reached hastily for the silver pen tucked into her boot. Perhaps there was still time to figure out its firing mechanism . . . !

She barely had time to get to her feet, however, before Noon was behind her, with his knife to her throat. "I'll take that," he stated with casual authority, snatching the disguised weapon from her fumbling fingers. "Stay back!" he commanded the surviving guard, who was only just scrambling back onto his feet after dodging the hurled *chakar.* "Drop your weapon or she dies!"

"No!" Komananov cried desperately. Her life didn't matter, not so long as the operation survived. The Sikh and the American could not be allowed to endanger the master plan any longer. She dropped the attaché case gently onto the pavement, hoping that Noon would leave it behind should he take her hostage as he fled. "Shoot him! Shoot him now!" she shrieked.

The soldier hesitated, no doubt reluctant to take responsibility for the death of a high-ranking KGB officer. The Sikh took advantage of his indecision to throw Komananov over his shoulder, as effortlessly as though she were a child, and dash for the unguarded entrance of the Tomb. "Seven!" he called out in English to the American, who was still providing cover for Noon by firing his stolen assault rifle at the soldier trapped behind the right-hand corner of the pyramid. "Follow me!"

His vibrant voice had a peremptory tone, leading the confused colonel to wonder just who was in charge, the Indian teen or the older American? She had little time to ponder such enigmas, though, as the racing Sikh took the stairs up the front of the Tomb several steps at time, his headlong pace unhindered, so it seemed, by the weight of the full-grown KGB agent draped over his shoulder. Komananov flailed madly, struggling to free herself, but could not break free of the Sikh's iron grip. Every lunging stride left her jarred and breathless, and she clenched her teeth to keep from accidentally biting down on her tongue.

"Leave be," he ordered curtly in Komananov's own tongue, "or I'll snap your spine!" Reaching the top of the steps, he turned beneath the square entrance of the Tomb. "Hurry!" he shouted to his American ally, once again switching to English. "We must leave this place at once!"

But Lenin's sacrilegious imposter, whose code num-

ber was apparently "Seven," was not ready to leave Red
Square just yet. In a startling display of speed and
marksmanship, he shot the rifle out of the hands of the
soldier peeking out from around the corner of the
Tomb, then spun around quickly and did the same to
the guard who had dodged the *chakar*. Blue sparks flared
along the grooved stock of the latter soldier's AK-74 as
the American's bullets blasted the rifle out of the
guard's grip. Suddenly finding himself empty-handed,
the soldier ran for safety, leaving Number Seven momentarily in control of the Square. Komananov's desperate hopes were dashed as the American snatched up
the attaché case she had already reclaimed from him
once before. *No! Not again!* she raged silently, while the
impatient Sikh urged his fellow terrorist to greater
speed. "Faster!" Noon called out from the entry to the
Tomb. "Hurry! Before reinforcements arrive!"

By now, in fact, the commotion in the Square had
caught the attention of the sentries posted along the
Kremlin walls. Searchlights beamed down on the
chaotic scene from the towers along the northeast wall
of the centuries-old fortress, revealing an appalling display of bloodshed and bodies. Snipers fired from the
towers at the American as he sprinted for the nearby
mausoleum. Clouds of dust and powdered rock, raised
by the thunderous impact of bullets colliding with cobblestones, trailed in Number Seven's wake, nipping at
his heels, yet the brazen American successfully gained
the shelter of the tomb, rushing past Noon, who
stepped aside just in time to let the older man dive over
the threshold of the violated mausoleum.

The Indian teenager dropped Komananov uncere-
moniously onto her feet, then waved his curved silver

dagger beneath her chin. "Watch her," he curtly instructed Number Seven. The kidnapped colonel could not help noticing that, horrifyingly enough, Noon did not seem at all short of breath, despite his strenuous exertions during the battle and afterward. He slammed the Tomb's heavy iron door shut with a single easy shove, then bolted the gate from the inside. For extra assurance, he took two *chakram*s off his arm and used them to jam the door closed, wedging them between the door and its frame, then folding the metal rings over the edge of the jamb with his bare hands.

Such strength! Komananov observed, impressed even amidst such dire circumstances. *Our Olympic coaches and trainers would give much to know what sort of diet and regimen produced such exceptional might and stamina!*

"There!" Noon pronounced confidently as he stepped back from the door. A single *chakram* remained threaded upon his brawny biceps. "That will do for now." Keeping his dagger at the ready, he approached his American partner. Komananov noted with some relief that Number Seven, at least, showed signs of fatigue. Beneath the last greasy remnants of his disguise, the American's bruised face was slick with perspiration, and his chest rose and fell heavily as he struggled to catch his breath. *Good to know,* the colonel thought bitterly, *that at least one of my captors is mortal.*

"Thank you, Noon," the older man stated in English, standing guard over the colonel with his borrowed rifle, the purloined attaché case resting at his feet. The blinding effect of the flashbomb had long passed, so that the American's vision had been restored. "I am grateful, if admittedly surprised, by your intervention." He arched his eyebrow quizzically. "I wasn't aware you were in Moscow."

"The name is Khan," the Indian corrected him brusquely. It seemed there was little love lost between the two foreigners. "I rescued you just as you once rescued me." A scowl marred the young man's otherwise handsome features as he recalled some prior encounter with the American. His body language was stiff and aggressively formal. "Now we are even."

Number Seven nodded grimly, acknowledging the other's cool assessment of the nullified debt. Then he gestured at Komananov. "Be careful of her earring. It may contain an explosive charge or some other mechanism." He gingerly rubbed his split lip and purpled jaw, wincing as he probed his broken teeth with a cautious finger. "Trust me, I know whereof I speak."

Komananov smirked, drawing some comfort and satisfaction from the injuries she had inflicted on the American. She stared coldly at the youth who called himself Khan as he reached out his hand and demanded her sole remaining earring. "Carefully," he added ominously, pressing the flat of his blade against her cheek. The captive officer grudgingly removed the camouflaged flashbomb from her ear and surrendered it to Khan. *Fine*, she resolved. She would have to find another way to achieve her liberty—and foil her foes.

Multiple footsteps pounded up the stairs on the other side of the jammed door. "Open up!" demanded a loud, angry voice that Komananov recognized as belonging to Colonel Rublev of the Kremlin's security forces. Rifle butts hammered the iron door from without, but the sabotaged door held fast against the barrage, at least for the moment. "Open up in the name of the State!"

"That door won't hold forever," Number Seven predicted. Slinging the strap of his rifle over his shoulder, he extended an open hand toward Khan. "Give me back my servo, and I'll get us out of here."

Servo? Komananov guessed that the American was referring to his ingenious pen-shaped device. She was not surprised that he wanted it back, perhaps even as much as she yearned to recover the attaché case upon the floor.

Frowning, Khan shook his head. "No," he stated unequivocally. "I will not be placed in your debt again." Shoving Komananov ahead of him, he pointed with his knife at the hallway leading to the Tomb's inner chamber. "This way," he insisted.

Apparently, the older man knew better than to argue with the insolent young Sikh, especially when there was a squadron of Russian soldiers pounding at the door. "Very well," he agreed, picking up the leather case before following Khan and the colonel down the murky corridor. "I confess, I'm curious to see how you plan to extricate yourself from this situation."

"I assure you, Seven, that I came prepared for every eventuality," Khan shot back, "including your own feeble attempt to find out exactly what the colonel and her co-conspirators are planning for tonight."

Does everyone *know about our operation?* Komananov thought, clenching her fists in fury and frustration. "You cannot stop us!" she spat defiantly. "Russia's true patriots will see to that. Gorbachev's hours are numbered!"

"Never mind your celebrated leader," Khan warned her, menace in his tone. He addressed her in fluent Russian, as opposed to the English he used when speaking to Number Seven. "It is your own future you should be worrying about now."

They reached the heart of the crypt, with its empty bier and raised glass sarcophagus. Komananov spotted her fur hat lying on the floor of the tomb, just where she had dropped it less than half an hour ago. The heavy blows and angry shouts of Colonel Rublev and his men barely penetrated the hush of the Tomb, sounding muffled and much too far away. Given the mausoleum's monumental solidity, it would not be easy to break into, Komananov knew, but where else could the fleeing terrorists go, now that they had arrived at the desecrated crypt? *We have reached a dead end,* she realized. *There is no escape.*

Instructing Number Seven to keep an eye on their captive, Khan strode toward the vacant bier and took hold of one of the decorative spears adorning the crypt. He twisted the sickle-headed lance clockwise, then pushed it forward about forty-five degrees. To her surprise, Komananov heard the sudden thrum of hidden machinery coming to life. Long-dormant gears screeched in protest as the heavy iron catafalque slid backward into the shadows, revealing a set of wide concrete steps leading down to another level below the burial chamber. The colonel's sky-blue eyes widened; in all her years of service to the State and its secrets, she had never heard a whisper about any hidden passageway beneath Lenin's Tomb. Judging from the bemused expression on Number Seven's face, she guessed that this revelation came as a surprise to the American as well.

"Aleksey Shchusev, the architect of the Tomb, included this concealed back door at Stalin's request," Khan explained rapidly. He directed his comments at Komananov as well, apparently quite aware that she understood English. "All the relevant blueprints and documents were supposed to have been destroyed, but I deciphered a coded memorandum hidden in the private diary of one of the construction workers, who later defected to the West during the purges of the 1930s."

"Excellent work," Number Seven commented, sincerely so it seemed. He took Komananov's arm and led her toward the waiting steps, where Khan lingered to make certain they were coming. "The existence of this escape route had escaped even my data files." Pensive gray eyes regarded the young Sikh with what struck Komananov as a genuine mixture of pride and regret. "I always knew you had enormous potential, Khan."

"Yes," the youth agreed bluntly. He thrust his silver dagger back into his belt. "And, more importantly, the will to use it."

Komananov felt like she had wandered into the middle of an old argument between the two men, who clearly shared an uneasy history of some sort. A teacher-student relationship gone wrong? *That appears the most likely scenario,* she surmised, attentively scrutinizing her captors for further evidence of any rift that she might be able to turn to her advantage. *Khan has the attitude of a former apprentice determined to outshine his one-time mentor.*

Unless, of course, this was all just an elaborate good-cop/bad-cop routine designed to soften her up for interrogation. Komananov had played such games herself, often to great effect, so she resolved to take nothing for granted, and to zealously guard her secrets no matter what nefarious tactics Seven and Khan employed.

Her suspicions were interrupted by the jarring sound of several kilograms of iron crashing to earth. *The front door,* she realized, even as she was dragged reluctantly down the underground stairway. Colonel Rublev had broken into the Tomb at last, but was he already too late?

"In here! Hurry!" she shouted, digging in her heels upon the concrete steps, in a possibly hopeless attempt to buy enough time for Rublev's soldiers to catch up with them. "Help! *Pomogite!*"

Snarling, Khan grabbed on to her arm and handily hurled her down the stairs, amazing her once more with his sheer physical strength. He then leaped to the bottom of the steps in a single bound and hastily pulled on a rusty metal lever mounted on the wall. The manual switch looked as though it hadn't been touched in decades, but Khan's formidable grip easily liberated the lever from its corroded housing, throwing ancient gears into reverse. Komananov watched despairingly as the ponderous catafalque slid back into place, cutting them off from the crypt above. A single lightbulb, naked and coated with dust, flickered above the lever on the wall, providing only a bare minimum of illumination to replace the light from the Tomb.

By the time Rublev and his men reached the inner chamber, she realized, there would be no hint at all of where the deadly terrorists and their hostage had disappeared to, except perhaps a discarded *ushanka* hat upon the cold stone floor. She could just imagine the consternation on Rublev's jowly face when he discovered that the murderous fugitives, who had littered Red Square with the bodies of dead Russian soldiers, had escaped immediate capture and retribution. Despite her own precarious situation, she did not envy Rublev the position he had been placed in. Someone would have to take the blame for this tragic lapse in security.

"Are you all right, Colonel?" Number Seven asked,

reaching out to help her back onto her feet. He spoke Russian, presumably as a courtesy. *Ah yes,* she thought disdainfully, *the good cop.* Pointedly rejecting his offer of assistance, she raised herself from the floor. Her body was sore and bruised from the fall, but, to her relief, nothing appeared to be broken. *Thank providence for small favors,* she thought, brushing dust and grit from her hands and knees.

The sputtering lightbulb revealed little of their new surroundings, but Komananov had the impression of a moldy underground vault or catacomb, little used and long forgotten. The air was dank and smelled of mildew and rat droppings. Vermin scuttled outside the meager swatch of light cast by the single bulb, while water dripped like a metronome somewhere in the darkness. Cobwebs shrouded the crumbling stone walls, and she flinched as a spider scurried across the toe of her boot.

Khan waited until the arachnid dropped back onto the floor, then crushed it beneath his heel. "There is an entire network of tunnels here," he explained in a condescending tone, "dating back to the days of the tsars. Successive generations of Russian leaders have added yet more hidden entrances and exits, including a celebrated one beneath the so-called Secret Tower on the Kremlin's southern wall." Komananov nodded grimly; she knew about that clandestine passageway, at least, along with every tour guide in Moscow. "I have a swift boat waiting by the river, not far from here," Khan added.

He knelt by the bottom steps, where the colonel now noticed a bulging canvas sack resting against the wall. The young Sikh rooted through the bag, coming away with a portable flashlight, which Komananov assumed that Khan had stowed here earlier. *Of course,* she realized. *This explains the way he suddenly appeared up above.* He must have used the underground stairway to enter the Tomb while she and the guards were occupied with Seven. She grimaced at the thought of the boyish assassin coming and going as he pleased in the very shadow of the Kremlin itself. *If I survive this,* she vowed, *I will see to it that every centimeter of these cursed tunnels is mapped and placed under the tightest guard!*

Khan had a more immediate agenda. He tossed the flashlight at Number Seven, who switched it on obligingly. A brilliant white beam, stronger and more steady than the faltering bulb, swept across the stony floor of the vault, surprising a plump, black rat who screeched and scurried from view. "Come," Khan instructed the others, pointing into the Stygian darkness ahead. He glanced briefly upward. "I doubt that our pursuers will uncover the means of our escape right away, but it might be wise to put a little more distance between us and our foes . . . before attending to the business at hand." A fierce look at Komananov made it clear that she was the "business" to which he referred.

"I agree," Number Seven said, shining the flashlight in the direction Khan had indicated. The incandescent beam exposed the arched entrance of a decaying, subterranean corridor stretching away into the shadows lying beyond the reach of the light. Stagnant puddles of filmy water created iridescent reflections of the radiance emanating from the American's flashlight.

"I was not asking," Khan asserted. Raising the hilt of his dagger, he shattered the dingy lightbulb at the foot of the stairs. "To inconvenience any who follow." Fragments of broken glass crunched beneath the tread of his boots as he led the party into the gloomy, timeworn tunnel. His shining blade slashed at the cobwebs across their path like a machete cutting through dense underbrush, yet shredded wisps of webbing still clung to Komananov's face and hair as she trudged grimly down the tunnel, a few meters ahead of Number Seven and his electric torch.

After they had marched for several minutes, a tense and uneasy silence hanging over the group, they came to an intersection where two deserted tunnels met at right angles, beneath an unadorned groin vault whose upper reaches were cloaked in shadows. A thin trickle of water ran down the nearest brick wall, irrigating slimy layers of mold and algae. Mice and insects burrowed in the niches between the decrepit bricks, where all or part of the mortar had crumbled away over time. In the middle of the crossing, a squat stone well, covered by a rusty metal lid, fed corroded lead pipes running along the bottom of the tunnel walls. Sludge leaked from the pipes, pooling in the cracks between the floor stones.

"This will do," Khan declared, raising his hand to halt the mute procession. The *chakram* on his upper arm caught the light of Number Seven's torch, as did the engraved steel band on his right wrist. He turned on Komananov and advanced toward her, knife in hand, backing her up against a damp, ooze-encrusted wall, whose inhospitable chill seeped into her bones even through the heavy wool layers of her greatcoat. Khan kept on coming, until his chiseled, sparsely bearded face was only a finger's length away from hers. "Now then, Colonel Anastasia Natalya Komananov, of the Committee for State Security, Third Chief Directorate, I want you to tell me everything you know about the plot to disrupt the summit conference now being held in Reykjavik." He pressed the tip of the blade against the hollow of her throat. "Refusal is not an option."

Ordinarily, she would have laughed at the notion that she, a high-ranking member of the world's most feared intelligence agency, could be intimidated by a teenage boy scarcely past puberty. But Khan, it was obvious, was no ordinary youth. His dark brown eyes held an intensity and firmness of purpose far beyond his years. Nor did she sense that he was bluffing; that icy determination left little room for mercy or squeamishness. "I do not know what you are talking about," she said, swallowing hard, which caused the sharpened tip of the dagger to scrape minutely against the taut flesh of her throat. "I know of no such plan."

Khan's expression darkened. "Do not toy with me, woman," he hissed, baring flawless white teeth. "I know that you and your confederates have a scheme to derail the summit meeting between Gorbachev and Reagan, endangering the safety of the entire world merely to keep your precious Cold War alive." His left hand clamped on to her wrist, squeezing it hard enough that she feared her bones might snap. "What I do *not* know are the exact particulars of your plot, but you will tell me those . . . now."

Khan twisted her wrist and Komananov winced in pain. In desperation, she looked past Khan's shoulder at Number Seven, who stood a few paces away, his stolen AK-74 still slung over his shoulder. His knitted brow and disapproving frown gave her hope that he might call a stop to her brutal interrogation. "Khan," he said sternly, taking a step toward Khan and the colonel.

The youth did not deign to look back at his American ally. "You may avert your eyes if you wish, old man. I know that doing what is necessary is sometimes too much for your humane and oh-so-civilized sensibilities."

Biting down on her lower lip, to keep from giving voice to her pain, Komananov prayed that Number Seven would not be so easily rebuffed. She could use a good cop right now, no matter what the American's ultimate agenda was.

"I'm disappointed, Khan," the older man said, shaking his head. His voice had the tone of an elder chiding an upstart child. "Your intellect is as impressive as ever, but you're still too quick to resort to violence, too easily caught up in the adolescent bloodlust of conflict and battle." He patted the leather attaché case in his grip, calling Khan's attention to the crucial item. "This case, which you overlooked in your eagerness to wage a one-man war against the entire Soviet Army, may tell us everything we both want to know about the conspiracy against Gorbachev—and without descending to savagery."

For an endless moment, Khan stood as silent and immobile as a statue, the point of his knife remaining at his captive's throat. Komananov held her breath as the youth sullenly mulled over Number Seven's words, too proud to admit any error, yet too intelligent not to recognize the rationality of the older man's suggestion. Komananov's heart pounded; she was afraid that the militant young Sikh would sooner cut her to ribbons than lose face in front of Number Seven.

Instead, he withdrew his blade and returned it to his

belt. Then he sulkily unwound his turban and used the durable strip of saffron-colored fabric to bind the KGB officer's hands behind her back. "So be it," he stated sourly, his thick black hair tied in a ponytail at the back of his neck. Leaving Komananov against the fungus-covered wall, he turned and nodded at Number Seven. "Let us see what you have then."

Komananov was tempted to make a break for it while Khan's attention was momentarily elsewhere. Re-alistically, however, she knew that she stood little chance of outrunning the incredibly athletic youth, es-pecially once she got beyond the indispensable radi-ance of the flashlight. The prospect of racing blindly through total blackness, her hands tied behind her back, perhaps stumbling without any way to break her fall or even to get back up again, was not an appealing one. Better, perhaps, to wait for another, more promis-ing opportunity. *Besides,* she reminded herself, *I cannot leave without the case and its papers.*

Number Seven laid the slender attaché case down upon the sealed stump of the abandoned well, wisely re-fraining from provoking Khan further. "I had a glimpse of the contents earlier," he informed his teenage ally. "What I saw was most disturbing. I believe Colonel Ko-mananov and her colleagues intend to do far more than merely derail the negotiations in Reykjavik."

He fumbled briefly with the clasp on the case, which Komananov had carefully relocked after recovering it from Number Seven the first time. "This might take a moment or two," he commented to Khan, "unless you'd care to give me back my servo now."

"That won't be necessary," Khan replied darkly. Snatching up the case before the older man could protest, he ripped the lid off the case with his bare hands. "There," he announced, throwing the severed lid onto the moldering stones at his feet. He smugly placed the bottom of the case back onto the top of the well. "I trust that was not too violent a solution."

"No," Number Seven conceded, a trifle wryly. "Sometimes the direct approach can be very effective." He lifted a folder from inside the ruptured case and started leafing through several pages of classified documents. "Just remember, Khan, some Gordian knots take more effort to untangle."

Khan grunted dubiously, choosing to ignore the American's unsolicited advice. "Let me see those," he said simply, reaching out for more of Komananov's private papers. The KGB officer winced to see her carefully guarded secrets handled so cavalierly. *If only I hadn't stopped at Lenin's Tomb,* she agonized, *instead of going straight to the Presidium!*

Number Seven handed over the folder to Khan, while picking up another sheaf of documents from the case. "Do you read Russian?" he asked the teenage assassin.

"Do not insult my intelligence," Khan answered indignantly.

Apparently undaunted by the Cyrillic alphabet, both men rapidly skimmed through the notes, memos, and timelines that Komananov had once thought safe enough to transport in person. Trading the papers between them, their simmering rivalry momentarily placed on hold by the enormity of what they found in the illicitly acquired papers, Khan and Number Seven nodded in unison as they grasped the true dimensions of the operation.

"Do you see what I mean, Khan?" the American said finally, raising his eyes from a confidential fax. "We are talking here about nothing less than the deliberate assassination of Mikhail Gorbachev—sometime tonight, followed by an immediate military coup, imposing martial law upon the nation in response to the general secretary's death." He cast a censorious glance at Komananov. "According to the plan, the colonel here was to take control of the executive offices of the Supreme Soviet, before the civilian government had a chance to rally against the coup."

Khan put down a fistful of papers, then clapped his hands together softly. "A most ambitious project, madam," he applauded her, a tinge of admiration in his voice. "I commend you for your daring, if not your reckless disregard for world peace." He tipped his head in an ironic bow. "But unless I am missing something, which I sincerely doubt, there is one crucial detail missing from your meticulous files and reports. How, exactly, is Gorbachev to be killed tonight? What is the means of assassination?"

Number Seven continued to sort through the documents, mounting concern deepening the lines of his craggy face. "I can't find any specifics regarding the killing either," he confessed. "Just repeated references to something code-named *Pobeditel Velikanov.* Roughly, 'Giant-Killer,' " he translated. "Perhaps that designation holds some clue to what is planned for tonight."

"We have no time for riddles!" Khan declared, sneering at the American. He fingered the knife at his side, and glared balefully at Komananov, who, shuddering, saw her brief reprieve slipping away. "Fortunately, I know an easier way to uncover the truth."

"Wait, Khan!" Number Seven exclaimed. His hand rested on the stock of the assault rifle slung over his shoulder, but he refrained from actually drawing the weapon. "Don't do anything rash."

"Rash?" Khan laughed out loud. "Are you mad, Seven? The future of the world hangs in the balance and you counsel restraint?" With lightning speed, he yanked his last *chakram* off his arm and set it spinning briskly upon a raised index finger. With his other hand, he drew his curved dagger once more. A look of deadly seriousness came over his adolescent face. "Do not try your luck, old man," he challenged the American, who had yet to unshoulder the AK-74. "I am younger, faster, and genetically superior . . . as you well know." Twirling faster and faster, primed for flight, Khan's *chakram* was a mesmerizing, silver blur. "Put down that rifle, slowly."

The colonel's heart sank as Number Seven carefully discarded his weapon as requested. "Listen to me, Khan," he exhorted his presumed protégé urgently, sounding determined to reason with the rebellious youth. "I know your ultimate intentions are good, that you have the best interests of the planet at heart, but, believe me, such barbaric means inevitably corrupt their ends. You cannot build utopia on a foundation of bloodshed and torture."

Sadly, Komananov knew that the American was wasting his breath. In Khan she recognized a pragmatic ruthlessness not unlike her own, and she knew that the strong-willed teen would not refrain from torturing the truth out of her because that was exactly what she would do were their positions reversed. *A shame we could not have recruited him first,* she mused.

"That's where you are wrong, Seven," Khan stated confidently, confirming the colonel's cold-blooded appraisal of his character. "Lectures on morality will not rescue Gorbachev in time, nor bring an end to the senseless chaos plaguing mankind." His unsheathed dagger furiously slashed the air. "Only action, swift and sure!"

There is no stopping him, Komananov understood at last, realizing that she was running out of time and options. Having supervised many a stringent interrogation in the soundproof cells beneath KGB headquarters, she had no illusions about the human animal's ability to resist torture—or Khan's willingness to do whatever was required to extract the truth from her. Sooner or later, he would obtain the answers he sought, even if he had to eliminate Number Seven first.

"*Nyet,*" she whispered, steeling herself for what was to come. There was only one course left to her, if the operation—and the State—were to survive. "Counterrevolutionary filth!" she suddenly screamed. "Foreign adventurists!" Shrieking like a rampaging Cossack horseman, she threw herself at Khan, who instinctively thrust out his dagger to defend himself. The colonel ran right into the waiting knife, deliberately impaling herself upon the cold steel blade.

"No!" Khan cried out in anger, pulling back his encrimsoned knife too late. *Da!* Anastasia Komananov thought triumphantly, feeling her lifeblood gush from her sundered heart. As her legs collapsed beneath her, and eternal darkness overcame the glare from Number Seven's shaky flashlight, she had only one last request of fate. *Please,* she pleaded with her last dying breath, *let*

*me be remembered in the pantheon of historic Soviet heroes,
and not just as a slinky femme fatale in that tawdry spy
thriller...!*

Grim-faced, Khan rose from the lifeless body of the
dedicated KGB officer. "She had great courage," he
granted, giving the dead woman her due. Unlike Evergreen, that scientist in Antarctica, she did not rise
again after breathing her last. Nor did Khan expect her
to; in the last two years, he had become much more familiar with violent death and its consequences. "A pity
such a superior woman had to throw away her life for
such an ignoble cause."

"This has been a costly affair, Khan," Gary Seven
said, contemplating the fallen colonel with a look of
profound regret. He looked older than Khan remembered, his face more haggard and etched with strain
and worry. "Perhaps more so than necessary."

"Spare me your pious recriminations, old man,"
Khan growled impatiently. If the meddlesome American had not delayed him with his constant carping and
protestations, he might have already wrested the truth
from the Russian witch! Nonetheless, he arrested the
spin of his *chakram* and returned the steel ring to his
arm. With Komananov beyond his power to interrogate further, there was no longer any reason to keep
Seven at bay. He wiped off his dagger on the fabric of
his trousers and tucked the blade back into his belt.
"Gorbachev remains in mortal danger, and there is
much to do before this night's work is over."

Searching through the pockets of his trousers, he
found the servo he had taken from Komananov outside
the Tomb. "Here," he said brusquely, lobbing the inge-

nious device back to Seven. "Summon your unnatural mist. We must get to Iceland at once, and I can think of no faster way to do so."

It galled him enormously to be dependent on Seven once more, but larger issues took priority over his wounded pride. The reckless arms race between the United States and the Soviet Union threatened the entire planet with apocalypse. Colonel Komananov's co-conspirators could be not allowed to jeopardize Mikhail Gorbachev's peace offensive. *I have my own plans for this world,* Khan brooded morosely, *and they do not include ruling over a radioactive cinder.*

If only he knew how Gorbachev's nameless assassin intended to strike! "Well?" he prodded Seven, glaring across the dank underground crossroads at the man whose path kept crossing his own at the most inopportune times. Khan had not expected to find Seven on the trail of Komananov's conspiracy any more than Seven had anticipated Khan's timely appearance in Moscow. "What are you waiting for? Death waits for Gorbachev in Reykjavik, and there is not a moment to lose!"

Seven managed a thin, infuriating smile. "You need not fret, Khan." He activated the servo, which beeped as he lifted it before his lips like a microphone. "I already have agents on the scene. . . ."

CHAPTER THIRTY-THREE

"IT IS GOOD TO SEE YOU AGAIN, MR. PRESIDENT," Mikhail Gorbachev said. "Permit me to introduce my translator, Ms. Radhinka Lenin."

"Thank you, Mr. General Secretary," the President said warmly. "And you, too, young lady."

Standing beside Gorbachev, Roberta smiled politely at Ronald Reagan and recast the President's reply into Russian, discreetly assisted by the automatic translator in her earrings. She still couldn't believe that Gary Seven had actually managed to get her this gig. *Boy, did he have to call in plenty of favors,* she recalled, *not to mention manufacture some pretty impressive phony credentials!*

It would be worth the effort, though, if her close proximity to the general secretary allowed her to keep an eye out for the assassin Seven had warned her about less than twenty minutes ago, right before the beginning of this reception. According to Seven, who had contacted her via servo from Moscow (where he had also run into Noon Singh, of all people!), the unknown killer would strike tonight, perhaps even within minutes. All of which put Roberta in the unenviable position of being personally responsible for the safety of Mikhail Gorbachev and, quite possibly, peace in our time.

Wonderful, she thought sarcastically. Trying not to be too obvious about it, while simultaneously keeping up with her duties as Gorby's translator, she scoped out the tony, high-powered affair in which she was currently playing a key supporting role:

Hofoi House was a modest municipal reception hall with white clapboard walls and a picture window overlooking the harbor. Formerly home (at different times) to the French and British consulates, the venerable building was also said to be haunted, although by whom Roberta was not quite clear. A skylight in the gabled ceiling provided an eye-catching view of the Northern Lights shimmering brightly overhead, as well as a potential access point for, say, a crazed ninja assassin.

No, Roberta reconsidered, letting her gaze waft downward from the ceiling, *I have to assume that the Secret Service, as well as its Soviet counterpart, have a tight watch on every exit and entrance.* The attack on Gorbachev, if and when it arrived, would not come from such an obvious direction. *I have to be on guard for something much trickier.*

Although formal negotiations were not scheduled to commence until tomorrow morning, tonight's cocktail reception was intended to provide the U.S. and Soviet delegations with a chance to socialize briefly, and for Reagan and Gorbachev to give each other some personal face time, before everyone got down to the serious business of nuclear arms reductions. At the moment, the spacious hall, whose wooden walls were decorated with paintings and tapestries illustrating Iceland's proud Viking past, was crammed with a mixture of American, Russian, and Icelandic dignitaries, plus a small army of aides and translators. A buffet table, draped in white chiffon, offered samples of various local delicacies, including shark, haddock, puffin, and creamy yogurt pudding. Two other Icelandic staples, freshly killed whale and seal, were conspicuously absent, no doubt in deference to international sensitivities, whaling and seal-bashing being touchy issues these days.

Near the end of the buffet, Iceland's own president, Vigdis Finnbogadottir, was entertaining both Nancy Reagan and Raisa Gorbachev. *That can't be fun,* Roberta thought sympathetically; rumor had it that the two First Ladies actively loathed each other, unlike their respective spouses, who had managed to hit it off, and form a good working relationship, when they first met in Geneva a year ago. Hopes were high for this second summit, which was probably what had put the hardliners at the Kremlin in such a tizzy.

Operation: Giant-Killer, Roberta mused, recalling the assassination plot's inconveniently cryptic code name. What on Earth could that be a reference to? David and Goliath? Her eyes nervously turned toward the picture window facing the harbor, where moonlight glistened upon the crests of rolling waves. Surely the bad guys weren't planning to kill Gorbachev with a rock hurled by a sling? But what else could "Giant-Killer" mean?

"I'm glad we have another opportunity to talk like this, face-to-face," Reagan said to Gorbachev. Roberta had to interrupt her worried speculations to translate the elderly president's remarks. A head taller, and a quarter of a century older, than his fellow world leader, the President addressed Gorbachev in a characteristically genial manner, rather like an uncle advising a favorite nephew. "I enjoyed our fireside chat in Geneva last fall, and think that we have a real opportunity here to further improve relations between our two countries."

"Yes, exactly!" Gorbachev agreed enthusiastically. Unlike his phlegmatic predecessors in the Kremlin, Russia's new General Secretary was an energetic and charismatic individual. He did not wait for Reagan's own translator, an attractive blond woman named Sommers, whom Roberta believed had once been a champion tennis player, to convey his assent to Reagan before continuing in the same vein. "It is our duty to rid the world of the terrible menace of nuclear weapons. As you yourself once wisely said, 'a nuclear war could never be won and must never be fought.' " He slapped his leg loudly for emphasis. "That is why we are here!"

Obviously, Gorbachev had no intention of waiting until tomorrow to make his agenda known. Roberta knew that more than idealism motivated the Russian leader's determination to achieve serious arms reductions; the Soviet economy was on life-support and could not afford to keep up with America in an escalating arms race, especially with Reagan talking about expanding that race into space with his controversial Strategic Defense Initiative, better known as "Star Wars."

"Whoa there, Mikhail," the President said, leading Roberta to hope that the handy-dandy translator in her ear could come up with the Russian equivalent of "whoa." Reagan held up his hands, as if to ward off Gorbachev's aggressive lobbying tactics. "I want to eliminate the nuclear threat as much as anyone on this planet, but we have to proceed carefully. There are still some important issues to be worked out here."

"Like your so-called missile defense system?" Gorbachev shot back, apparently intent on pressing the issue. "Let us not mince words. I am prepared to offer you *significant* reductions in our nuclear arsenal in exchange for your promise not to test or deploy any space-based military weapons systems. Such an agreement is crucial if we are to achieve a lasting peace between our two nations."

Reagan's voice took on a stronger, firmer tone. "That program is a *defensive* system, Mr. Gorbachev," he said sternly, kind of like when he took control of the microphone during that presidential debate years ago. Roberta recognized this as his "I paid for that microphone" voice.

"Which would give you a first-strike capacity against us!" Gorbachev shot back. His face flushed angrily, not quite matching the beet-red birthmark on his forehead, which curiously resembled the outline of South America. "This is totally unacceptable."

To be honest, Roberta had her own reservations about Reagan's Strategic Defense Initiative. The whole idea struck her as only slightly less scary than that orbital nuclear platform that Gary Seven sabotaged way back in '68, when he first arrived on Earth. *The more things change, the more they stay the same,* she reflected rue-

fully. What was it Seven had said when Reagan originally went on TV to hype his proposed missile-defense
program? *Oh yeah,* she recalled, hearing Gary Seven's exasperated voice in her head: "How many times do I
have to scare you people out of extending your arms
race into space . . . ?"

Don't blame me, she thought. *I voted for Mondale.*

Fatigue swept over her as she dutifully waited for
Reagan's response, while also trying unsuccessfully to
anticipate the nameless assassin's strategy. If only she
wasn't so jet-lagged, having flown all the way to Iceland
with the rest of the Soviet delegation. Reykjavik was a
logical spot for the summit, being equidistant from
Moscow and New York, but it had still been a long trip
across at least three time zones. *It's already past eight,
Moscow time,* she calculated, wondering if Seven and
Noon had parted company yet. *Thank goodness that, at
the very least, Noon turned up in Moscow and not here;* she
was under enough pressure without having to deal with
that cocky teenage superman to boot.

"Perhaps we should save this discussion for the bargaining table," Reagan suggested, not unreasonably.
Switching back into avuncular mode, the former movie
star flashed his most irresistible smile. "I think I know
just the thing to sweeten this conversation," he said
with a grin.

The President snapped his fingers, and, on cue, a
youngish aide rushed forward, bearing a clear glass jar
packed to the brim with brightly colored jelly beans.
Roberta resisted a temptation to roll her eyes. *Of course,*
she thought; the whole world knew that Ronnie loved
his jelly beans.

Reagan took the glass container from the somewhat

nervous-looking aide and offered it to Gorbachev. "A gift," he explained, with a twinkle in his eye, "from one friend to another."

His charm offensive had the desired effect, or perhaps the canny Gorbachev simply made a strategic decision not to push his luck any further. In any event, the Russian leader smiled back at Reagan and graciously accepted the gift. "*Spasibo,* Mr. President," he said vigorously, handing the heavy jar over to Roberta to hold. "These look very tasty indeed!"

Roberta had to admit the glossy, rainbow-hued candies looked a lot more appetizing than, say, the highly pungent shark pieces on the buffet table. She was not at all surprised when Gorbachev, being a good sport, lifted the lid off the container in her hands, then scooped out a handful of gourmet Jelly Belly jelly beans. "Perhaps I should save some of these 'beans' for our Ministry of Agriculture," he quipped, pausing as he raised the candy toward his lips so that the official summit photographer could record the moment for posterity. Reagan chuckled appropriately.

Beans, Roberta thought, the word lodging in her brain as she started to step aside to give the photographer a better shot (and keep her cover from being blown). Something about the word bugged her, and not just because the automatic translator was taking its own sweet time figuring out how to say "jelly bean" in Russian. *Beans,* she repeated, free associating. Jelly beans. Magic beans. Jack and the Beanstalk. Jack the Giant Killer. . . .

Ohmigosh! she realized with a start. *Giant-Killer . . . of course! It's the beans! The KGB must have poisoned the jelly beans!*

She quickly looked across the room at the anonymous, nondescript aide who had delivered the jar to Reagan. The man's face was slick with perspiration as he stared at Gorbachev with a look of horrified fascination. He wasn't just nervous, Roberta concluded instantly; he looked guilty as hell, like a man who saw his own soul being damned right in front of his eyes. *They made him do it,* she realized beyond a shadow of a doubt. *The KGB got to the Gipper's gofer!*

A flashbulb went off, practically in Roberta's face. Reagan and Gorbachev smiled for the camera, and she knew that Gorbachev was only seconds away from tossing a whole handful of poisoned jelly beans into his mouth. His enemies in the Kremlin would no doubt try to pin the blame on the United States, she guessed, maybe even on Reagan himself. Talk about a diplomatic catastrophe! *I have to do something right away,* she thought frantically, *preferably without causing a major international incident.* . . .

"Watch out for that cat!" she yelled as shrilly as she could, startling Gorbachev and alerting Isis, who came racing out from beneath the buffet table with a strip of dried haddock between her jaws. The speeding feline zoomed straight across the room and up Gorby's leg, causing him to let go of the jelly beans in surprise and giving Roberta the excuse she needed to "accidentally" drop the entire jar onto the hardwood floor, where it shattered in an explosion of glass and tainted gelatin. "Oops!" she said in Russian, not that anyone was listening except maybe the American translator, Sommers, who reached out quickly to steady Roberta. *Wow,* she thought, surprised by the ex-tennis champ's strength, *that's quite a grip she's got.*

Letting go of Gorbachev's leg, Isis twisted in the air, landing on her feet in the middle of the crowded reception hall. Freaked-out diplomats scurried away from the demonic black cat, while Secret Service agents and their Russian competitors raced each other to capture the unsanctioned feline, diving for the floor and getting in each other's way even as Isis made a break for it, disappearing under a twelfth-century Viking couch. "There it went!" Nancy Reagan shouted helpfully, pointing at the gap between the couch and the floor with a forkful of broiled puffin. "Don't let it get away!"

Giddy with relief that disaster had been averted, Roberta fought hard not to giggle as she watched the First Lady's antics with undeniable amusement. Nancy was notoriously superstitious where astrology was concerned. *Wonder how she feels about black cats?* Roberta thought.

Unnoticed in the confusion, she discreetly toyed with the servo in the pocket of her gray serge business suit, locking an exceiver signal on the intricate circuitry in Isis's sparkling silver collar, so that, by the time the incensed bodyguards succeeded in dragging the hefty whalebone couch away from the wall, there was no sign of the cat at all, merely a wisp or two of a faintly ectoplasmic blue mist. "Good heavens," Roberta blurted out loud. "This place really *is* haunted!"

She glanced down at her feet, where the deadly jelly beans were now strewn amid slivers of broken glass. "I'm so sorry, Mr. President, General Secretary," she said ingenuously, shrugging her shoulders sheepishly. "That animal just came out of nowhere!"

"No harm done, young lady," Reagan assured her. He and Gorbachev both looked anxious to put the bizarre incident behind them. *Somehow I'm guessing this won't make the official press release,* Roberta thought, figuring that all parties involved were pretty much equally embarrassed. "So, Mikhail," Reagan said expansively, taking Gorbachev by the arm and guiding him toward the buffet table. "What do you say we sample some of our hosts' fine cuisine?"

Translating on the run, Roberta hustled to keep up with the gabbing world leaders, sparing only a second to glance over her shoulder at that suspicious-looking young aide, who looked on the verge of fainting, perhaps from relief that he hadn't actually killed the leader of a major world superpower. *I'll have to tip off our contact in the CIA about that guy,* she realized, making a mental note to do so at the earliest possible opportunity. *Or maybe Seven will want his friend McCall to "equalize" the culprit?*

In the meantime, she quietly congratulated herself (and, okay, Isis) on a job well done, even if she suspected that it would take more than some briny hors d'oeuvres to bridge the gap between Reagan's and Gorbachev's positions on SDI. That was their negotiators' problem, though, not hers. She had succeeded at the absolutely essential task of keeping Gorby alive.

How's that for a new twist in espionage? she thought, a mischievous smirk creeping onto her face. *This has to be the first time an undercover agent has ever saved the day by spilling the beans!*

CHAPTER THIRTY-FOUR

THE BERLIN WALL WAS COMING DOWN, AND ROBERTA was stuck watching it on TV. CNN, to be precise, which she was monitoring via the Beta 5. On the super-computer's circular display screen, hordes of ecstatic Germans, from both East and West, celebrated atop the now-obsolete Wall, while others went at the hated, graffiti-covered barricade with picks and hammers. Honking horns, pealing bells, and jubilant cheers joined with the pounding techno music blaring from dozens of boom boxes to effectively drown out the earnest efforts of on-site news commentators to provide a historical context for the riotous festivities. Tears flowed, and champagne bottles popped, as the city, divided for nearly three decades, came together once more.

It looked like one heck of a party, and Roberta was sorely tempted to get in on the action. Leaning back in Seven's well-worn suede chair, her feet upon the now-creaky walnut desk, she eyed the empty matter-transmission vault speculatively, then sighed and shook her head. As much as she wanted to hop the Blue Smoke Express to Berlin, Seven was counting on her to hold down the fort while he and Isis finished off their mission in Bulgaria, where even now they were working behind-the-scenes to insure that the collapse of that country's thirty-five-year-old Communist government took place in a peaceful manner. Seven and the cat been gone for hours now with no word, but Roberta wasn't too concerned yet. So far, the Iron Curtain appeared to be melting away with surprisingly little blood and thunder.

Who would have ever imagined it? Roberta thought, agog at the rapid-fire changes transforming the face of Eastern Europe. She and Seven had been working overtime for weeks now, trying to keep one step ahead of what appeared to be the complete and total meltdown of the Warsaw Pact. Not that she was complaining, of course; she still had vivid memories of being chased toward the Berlin Wall by barking guard dogs and trigger-happy East German soldiers, like that time she and Seven pilfered those files from the Russian Embassy. *Good grief,* she thought, with apologies to Charlie Brown. *Was that really fifteen years ago?*

Roberta suddenly felt very old. She had turned forty a few months ago, and though her shoulder-length hair was still honey-blond, the color came out of a bottle these days. She liked to think that she'd held on to her figure, though; if nothing else, saving the world on a near-weekly basis gave her plenty of exercise. *It's certainly been an interesting couple of decades,* she reflected philosophically. She'd traveled the world (and several places beyond), visited both the past and the future, risked her life a couple zillion times, and, most important, helped make the world a better place.

After a rocky start, what with AIDS and the Iran hostage crisis and all, the eighties seemed to be ending with peace and democracy and positive vibrations breaking out all over, as if the entire world had just taken a Prozac. *So much for the Cold War,* she mused, munching on a slice of pineapple pizza and trying not to drip any melted cheese onto her turtleneck sweater and old bell-bottoms. *Wonder if this means that Seven and I are finally out of work?*

As if in response to her unspoken query, the door to Seven's office came open with a bang. A single powerful kick was enough to knock the wooden door, which Roberta had conscientiously locked before rotating the Beta 5 out from its hiding place behind the bookcase, right off its hinges. Caught by surprise, with her feet still awkwardly perched on top of the desk, she choked on her pizza as a trio of intruders barged into the office, led by a bearded young man wearing a snow-white turban and a red Nehru jacket. Roberta recognized the invader at once, even though she hadn't laid eyes on him for at least five years.

"Khan!"

She reached wildly for her servo, resting atop the desk, where she had actually been using it as a pen, to scribble down notes on a memo pad, but a single gunshot shattered the polished obsidian desktop directly between her and the servo, making her yank her hand back abruptly. Looking up in alarm, she spotted a Glock automatic pistol, complete with silencer, in the youthful superman's grip. *Guess he's graduated from killer Frisbees,* she noted acerbically, recalling Seven's description of the deadly *chakram*s Khan had employed in Moscow a few years back.

"No tricks or ill-considered heroics, please," he warned her calmly, striding confidently toward her. He pocketed the servo while keeping the Glock aimed directly at her heart. "Good evening, Ms. Lincoln." He boldly looked her over, his dark eyes appraising her without a hint of shame or discretion. Roberta was suddenly grateful that she'd gone with the bell-bottoms instead of a miniskirt today. "The years have been kind to you."

"Thanks," she said coolly. Shoving her chair back from the desk, she carefully lowered her feet to the carpet. "You're looking good, too, I suppose. Aside from the ugly black gun, that is."

Khan would be nearly twenty now, she calculated. No longer the wide-eyed teen Seven had rescued from Delhi years ago, let alone the strangely charismatic toddler she had first met at Chrysalis way back in '74, he had only grown more impressive—and dangerous— over the intervening years. Magnetic brown eyes looked out on the world with complete assurance, while his deep voice and assertive manner were those of a born leader. Beneath the mandatory black beard, a Sikh tradition, his once-boyish features had evolved into those of a strikingly handsome young man. He could have been a model or movie star, Roberta figured, had not his lab-approved DNA and overweening arrogance steered him toward more grandiose and unsettling ambitions.

Although Khan had been keeping a low profile since killing all those Soviet soldiers outside Lenin's Tomb in '86, Seven had tried, with mixed results, to keep track of the Indian superman's activities over the past few years. Unconfirmed rumors and reports had placed Khan all over Asia and the Indian subcontinent: inciting the 1987 pro-democracy uprising in South Korea, fighting alongside the Afghan rebels in their guerrilla war against the Soviet Union, and, perhaps most ominously, personally arranging the mysterious 1988 plane crash that killed General Zia ul-Haq, the leader of Pakistan's military government, leading to the eventual return of democracy to India's nearest neighbor and rival.

Granted, not all such reports proved accurate. At one time, about four months ago, she and Seven had come to believe that Khan had, in fact, perished during the bloody government crackdown in Tiananmen Square—until equally unverifiable reports credited him with the supposedly "natural" death of the Ayatollah Khomeini on the very same day. Still, even if only half of what they had heard was true, Khan had certainly been keeping busy since '86, albeit in a sneakily covert way.

Sarina Kaur would be very proud of her son, Roberta thought, *which isn't necessarily good news for the rest of us.* Her gaze crept furtively toward the green translucent cube resting atop the desk like a snazzy crystal paperweight. The cube was actually a portable, artificially intelligent interface with the Beta 5. *If I can just get my hands on that cube for a few moments, I might be able to send a distress signal to Seven—or even Isis!*

"So who are your new buddies?" she asked Khan, stalling for time. She tipped her head toward the two strangers flanking Khan. They looked like hired muscle to her, with beefy bodies and silent, sullen expressions. One was Arab in appearance, while the other looked African, but they were both too homely and thuggish-looking to be genetically engineered, which provided Roberta with some small measure of relief. One new-and-improved *Ubermensch* was more than enough.

"Why, these are but two of my many followers," Khan said grandly, introducing the brutish pair with a sweeping gesture. "They share my vision of the new world order to come, in which, at long last, the suffering masses of humanity will be governed by those, such as myself, best equipped to manage world affairs." He glanced over at the Beta 5, which continued to display televised images of festive Germans dancing upon the disintegrating Wall, and nodded in approval. "This is my moment, Ms. Lincoln. In the imminent collapse of the once-mighty Soviet Union, I see a power void crying out to be filled by a new breed of superior men and women. The time draws near when I, and others like me, shall be able to step from the shadows to claim our rightful place as the destined rulers of humanity."

And the really scary thing is, Roberta thought with a shudder, *he might actually be able to pull it off.* But what was Khan talking about when he referred to "others" like him? Did that mean he knew where all the other Children of Chrysalis were hidden, scattered throughout the world? *Please, God, no!* she prayed. The very last thing the world needed was for Khan to unite his superhuman brothers and sisters in a joint effort to take over the planet!

If Seven were here, she guessed, he would probably let Khan know in no uncertain terms what a bad idea it was to place total world power in the hands of a small genetic elite. *He'd be right, too,* she acknowledged, *but I don't think Khan is in any mood to listen to anyone but himself.*

"What do you want here?" she asked Khan defiantly. Hiding her apprehensions behind her best poker face, she tried to match Khan's fearless bravado with some attitude of her own. "I ought to warn you. Gary Seven, and a whole squad of new recruits, are due back here any minute."

Khan laughed at her desperate bluff. "Don't be ridiculous, Ms. Lincoln. Seven is in Bulgaria; my spies spotted him there less than twenty minutes ago, along with that remarkably long-lived cat of his." His gaze shifted to the empty matter-transmission vault. "Still, we are quite prepared should he attempt a sudden return via that quite miraculous device." He crossed over to the open door of the vault, where he proceeded to physically rip out the switches and knobs controlling the transporter. With just one hand, he tore apart the dense solid-steel plating, exposing the flashing crystalline circuitry beneath. Then he stepped back and fired his gun directly into the naked apparatus. Fiery red sparks flashed as the delicate instrumentality was disrupted by a round of 9mm ammo.

Roberta's heart sank. Nobody was 'porting anywhere, she realized, until some serious repairs were made. *Guess I'm not getting to Berlin tonight.* "Okay, now what?" she asked Khan glumly.

"Now you remain quietly seated," he informed her, "while I help myself to some key information that I suspect your sanctimonious employer had no intention of ever sharing with me." He looked at his looming flunkies, then nodded at the unarmed woman behind the desk. "Watch her," he ordered curtly, putting away his gun. He turned his back on Roberta and marched over to the Beta 5. The big Arab lumbered around the desk so that he could stand right behind the worried hostage. Meaty hands landed heavily on her shoulders, driving her deeper into the black suede chair.

"Hey, watch the hands, Bluto!" she protested indignantly, eliciting only a grunt in response. Khan's other henchman stood, his arms crossed belligerently, in the empty space where the kicked-in door had once stood, blocking the only exit from the office now that the transporter had been disabled. *This isn't good,* Roberta thought, taking stock of her increasingly precarious situation. The green cube tantalized her, glinting atop the desk several inches away, not far from the spidery network of cracks radiating from the bullet hole Khan's automatic had left in the desk's black obsidian surface. The cube was easily within reach, if only the giant Arab were not watching her like a hawk. *So near and yet so hard to get. . . !*

Khan faced the Beta 5. He stroked his thick black beard as he inspected the protruding control panel. Roberta found it hard to imagine that he could actually figure out how to operate the alien supercomputer, but, then again, who knew what his genetically engineered intellect was capable of?

"Computer!" he commanded imperiously. "Cease transmission."

Multicolored strips of light blinked above the control shelf. "Voice pattern unknown," the Beta 5 announced. "Please identify."

Roberta experienced a surge of hope. If anything on Earth could stand up to Khan Noonien Singh's indomitable will, it would be that snooty supercomputer. She still had no idea what exactly Khan wanted from the Beta 5, but she crossed her fingers and prayed that the computer would guard its precious data files like a mother Horta protecting its eggs.

Khan scowled, not used to being disobeyed, then fished a small electronic patch from his pocket and placed it against his throat. When he spoke again, his voice was a dead-on re-creation of Gary Seven's somber intonations. *Hey,* Roberta protested silently, *I thought only Seven could do that trick!*

"Computer," he began again, this time sounding far too much like Seven. "Cease transmission."

To Roberta's chagrin, the deception appeared to work. "Voice pattern acknowledged. Identity confirmed, 194." A series of electronic beeps accompanied the blinking lights. "Ceasing transmission."

CNN disappeared from the monitor, leaving the white circular screen blank. Khan nodded in approval, smiling coldly. "Computer, assemble all data concerning the status and current whereabouts of the genetically modified children conceived in India during the early 1970s. Check references for Chrysalis, Rajasthan . . . and Dr. Sarina Kaur."

"No!" Roberta blurted loudly, realizing what Khan was up to. *He wants to find the other superkids!* "Computer, override previous command! Maximum security!"

The hulking Arab snarled and clamped an immense hand over her mouth. The other Terminator clone stalked toward Roberta angrily, raising his hand as if to strike her across the face. *These guys remind me too much of my old sparring partner, Carlos,* she decided, wincing in anticipation of the blow.

"Hold!" Khan barked, fingering the patch at his throat so that he reverted to his own voice for the moment. He waved his hand, and the African enforcer retreated back to the doorway. "There is no need to injure a defenseless woman. Yet."

Roberta's sigh of relief was muffled by the intrusive palm covering the bottom half of her face. *Nice to know Khan still has some scruples,* she thought, even as she wondered how long his forbearance would last if he didn't get what he wanted. *He's not getting anything out of me without a fight,* she vowed.

"See to it she remains silent," Khan added, turning his attention back to the Beta 5. He took a deep breath, preparing himself, then spoke once more in Gary Seven's voice. "Computer, resume search for data concerning the Chrysalis Project and all surviving offspring engineered during its years of operation."

The computer beeped testily. "Unable to comply. All data relating to Chrysalis Project has been classified Highly Confidential. Zeta-level security protocols required to access data."

Khan frowned and shot a murderous glance at Roberta, who felt her projected life span shrink accordingly. "Computer," he insisted firmly. "This is Gary Seven, 194. Disregard prior command by subordinate Roberta Lincoln. Access data immediately."

"Prior command irrelevant," the Beta 5 stated stubbornly, not making things remotely easy for Khan, bless its obstructionist algorithms! "All material relating to Chrysalis was classified Highly Confidential by Supervisor 194 as of Terran date December 4, 1984. Zeta-level protocols required."

Snarling, Khan clenched his fists in frustration while Roberta savored his apparent defeat. *How about that?* she thought, impressed by Seven's obvious foresight. *December '84 . . . let's see, that would have been right after that big blowup in Antarctica—and that horrible disaster in Bhopal. Seven must have locked the Chrysalis files down tight as soon as he realized that Khan was likely to become a problem.* Beneath the hand clamped over her face, a sassy grin appeared. For all Khan's brilliance and Taj Mahal—sized ego, Seven was already way ahead of him!

But the determined wunderkind refused to give up. Concentrating with fierce intensity upon the Beta 5's control panel, he began operating the instrument. Slowly at first, then with increasing speed and confidence, his fingers danced over the controls, flipping switches and keying in commands at a frightening pace. In response, the blinking colored lights started flashing faster and faster, while the Beta 5's high-pitched electronic voice acquired an almost hysterical tone.

"Error! Error!" the computer chirped. "System parameters under attack. Halt! Cease illegal operations immediately. Error! Reporting unauthorized breach of autonomous analytical criteria. Stop! Halt! Error! Security protocols degrading. Error! Error! Error. . . ."

I don't believe it! Roberta thought aghast. *He's hacking into the Beta 5!*

She didn't think it was possible, but within minutes the computer's frantic protests fell silent while Khan continued to manipulate the Beta 5's controls as though he were some cyberpunk computer cowboy straight out of a William Gibson novel. "Accessing all relevant files on Project Chrysalis," the Beta 5 reported robotically. Roberta half-expected the lobotomized computer to start singing "Daisy" at any moment. "Preparing storage medium as requested."

Greenish radiation flashed briefly and a high-density compact disk materialized in the replicator tray next to the controls. Khan plucked the CD from the tray and held it up to the light, beaming triumphantly. "Excellent," he pronounced, giving the Beta 5's control panel an affectionate pat. For a moment, Roberta thought he was done ransacking the computer's confidential files, but then Khan returned to the keyboard on the control shelf.

"One more thing," he added, almost as an afterthought, while manually overriding the computer's better judgment and inhibitions. "Access all files regarding ozone manipulation technology, developed by Dr. Wilson Evergreen, circa 1984. Include all relevant technical specifications and diagrams."

Roberta groaned inwardly. *This just keeps getting worse and worse,* she lamented. Not content to loot the Beta 5 for the current addresses of all his genetically souped-up siblings, he now wanted the know-how to control Earth's ozone layer if he felt like it. *And there's nothing I can do to stop him!*

The brainwashed computer beeped obediently, and another CD was conjured up in a bright green flash. Khan tucked the two bootleg disks into the interior of his jacket and nodded in satisfaction. "That will do . . . for now," he declared, peeling the adhesive patch off his throat, and drawing out his Glock once more.

Realizing what he intended, Roberta attempted to leap from her seat, but the huge Arab henchman shoved her back down forcibly. "No! Wait!" she cried out, but her terrified pleas were muffled by the thug's immovable palm. She could only look on in horror as Khan fired the automatic weapon at the Beta 5. The blank viewscreen exploded into white Plexiglas shards, the prismatic radiation gauge above the monitor was shot to pieces, and acrid gray fumes rose from the perforated black screen against which the vibrant colored lights had previously flickered in time with every pulse of the Beta 5's cybernetic synapses. Roberta felt as though an old friend, albeit a somewhat cranky one, were being murdered right before her eyes.

Khan emptied his pistol into the computer, then coldly walked away from the butchered machine. He gestured at the Arab, who responded by finally lifting his huge hand off Roberta's lips. "You monster!" she raged at Khan, tears of anger leaking from her eyes. "Whatever happened to the precocious little boy I met in India so many years ago?"

Khan accepted her fury calmly. "He is fulfilling his destiny, Ms. Lincoln. That is all."

On an end table by the couch, the fax machine clattered noisily. Curious, Khan strolled over to the brand new appliance and tore the newly printed message from the machine. His dark eyes quickly scanned the communiqué and he chuckled softly to himself before striding back toward Roberta with the curled fax paper in his fist.

"This appears to be the text of a resignation speech to be delivered by President Todor Zhivkov of Bulgaria. Written by Gary Seven, of course. He wishes your editorial input, Ms. Lincoln, before delivering the final text of the speech to his contacts in the Bulgarian government." Khan shook his head and sighed theatrically. "Seven was always good at making speeches, I'll give him that. A shame he can be so fainthearted when the sword is required."

Khan tossed the crumpled fax onto the floor. "I have a message as well, Ms. Lincoln, which you may deliver to your employer when he returns to America. Tell him I have no objections if he continues to perform good works here and there about the world, scribbling insignificantly in the margins of history." Roberta couldn't tell if he meant to be conciliatory or just condescending. *Probably the latter,* she supposed. "After all, our ultimate goals are largely the same."

"I wouldn't be so sure of that," Roberta said acidly.

Khan ignored her barb. "Nevertheless," he said, his voice taking on a more menacing tone, "warn the indefatigable Mr. Seven that he must in no way interfere with my operations and activities in the months and years to come. I shall be stepping out onto a larger stage, Ms. Lincoln, and I will not tolerate either you or your employer getting in the way of my inevitable ascent."

A bright green glow suddenly emanated from within the stationary cube upon the desk, which also beeped insistently. *Seven's doing,* Roberta guessed, no doubt in response to his discovery that the transporter would not respond to his signal. *He must be trying to activate the transporter via the remote interface, not realizing that Khan has pretty much wrecked the primary controls.* Unfortunately, there was nothing she could do to help Seven out at the moment. Khan had even taken her servo.

Intrigued, Khan picked up the glowing cube and inspected it quizzically, turning it over in his hand. "Another of Seven's amazing toys?" he asked. When Roberta declined to answer, he merely shrugged and held the cube up before him. "No matter," he declared. "My message remains the same." He squeezed the crystal cube tightly within his fist, until the alien device imploded under the pressure. Releasing his grip slowly, he let the powdered remains of the cube rain softly onto the carpet. "I trust I make myself absolutely clear?"

Crystal, Roberta thought, nodding unhappily. *Or what's left of it.*

"Then my business here is concluded." Khan clapped his hands together and his bullying minions marched out of the office. "Farewell, Ms. Lincoln," he said, bowing courteously as he lingered in the doorway. "Let us hope we need not meet again."

She waited until she heard the outer door slam shut before rising shakily from Seven's chair. Pale and wobbly, she swept her shell-shocked gaze over the devastated office, which seemed everywhere to display the aftereffects of Khan's destructive wrath: the broken door lying flat upon the floor, the smoking shell of the bullet-ridden Beta 5, the mangled transporter controls, and the pulverized residue of what had once been the chirpy little green cube.

And to think that, less than an hour ago, I thought the whole world was hunky-dory. A chill that had nothing to do with temperature swept over her and she hugged herself as though she were standing outside in a bitter wind blowing straight from an underground cavern buried deep beneath the deserts of western India. The Cold War might have ended, but somehow, standing in the ruins of the violated office that had been her home away from home for over twenty years, Roberta Lincoln knew that the worst was yet to come. . . .

CHAPTER THIRTY-FIVE

"Good Lord, Jim, it's a planet of Spocks."

McCoy joined Kirk at the table, arriving a few minutes late at a banquet being held in honor of the Paragon Colony's distinguished guests. The feast was taking place at a roomy outdoor plaza beneath the great green dome protecting the colony from the planet's unforgiving environment. Strategically planted redwoods rose like Doric columns around the perimeter of a rectangular courtyard, mimicking the look of some ancient Grecian temple. Polished basalt tiles, doubtless mined from the volcanic plains outside the dome, gave the floor a glossy black sheen, while Regent Clarke and her honored guests, including Kirk and McCoy, dined at an elevated pine table surrounded by easily a dozen smaller satellite tables. McCoy sat down at the vacant seat to Kirk's right, his medical tricorder still hanging from a strap over his shoulder. "I mean it, Jim! I just spent the last several hours reviewing the colony's medical records, and you've never seen such a terrifying glut of physical and mental fitness. Muscular density, cardiac strength, respiration, you name it . . . everyone here would be in the upper percentile, health-wise, on any other planet in the Federation. They have superior recall and cognitive functions, too. You should see what sort of enormous calculations these people can effortlessly perform in their heads." McCoy's expression soured. "Like I said, Spock would feel very at home here."

"Hello, Bones. Good of you to make it," Kirk replied wryly. He knew the doctor well enough to realize that "a planet of Spocks" wasn't exactly a ringing endorsement where McCoy was concerned. *Better a world of Spocks than a planet of Khans,* the captain reflected, making a mental note to take a closer look at McCoy's medical findings later. He was curious to get the doctor's impressions of the colonists' overall psychological stability, although he could hardly grill Bones on that subject right in front of their hosts.

McCoy nodded deferentially at the regent as he settled in at the table. "My apologies for my tardiness, ma'am," he drawled. Like Kirk, he was decked out in his full dress uniform, metallic gold piping sprucing up his blue medical tunic. "An occupational hazard, I'm afraid."

"So I understand, Doctor," Masako Clarke said graciously, "although, thankfully, we have little need for physicians here, having largely eradicated disease and disability, except in the extremely aged. We've made considerable strides in geriatric medicine as well, which I'm sure our medical researchers will be happy to discuss with you later."

"Thank you, Madame Regent," Kirk said, seated between Clarke and McCoy. Gleaming bone plates and utensils rested atop the pristine silk tablecloth. "That's very generous of you."

"Masako, please," the regent insisted once more. "And my motives aren't entirely altruistic, I fear. I have a favor to ask of you as well. Our scientists would dearly like to obtain DNA samples from you and your crew, Captain, just in case any interesting mutations have developed in the human species since our ancestors left the Federation."

Seated to Clarke's left, Koloth chuckled disparagingly. "You may be disappointed with what you find," the sardonic Klingon commander remarked. For this formal occasion, he wore a silver sash, adorned with glittering medals, across the chest of his military uniform. "It is the indisputable opinion of the finest Klingon minds that the human genome has actually *degraded* under the decadent regime of the Federation. Survival of the fittest, the fundamental principle of evolution, has, alas, been supplanted by a debilitating doctrine of 'survival of the mediocre,' in which the weak and infirm are coddled by a system unwilling to cull even the most unworthy specimens from its collective gene pool. Unlike the Klingon Empire, of course, whose bloodlines are kept strong and vigorous by the bracing demands of honorable combat."

McCoy bristled at Koloth's snide attack on humanity's genetic health. "Indisputable, my aunt Fanny. That's pure Klingon propaganda, and bad science to boot! The evolutionary progress of a sentient species is measured by a heck of a lot more than the ability to swing a *bat'leth* or fire a disruptor. Some of the greatest advances in human thought and civilization have been brought about by individuals who would have been dismissed as genetically unfit by less discerning minds. Stephen Hawking, for instance, or, more recently, Dr. Miranda Jones, a blind woman who became the first human being to achieve a telepathic link with a Medusan."

"A few freak instances," Koloth insisted, dismissing McCoy's arguments with an airy wave of his hand. "The exceptions that prove the rule." A self-amused smirk displayed the pleasure the wily Klingon took in baiting the cantankerous MD. "A human expression, I believe."

Kirk couldn't resist joining the fray. "If Klingon evolution is on such a fast track already, then you obviously have no need for the Paragon Colony's advanced genetic engineering techniques." He quickly changed the subject in an attempt to get the last word. "By and by, I can't help noticing that your second-in-command, the ever-charming Lieutenant Korax, is not gracing us with his presence this evening."

In fact, an empty seat gaped next to Koloth, creating a gap between the Klingon captain and the local dignitary at his left. "Ah, yes," Koloth acknowledged, "I regret to say that Korax is indisposed at the moment." Not far away, Koloth's bodyguard—the bald warrior with the scarred face—shared a separate table with Lieutenant Lerner and a couple of members of the colony's own security forces. The human and Klingon soldiers glowered at each other in silence as they gnawed on the appetizers provided. *Must be a tense table to dine at,* Kirk suspected, feeling sorry for Lerner as well as for the unlucky colonists trapped in the middle of that miniature cold war.

"What a shame," Kirk commented sarcastically about Korax's absence. "But, of course, we understand, given how delicate his health must be. I do hope that his fragile system recovers from his unfortunate 'indisposition' eventually."

Koloth scowled, annoyed by Kirk's tweaking. "I never said anything about his health," he began indignantly, only to be interrupted by the arrival, on several ivory trays, of the first course of the banquet. A parade of servers, in smart white uniforms, delivered the colony's bounty to the table, while Koloth fumed silently.

The appetizers consisted of soup and salad, for the humans, and a skewer of nearly raw meat slices for the Klingons. Having worked up an appetite researching the Eugenics Wars, Kirk gladly sampled the fare, only to find both the onion soup and the Uranian salad dressing surprisingly bland. Almost tasteless, to be honest. The soup was thin and watery, while the vegetables and greens making up the salad tasted as though they had been deliberately leached of flavor. *They may be whizzes at genetic engineering,* Kirk thought, doing his best to conceal his lack of enthusiasm for the pallid gruel, *but Sycorax's culinary arts leave something to be desired.*

"I do hope your meal isn't too rich or spicy for you," Masako Clarke asked solicitously, not to mention surreally. "I expressly instructed our chefs not to prepare anything that might overtax your unrefined palates and less efficient metabolisms, but please let me know if you'd prefer simpler, less exciting fare."

Less exciting than this? Kirk thought, his mind boggling at the notion. The colony's chefs had clearly overcompensated, just as it was becoming quite obvious that the regent, and perhaps all of her genetically enhanced con-

stituents, had an exaggerated sense of their human forebears' intrinsic deficiencies. *Just like Khan,* he thought
ominously. *He ultimately underestimated us, too.*

"This is more than acceptable, thank you," Kirk said
diplomatically, while McCoy grinned in amusement. Farther down the table, Kirk caught Koloth toying unen-
thusiastically with his shish-kebob. Judging from the
dubious look on the Klingon's face, Koloth found his
own meal no more appetizing than Kirk's. *That's probably
the one thing we can both agree on,* the human captain
thought, dutifully downing another tepid spoonful of
soup.

"Yes, an excellent repast," Koloth lied shamelessly,
"fit for a gourmet. Your chefs are to be commended."
He clapped his hands together imperiously, and his
bodyguard rose from the adjacent table, bearing a package wrapped in a protective black leather sheath. Immediately on guard, Lieutenant Lerner moved to block the
swarthy Klingon soldier, but, at Kirk's signal, backed off
and let the bald warrior approach the elevated table.
Kirk couldn't imagine that Koloth would attempt anything overtly threatening at such a formal occasion, yet
he nonetheless watched warily as Koloth accepted the
parcel from his subordinate and proceeded to remove a
tapered glass bottle from the sheath. "If you have no ob-
jection, Madame Regent, I've taken the liberty of securing a libation worthy of such an exquisite feast." A clear
blue fluid sloshed within the bottle. "The finest Romulan ale, with my compliments."

Kirk frowned. Apparently the recent alliance between the Klingons and the Romulan Star Empire had
yielded more than just an exchange of military technology. He kicked himself mentally for letting Koloth gain

a momentary advantage on him. *Too bad there's no way Scotty can beam me a bottle of his best whisky, what with the force field surrounding the dome.*

"Thank you, Captain," Clarke said, accepting the proffered vintage. The bottle was passed around the table so that everyone could fill their wineglasses with the sparkling blue ale. Lifting a cup to his lips, Kirk had to admit that the potent nectar was a good deal more satisfying than anything yet served at the banquet.

The piquant ale also met with McCoy's approval. "Now, that's what I call a drink," he admitted, smacking his lips. "Hard to believe that such an intoxicating brew was actually concocted by some distant cousins of the Vulcans."

"The Romulans, for all their faults, can hardly be compared to their cold-blooded, overly ascetic ancestors, Doctor," Koloth observed, and Kirk wondered if, back on the *Enterprise,* Spock's ears were burning. "Like my own people, they appreciate that existence is a never-ending battle for supremacy and survival. To the victor go the spoils—including this delightful vintage." He raised his cup in a toast. "To our hosts, and their own laudable pursuit of superior strength and cunning."

Feeling outmaneuvered once more, Kirk had no choice but to join the calculating Klingon in raising his cup to Regent Clarke and her people. He countered, however, with a toast of his own. "To a new future of better understanding and cooperation between our respective peoples."

And to avoid the mistakes of the past, he added silently to himself. The insights he'd absorbed from his ongoing immersion in the history of the twentieth century haunted his thoughts, casting a sinister light on even the regent's questionable pride in her staff's cuisine. It was clear from his studies that supermen such as Khan and Gary Seven had been capable of enormous good in the distant past, and yet the seeds of Khan Singh's ruthless ambition had blossomed early on, despite the deliberate efforts of Gary Seven to channel the young Khan's remarkable talents toward the greater good of humanity. *What was it Spock once said about Khan and his fellow supermen?* Kirk tried to recall. The heady Romulan ale wasn't helping his memory any, but he soon remembered Spock's prophetic assertion that "superior ability breeds superior ambition."

As history knew too well, Earth had paid a terrible price for that ambition. Would the same apply to the Paragon Colony, or any future superhumans created via their genengineering techniques? How long would Khan's spiritual descendants be content to exist merely as part of the Federation, before aspiring to take control of the many worlds and cultures under Starfleet's protection? Masako Clarke and her people seemed amiable enough, but how could he be sure that, allowed to spread beyond Sycorax's planetary boundaries, the Paragon Colony's philosophy and influence would not pose a greater threat to galactic peace than the Klingons and the Romulans combined?

I can't, Kirk realized soberly. *Not yet.*

An uproar at the far end of the plaza intruded upon Kirk's somber musings. Along with the other attendees of the banquet, including the regent herself, he looked on in surprise as two imposing colony members, no doubt bred for their intimidating stature, marched toward the main table, dragging with them a struggling figure whom Kirk quickly identified as Korax. "Let go

of me, you misbegotten *targs*!" the irate Klingon lieutenant snarled, his wrists handcuffed together. A black
eye and split lip suggested that Korax had not surrendered to the colony officers without a fight. "You will
regret this, Earthspawn! I swear by Kahless's name that
I will have my revenge!"

Masako Clarke rose from her seat with a look of consternation. "What is the meaning of this?" she demanded. By contrast, Kirk observed, Koloth looked less
surprised than annoyed by his first officer's capture.

"We caught this outworlder inside the primary
forcefield generator, trying to download classified information about the colony's defenses," one of Korax's
captors announced. Like the accused spy, the security
guard's face bore evidence of a violent struggle. Kirk
was somewhat relieved to note that genetically engineered supermen were evidently just as capable of receiving a bloodied nose as anyone else.

Clarke's face hardened and she sternly confronted
the Klingon seated beside her. "Is this true, Captain
Koloth?" she asked indignantly.

The Klingon commander was the very picture of
wounded innocence. "Madame Regent, you must believe me! I am utterly appalled to even think that one of
my men might be so misguided as to abuse your generous hospitality." He rose from his chair and shook his
head theatrically at Korax, who endured the rebuke in
surly silence. "I assure you, Regent, that, if these charges
are true, Lieutenant Korax will be severely disciplined."

Kirk suspected Koloth of telling only half the truth.
If Korax was punished at all, he surmised, it would be
for getting caught rather than for the espionage itself.
Kirk had not forgotten Koloth's involvement in the

plot to poison grain vital to the survival of the Federation colony on Sherman's Planet. Compared with that, what was a little unauthorized snooping?

Clarke wasn't buying Koloth's act either. "I think it would be best," she addressed the Klingon commander frostily, "if you and your people departed Sycorax immediately." She capped the bottle of Romulan ale and handed it back to Koloth. "And you can take your gift with you."

"With all due respect, Regent," Koloth warned, letting a hint of steel show through the velvety facade of his impeccable etiquette, "I urge you to reconsider this decision. The Klingon Empire is not about to let this minor . . . misunderstanding . . . get in the way of our long-term interests where your colony is concerned."

To her credit, Clarke refused to be cowed by the Klingon's veiled threat. "These security officers will escort you back to your shuttlecraft, Captain," she stated forcefully. "I believe our negotiations have concluded."

Koloth nodded, accepting the inevitable, for now. "Very well," he acceded, returning the rejected bottle to its sheath. "You may come to regret your actions this evening," he informed the regent darkly, before dipping his head toward Kirk and McCoy. "Farewell, Captain, Doctor. No doubt we shall meet again."

Flanked by an entire team of armed security guards, who had arrived on the scene within seconds of the regent's pronouncement, Koloth and his men were led out of the plaza. "I don't like the look of this," McCoy muttered quietly to Kirk. "It's not like the Klingons to give up so easily."

"They haven't," Kirk said with total confidence.

While he remained undecided regarding the Paragon Colony itself, he was certain of one thing.

They had not heard the last of Koloth and his forces.

"Your chief engineer beamed *what* onto Koloth's warship, Captain?"

"Tribbles," Kirk repeated, grinning at the memory. He had been entertaining the regent and the other diners at the table with the story of his earlier run-in with Captain Koloth at K-7. At least forty-five minutes had passed since the Klingons had been summarily ejected from the colony, and the banquet was winding toward its conclusion. A bowl of ice cream—vanilla, of course—rested on the tablecloth in front of Kirk as he wondered how to best convey the insidious cuteness of the purring tribble hordes.

Suddenly, an explosion rocked the floor of the plaza. Plates and glasses rattled at every table and, through the branches of the redwoods surrounding the dining area, an enormous orange fireball could be glimpsed rising over the trees maybe three-quarters of a mile away. Kirk leaped to his feet, reaching instinctively for his phaser, only to remember that he had come unarmed to the formal state dinner. Of the three Starfleet officers present at the banquet, only Lieutenant Lerner was ready to repel any immediate assault. Kirk was proud to see that the security officer already had his weapon out, and had taken a defensive position in front of the regent's table.

As yet, however, there was no sign of an attack, aside from the initial explosion. Billowing black clouds of smoke continued to rise beyond the trees, and Kirk could smell the blaze from where he was standing. Strident klaxons sounded in the distance, audible even over the hubbub of excited and frightened voices echoing throughout the outdoor plaza, as the colony's fire department and other emergency services went into action with admirable speed, but Kirk was utterly convinced that the explosion had been no mere accident. *This is Klingon work,* Kirk thought, clenching his fists at his sides. *I'm sure of it.*

An anxious-looking aide, his face pale, hurried to the regent's side and whispered hastily in her ear. Clarke's own face blanched at the dire news she had clearly just received. "Oh, no!" she whispered, her worried gaze glued to the unchecked smoke and flames on the horizon. "I never thought . . . "

"What is it, Madame Regent?" Kirk asked, determined to find out what had the regent so dismayed. "If there's any assistance we can provide . . ."

"Yes," McCoy added emphatically. As always, he was a doctor first. "Please let me help treat the wounded."

"Thank you, Doctor," Clarke said sincerely, "but I'm afraid the situation is even more serious than it appears." She lowered her voice to avoid inciting a panic. "The explosion occurred at our primary deflector array. According to early reports, an entire bank of forcefield projectors has been destroyed, threatening the structural integrity of the dome itself." Her gaze rose reluctantly toward the bioorganic blister vaulting high above their heads, the colony's principal line of defense against the toxic atmosphere outside.

The deflector array, Kirk acknowledged, *exactly where Korax was captured less than a hour ago.* This was conclusive evidence of Klingon sabotage as far as he was concerned. Obviously, Korax had been up to more than simple snooping. *Probably a photon grenade,* he theorized, *activated by remote control once Koloth's shuttle was safely clear of the dome.*

"Look!" Gregor Lozin pointed up at the roof of the dome, a look of outright fear replacing his usual suspicious scowl. Blue flashes of Cerenkov radiation crackled along a sizable segment of the huge chartreuse hemisphere, providing dramatic proof that the colony's vitally needed forcefield was already weakening in spots. Suddenly, the translucent dome looked perilously thin and fragile, especially compared with the hellish heat and pressure threatening to break through the life-preserving barrier.

"How long," Kirk asked Clarke softly, "can your dome hold up against the pressure, without the additional protection of the forcefield?"

The regent had the hopeless-yet-steadfast demeanor of a ship's captain fully prepared to go down with her ship. "Hours," she said despairingly. "At most."

Continued in
STAR TREK®
THE EUGENICS WARS
The Rise and Fall of Khan Noonien Singh
VOLUME TWO

AFTERWORD

Historical Notes on
The Eugenics Wars, Volume One

When the original *Star Trek* television series first alluded to the fearsome Eugenics Wars of the 1990s, probably none of the show's writers or producers guessed that we would still be concerned with such matters all the way into the twenty-first century. Regrettably, many of the vital details regarding the rise of Khan Noonien Singh remain unrecorded by contemporary historians, but it may interest some readers to note where and when the events chronicled in this volume intersect with the "official" history of the late twentieth century. . . .

Chapter One: Zealously guarded, the Berlin Wall still stood as a symbol and artifact of the Cold War in March 1974, as it would for many years to come.

Chapter Five: Think Dr. Lozinak's glow-in-the-dark mouse is just a whimsical figment of my imagination? So did I. Imagine my surprise on discovering that, in fact, a bioluminescent bunny rabbit was born in France in February 2000, the creation of a transgenic "artist" who added the green fluorescent protein of a jellyfish into the DNA of an albino rabbit, producing a mammal that glows bright green under the right kind of light. Little did he know, of course, that the Chrysalis Project had beaten him to the punch over a quarter of a century earlier. (For more info on the glowing bunny, check out: www.ekac.org/gfpbunny.html.)

Chapter Six: As mentioned by Gary Seven, one of the real-life founders of modern genetic engineering was Har Gobind Khorana, an Indian-born biochemist. Khorana won the Nobel Prize in 1968 for his work on the chemistry of the genetic code, and later led the team that first synthesized a biologically active gene. (No doubt Khan's mother was one of his students. . . .)

Chapter Seven: The smallpox epidemic that Roberta alludes to actually occurred in India in 1974, killing approximately ten to twenty thousand people.

Chapter Eight: Metal detectors were indeed a new fixture at airports in 1974, in response to a wave of real-life skyjackings.

Chapter Twelve: As mentioned by Sarina Kaur, the Soviet Union did, in fact, launch a major germ-warfare program, "Biopreparat," in 1974, despite having signed the Biological Weapons Convention shortly before. The program ultimately employed approximately thirty-two thousand scientists and staff, and really did develop special refrigerated warheads capable of delivering smallpox or bubonic plague to target sites within the United States and Europe.

Chapter Fourteen: Although such stories have been repeatedly denied by the U.S. government, rumors that an alien spacecraft crashed at Roswell in 1947 persist to this day.

Chapter Twenty-three: On May 18, 1974, there actually was an underground nuclear explosion beneath the desert in Rajasthan. The Indian government claimed it was a peaceful atomic test, but we know better.

Also: In July of 1974, the U.S. National Academy of Sciences called for a temporary moratorium on genetic engineering, prompted no doubt by the discreet efforts of Gary Seven.

Chapter Twenty-six: Sadly, the bloody riots in Delhi following the 1984 assassination of Indira Gandhi are a matter of historical fact.

Chapter Twenty-nine: The existence of the ozone hole over Antarctica became public knowledge in 1985, not long after Gary Seven's mission to the South Pole. The space shuttle *Discovery,* which debuted in 1984, did not "officially" start conducting classified military missions until '85, but clearly *Discovery* must have launched Dr. Evergreen's top-secret satellite a few months earlier than that.

Chapter Thirty: The 1984 chemical leak in Bhopal, India, remains one of the worst industrial accidents in history. The final death toll has never been accurately determined, but fatalities numbered in the thousands, with maybe fifty thousand more victims permanently disabled. Small wonder the young Khan was so outraged by the disaster.

Chapter Thirty-one: Area 51, in Nevada, has long been rumored to be the repository of the U.S. government's most top-secret UFO research projects.

Chapter Thirty-two: Although better known these

days as the trademark weapon of *Xena: Warrior Princess,* the *chakram* is, in fact, a traditional Sikh weapon whose use dates back to at least the sixteenth century. Khan surely would have been schooled in its use, even before *Xena* reruns began airing in Delhi. The wheel-like *chakar* is also unique to the Sikhs.

Also, at least one hidden tunnel is known to run beneath the southern wall of the Kremlin, providing an escape route to the nearby Moskva River. The secret passage beneath Lenin's Tomb, however, has so far managed to stay out of the guidebooks.

Chapter Thirty-three: Mikhail Gorbachev was already shaking things up in the Soviet Union by October of 1986, when he met with U.S. President Ronald Reagan in Reykjavik in the hope of convincing Reagan to halt development of the "Star Wars" missile defense system. But Reagan's commitment to his Strategic Defense Initiative, along with his predilection for jelly beans, is a matter of historical record. As a result, the summit ended in a stalemate, just as "Radhinka" feared.

An intriguing aside: In her 1990 biography of Gorbachev, *The Man Who Changed the World,* author Gail Sheehy cites an unnamed American diplomat who describes Gorbachev and two of his chief advisors as the "the 'Star Trek troika'—Gorbachev as Captain Kirk, the sage and driving force; [Alexander] Yakovlev as Dr. Spock [sic], the unemotional conceptualizer; and [Eduard] Shevardnadze as McCoy, the moral force." One can only wonder if Gary Seven and Roberta noted the resemblance as well!

Chapter Thirty-four: The Berlin Wall came down on November 9, 1989, over fifteen years after Gary Seven first became aware of the Chrysalis Project. On the very next day, the Communist leader of Bulgaria stepped down peacefully, thanks to Seven's behind-the-scenes meddling. The Cold War had ended, but Khan Noonien Singh was just getting started. . . .

That covers the key events of Volume One. Just wait until we get to the nineties!

—Greg Cox
February 2001

SNEAK PREVIEW

STAR TREK®
THE EUGENICS WARS

The Rise and Fall of
Khan Noonien Singh

VOLUME TWO

By Greg Cox

In Stores Now!

MUROROA ATOLL
TUAMOTO ISLANDS
FRENCH POLYNESIA
JUNE 14, 1992

One hundred and seventy feet above the concrete launch pad, Roberta Lincoln crawled out onto one of the horizontal swing arms of the towering rocket gantry. A small green gecko scurried out of her way as the fortyish American woman clambered on her hands and knees across the steel bridge toward her target: an Ariane rocket primed for takeoff.

The more things change, the more they really do stay the same, Roberta thought wryly. Twenty-five years ago, her longtime friend and supervisor, Gary Seven, had crept across a similar elevated platform to sabotage another rocket launch. His mission then had been to prevent a weapon of mass destruction from being launched into orbit, initiating a full-scale outer space arms race. A quarter century later, Roberta's agenda was pretty much the same. *The only difference is that this time I'm the one performing without a net.*

Just to play it safe, however, she clipped one end of a safety cord to the metal grating beneath her, keeping the other end securely attached to her belt. A cool, dry wind rustled her honey-blond hair as she came within reach of the powerful European booster rocket, designed to place commercial satellites in orbit high above the Earth. Roberta briefly wondered what kind of bribes and/or extortion Khan had employed to get his hands on the Ariane, let alone transport it to this remote launch site in the South Pacific, previously occupied by the French government's now-defunct nuclear testing program.

From her lofty perch upon the gantry, Roberta could look out over the entire atoll: a circular ring of greenery surrounding a large moonlit lagoon. Leafy palm trees and mangroves covered much of the island, although she could also spot the lights of the Mission Control center, nestled amidst the lush tropical flora.

"Let's just hope they don't spot me," she whispered to herself, acutely aware that her green camouflage shorts and tank top, which had blended perfectly with the tropical shrubbery on her way here, now clashed alarmingly with the industrial-red paint job on the rocket gantry. According to their most recent intel, Khan himself intended to be present for this launch, and Roberta sincerely hoped to get in and out of Muroroa without actually running into the man himself.

The last thing I need right now is a reunion with that smug, so-called superman, she thought. She and Seven had their hands full these days, coping with the crisis in Bosnia, not to mention all the other international mischief stirred up by Khan and his genetically engineered siblings. In their eagerness to assert their self-proclaimed destinies as rulers of the Earth, the Children of Chrysalis, as Roberta still thought of them, had sparked civil wars and unrest all over the globe, in Eastern Europe, Liberia, Somalia, Peru, and elsewhere. This had not made her and Seven's primary mission—preventing World War III—any easier. *And to think that, after the Cold War ended, I had briefly thought that Seven and I could retire!* If anything, their job had gotten even more complicated since the Berlin Wall came down.

And now Khan had to up the ante with this stunt! Roberta scowled and glanced toward the horizon, glimpsing a faint rosy tint where the night sky met the Pacific. The Ariane was scheduled to launch at dawn, so Roberta knew she had to act soon; the sun rose very quickly this close to the equator.

Her all-purpose servo device, cunningly disguised as a silver fountain pen, projected a beam of white light onto the outer casing of the Ariane's main rocket, which was flanked by two solid-fuel boosters, intended to provide the initial thrust upon lift-off. According to the diagrams she'd memorized earlier, the rocket's primary guidance system was just behind the metal panel directly in front of her, bearing the snazzy blue logo of Arianespace, the French manufacturer of the rocket. Roberta's plan was to tweak the controls so that the rocket would self-destruct harmlessly in the upper atmosphere, taking its insidious cargo with it. With any luck, Khan's latest scheme would be over before it even began.

That was the plan, at least. Trying hard not to think about the twenty-five tons of liquid hydrogen stored beneath her, just waiting to be ignited, she switched the servo to laser mode and began cutting a hole in the side of the rocket with what she hoped was surgical precision. The ruby-red beam traced a charred black line around the company logo, quickly forming a complete loop. Roberta gave the melted metal a few minutes to cool, then carefully lifted the newly created circular segment away from the rest of the rocket, revealing the intricate circuitry beneath.

Pretty smooth, she congratulated herself. A few deft moves and—voilà!—Khan's high-tech hardware is more exposed than Sharon Stone. Grinning triumphantly, she cautiously laid the displaced metal disk aside, making sure it wouldn't topple off the edge of the gantry, and turned her servo back into a flashlight. She gripped the slender silver instrument between her teeth, to keep the incandescent beam focused in front of her, then reached carefully into the electronic innards of the Ariane satellite launcher.

A high-voltage jolt caused her entire body to stiff-en in shock. A moment before she lost consciousness, she thanked heaven for the safety cord binding her to the steel platform. At least she wasn't going to fall to her death! . . .

"She's waking up, Your Excellency," a gruff male voice intoned, penetrating the fog receding from her brain. Roberta struggled to lift her eyelids, half-surprised to find herself alive and not electrocuted.

She suspected the good news ended there.

"Thank you, Joaquin," a familiar voice replied, confirming Roberta's worst expectations. *Oh no!* she thought, genuine apprehension sending a chill through her recently dormant body. As far as she could tell she seemed to be lying sideways on some sort of couch or cushion. *Not him!*

Blinking, she opened her eyes to see a tall Indian man looking down at her with an amused expression on his strong, handsome features. Piercing brown eyes inspected her as they might an exotic animal securely caged in a zoo; that is, with total confidence and an unchallenged sense of superiority. He was clean-shaven, with thick black hair tied neatly behind his head, and wore a spotless white Nehru jacket with matching cotton slacks. "Ah, Ms. Lincoln," he greeted her with a mocking pretense of warmth. "How good of you to rejoin us!"

"Hello, Khan," she said icily. Raising herself to a seated position, she tried to stand up, but found her legs still a little too wobbly. A quick glance around revealed that she was in a luxuriously appointed office decorated with traditional Polynesian art. An original Gauguin hung on one wall, while an authentic Melanesian wood carving of a cruising shark sat atop an executive-size desk. A colorful mat, woven from dyed pandanus fibers, carpeted the floor. Roberta did her best to meet Khan's gaze defiantly, despite a profusion of tropical butterflies in her stomach. "Long time, no smirk."

Looming a few feet behind Khan, a large, muscular brute with a sullen expression and light-brown hair glowered at Roberta. A plain black T-shirt was stretched tautly over a Schwarzenegger-size torso, above a pair of simple gray slacks. Compared to Khan's crisp, snow-white suit, the scowling bruiser's attire was dull and unremarkable, except for a large brass belt buckle that bore the visage of a snarling grizzly bear. "You will address His Excellency with more respect!" he warned her balefully, raising a meaty hand as he stepped toward her ominously. She flinched in anticipation of the blow, which would no doubt carry the full force of genetically augmented bones and sinews.

But Khan shook his head, dismissing his henchman's concerns with an airy gesture. "No need to stand on formality," he insisted. "Ms. Lincoln and I are old friends." He smiled coldly at her. "Isn't that so?"

"What's up with the close shave?" she asked him glibly, stalling for time while she recovered from her shock-induced trip to dreamland. "The last time I saw you, back in eighty-nine, you were sporting a respectable-looking beard. I thought that was mandatory for all male Sikhs?"

Khan nodded, smiling appreciatively. "Very good, Ms. Lincoln. I applaud your cross-cultural erudition." He thoughtfully stroked his smooth and stubble-free chin. "With all due respect to my heroic Sikh ancestors, however, I eventually came to the conclusion that I should not be bound by the traditions of the past. I am a new breed of human being, after all. A new and superior kind of warrior. Thus, on my twenty-first birthday, I shaved off my beard, in recognition of the revolutionary turning point that I, and the others like me, represent in the history of human evolution. Henceforth, I resolved, I would make my own traditions, chart a new path for mankind."

"I see you're still as humble as ever," Roberta observed dryly. As discreetly as possible, she searched her pockets for her servo, but the versatile device eluded her fingers. Had she dropped it back on the gantry, or had Khan and his people confiscated it? "Frankly, I always kind of hoped that your delusions of grandeur were just a phase you were going through, something you'd outgrow eventually." She stopped fishing for the servo and started looking for an escape route; from what she could see, the office had only a single exit. "I guess that was wishful thinking."

Khan scowled, his bogus bonhomie slipping. "Hardly delusions, Ms. Lincoln," he said curtly. "Or have you forgotten how easily I have eluded you and the enigmatic Mr. Seven these past few years, despite the considerable resources at your command?"

True enough, Roberta conceded. Using data stolen from Seven's advanced Beta 5 computer, Khan had even found a way to protect his strongholds against transporter technology, forcing her and Seven to use far more primitive techniques in their periodic attempts to infiltrate Khan's hideouts and headquarters. Just to reach Muroroa, in fact, Roberta had needed to teleport to another island, several miles south of this one, then brave the treacherous currents and coral reefs in an outrigger canoe until she came close enough to the forbidden atoll to jump overboard and scuba-dive the rest of the way, dodging sharks, moray eels, and poisonous jellyfish as she swam to shore not far from the rocket launch pad. A damp wetsuit along with a set of oxygen tanks were presumably still hidden amidst the sword-shaped leaves of the bushes at the edge of the shore. Sadly, the scuba gear was too far away to do her much good at the moment. *Some South Seas vacation this is turning out to be,* she thought sarcastically.

"Maybe we've been keeping our eyes on you all along," she challenged Khan, then wondered if she had said too much. What if Khan demanded to know the name of her chief informant? "Imagine our disappointment when we found out what you were up to here. Even Seven never thought you'd go this far. . . ."

Khan's faced hardened. "Seven has always lacked vision," he said scornfully. "That is why he is content to skulk in the margins of history, when he possesses the means to do so much more. And why I broke with him years ago. The problems of the world require bold, decisive action, not timid, cautious half-measures of the sort you and Seven specialize in."

Roberta didn't back down. "We put out fires. You start them. That's a big difference, as far as I am concerned."

"Fire can be a transforming force, Ms. Lincoln," he stated, "clearing away the rotting debris of the past and making room for new growth." He lifted the carved wooden shark from his desk, crushed it to splinters within his fist, then wiped the dusty residue from his palms. "But enough philosophical debate. Your presence raises crucial questions: Where exactly is Gary Seven at this moment? Can we anticipate his arrival as well, in an attempt to rescue you, or perhaps complete your mission?"

I wish, Roberta thought. In fact, Seven was currently attending a key environmental summit in Rio, while recovering from injuries sustained during the fall of Kabul a few months back. Despite his own superhuman physique, the result of years of selective breeding on a planet light-years away, Seven was in no shape to stage a commando raid on the secluded and well-protected island.

"For someone with a superior brain," she told Khan, "your math needs work. Seven is in his sixties now; he lets me handle all the house calls."

This was a slight exaggeration, but close enough to the truth that she hoped Khan would buy it. Over the years, she had indeed taken over more and more of the field work, leaving Seven to concentrate on the big picture. *One of these days, we really do need to bring in a new junior operative,* she mused. *Heaven knows I could use some backup right now.*

"So Seven is finally feeling his years, is he?" Khan's voice assumed a magnanimous tone, leading Roberta to suspect that he had taken her protestations at face value. "In a way, this saddens me. In his own fashion, he was a worthy adversary."

A buzzer sounded behind Khan and he strode across the spacious office to answer the intercom on the desk. "Khan here," he declared crisply. "What is our status?"

"We're about ten minutes from launching, sir," a disembodied voice spoke from the intercom. Roberta thought she detected a trace of Scottish accent, along with the distinctly deferential tone. Her heart sank at the implications of the announcement. She hadn't prevented the launch at all; the Ariane was still ready to deliver its obscene payload into orbit. *I've failed,* she realized.

"Excellent," Khan pronounced, switching off the intercom without waiting for a reply. "I'm happy to say, Ms. Lincoln, that your feeble attempt at sabotage cost us merely half an hour, not nearly enough time to cause us to miss our launch window." Stepping away from the desk, he stared down at her like an adult scolding a wayward child. "You should have remembered that you were dealing with an intelligence deliberately engineered to exceed your own; anticipating sabotage, I had the foresight to install a fail-safe device into the Ariane's guidance systems against any such interference." He smiled condescendingly, pleased by his own remarkable foresight. "My apologies if my countermeasures came as something of, well, a shock to your system."

Very funny, Roberta thought acidly. "Well, as surprises go, it wasn't exactly up there with *The Crying Game.*" She'd be damned if she was going to feed Khan's already gargantuan ego. "But, yeah, I suppose it caught me a little off guard."

Too bad my informant failed to mention Khan's sneaky little safety precaution, she lamented. *Guess that was one secret Khan was keeping under even tighter wraps than usual. . . .*

"Your spirit is admirable," he acknowledged, annoyingly unshaken by Roberta's faint praise, "even if your accomplishments are not." He marched toward the office's only exit. "Bring her," he instructed Joaquin, who grabbed her roughly by the arm and yanked her to her feet. His bruising grip reminded her of Carlos, the hulking guardian of the old Chrysalis Project—and one of the project's earliest genetic experiments. She wondered if Joaquin's muscles had been souped-up with gorilla DNA, too.

Following Khan, Joaquin dragged her out the door. A short flight of steps later, they arrived on the roof of the Mission Control building. The sun was newly risen, Roberta noted, providing her with a panoramic of view of the picturesque island and its enclosed lagoon. Rising high above the swaying palm trees, on the opposite side of the tranquil blue waters, the Ariane and its attached launch tower looked incongruous amidst the idyllic South Seas scenery. Observing her gaze, Khan threw out his arms expansively. His pristine white suit reflected the bright morning sunshine. "Welcome, Ms. Lincoln, to Chrysalis Island!"

Look for STAR TREK fiction from Pocket Books

Star Trek®: The Original Series

Star Trek: The Next Generation®

Star Trek: Voyager®

Enterprise®

Star Trek®: New Frontier

Gateways #6: Cold Wars • Peter David
Gateways #7: What Lay Beyond: "Death After Life" • Peter David
#12 • *Being Human* • Peter David

Star Trek®: Starfleet Corps of Engineers (eBooks)

Have Tech, Will Travel • John J. Ordover, ed.
 #1 • *The Belly of the Beast* • Dean Wesley Smith
 #2 • *Fatal Error* • Keith R.A. DeCandido
 #3 • *Hard Crash* • Christie Golden
 #4 • *Interphase, Book One* • Dayton Ward & Kevin Dilmore
Miracle Workers • John J. Ordover, ed.
 #5 • *Interphase, Book Two* • Dayton Ward & Kevin Dilmore
 #6 • *Cold Fusion* • Keith R.A. DeCandido
 #7 • *Invincible, Book One* • Keith R.A. DeCandido & David Mack
 #8 • *Invincible, Book Two* • Keith R.A. DeCandido & David Mack
 #9 • *The Riddled Post* • Aaron Rosenberg
#10 • *Gateways Epilogue: Here There Be Monsters* • Keith R.A. DeCandido
#11 • *Ambush* • Dave Galanter & Greg Brodeur
#12 • *Some Assembly Required* • Scott Ciencin & Dan Jolley
#13 • *No Surrender* • Jeff Mariotte
#14 • *Caveat Emptor* • Ian Edginton

Star Trek®: Invasion!

#1 • *First Strike* • Diane Carey
#2 • *The Soldiers of Fear* • Dean Wesley Smith & Kristine Kathryn Rusch
#3 • *Time's Enemy* • L.A. Graf
#4 • *Final Fury* • Dafydd ab Hugh
Invasion! Omnibus • various

Star Trek®: Day of Honor

#1 • *Ancient Blood* • Diane Carey
#2 • *Armageddon Sky* • L.A. Graf
#3 • *Her Klingon Soul* • Michael Jan Friedman
#4 • *Treaty's Law* • Dean Wesley Smith & Kristine Kathryn Rusch
The Television Episode • Michael Jan Friedman
Day of Honor Omnibus • various

Star Trek®: The Captain's Table

#1 • *War Dragons* • L.A. Graf
#2 • *Dujonian's Hoard* • Michael Jan Friedman
#3 • *The Mist* • Dean Wesley Smith & Kristine Kathryn Rusch

Star Trek: Odyssey • William Shatner with Judith and Garfield Reeves-Stevens
Millennium Omnibus • Judith and Garfield Reeves-Stevens
Starfleet: Year One • Michael Jan Friedman

Other Star Trek® Fiction

Legends of the Ferengi • Ira Steven Behr & Robert Hewitt Wolfe
Strange New Worlds, vol. I, II, III, and IV • Dean Wesley Smith, ed.
Adventures in Time and Space • Mary P. Taylor, ed.
Captain Proton: Defender of the Earth • D.W. "Prof" Smith
New Worlds, New Civilizations • Michael Jan Friedman
The Lives of Dax • Marco Palmieri, ed.
The Klingon Hamlet • Wil'yam Shex'pir
Enterprise Logs • Carol Greenburg, ed.
Amazing Stories Anthology • various